SHADOWCOP

SHADOWCOP

Hal Barwood

Murder in the California Foothills
a ghost story

Shadowcop

Copyright © 2013 Hal Barwood
All rights reserved
A Finite Arts Book
Published by Finite Arts, Portland, Oregon
version 3.2

ISBN 978-0-9911566-1-0

This is a work of fiction. The California foothills are real, but the settings depicted herein are either fictional in themselves or fictional in detail. All the characters in this fictional world are fictional products of the author's imagination . . . except, possibly, the shadow.

Acknowledgements . . .

Many thanks to the readers who bravely trudged through early versions of this tale — most helpfully Barbara, Jonathan, and Tobias Barwood, Bob Bates, Betsy Blanchard, Curt Blanchard, Robert Dalva, Joan Kvitka, Muriel Murch, Janet Robbins, and Matthew Robbins. The advice offered was priceless. All failures to heed it and other mistakes are the author's.

Many thanks as well to Officer Andy Litzius and Sergeant Dan Maciel of the Placerville Police Department for demonstrating some real law enforcement and helping lay the foundation for another foothill story.

About the Author . . .

Hal Barwood is a veteran writer with multiple movies and videogames under his belt. Find out more here . . .

www.finitearts.com

for

Barbara

for a lifetime

Table of Contents

Part ONE

1

"SAY YOUR NAME ...?"

"Mary Ann Sarzo."

The young woman stood in front of a worn-out oak desk in the worn-out offices of the Golden Hills Tri-Town Police Department, facing the chief.

"What kind of name is that — some sort of Hungarian moniker?" growled the man without looking up from the stack of papers on his blotter. He looked really old to her, sixty at least, with grey hair cut in a buzz, big shouldered, beefy rather than fat.

She bit her lip. "I don't know. All-American, I guess. Mom and Dad were born here, anyway."

"Didn't say they weren't." Now he looked up, looked her over. Young, not too tall, late twenties, he guessed. Fair hair pulled back in a clip, black-frame glasses shielding dark eyes, a sharp little nose, collared shirt over tee and jeans. Small of breast, wide of hip. Nervous but cute, he thought, in a plump sort of way.

"How'd you hear about our little world?"

"In the Journal. You know, you placed an ad."

"Jesus, CAFOP, that thing."

She nodded. "And the Miners Weekly. I live up in Placerville."

"It's true, we're understaffed. Vera — the mayor — is after me. Our old-time lifer fell under a truck, picked up a disability, and decided he liked Oregon better than the Sierra Foothills. So here we are."

"I don't think I'd fall under a truck."

"You did go to cop school? Completed POST? Say yes, I hope."

"Yes."

"Where?"

"Butte College, up in Oroville. It's there on your sheet."

The chief drummed a pencil against the desk. "Okay, but you don't look much like a police officer to me." She cringed and opened her mouth to protest. He raised his hands, palms out. "Save the feminist outrage, so you're a woman, I don't care. Why do you want to join up? Military background? Finish high school? Previous employment? — I don't see any details here."

"My last job was behind a counter at DQ. I managed the place, handled the drive-throughs, all that swirled ice cream. I'd rather wear a gun than a headset. I applied up in Placerville and down in Jackson, but they're not hiring. You are."

The chief noticed a faintly aggressive resistance to his deliberate intimidation and almost smiled. "What about those glasses?"

She whipped them off. "I've got contacts."

"Can you shoot?"

She started to feel that this crude old hulk was actually considering her and decided not to lie. "I passed all my tests. I can field-strip anything. But the truth is, I can hit a barn door and not much else. That's my weak spot."

He thought for a moment, savoring her unexpected, undeveloped, but undeniable poise, then commanded, "Repeat after me: 'Expect snow accumulations above 2500 feet.' "

"What? In the summer?" She swallowed. "Expect snow accumulations above 2500 feet."

He nodded grudging approval and held out a piece of paper. "Now, read this out loud for me." She took the sheet with shaky fingers, studied it briefly without the slightest understanding, cleared her throat, and recited:

"Tri-Town travel update for nine AM. Snow turning to rain after eleven AM. Exercise caution on County Road 520. Exercise caution at higher elevations on all roads and streets throughout the Tri-Town Area. Clear on 49 to Placerville. Clear on 88 to Jackson. Alert ending two PM. Stay tuned to 1610 for changes."

"Read it again." She did so and then placed the paper back on the desk — enough of that nonsense.

The chief tilted his head to one side and studied her. "*Mary Ann SARZO . . .* " He rolled the name around in his mouth. "You've got a nice voice. Vera will love this — she can't get enough of our travel alerts. Thinks if we're on the radio, we're famous, a genuine reality show."

"The mayor, you said?"

"Vera Teasdale. She runs this little strip of heaven — Applefield, Ragtown, Tarvolo. From the Whiskeyjack right down to the reservoir, she's the boss. So, uh, you're hired. Maybe you can't shoot, but with our crime rate the traffic reports are more important, and you'll be fine."

"I'm supposed to be a radio voice? Like a disc jockey?" It took a moment for the news to sink in. "Okay, if you say so." Then she almost bounced into the air. "Oh my God, I've got a job!"

"Driving a desk for me. I'm Hector Ibañez, chief of police around here, for what that's worth. Welcome to the California gold country — and here's my training lecture, short and to-the-point — don't fuck up." He held out his hand, big as a bear paw. She took it firmly and squeezed, trying to act like an adult.

▼

After the instructions on buying her uniforms, after taking her service oath, Mary Ann was grinding through reams of paperwork at her new desk when the rattle of the station door shifted her attention to a young patrol officer who bounced into the office, stripped off his hat, his duty belt, his jacket and tie, and deposited them all in a rusty green locker. She began to wonder if he would notice the stranger, and eventually he did.

"Well, hello, there. You the new hire?"

"I guess so. Chief thinks I'm going to be a radio star."

He cackled, his big grin splitting a wide and handsome face. "He wants to stay on Teasdale's good side. Don't blame him."

An awkward moment passed as the two exchanged appraising looks. Then, "Hey, I guess we should, uh, introduce ourselves and so forth: I'm Bobby Rainwater, local cop." The name confirmed her tentative first impression — what do you know, a Native American.

"Mary Ann Sarzo. Nice to meet you. What about a weapon?"

"You don't have one?"

"Local policies are all different, so no, I thought it best to wait until someone actually hired me."

"When do you start? Monday? Buy one down in Jackson is the rule, I believe."

"Okay, in that case I'm done here. Gotta go before my fingers fall off. See you Monday."

She stood up, stacked the forms she had been filling out, and dropped them on Chief Ibañez's now-vacated desk.

"Hey, wait a minute." He raised a hand to stop her. "Got a car? I could use a lift. My ride's in the shop."

Mary Ann opened the door of her battered old two-door Honda Civic for Officer Rainwater and dropped into the driver's seat. He pointed to a signed intersection, and off they went, down from Applefield toward nearby Spring Valley, the oldest settlement in the county, and known since gold fever days as Ragtown. Bobby watched her stir the stick shift in and out of gears as they descended the switchbacks, more appreciative of the car than its owner would ever be.

"Wash this thing, install a decent air cleaner and glass-packs, you could tune her up. She's a classic," he said.

"After my first paycheck, I'm buying an Elantra, thank you very much. With an automatic."

"Oh, no, don't do it. That 100,000 mile warranty you see on TV is bullshit."

They pulled onto Ragtown's main drag, little more than a wide spot in the narrow highway. At the far end a ramshackle garage in urgent need of paint stood with its entry agape. This was Mike's Motors, the only repair shop within thirty miles. Halfway inside sat a beautiful metallic blue 1969 Mustang hardtop. As they approached, the proprietor, clad in a white undershirt exposing tattooed muscles, slammed the hood down and waved them over.

Bobby did the honors. "Mary Ann Sarzo, Morning Star Russell. She's our new cop. He's the best mechanic in town. Only one, actually."

Russell wiped his hands on a greasy towel, nodded, smiled a ragged smile and offered a hand. "Call me Mike. I was born in a commune, don't hold it against me."

Mary Ann regarded him with distaste. She braved a quick shake and forced a little laugh. "Don't worry, I won't."

She fidgeted while Bobby paid for his service work. Then, as he took the keys from Russell, he turned back to her. "Say, how about we go for a beer over to the Palomino?" She looked doubtful. He gave her a million-dollar grin. "It's just up the road, it's Friday night and all, take five minutes." He pointed at the Mustang. "I'll drive."

Mary Ann hesitated. The boy was gorgeous, better-looking than anyone she had ever dated. And, in his rural way, she thought, unexpectedly charming.

She smiled and held up a hand, forefinger extended. "One beer. Celebrate my new job."

He opened the passenger door. "Hop in."

She pointed at her own car. "Tell you what — I'll meet you there."

▼

The Palomino was quiet when Mary Ann walked in. The blackboard at the entrance promised live music by the Tailings, a local country-rock group, but they had yet to arrive. Bobby Rainwater was already sitting at the bar, sipping a beer. He handed her a Corona Extra as she slid onto the stool beside him. They clicked bottles together in a little toast.

"Here's to police work," she said, "now that I've got it."

He chuckled. "You trained and all?"

"Oh yeah, up in Oroville."

"But this is your first actual duty, being sworn, and so on."

"Yeah."

"Been around cops much?"

"Not really. Well, my teachers. Some of them were real cops. Dad's military. Same thing, I'm guessing."

He smiled. "Don't be so sure. Help is hard to find up here in the sticks."

"Meaning what? Who cares if I'm any good, just fill a slot?"

"You'll see when you meet the rest of us. What the mayor calls her 'force.' "

"Is there a problem?"

"Not really. But I'm not sure how our boys would measure up in the Big City, know what I mean? I think one of them would just as soon own a U-Haul franchise, and the other one wants to build houses."

"But you're a different animal."

"Oh yeah. I'm a cop. Inside and out. Always wanted to be."

"Pardon me, but you're Native, right?"

Bobby flexed his fingers, regarded her with deep brown eyes. "Unh-huh."

"And you want to lay down the law for white folks?"

"Sure do. My family, they need to wake up to the future. How about you?"

"Well, it beats running a Dairy Queen and wrangling the brats who work there." Mary Ann took a big swig of her beer. "I'm not tuned to the indoor life."

"And yet you just signed up to shuffle a lot of paper."

"I guess so. But that's temporary. You wait."

"That's what I like to hear. Ambition . . . that's important, does a person good."

"How about you, the cop critic? What's your lofty goal in life?"

"Live through the boredom here, I guess, then head downhill, join a real department. After that, apply to the FBI."

She gave him a wry grin. "Unh-huh. Too good for the rest of us."

He waved a cautionary finger. "Well, there is the chief. Stay on your toes, he's an old-school pro, and he can be" — Bobby struggled to find the right word — "excitable," he decided.

"I'll remember."

He drained his beer, looked at Mary Ann's. "*Uno más?*"

"Mmm, *no más*, thanks."

By now the Tailings had arrived. They had their amps set up and were tuning their instruments. What promised to be dueling guitars were screaming and wailing in experimental discord. Bobby turned on his charming smile. He leaned close to make himself heard over the din.

"Now, you're new in town, but I know all the decent places to eat around here. What do you say we protect our hearing from further loss and go get some supper?"

Mary Ann was flattered by Bobby's attention, but she knew where this was going. She imagined the ugly situations that could easily emerge in the department. A long moment passed.

"Come on," he urged with another smile, "you don't have anything better to do."

She laughed. "Ha! What makes you think I don't have a date lined up?"

"I can tell."

His accurate observation made her blush. "Be that as it may. Sorry, nothing personal. I've got this, uh, policy — never date co-workers."

"You just made that up."

She giggled. "True, but it still holds."

"I understand. Okay, that's probably best. Welcome to the department anyway. See you on the holodeck." He tapped the bar and ambled outside to his waiting Mustang. She heard the engine start and the car roar off down the road toward Jackson.

2

BRIGHT AND EARLY Monday morning she arrived in the Golden Hills Tri-Town police station to find Chief Ibañez and Officer Rainwater waiting for her with frowns on their faces.

"Where's your uniform?" asked Ibañez.

"I haven't bought anything yet. I thought — gear, gun, do it all at once."

"Well, okay, that's good. I'd like Bobby, here, to tag along, make sure you get everything right. Vera, our honorable mayor, thinks dressing well promotes morale."

Bobby insisted on driving, and soon they were winding down through the hills toward Jackson. Mary Ann thought they were traveling at an unnecessarily stately pace, given Bobby's powerful old Mustang.

"This the fastest you ever go?" she inquired.

"You'll learn. Think about getting nailed for speeding when you are a cop. The embarrassment." He shook his head.

"Oh yeah, right." She slumped down in the passenger seat, plenty embarrassed.

"On the other hand, when you light up in an emergency, then you can move. Every now and then a call comes in while I'm off duty, and I got this little fireball here, see?" He reached under the dash and pulled out a red globe attached to a big black suction cup. "It goes on the roof, there's a bunch of LEDs inside that flash pretty good, and I let this pony run."

"How fast?"

"Hundred or better. On the clock, anyway. Car's in good shape, but she hasn't been restored."

Mary Ann smiled. "Hey, maybe we'll have an emergency."

"Let's wait till you're armed and dangerous, okay?"

At the Foothills Gun Emporium the ancient salesman showed Mary Ann an array of law enforcement weapons. "Take your pick, young lady. Every one of these will stop your angriest, raging, drug-induced malefactor as cold as a side of beef in the freezer."

Mary Ann was trying to figure out which one would likely scare someone the most without her actually having to pull the trigger when Bobby stepped forward.

"Let's see that little Beretta there."

The salesman brought out a Beretta Px4 Storm.

"Geez, that thing is huge. I won't be able to lift it," worried Mary Ann.

"No, no, that's the .45. Show us the compact 9-mill."

The salesman obliged. Mary Ann hefted it.

"Now I carry a big Ruger," said Bobby. "But see, what I like is, the Beretta looks deadly, but it's kind of small, perfect for a woman — no offense. Anybody facing that is going to think, 'you know, she'll damn well use it.' "

"And then maybe I won't have to."

"That's the attitude. But just in case, you got fifteen rounds in there."

"Thanks. I'll take it."

▼

Back up the slope in Applefield, in the Tri-Town Police station, Mary Ann stepped out of the woman's restroom in full regalia. She did a 360 degree turn for Ibañez.

"Think I'll promote the morale around here?"

"Won't hurt it, anyway. Let's see your weapon."

Mary Ann drew her little Beretta and handed it over. Ibañez examined it, worked the slide, popped the clip, slammed it back into place.

"This was Bobby's idea, right?"

"Yes sir. Small but effective."

"Looks like a popgun to me. However, if life treats us right, this will be pure decoration, like your badge. Just the same, make sure you learn how to use it."

"Yes sir."

"Okay, then — there's your desk. Better get rolling, there's papers to file."

3

ONE MONTH LATER.

Trees were already losing their leaves in the dry heat of late summer. Mary Ann's little Honda spun them into the air as she worked her way up and out of the Whiskeyjack River canyon that stretched between Placerville and her new job. She was in a thoughtful mood, reconsidering her dating "policy" and wondering if it needed a tweak or two in the case of Bobby Rainwater. She was beginning to regret pushing him away. He was good-looking, unfailingly courteous, bright enough to hold down a real job, and from what she had heard he was pretty good at it. Also — sigh — sex was just a rumor to her and had been for more than a year.

As she crested the south rim of the canyon, her mobile phone warbled. She pushed an earbud into her ear and touched the screen.

"This is Officer Sarzo."

"Mary Ann? Ibañez. You're on your way to work, right?"

"That's affirmative. Ten minutes away."

"Look, we got an accident called in up on 520. Car out in the oaks. I'd send Wade, but you're a lot closer. Wheel by there and find out what it's all about, okay?"

"Does this mean I'm allowed out in the field now?"

"I'll think about it. Call me when you reach the scene."

She swung left onto County Road 520 and motored through a quarter mile of tight uphill turns. Then, as the country widened out, she spotted the accident. There, sitting just off the pavement in a gravel turnout, was a familiar metallic blue 1969 Mustang under the gnarly oak trees. She hit the brakes, stopped, and jumped out. As she approached from behind on the passenger side, she could see someone slumped at the wheel. Her heart did a little flip-flop.

"Oh my God, Bobby — !"

She ran around to the driver's side. The door wasn't tightly closed, and without thinking, she yanked it wide open. Bobby sagged outward into her arms. As his head lolled toward her she could see blood on his neck and police blouse and a tiny bullet hole just behind his right ear. She let him pivot out of the car and reached down for a pulse. Not a chance. She felt his cheek. Spooky cold. A sudden rush of adrenaline pounded through her chest. She bounded away from the Mustang and held up her hands.

"Shit!" Now she had blood all over them.

The car, apparently freed from Bobby's brake foot, rolled slowly forward, dragging Bobby with it, and smacked into a tree.

She was still holding her bloody mobile phone at her side when Chief Ibañez pulled up in his black & white Ford Explorer. A moment later, another cop, Wade Gawley, appeared in a Crown Vic. They both looked at her with concern: she was white as a sheet, in a daze, eyes vacant.

"Use this." Ibañez handed her a towel. The two older cops circled the Mustang, looking for — what?

"Heh, the bumper's got a crunch where it hit." Gawley said.

"Not much of a dent, you ask me. And the tree sure as hell didn't cause this," snorted Ibañez, gesturing toward Bobby's body, still awkwardly posed upside down, half in and half out of the car. He looked at Mary Ann. "Holster's empty. You see a service weapon when you got here?"

"No, sir, I didn't."

"But you looked. You opened the door."

"Yes, sorry, guilty as charged. I saw it was Bobby," she explained with a wail.

"Get a grip. You failed to secure the automobile."

"Yes, that too. Sorry, sorry, I'm sorry." She did her best to straighten up and look like a police officer.

"You ran all around the damn thing. Your footprints and fingerprints will be all over the crime scene." His face reddened. "You call this police work? The boys down in Jackson will be fucking overjoyed." He tilted his head toward the sky. "Fuck!"

Mary Ann blanched all over again. Then she turned on her heel, popped the door of Gawley's Crown Vic, and returned with a digital camera. She angrily began taking pictures.

Ibañez cocked an eye. "And what are you doing?"

"Documenting the crime scene. Before I fuck it all up completely."

"Well, then, get some of the footprints, for Christ's sake."

Gawley chimed in: "And that bent-up bumper."

4

AMADOR COUNTY Sheriff's Deputy Terry Gardner carefully sifted through Mary Ann's photos, now printed up as 8x10 glossies, before offering any opinion. Ibañez had called the case into the county seat down in Jackson, and an hour later Gardner, the senior man in the Sheriff's Investigations Bureau, was in the Golden Hills Police station taking charge.

"Tell me, Miss —"

"Sarzo." Mary Ann looked him over. Thirty-five or so, curly hair, lean and handsome in a cool mature way, with sparkling blue eyes regarding her closely.

"Right. Officer Sarzo. Tell me, was the driver's door closed when you got there?"

"I'm not sure. It might have been ajar."

"Ajar?"

"I don't think it was tight when I grabbed the handle. It just sort of fell open. Why?"

Gardner held up one of her photos. "That Mustang wasn't in any accident. It might mean our victim was about to get out and talk to somebody. Or, he might have been waiting for someone to show up, and whoever did the deed opened the door and released the handbrake. Please tell me you didn't touch the brake lever."

She grimaced. "I guess that's the only thing I missed."

"How long have you been with Golden Hills Tri-Town?"

"Just this month. I'm really new. And usually I'm just running the shop here. I was on my way in."

"So you don't know if Officer Rainwater was mixed up in anything?"

Ibañez held up a cautionary hand. "Whoa. It's a helluva thing, this thing. We're usually pretty quiet up here in the hills. And Bobby was as close as you ever get to an honest man. He never crossed the line. Except, I think Wade got him for speeding once before he joined the force."

Gardner nodded assent. "Point taken. Had to ask."

Ibañez opened his laptop and swung the screen around. "We've got the report online." He played the call. The voice was muffled, possibly altered. They all strained to make sense of the muddy MP3. "Reported as an accident, although we know otherwise, so whoever this voice unknown might be, he just wanted us to find the body sooner rather than later."

Gardner stood up and peered into Bobby's locker. "No service weapon here. None at the scene. Where the hell is it?"

Mary Ann wondered about that too.

5

AFTER GARDNER gathered up the photos and departed, Mary Ann brooded miserably at her desk. Ibañez eventually lost patience.

"Jesus Christ, Mary Ann, stop feeling sorry. Go do the weather report."

Near the end of the day she opened Bobby's locker, felt around inside, and discovered a house key. Tucking it into her holster, she left the office by the rear door, stepped into her assigned vehicle, the department's oldest, an ancient Jeep Cherokee SUV done up in Golden Hills Tri-Town Police paint, and headed for Jackson. Two miles outside of Ragtown she consulted a hastily scribbled note, turned off on a paved back road, and drove to Bobby's house, a tiny white bungalow with a tin roof set back among oaks and brush.

She parked the Cherokee and sat for three minutes before she dared open the door and step out. No lights were visible inside the building. Her arrival seemed to have had no effect. So she unsnapped her holster, loosened her pistol, and cautiously made her way around the house to a back door. There she tried the key. It snicked into the lock and turned easily. The door creaked open. Holding her breath, and with heart pounding, she eased inside.

The interior was well-kept and cheerfully illuminated by large windows. A coffee cup and the plastic tray from a recent microwave dinner marred the perfection of an otherwise spotless kitchen. Mary Ann opened the refrigerator. Milk, cheese, eggs, a six-pack of Sierra Nevada beer. A couple of Coronas lying on their sides. Nothing unusual. Same thing in the freezer. Ice cubes, several more boxed microwave dinners, a quart of low-fat vanilla caramel ice cream.

Mary Ann stepped into the tiny living room. On a low table in front of a cushy sofa were magazines. *Sports Illustrated, Car and Driver, National Geographic.* Also an empty bottle of Corona. A Sacramento Kings warmup jacket was folded over the back of a chair. She stopped. What was that? Did she hear something, aside from her own breathing? She unholstered her gun. Invading what seemed like such a comfortably lived-in space gave her the creeps. The belongings of her dead colleague seemed to keep him alive.

"Bobby?" she called, in a plaintive voice.

The name reverberated through the house, but there was no reply.

In one corner of the room she found a tactical gun case. She opened it. Empty. Nearby was a small desk, with a portable filing cabinet tucked underneath. She opened the single file drawer. Taxes, credit card records, and auto repair receipts were stuffed into the folders. The tiny desk drawer contained the usual assortment of paper clips, pencils, and pens. And something else — a check for $5,000 made out to Robert Rainwater. She picked it up. Printed in the upper left corner was the name and address of the account holder — *The Hilltop Band of the Hokyut Nation*. It was dated in May, two months previously. The signature was done with a flourish, and was, to her at least, unreadable. Why, she wondered, would a check for such a substantial sum go uncashed?

Two minutes later she was back in the yard. Aside from the check, she had found nothing to suggest a reason for Bobby's murder, and she had certainly not found his service weapon. She didn't know if her efforts proved anything aside from her own possible incompetence.

As she came back around the house, she stopped short. Standing in the driveway was a black & white police Explorer, and leaning against the door was Chief Ibañez.

"Hello, Chief."

"Officer Sarzo. What in hell are you doing here?"

"Well, we didn't find Bobby's gun, so I thought . . . "

". . . you thought, why not ruin the investigation altogether by an unauthorized search of the victim's residence."

She slumped, feeling idiotic. "I guess that's about the size of it."

"Jesus H. Christ on a lava lamp. Get out of here. Stay out of trouble. Stay out of danger." She arched her eyebrows, and he scowled back. "That's right, Miss Rookie of the Year. Danger. Something mighty odd just happened, and who says it's over?"

Sheepishly, she handed Ibañez the $5,000 check. "This should be secured. Bobby never cashed it. Did he have a lot of money?"

Ibañez took it with barely a glance. "Not any more. My new hire stole it all."

She produced the key to Bobby's house. "I didn't break in, if that's what you're wondering."

"Go home, Sarzo."

But she didn't go home. As the sun was going down across the Big Valley, she wound her way back up County Road 520 to the scene of

Bobby's "accident." By now the area was thoroughly picked over by the Tri-Town cops and Gardner's team. What harm could a few more footprints do?

She scoured the grounds, and again came up empty. She was annoyed with herself for working so hard to find the dead cop's gun, and also for harboring the vain hope that finding it would restore some respect in Ibañez's flinty eyes. But very likely the killer took it, she thought. And who cared, really? Bobby had no further use for the thing.

▼

Back in Ragtown, back in civilian clothes, she nursed her sorrows at the Palomino bar. The night was warm, the music loud, the customers sparse. She didn't know a soul. Mindful of her obligations as a duly sworn officer of the law, she was careful not to order a second Corona, and she was just getting ready to call it a night when Morning Star Russell sauntered in. He was wearing a bright yellow and red Hawaiian shirt. He had bathed and shaved. He looked presentable. He ordered a margarita, took a sip, scanned the crowd. When his eyes fell on Mary Ann, he lifted his glass in greeting, ordered another margarita, and steered himself in her direction.

"Mike."

"Evening, Officer. Sorry to hear the news."

"Yeah, Bobby had a bad accident." Until the police found something to go on, she thought it best to stick to the innocent version of events.

Russell rolled his eyes. "Some accident. I've got his car down in the shop, and there's a tiny ding in the right front bumper."

"Well, I'm new at this, and I say, leave it to the experts."

Russell nodded. "That's best. Could be he had enemies, you know? Like on CSI. Don't let the tourist trade fool you. Stuff happens up here in the hills." He took another sip of his margarita and held the other out to Mary Ann.

"Sorry, I can't. Thanks for the offer."

"What's the problem, too much salt? You're not on duty."

"No, but I am on probation for six months, and I like my new job."

"Well, here's to Bobby Rainwater, and to better times, and whatever the hell that might mean." He drained his glass, then started on the second one. She clinked the neck of her Corona against it.

"Hear, hear."

"Say, his car. Blue Mustang? I'm told his brother will inherit, and I'm sure he wants to sell the thing. Have any interest? It's well-maintained, by yours truly. I can get you a real good price."

Mary Ann felt a wave of anguish wash through her. All social impulses vanished. "Jesus, is the man even buried yet? Look, I'm on my way home, and I've gotta make a pit stop. I'll think about the car."

She slipped off her barstool and retreated toward the restrooms. Inside she found a stall, sat down on the seat, and cradled her head in her hands. Earlier in the day she had occasionally felt entirely useless. Now those moments seemed like the height of self esteem.

And Bobby. Bobby was gone. Gone for good. No chance to reverse her no-dating policy in his case, and she wished she had. Her eyes were misting. She let tears spill, let them wash away some of her guilty regrets. Then abruptly she gritted her teeth, yanked a wad of toilet paper from the holder, and wiped her face.

"Whoo. Stop it, stop it, stop it."

She dragged herself to the dimly-lit wash stand and stared into the dingy mirror. It was cracked, and some disenchanted young thing had scratched crude words of wisdom into the glass — *no matter how big it is, it's just a prick, and so is he.* The cracks and letters broke her reflection into multiple facets. Someone else had left a cigarillo smoldering on the sink. Wisps of tobacco smoke rose lazily upward. The result made her look strange. She frowned.

Wait a minute, what was that? She began to sense another face staring back at her. As the hairs rose on her neck, she whirled around to see who might be behind her. Nobody. She turned back to the mirror. Hmm. The crazed wide-eyed reflection was merely her sorry self, paler now in the weak light. Relax, girl.

Then, a shift in color, a refracted jaw line, another wisp of smoke — and there it was again! — an apparition, shadowy, elusive, shimmered into view near her own. She stared long and hard. It wavered, but did not go away.

"All right, wiseguy, who the fuck are you?"

To her surprise, as if in reply the image in the mirror shrugged its shadowy shoulders. A reticulated mouth opened and silently formed an unintelligible word. Her blood ran cold.

6

MARY ANN'S HOME was a rented trailer on the woodsy edge of a clean but run-down RV park on the outskirts of Placerville. Here she hurried from her encounter in the Palomino toilet, vaulting from her car and running for the entrance as if pursued by demons. Maybe she was, she thought. She banged the door shut behind her and turned on all the lights, opened the fridge, found a beer, then collapsed into an easy chair she had bought second hand from Dunnigan's Affordable Luxury Consignments downtown. Now that she was safe at home, she felt giddy with relief. She giggled out loud. Then, sobering, she jumped up and bolted the door, just in case. She squinted suspiciously into the night outside her windows, peering into the woods and ranch land beyond her trailer. Nothing stirred among the rusted truck carcasses and abandoned farm implements, faintly visible in the light of a quarter moon. Satisfied, she checked the bathroom, slowly and deliberately moving into view of her mirror. Nothing but her own slightly addled reflection appeared before her. She realized she was holding her breath and let out a sigh of relief.

Back in the kitchenette, she elected to pour her beer into a glass. As she removed a tumbler from the cupboard, a shadow seemed to pass across the rest of the glassware. Did she see something? Refusing to panic, she resolutely closed the cupboard and turned on her old TV set, prepared for any show, as long as it was distracting. She flipped through the channels, passing several blanks, and stopped on a re-run of *ER*. She took a sip of beer, then another, settling down now for the evening.

But wait. Something nagged at her. Frowning, she backtracked through the blanks to Channel 23. It was supposed to belong to HBO, and she did not subscribe, not even to basic cable. But it wasn't quite blank. A shadowy shape was moving around there among the digital TV artifacts. She felt herself go numb as the shape became distinct and slowly resolved itself into the silhouette of a face and upper torso. A half-visible hand waved at her.

"Ahh!" Mary Ann let out a shriek and leaped from her chair, spilling beer all over the trailer's well-worn carpet. She snapped the TV set off, moved to her duty belt where it dangled from a hook by the door, unfastened the holster, and placed her pistol on a side table within easy reach. Then she turned out all the lights and checked the windows again. Trailers and trees could be recognized by their outlines, and all was calm.

"Oh boy, oh boy, oh boy," she mumbled, returning to the TV set. She sat across from it with her hand poised on the remote for several minutes, considering the situation, working up her courage. Finally she took a deep breath and pressed the power button. Digital noise filled the screen, but nothing spooky appeared. She turned the volume down to zero and adjusted the aluminum foil on her rabbit ears. Still nothing. Maybe she was just hallucinating, overly jumpy after a rough day at the office. She clicked to the next channel and stared as if hypnotized at the indistinct form of a person, bobbing and waving amid the static. Her skin prickled. She thought her heart would stop. "Okay, I see you."

The figure pointed two fingers at its eyes, then swung them around toward her. "And I guess you see me too."

The apparition nodded. "What, uh, what do you want — whoever you are?" The apparition nodded again, held up a hand posed in the shape of an upside-down gun and then, with its other hand, placed a finger through an imaginary trigger guard. "What is this, charades?" The apparition nodded a third time and repeated the little demonstration.

"Okay. I'm talking to a ghost, right? Ha ha. It's perfectly natural, happens every day, all the time. And, when I'm not completely terrified, I'm thinking, one hand is a gun. Am I right for $64,000 dollars?"

Vigorous nod from the shadowy TV presence.

"Oh, God. And the other hand is, is — it's a hook, holding up the gun." Sad shake of a blurry head. "No? Well, then it's, uh, I dunno, it's a . . . something. Shit, I have no idea."

A shrug, a pair of hands thrown up in symbolic frustration, and as mysteriously as it appeared, the image faded away, leaving behind an unrelieved tissue of digital noise on her screen, sparkling and popping in random fashion.

Mary Ann sat staring at the TV set. She was scared, and she was mystified, and she was annoyed with herself. She exhaled a long grumbling moan. Then her eyes popped wide open. She stood bolt upright. Suddenly, as if by some telepathic inspiration, she understood what the hook-like gesture meant. "Hey, wait, come back — it's a tree branch! The gun is hanging from a tree branch."

7

BY SEVEN AM the next morning, Mary Ann was back at the turnout on County Road 520, still shaken by the previous night's events, but alert and determined in spite of a sleepless night.

One by one she examined the oak trees bordering the area. On the back side of the fifth one, hidden from the road, was Bobby's Ruger SR9 handgun, hanging from a twig just above head height. She let out a little squeak. She didn't know what to feel — a fortunate tip had uncovered a major clue, but the tip was supplied by someone she could not name or explain.

She instinctively reached for the gun, then caught herself and drew back. No more stupid mistakes, girl. She pulled out her not-so-smartphone and snapped several digital photos of the weapon in place. Then she opened the Ziploc plastic bag she had foreseen might be needed, thrust a downed oak branchlet through the trigger guard, levered the Ruger into the bag, and sealed it shut.

As she entered the Golden Hills Tri-Town Police station, carrying Bobby's bagged gun as she might a turd, Wade Gawley, heading the other way, failed to notice. "Hi, Mary Ann — got three speeders down on 49 already this morning. You should try hanging out at Spencer's Corners, the fish just line up to be caught."

"That's great, Wade."

She dropped her find on Ibañez' desk. The chief raised his eyebrows. "Is this what I think it is, all bagged up?"

"Yes, sir. And I didn't touch it."

"That's good, there's a sigh of relief. Where on Earth . . . "

"Hanging on a tree, like fifty feet from where we found the car."

Ibañez picked up the bag and inspected the weapon. "Gardner will want this. He's got no prints from the brake lever, none from the car. Well, except yours, all over everything." He scowled in frustration. "And you knew where this thing was hidden." He looked up at her. "Maybe you're the shooter."

Mary Ann forced herself not to rise to the bait. "Do you think the actual perp used Bobby's own gun on him?"

"Don't be silly. This thing would have blown his head off, and there was no exit wound. No, whoever it was used some sort of mean little .22."

Mary Ann's discovery was giving her confidence a boost. She pressed on. "Well, hanging in the tree like that, it's a sign, right?"

Ibañez sighed. "Barking dog. The damn thing is trying to tell us something — fire in the barn, Timmy!"

"But what?"

"Advertisement like this, as I read it, probably means something like 'don't tread on me.' Could be, dare I say it, drugs. Most runners hide in their holes. This feels like an operation. Organization, money, outsiders. Terry Gardner can have the case, thanks, and keep the change."

"Want me to run the gun down to Jackson?"

"Right after your traffic update. Vera tells me she likes you, by the way. At least you're doing something right." She gritted her teeth and turned toward her corner desk.

"Be damn careful from now on, Sarzo. This sort of thing happens all the time down in the Big City where I come from. Around here, I can't remember when. I doubt Bobby was killed because he was in the wrong place at the wrong time, or because he was screwing somebody's wife. Although, knowing Bobby, I guess he might have been."

8

AT THE AMADOR COUNTY Sheriff's Office, Deputy Terry Gardner accepted the bagged Ruger politely and expressed his heartfelt gratitude after learning that Mary Ann had been smart enough not to touch it.

"Was it fired?" He wondered.

"Probably. I'm sure he used it down on the range."

He cracked the seal and held the opening up, first to his nose, then to hers. "Take a whiff, what do you think?"

"I can't smell a thing."

"And?"

"So, no, it hasn't been fired, at least not for a while."

"Very good, Officer." Gardner appeared to conclude that Mary Ann was, all in all, an okay cop. "You know, this case hasn't given us much to go on. Thanks to you, we've got a gun. We're lucky, we'll find a print on the piece, but whoever stuck it in that tree probably wiped it."

"Ibañez thinks it might be a drug gang. He's worried." She sounded worried too.

"Your chief, what a guy. I guess he thought moving up to Applefield meant retirement. But hello, Earth calling, we knocked over a meth lab last week, just down the road a mile or two."

▼

On her way back up the hill from Jackson, Mary Ann tuned her radio to 1610 to hear how she sounded issuing traffic advisories. After the preliminary beep and formal FCC notifications, her voice chirped merrily from her tinny loudspeaker. She relaxed her white-knuckle grip on the wheel — she had been bracing to hear some ghostly whisper from the void.

"Weather is sunny and bright today, and traffic is flowing smoothly on all roads throughout the Tri-Town Area. Temperature will reach ninety-five degrees this afternoon, so put those tops up when you park your convertibles, you tourists out there."

She smiled. Coming through the ether she sounded poised, alert, and ten years older. Her first reports had been pinched and constrained by the broadcast format, but after a few weeks wrestling with the most boring task of her life, she let things loosen up. No one complained. She wondered if any single soul, aside from Mayor Teasdale, had ever heard her speak on the air.

In Ragtown she pulled into Mike's Motors. Bobby's Mustang was there under a tarp, alongside exposed oil barrels and discarded tires. Other cops had already been through it, but she wanted to satisfy her own curiosity. She peeled the tarp back. As she leaned toward the window, something flickered in the driver's side mirror. She jumped back as if scalded and turned around, hand on the heel of her sidearm.

"Hey, take it easy, Officer." It was Morning Star Russell, not a ghost.

"Jesus, Mike, you scared me."

"Nice car, right? I don't want you to think I've been careless. Battery was already dead when I towed her in."

Mary Ann noticed that both front windows were down. She opened the door, turned on the lights. No glow. She paused and surveyed the instrument cluster. Dead. Then she noticed the turn signal on the left of the steering post. It was tipped upward, positioned to indicate a right turn. She pointed it out to Russell. "You set this?"

"No, ma'am, I didn't. Everything is just like you found it. Any leads on Bobby's killer?"

"Not that I know of."

Russell slowly toweled the oil off a socket wrench. He eyed her coolly. "Could have been Bobby got in somebody's way. I've got friends around here, and not all of them are entirely on the up and up, if you know what I mean. I hear stories."

"I'll bet you do," said Mary Ann.

"Things like this? Hard to solve."

"And why's that?"

"Too big. Bigger than Bobby, anyway. Bigger than your whole department. You want to stay on your toes. This kind of trouble could spread."

Mary Ann scowled. "What do you know about Bobby's murder?"

"Nothing, really."

"If you have information, you're a material witness. Withholding evidence, that's obstruction of justice. A crime."

Russell grinned and held up his hands in protest. "Nothing material here, your honor. Just idle speculation."

"You should talk to the sheriff."

"I just might. Now, Bobby's car. What do you say, going to buy her?"

Mary Ann was trying to grasp the import of Russell's odd warning.

"I'm still thinking."

9

THE HILLTOP BAND of the Hokyut Nation owned a parcel of reasonably flat acreage bordering the Whiskeyjack River some five miles up a gravel road from Ragtown. A few locals said their meager holdings extended right into the national forest, but most doubted that. No one, with the possible exceptions of Grandmother Rainwater, the ancient matriarch of the group, her grandson Billy, the present leader, or the Amador County Registrar knew for sure. The Hilltop Band wasn't wealthy, or very numerous either. Counted liberally, perhaps twenty individuals could claim membership — an uncertain assortment of second cousins, nephews and nieces, each possessed of a genealogy that baffled local officials. The Federal government seemed equally bewildered, and had persistently refused to recognize the group.

Billy Rainwater was out to change that, but on this day it was his duty to pause in remembrance of his fallen younger brother, killed in the line of duty with the Golden Hills Tri-Town Police Department.

At 2:00 PM Mary Ann Sarzo joined her fellow officers at the grave site, overlooking a dry creek bed on The Hilltop Band's modest burial ground. Quite a gathering. Among the unfamiliar faces she noticed an erect older woman with a wreath of silver hair tucked under a black pillbox hat and an orange-and-green Hermès scarf wrapped around a stylish black jacket. She was standing beside Grandmother Rainwater, keeping the tribal icon on her feet with a tight grip and quiet determination. Mayor Teasdale? Mary Ann was sure it was. Just behind the pair of women stood a tall, dignified gentleman in a blazer and maroon tie. He looked uncomfortable. Mary Ann thought he would much rather be playing golf over in Tarvolo.

Chief Ibañez leaned toward her. "Stop rubbernecking, Sarzo. I'll introduce you after the show."

Mary Ann took this rebuke, milder than usual, as encouragement. "I had a good look at Bobby's Mustang yesterday. He had a turn signal going that was still set when the battery died, so he pulled off the road on purpose. Want to hear my theory, Chief?"

Ibañez was watching the mayor. It took him a moment to respond. "You? You have developed a theory of the crime?"

"He was pulling over to stop and talk to someone. That means he knew the guy — or thought he did. His windows were down on a hot summer night, and someone sneaked up on the passenger side and shot him. So this was planned, and not some random act of modern American violence we read about all the time."

"Of course not. He was hit." Ibañez sighed. "You're a cop now. Ease up on those police academy theories. Try to take the next step. And remind yourself now and then that this case belongs to Deputy Gardner, for the love of God."

Mary Ann gulped. "Yes sir."

Ibañez removed his hat, scratched his head, flung out an arm. "And get out to the range and practice up on your marksmanship."

"Yes sir, I'll do it," said Mary Ann.

He put his hat back on. "Damn well better. It's important, don't fuck around."

Now Billy Rainwater came forward, nodded to his extended family, opened his arms, and addressed the assembly from the edge of a freshly dug grave.

"Our brother Bobby was a good and useful man, a dedicated police officer, and a pillar of our tribe. We're told he was murdered. Perhaps he was, perhaps by mistake, perhaps by someone desperate to avoid arrest, or perhaps because he upheld our sacred commitment to our land, our heritage, and our drive to achieve economic independence. We may never know."

This was the first time Mary Ann had a good look at the older Rainwater. He reminded her of Bobby, but he gave off a theatrical vibe that made her think he'd be a good vacuum cleaner salesman.

"Today, we put Bobby's death aside to focus on his life, a life of joy in his chosen work, a cheerful life that will, we fervently believe, continue on into the spirit world, from where he will reach back and gently guide us forward.

"So, let us commit his mortal body to the earth, and shovel dirt on his interment, knowing that his immortal spirit soars on high, and be comforted."

Mayor Teasdale led Grandmother Rainwater to the edge of the grave. With Billy's help the old woman managed to dribble a few clods of dirt onto the simple coffin.

"Amen."

Mary Ann followed Wade Gawley and Chief Ibañez to the grave, and each added their own bits of soil. Then everyone headed downhill to their cars, pickups, and SUVs.

"I thought there'd be a pastor. Aren't the Hokyuts Christian?" whispered Mary Ann.

Ibañez gave her a cynical shrug. "That's Billy for you. He's a star. Hang on a minute." He walked over to Rainwater, who was busy accepting condolences, shaking hands, making little bows of acknowledgement, and handed an envelope to the Native leader.

"Sorry about your loss, Billy. Here's an item that was found among Bobby's effects. Nobody wants to put it through some ridiculous chain of evidence."

Rainwater took a step backward in surprise. He accepted the envelope with obvious reluctance, tore it open, and peeked inside. When he realized what it was, he recoiled, evidently startled.

"Thank you, Chief. Very kind," he said, recovering.

Ibañez rejoined Mary Ann.

"That was the check I found, right?" she guessed.

"Yup, no point in formality there."

"When you handed it over, he jumped, did you notice?"

"I did. He's a strange one."

"I'll say," she agreed. She puckered up her mouth in confusion.

He looked at her. "What?"

"Something fishy going on, right?"

"Not sure. I Just wanted to see how he'd react."

As the crowd thinned, the mayor and her dignified gentleman companion fell into step with her cops.

"Vera! Gordon! Nice to see you here," said Ibañez.

"Is this our new radio announcer?" Teasdale inquired with a smile.

"That's right, meet Mary Ann."

"Officer Sarzo, is it?"

Mary Ann nodded deferentially.

"How nice to put a face with your voice," said Teasdale. "You've certainly breathed some life into our little weather station. Keep up the good work — it does more for tourism around here than the Chamber of Commerce ever will, don't you think so, Gordon?"

Ibañez smoothly offered another introduction. "Gordon Hollinsworth is the Golden Hills town attorney, among other pursuits. Gordon, this is our new police officer."

The dignified gentleman inclined his head. "I'll have to give you a listen, young lady. Keep the weather in line for us, and tourism will take care of itself."

As quickly as they appeared, with a nod and a wave the pair veered away toward the mayor's blue Volvo SUV. Hollinsworth gallantly assisted the mayor aboard. As she pulled away down the gravel track, Billy Rainwater caught up with him and touched his sleeve. Hollinsworth turned around and produced a jovial smile.

"Billy — excellent sentiments on behalf of your brother. So sorry about this entire affair."

"Mr. Hollinsworth. Talk to me." Rainwater led Hollinsworth aside for a private conversation. Mary Ann, pausing at a table where lemonade and snacks had been set out, watched the pair walk away out of earshot.

"I know these things take time," Rainwater began when they had separated themselves from the gathering. "And I've been waiting patiently — for months now. What about my casino?"

"You're set on this, I know, but it's no slam dunk, Billy. The commissioners don't want to think about it. And no one wants to drive five miles up a dirt road in Ragtown to pull the handle on a slot machine."

Billy scuffed the dirt with his toe and tilted his head toward heaven as he absorbed the little lecture.

Hollinsworth pointed at Billy's chest. "You need to get into Auburn, or Placerville at least."

"Money's flowing now. We've got backers."

"Do you really? That's a development, that's good news. But that only takes you so far. You'll never get approved unless you agree to build on tribal land. You need a land swap."

"Then make it happen."

Hollinsworth reddened. "Billy, my friend. What do you think I've been doing?"

"Fuck all, it looks like, pardon my French."

"Now hold on, hold your horses. There's also the awkward problem of Federal recognition of the tribe."

"We're completely legit."

"Of course you are."

"Those Maidu bastards — they're lobbying against us, I know it."

Hollinsworth blew out a big sigh. "I've heard it rumored. Please understand — this casino business, it's all political now. We've got to act before the gambling issue overwhelms us."

"Then tell me, please, what is it I've got to do that I haven't been doing."

"You've got money? Put it where your mouth is."

"You mean bribes?"

"This is the USA, Billy. No bribes here. Let's just say you're going to pay top price on every transaction. Get used to it."

"How much?"

"Hundreds of thousands, Billy. Millions. But for now, ten thousand dollars to retain my services. Think of it as a poker buy-in."

"Your office?"

"Tell you what. Vera's giving a party to celebrate the civic renewal of Applefield and the Golden Hills Tri-Town Special District. There'll be some interesting people there. You're invited."

As Rainwater angrily stomped away, Mary Ann noticed his arms flying up and down in apparent frustration. Talking to himself, she thought.

10

THE FOOTHILL SHOOTING CENTER was a private operation
that rented its facilities to several foothill law enforcement agencies. It was
only a fifteen minute drive from Mary Ann's trailer in Placerville, so she
was on the pistol range early instead of in the Applefield station.

As she reeled in the B27 target from her first clip, Terry Gardner
appeared, pushing .40 caliber S&W cartridges into his Glock 22. He
whistled when he saw the pattern.

"Whoa. At least you got some of your shots on the paper. And look,
one of them actually hit the silhouette."

Mary Ann removed her ear protectors. "Yeah, I'm just terrible." She
was almost fainting with embarrassment.

Gardner's blue eyes were sparkling. He indicated for her to go again.
"Let me watch you."

Mary Ann reloaded, attached a clean target, ran it out to the ten yard
line, adjusted her safety goggles, and, grasping her Beretta with both
hands, let fly. When she reeled in the target the result was no better than
her first attempt.

Gardner pulled on his own goggles and ear protectors and set up next
to her. "Now me." He ran his target out to the fifteen yard line and fired
off ten rounds at measured intervals. Mary Ann jumped back. His Glock
was so much louder than her little Beretta. When he reeled in the target it
revealed a pattern grouped tightly around the center X. Now it was Mary
Ann's turn to whistle.

"Wow. What am I doing wrong?"

"First thing, you're just supporting your gun hand with your left. You
should wrap your fingers around your shooting hand, pull back, make a
brace." He studied her. "And, more important, you're scared shitless."

"Yeah, true."

"Well, you want the bad guys to be scared, not you, so be brave. If you
can't do that, pretend!"

Mary Ann reloaded, gritted her teeth, and fired off another clip. This
time the target showed two rounds within the eight ring.

"Okay, that's better," said Gardner, then reconsidered. "Well, a little
bit. Know what? You're never going to be any good with a gun, so the best
thing is — stay out of trouble. Lots of cops never fire their weapons in the

line of duty. My advice, be one of them."

"I guess. But I feel like a jerk."

"Hmm. Why'd you join up, anyway?"

"My dad is a sergeant in the army. Where, I don't know. Germany? Afghanistan? I haven't seen him since high school. I wanted to be like him, I guess." She made a face. "But I have this disqualifying problem."

"And that is?" Gardner pushed his goggles up onto his forehead and squinted at her.

"Seizures. When I was a kid. I'm fine now, but they know."

"They know everything. Are you on medication?"

"No. I haven't had the shakes since puberty."

"And you're legal to drive?"

She shrugged. "Sure."

He smiled. "So, instead of Private Sarzo, it's Officer Sarzo. Does Ibañez know?"

"I don't think so. He didn't ask."

"Don't tell him."

Mary Ann dropped the empty clip out of her Beretta. "What about Bobby? How's the Rainwater case coming?"

"The investigation is proceeding, as we say to the media. I can't really talk about it."

Mary Ann thought back to the memorial service. "Have you looked at his brother, Billy?"

"And why would I?"

"Well, they're related, and I don't know about that guy."

"Meaning?" Gardner was willing to listen.

"Well, he's kind of slick, for starters. And Bobby had a check from him sitting in his desk drawer. Uncashed. It was two months old."

"A check? So? Some people are careless with their banking habits."

"Five grand?"

Gardner stared at her. "Yeah, well, who knows?"

"Maybe there was a dispute. Maybe he's the one Bobby pulled over for," she persisted.

"Interesting theory, I'll give you that." Gardner pulled his goggles back down and ran out another target. "Say, later, when we're both exhausted from the day's police work, what about dinner?"

Mary Ann acknowledged the invitation with a smile and briefly considered the idea. But Deputy Terry Gardner, although a handsome dude, was almost ten years older. She thought he might have dated more than his share of women. "Oh no, I can't." She made a rueful face. "Um, it's policy — never date co-workers."

Gardner nodded. "Got it. I understand. No harm trying, right?"

"No harm no foul."

Part TWO

11

BILLY RAINWATER thought it prudent to get an independent opinion of his casino prospects, so he climbed into his beat-up Toyota Tacoma pickup truck and drove down Route 49 to Angels Camp, where a distant relative, Hannah Crowfoot, held forth as a Native American spirit woman, telling fortunes in a small shop on Bush Street, just off the main drag.

The small sign above the door of her establishment, a weather-beaten private house surrounded by overgrown flowers and shrubs, advertised *Readings & Spiritual Advice*. Rainwater knocked and entered a dimly lit foyer. The faint odor of chicken broth mixed with the perfume of an oil-fired space heater and cat urine tickled his nose. On a side table beside a grandfather clock was a small bell and a notice: *Ring for Service*. He picked it up and rang it gently without result. Twitching at the clangor, he rang it more vigorously, and was rewarded with slow and heavy footsteps. A moment later Mrs. Crowfoot appeared. She was short and broad, with strands of grey hair escaping from a long ponytail. She had on thick-lensed glasses and was using a blind person's white cane to tap her way into the foyer. She squinted at her visitor.

"William? William Rainwater?" She wasn't quite blind.

"Yes, ma'am. It's Billy."

"William, Billy, how nice. How are things up on the Hill?"

"Remember my brother Bobby? He got shot."

"I read about that. Tragic." She sighed. "That can happen when you become a white boy."

"Don't I know it."

"What brings you all the way down to see me?"

"The Hilltop Band is planning to build a casino."

"Not in Ragtown?" She was aghast at the impossible notion.

"Of course not. We have investors. We're in the process of acquiring property."

"I see."

"I don't think Bobby wanted us to go ahead with it."

Mrs. Crowfoot leaned forward to scrutinize Rainwater. "Is that why he got shot?"

"Well, I wish he had been on our side, we need to stick together on the big things — tribal unity, it's important. But I don't see a connection."

"Family and all," she nodded, understanding.

"But doubts cause doubts. Can we pull it off?"

"You mean, what do the spirits say?" She folded her hands over her shapeless black shift.

"I guess. I'm not much of a believer in this sort of thing — you know that we joined the Church of God's Blessing, right? — but I don't want to chance anything."

"You foolish people. It doesn't matter what you believe." She pointed to a doorway covered by a heavy curtain printed with a wild animal motif. She pushed a coyote out of the way and indicated a seat at a small table in the center of a small room. Rainwater sat, and Mrs. Crowfoot drew heavy curtains over the windows. She lit the burner on a small Sterno-powered brazier and placed it in the center of the table. Into this she dropped small bits of incense. Blue and yellow tongues of flame licked upward. She eased into an upholstered chair opposite Rainwater, adjusted the flame, and brought forth a half dozen feathers from a red-tailed hawk, which she fanned out above the fire.

"State your question," she ordered.

"I, uh, will we, the Hilltop Band, be able to fulfill our long-held dream and find the land to build our casino? How's that?"

"Good, good. I am consulting." She held the feathers together in a bundle, then let them drop, shafts downward, onto the table. The feathers flopped outward in a roughly circular pattern, which she appeared to study. After a minute of silence, Rainwater cleared his throat. After another minute, he shifted his weight. He tapped the table edge.

"What's the verdict?" he blurted.

"Shhh!"

She leaned forward and fanned smoke from the little flame over the hawk feathers with what looked like a woven basket cover, probably an heirloom. Two of the six feathers flipped over across the others.

"Here is your answer. Look how the feathers fell symmetrically. There is no clear path. When touched by the spirits, they gave way to the north. That way is open."

"What does it mean?" Rainwater was impressed by the little show.

"Your way is north, but your way will be hard."

"How so?"

"You see how one of the feathers fell across the other?"

"These?" He pointed.

"That's right. They are a warning. Pitfalls lurk. Bad things are waiting to happen."

"I don't believe it," said Rainwater stoutly, taken aback by her unfavorable reading.

She held up her hands. "You don't have to. I'm not always right. But this much I do know — you can't afford many mistakes. Forget the church, call on your heritage and let the spirits of the land guide you."

She blew out her little fire, then rose and opened the curtains. Rainwater stood up with her, unnerved by the ceremony.

"How much?"

"Because we are kinfolk, twenty dollars."

He opened his wallet and extracted two tens.

"Better yet — if you see a tom turkey running wild on the Hill, shoot it, and bring it to me in time for Thanksgiving."

He put one ten back in his wallet and stuffed the other into the woman's hand.

"Thank you. I'll do it."

Mrs. Crowfoot regarded her third cousin twice removed with concern. "You were hoping for clear sailing, I suppose."

Rainwater nodded unhappily. "Who wouldn't?"

"Understand, I'm not judging. I see what I see. So . . . if you want my best advice, try another path."

"Nothing doing. Whatever it takes. That casino — it's our future."

He was adamant.

12

"ALL RIGHT, OFFICERS. Vera wants traffic control at her party tonight, so I volunteered you two." Ibañez was sitting on the edge of his desk, arms folded, holding forth at the daily muster of the Golden Hills Tri-Town Police force. Wade Gawley and Mary Ann stood in front of him.

Gawley squirmed. "Man, I'm supposed to be down in Lodi tonight. What's wrong with Rick?" Ricky Moss was the only other member of the unit. Gawley resented his casual ways.

"Well, Wade, he's down there right now at the dentist, having a molar crowned. At least, I think that's what he's doing. I sure hope you two don't know the same woman."

Ibañez moved to a map on the wall and pointed out some Applefield details. "Vera wants us to park cars behind the Miners Market over here. So one of you can stand in her drive to route the guests, and the other at the lot to reassure the nervous ones that they won't get towed. It's only a block up the hill to the Teasdale property, so it's not a big deal. And, since you're not on duty, this is a paid gig."

Gawley blinked. "How much?"

"Couple of hundred. Next time at McDonald's, you can super-size those fries."

▼

As evening descended on the foothills, cars began arriving at Mayor Teasdale's sprawling brick and stucco mansion overlooking downtown Applefield. Mary Ann was in the driveway directing everyone to the grocery store parking lot. She was astonished by the expensive sheet metal on display in a region where money was hard to come by. Everything from a fancy Porsche something-or-other to a herd of elephantine sport utility vehicles. Nothing less than a hybrid Prius driven by someone whose expensive taste was overridden by environmental concern.

Up above, Mary Ann could hear laughter and the rhythms of a mariachi band. It sounded like everyone was having a wonderful time, so she climbed the drive to have a look.

And indeed, most everyone was. Once she was sure her guests had a beer or margarita in hand, Mayor Teasdale stepped out into her fashionably landscaped back yard, where a large tent had been set up to hold the food and drink. There she took up a position beside a tall shape heavily draped in green canvas. She raised an arm and called for attention.

"My friends, welcome. I know that you are all as proud as I am of the revival of the Tri-Town Area. It wasn't until my husband Daniel passed on that I discovered my life's work, but since then I have labored tirelessly toward this day, when we can declare our economic and cultural success. Here's to the Golden Hills." She raised her glass. Fifty guests let out a cheer and did likewise.

"To commemorate the moment when tourism became the new gold rush, we are tonight dedicating a statue by the renowned Santa Fe sculptor, Barry Klesko. Appropriately, it's a lone prospector, panning hopefully for a better tomorrow."

She gestured to her left, and Mary Ann observed a suave-looking Latino man step forward. He was wearing a pink golf shirt over white slacks. A white ribbed sweater was draped across his shoulders. He had long dark wavy hair and a dark mustache. Mary Ann thought he looked forty-ish and a little bit exotic, probably not from this country. She moved forward for a better view.

"Next week we'll set this fellow up in the Applefield town square, but first let's take a look. To perform the unveiling, I turn to Salvador Cruz." The mustachioed man waved to the crowd. "You know him as the owner of the Golden Fleece Ranch, where he's raising alpacas, but I know him as a generous patron of the arts who has expressed his love for our country by financing this fine statue."

Mayor Teasdale extended her arm, and Cruz bowed his head. "Go on, Sally. Show them." Cruz dutifully tugged at a rope, and the canvas fell away from the tall shape, revealing the life-size bronze statue of a weather-beaten gold prospector in a crumpled hat. He was speculatively stirring his fingers in a gold mining pan. Water bubbled from the pan into a pool at his feet. From Mary Ann's distant and aesthetically limited perspective, the statue seemed startlingly realistic, a stunning creation. That it was also a water fountain struck her as amazing.

Howard Turnbow, standing a lot closer, had a different opinion. "What kitsch, Gordon. How could she?"

"Now Howard, you know how hard Vera worked for this." Gordon Hollinsworth, in his capacity as town attorney, was on good terms with everyone who mattered in the Golden Hills Tri-Town establishment, including Turnbow, who was Teasdale's longtime political opponent.

"Jesus, it's something the ski crowd could buy from a Tahoe City gallery, and then to go and beg money from this, this . . . Mexican!"

"He's a citizen, Howard, same as you or me," said Hollinsworth.

"Is that so? Are you sure about that?"

Hollinsworth gritted his teeth. Turnbow was skeptical about everything, up to and including tomorrow's sunrise. "I'm sure, because I made sure. I wrote up all the papers, got him approved by an act of Congress. Forget that five-year crap."

"See, that's what happens when you let all these illegals in. Now they're everywhere." Turnbow pointed to his empty glass and headed for the bar. Hollinsworth shook his head watching him go.

"You know, with enemies like that, Teasdale could be mayor until she's a hundred."

Hollinsworth spun around to find Billy Rainwater at his elbow. "Christ, Billy, say hello. I almost spilled the mayor's very expensive scotch."

"You mentioned interesting people the other day. You mean this guy Cruz?" Rainwater awkwardly passed an envelope thick with cash to Hollinsworth, who tucked it into his blazer with a little nod of acknowledgement.

"Let's have a chat with Vera first, what do you say?"

Hollinsworth led Rainwater across the lawn to the mayor, who was surrounded by chattering rich folks from the gated community of Tarvolo, and took her aside. Her cheeks were glowing.

"What do you think, Gordon? Isn't he beautiful?"

"The statue — very nice, a nice addition to the community."

"No, you ridiculous man, Sally Cruz. He is our benefactor tonight." She took a long pull on her second margarita.

By this time Mary Ann's curiosity had brought her onto the lawn, from which vantage point she could eavesdrop on half a dozen conversations. No one seemed to notice.

"Vera, this is Billy Rainwater. He's the tribal leader of the Hilltop Band over in Ragtown."

"Hello, ma'am. Love the statue."

Hollinsworth swirled his scotch. "I've been thinking. Billy wants a casino. The state will require that it be built on tribal land."

"In Ragtown? Don't be silly."

"My point exactly. He needs a land swap. Now you've got that thirty acre parcel up in Auburn, just sitting there collecting hubcaps off the Interstate. While Billy and his Band here, they own in deed perfect twelve hundred acres just up the road. A chunk of that would make a nice trade, don't you think? Help move the Tri-Town Area forward, yes?"

Mayor Teasdale's bright face clouded slightly. "Land swap."

Rainwater piped up. "Yes ma'am, ancestral land. We own right along the Whiskeyjack and butt up against Tarvolo and the lake on the other side. Prime development possibilities."

"I couldn't consider an even trade. There's a condo developer interested in my Auburn property." The mayor's mood seemed to darken.

"Hold on, Vera, there would be a cash settlement as well, of course."

"How big?" Now she was all businesswoman.

"A significant cash payment. We're not finalizing here, just establishing a framework." Hollinsworth shaped the deal in the air with his hands as if outlining a voluptuous woman.

"Owing to the differential locations," added Rainwater.

Mayor Teasdale set her margarita glass on a little table and smoothed her grey silk dress. "It's something to think about. But the truth is, I'm trying to lure my daughter and her bio-tech husband back up here to God's country. They're rotting away down in San Diego, and I know Douglas would jump at the chance to run a bed-and-breakfast on that piece of land. Have you considered the hotel here in town?"

With that she floated away to her other guests.

"Will she go for it?" asked Rainwater, looking mighty depressed.

"I've got another idea," replied Hollinsworth. He knocked back the rest of his drink and swiveled toward the bar, where he approached a spry-looking older man in a plaid cowboy shirt and sprightly straw hat.

"Bob Brannan, my man," boomed Hollinsworth.

"Hello, Gordon. Helluva party, what?" Brannan hoisted his beer in salute.

"Yes indeed. Vera's on her game tonight." Hollinsworth rubbed his hands together. "Bob, you probably already know Billy Rainwater, the distinguished chief of the Hilltop Band. He and his tribe are looking to build a casino here in town, terrific potential for our community, don't you think?"

Brannan set his beer down on the serving table. "What's this all about?"

"Well now, the state and the Feds won't hear of such a thing, no matter how attractive economically, unless the facility goes up on tribal land."

"And . . . ?"

"The situation on their ancestral homeland is unfavorable. Dirt road, inconvenient access, you know what I'm talking about."

"And this involves me . . . how?" Brannan's indifference was dissolving into mild curiosity.

"The Hilltop Band is willing to consider a land swap. Your hotel and grounds for a significant portion of tribal holdings on the Whiskeyjack."

"We own right along the bank there, Mr. Brannan," said Rainwater. "And, as I understand it, you'd be thankful for an opportunity to retire down to Tucson."

"What in tarnation would I do with tribal land?"

Rainwater was quick with his pitch. "Development, Mr. Brannan. We butt up against Tarvolo too. Lots of rich folks are looking to locate first and second homes here in the foothills."

"Well, everybody knows I've got a son down there in Arizona. But . . ." He regarded his beer thoughtfully. ". . . I'd need an inducement. I can't retire on development opportunities."

Hollinsworth nodded sagely. "Of course not, Bob. We're prepared to make a substantial cash payment, in addition to, say, 150 acres."

Brannan finished his beer. "Well, that's quite an offer. If you're serious, see me during business hours, and we'll talk." He touched his hat and moved away.

Mary Ann looked over the rest of the well-heeled guests. She was admiring their outfits when she noticed Terry Gardner circulating through the group, looking very well-to-do himself in civilian clothes. She was surprised to see him there.

"Hi, Terry. What brings you up this way?"

"Networking. Lot of money strolling around tonight. Might run into a business opportunity." He fingered the lapels of his linen blazer, adjusted his dark knit tie.

"Being a sheriff not exciting enough?"

He grinned. "Well, if I really wanted to be *the* sheriff, I'd have to campaign for the job and get elected. I'm no Teasdale."

"I guess not," she said.

"Nothing's forever, Sarzo. Always keep an eye peeled." He winked and maneuvered away into the crowd. She watched him go, mildly disillusioned to think a cop could ever imagine another life.

Bored at last by the nattering of tipsy rich people, Mary Ann circled back to the upper end of the Teasdale driveway and was standing there as Rainwater and Hollinsworth moved to leave the party. She watched idly as they paused to chat with the Golden Hills' new social lion, Salvador Cruz. Apparently Rainwater was already acquainted with the man, because they shook hands like old friends.

As a jolly Hollinsworth and mournful Rainwater passed by on the way to their cars, movement from the direction of the mayor's garage caught Mary Ann's eye.

A light went on inside the Range Rover parked there, revealing a figure busy looking for something. Mary Ann unsnapped her holster, placed her hand on the grip of her pistol, and sidled toward the vehicle.

"Hey, you, buddy. Step away from the car."

The figure jerked upright. "And keep your hands where I can see them." The figure backed out of the Range Rover and turned toward her.

"Oh my God, Chief Ibañez. Sir."

"Evening, Mary Ann. Some party, huh?"

"What are you doing here? You're on duty tonight."

"Oh, just making sure everything's okay with our friend Señor Cruz, Hollinsworth's model citizen. This is his car. Don't want anyone planting any bombs." He gestured toward the open door with a hand holding several pieces of paper.

Mary Ann was shocked. "You are breaking and entering."

Ibañez looked at her with disdain. "I didn't break anything, young lady. This guy Cruz, he bought his ranch with cash I heard, and I'm sure he paid Gordon plenty for his citizenship papers. Vera thinks he loves his adopted country — generous gratitude, and so forth — but where did all the money come from? He's a bad guy, or I'm no cop."

"If you say so, Chief. But, whoa, you probably ought to close that door."

Ibañez let the slips of paper he had gathered fall onto the Range Rover's passenger seat, slammed the door shut, and stalked off down the driveway. "Just remember, keep an eye on the guests when they leave. Friends don't let friends drive drunk."

Mary Ann watched him go, then peered into the Range Rover, wondering what in the paper pile could have drawn the attention of her boss. As she did so, a shadow flickered across the glass. She gasped and stepped backward. The shadow stabilized, became an apparition, beckoned her with a finger. Involuntarily, she leaned forward. The apparition shook its head, tapped its chest, made a cutting gesture.

Mary Ann scowled. "Who are you, what do you want?"

The ghostly shape repeated its movements, shaking its head, tapping its chest, sharply slicing the air with the flat of a ghostly hand.

"No something, don't something. What?" she whispered.

Once again the shape repeated the sequence of movements.

"Don't, what, trust you? Believe me, that's no problem."

The shadowy head wobbled on a shadowy neck, and shadowy hands flew up to take in the world.

"Don't trust, um, anybody?"

The apparition held up a hand with thumb and forefinger touching each other in the classic sign of affirmation.

"Not the mayor?"

The apparition made a thumbs-down sign.

"How about this guy Cruz?"

Thumbs down.

"Deputy Gardner?"

Another thumbs down.

"Or even Chief Ibañez?"

Thumbs down yet again.

"Geez, you are one suspicious ghost."

The apparition nodded and faded from sight. Mary Ann sagged back against the Range Rover, thoroughly drained by the very strange encounter.

13

EARLY NEXT MORNING Mary Ann called in sick to the Golden Hills police station and informed Officer Moss that she thought her head would clear after lunch. Then she parked in front of the Ragtown Book Nook and waited for it to open. Finally a little bell tinkled, and the glass door angled inward. A hand flipped a sign hanging in the window from *Closed Book* to *Open Book*.

Mary Ann jumped out of her Honda, then slowed herself down for a dignified entrance. Inside, overhead fluorescent lights made the shelves and titles bright and shiny. No one seemed to be taking care of the merchandise, so she started browsing. Within a minute she knew she was lost. There were sections for Gold Mining, History, Mystery, Romance, Science, Fiction, and even Science-Fiction, but nothing obvious about ghosts. She coughed and scraped a foot. Immediately a plump woman of sixty or so flew out of a back office to greet her.

"Hello there, something I can help you find?" She lowered bright red glasses onto her ample chest, where they dangled from a beaded chain, and peered inquisitively at her customer.

Mary Ann was as embarrassed as if she were about to discuss condoms and diaphragms. "Um, I've never been in your store before. It's nice."

"Why thank you." The woman smiled a kindly smile.

"And, um, I was wondering . . . do you have, like, an Occult section maybe?"

"Looking for . . . ?"

Mary Ann bit her lip. She didn't want to reveal anything, lest she become known as a madwoman. But she sensed that this person might be on her side, so she confessed. "Ghosts, I guess. Real ones."

"Oh, that stuff is all over in Non-Fiction."

Mary Ann looked over the titles available — *Ghostly Garrets, The Haunted Hills, 47 Weatherly Place, My Life with the Dead,* many others — and felt confusion overwhelm her.

The woman studied Mary Ann from afar, and when she could discern no progress whatsoever, edged over beside her. "What's the problem? You don't look very well."

"Know anything about ghosts?"

"Not that much. The nearest haunted houses, so-called, are all down around Sonora."

"Ever see one?"

"No, and I hope I never do. I don't want the shade of some disappointed prospector waltzing through my bedroom window, thank you." She put her glasses back on to inspect Mary Ann's face and noted her pallor. "Ah, but you have seen one, I'm guessing."

"Or something a lot like one."

"Oh my. You're the new cop in town, right?"

"Yes, Mary Ann Sarzo."

"Welcome to Ragtown. I'm Lorraine Wagstaff, the only woman dumb enough to sell books around here. I own this place. Don't worry, nothing about our little chat will get back to your hard-ass police chief, if that's what you're worried about."

"I am worried about that, somewhere way down on the list below" — she made quote signs in the air — "actually seeing a ghost."

"Hmm. Could be you're hallucinating, you know. Any illegal substances involved?"

"Are you kidding? With a cop?"

"I'll take that as a 'no.' Double-checking the rational possibilities, hope you don't mind."

Mary Ann just stared at her.

"Okay then, if you're serious, stay away from the sensational titles. You probably ought to start with *Charter's Guide to the Supernatural & Atlas of Otherworldly Maps*."

Mary Ann smiled. The bookstore proprietor was obviously becoming curious. "I thought you didn't know much about this stuff."

"I only know what I read. You're an eyewitness. Look at me, I'm getting all excited. What was it like, anyway, a glimpse of the supernatural?"

"Like everyone says — real spooky."

14

MAYOR TEASDALE was in her office, poring over a pile of paper, scribbling notes, writing entries in her log book, making the hundreds of little decisions that kept the Tri-Town Area in business. She paused over a proposal from her chief of police, read it a second time, then picked up the telephone and punched a number on her speed-dial list.

"Hector? It's me."

"Morning, Vera. What can I do for you?"

"I'm looking at your proposal for a new hire to replace what's his name, Officer Rainwater. The man who was killed. And I can't approve it."

"Beg pardon? We're down a man, below manifest. It's in the budget."

"Yes, I know, but we're not seeing the tax revenue I thought we would this year. Have you looked at the housing market? Bob Brannan has asked to have the assessment on his hotel reduced. Businesses are hurting up and down the highway. We lost a souvenir shop on Main Street this month."

"So?"

"So, go with the staff you've got. Until next fiscal year, then the Council and I, we'll do some juggling."

"You're asking me to reduce our police presence, drop our guard."

"Yes, yes, just for a few months."

"You realize we've got a murder on our hands?"

"Of course. The first in how long? Before my watch, anyway. The sheriff will take care of that."

"I'm aware that money is tight. But I've got to recommend against this."

"My decision, Hector. I'll take the blame if there is any."

"I'm not worried about blame. Safety, that's my concern."

"You sound more like an old lady than I do. There's no choice, really. I probably should have stepped in before you hired that nice young woman. Relax, we'll be fine."

She put down the phone, wrote *not approved* on the new-hire request, shoved it aside, and moved on to the next issue in a long list.

▼

That same day in Applefield, Billy Rainwater parked his pickup truck in the Miners Market lot, then opened a mobile phone and made a call.

After a brief and cryptic conversation, he snapped the thing shut, yanked a backpack out of his truck, and set off between buildings, past the newly installed prospector statue in the town park, past a rubbish can at the park boundary, where he casually deposited the mobile phone, and on toward the local branch of the Bank of America.

There he spoke briefly to a teller, who led him through a gate into the safe deposit anteroom. Once behind the gate the teller signaled him to wait for a customer already inside the vault to exit. Rainwater set his backpack down on the counter and stood by patiently.

Presently the customer emerged from the vault, also carrying a backpack, which he deftly switched with Rainwater's as he passed by. The customer was none other than Salvador Cruz.

A few minutes later, Rainwater returned to his pickup. He got behind the wheel, opened another mobile phone, made another call.

"Hello, Millwood? Rainwater. I'm having terrific luck up here. I've got some color for you, and I'm in the area. When's a good time to come in?"

While he was talking, Cruz drove by in his green Range Rover without so much as a glance.

15

ARRIVING HOME from a late shift, Mary Ann checked her mailbox and discovered a postcard from one Sergeant Sarzo. She dashed inside, poured herself a glass of cheap red wine, and read it aloud, savoring the brief message:

Dear Daughter —

I know you've got a big occasion coming up. Number 27, right? Hope this card reaches you in time for a Happy Birthday. Understand you're in police work these days.

Don't get shot.

— love, Dad.

She raised her glass to her absent parent and downed a big gulp.

"Yo, Dad, thanks, that was last year, now I'm 28, my birthday was a month ago, and where the fuck *are* you, Mr. Lifer?"

She frowned back tears and flipped the card over. The image on the front side was anonymous, a tight close-up photograph of roses. She looked at the postmark: APO 31905. She knew that meant Fort Benning, Georgia. She also knew it meant nothing. Every year her distant father sent her cards at Christmas and on her birthday, and the cards always came from Fort Benning. Several times she had tried to track him down through the various commands, divisions, battalions, regiments, and brigades based there, without success. On the other hand, when she sent mail his way, she included the 75th Ranger Regiment in the address, and some of her letters apparently got through, because his cards, like this one, often showed vague knowledge of her activities.

Feeling completely rejected and dejected, she downed the rest of her wine in one swallow and crossed the kitchen for a refill. As she reached for the bottle she stopped short. A shadowy form was moving in the little glass window of her microwave oven.

"Hello, Mr. Ghost Guy. Welcome to happy hour at the Placerville Gardens RV Park & Resort." She poured herself a generous slug of wine and recklessly knocked it back. "Cheers to ya."

The form took on human shape and held up both hands in a stop gesture. It drew a finger across its throat, feigned collapsing. Mary Ann just stood there. The shock of encountering this thing, this apparition, hallucination, ghost, or whatever the hell it was, was wearing off. She folded her arms and waited.

Again the figure acted out its little pantomime. Mary Ann continued to watch in silence. The figure repeated its performance for a third time, then cupped its hands to an indistinct mouth, appeared to shout, and threw its hands outward in urgent silent appeal.

Mary Ann's skin started to prickle. She didn't know how she was able to decode the figure's ambiguous movements, but mysteriously, somehow she could. "Oh my God, another murder."

The figure nodded gravely.

"Where?"

The figure traced an *R* in the air with an outstretched finger.

"Ragtown."

The figure gave her a thumbs-up and vanished.

16

MARY ANN brought her little Honda to a screeching halt halfway along the stretch of road that passed for Ragtown's Main Street. She set her emergency flashers blinking, checked her rear-view mirror to be sure the ghost wasn't hitchhiking with her, and stepped cautiously onto the pavement for a look around. She noticed a couple of late night barflies idly watching her from the front steps of the Palomino. Otherwise the street seemed deserted. A few doors down, an alley ran between the local convenience store and a private house. She fired up her police-issue Maglite XL50 and moved warily into the dark and narrow passage.

Twenty yards in she came to a rusty dumpster. Just beyond it the powerful beam of her flashlight revealed a confusing heap of clothing and human remains surrounded by a family of raccoons. They were cackling and grunting. One of them appeared to be tugging on what she imagined human intestines might look like.

"Ughh."

She lurched back a few steps. Suddenly she felt her stomach heave. She turned, bent over, and vomited into a jasmine-covered chain link fence.

Wiping her mouth on a sleeve, she staggered back onto the street, hit a button on her mobile phone, and called 9-1-1.

"Hello? This is Officer Sarzo. I'm in Ragtown, on the highway here. We have what looks like an unconscious male, indeterminate age, lying in an alley. Possibly deceased. Um, that's Sarzo, S-A-R-Z-O. Golden Hills Tri-Town Police. Emergency? Good God, yes. Call the duty desk right away, please. Call Chief Ibanez if you can reach him, and send an ambulance with a squad to clean up this mess."

She opened her trunk. Her experience, brief as it was, had already taught her to keep a few police items handy. She pulled out a roll of yellow tape with the words, *POLICE LINE DO NOT CROSS*, repeated endlessly along it.

She tied one end of the tape to the convenience store porch railing, and was starting to unroll it when a bright yellow Toyota FJ Cruiser SUV pulled up. A young man about her age hopped out and ran over. He had hazel eyes under long shaggy hair and a beard trimmed short. He was dressed in half-length cargo pants and tee-shirt, and he was brandishing a video camera.

"Hi, you just made the 9-1-1 call? I was over at Mom's, and, lucky me, my scanner was on. Let's see what you've got here." He started into the alley.

Mary Ann placed a hand on his chest to stop him. "Sorry, sir, this is a police matter. Here, help me get this tape up." She handed him the roll and pointed to the chain link fence edging the alley.

He tied it off. "Now look, I'm a journalist. I edit the local newspaper, *County Courier?*"

"I've heard of it. That means you can read, right? So read the tape you just rolled out — do not cross."

In frustration he turned on his video camera and pointed it at her. A bank of LEDs mounted on top bathed Mary Ann in harsh white light. "Tell me, ma'am, what is the nature of this police action?"

She held up a hand to ward off the glare. "I'm not sure. And, until we know more, we have to treat this location as a crime scene."

"Are you actually a cop?"

"That's right."

"Is this some kind of undercover operation?"

"No."

"Then why aren't you in uniform?"

"I was off-duty when I got a tip we might have a crime here."

"What kind of crime, officer?"

"That is still to be determined. Ask Chief Ibañez when he arrives. And turn that thing off."

He studied her coolly in the blinding beam of his camera light. He thought she was kind of pretty and very shapely in a fills-her-jeans-well sort of way. He was impressed by her sense of authority. Her police manner seemed recently acquired, however, and in need of some practice.

"Hey, off . . . please."

He snapped the camera off. "Sorry."

"Don't worry, you'll get your story. It'll be a scoop."

He laughed grimly. "Unless the *Sacramento Bee* has a reporter hanging around the Palomino."

A Golden Hills Tri-Town Police Explorer roared up beside them, and Chief Ibañez got out. He buckled on his duty belt as he ambled over.

"Officer Sarzo. Why am I running around Ragtown in the middle of the night?"

"Better have a look."

Together they made their way back into the alley.

Ibañez whistled when they reached the dumpster. The raccoons were still tearing at the corpse, if that's what it was.

"You there! Git!"

He kicked one of the raccoons, whipped out his baton and took a swing at the others. Grudgingly they backed away, chittering unhappily.

Mary Ann held a hand over her mouth as they looked more closely at the rumpled mess in front of them. Then she gagged and bolted for the street.

This annoyed Ibañez almost as much as the raccoons. "What's the matter, Sarzo? You're a cop, this isn't the worst thing you'll ever see. Learn to deal, for Christ's sake."

But Mary Ann was back right away with a pair of digital cameras. She handed one to Ibañez. "Let's document the scene."

Ibañez almost smiled. "Don't touch anything," he warned.

"You either," shot back Mary Ann.

17

IN THE GOLDEN HILLS Tri-Town Police station, morning sun was blazing through tall and dirty windows, lighting up a cloud of dust motes. The ancient air conditioner was already whirring.

Wade Gawley flipped through the stack of photos Mary Ann and Ibañez took the night before. "I can't look at these. I just had breakfast." He passed them on to Ricky Moss, who lingered over every one, not the least bit disturbed by the grisly details.

Ibañez recited the facts of the case aloud, as if memorizing the important points. "The victim is one Morning Star Russell, identified by a driver's license found in the wallet in his pants at the scene, but the photos are clear enough, and it's obvious. Lived in Ragtown, owned the local garage, known to one and all as Mike. Son of Ernest and Sunshine Russell. Known to smoke grass, snort coke, maybe worse. Cause of death appears to be knife wounds, but we won't know for sure until the county ME weighs in. Motive could be robbery — if there was any money in that wallet, it's gone now. Sarzo, you found the body and dialed 9-1-1. How did that happen?"

"I got a tip."

"Phone call? Man or woman? Recognize the voice?"

"Um, man, I guess," she lied. "Pretty hard to understand."

"Hmm. No one was waiting at the scene. Could have been the perp calling. So, people, any idea who killed our beloved mechanic?"

Moss looked up from the photos. "We heard rumors of a meth lab a while back, but we never developed any evidence."

Gawley brightened. "I nailed him for speeding three different times."

"Jesus, Wade, you didn't kill him for going ten over. And I doubt meth zombies had it in them."

Mary Ann curled her lip. "I saw intestines."

"Those damn raccoons."

She shook her head. "Unh-unh. They're too small to rip open skin that's not — oh, God — all rotted and decayed. Take a look at those pictures. He was cut open."

Ibañez rolled his eyes. "Are you nuts? He was stabbed. That opened him up for our furry friends."

Mary Ann held her ground. "I don't believe it. There's a slice there from top to bottom. Everything is hanging out."

"So whodunnit, Miss Crime Theory? The butcher, the baker, the candlestick maker?"

Mary Ann scowled. She considered the matter for a moment. "The butcher," she said.

Ibañez shrugged, picked up his desk phone, and dialed a number. "I'll forward your professional conclusions when I pass this on to Jackson and the capable hands of Deputy Sheriff Gardner. Now, all of you, off to work. Write some tickets."

18

MARY ANN decided that Lorraine Wagstaff, the Book Nook's motherly proprietor, had to become her friend. Anything less, and her eerie confession was going to turn into gossip and come back to haunt her, of that she was sure. So she made a habit of dropping in from time to time to scan magazines, buy the occasional cheap novel, and chat. Today found her skipping lunch in order to discuss her paranormal research in Lorraine's private office.

"So I glanced through that book, *Charter's Guide*. He writes about some very weird shit."

"Well, my dear, you saw some very weird shit."

"Oh yeah. Still seeing it, by the way."

"This happens regularly?"

"No, but that's how I found Mike Russell's body. What that guy Charter calls an 'ectoplasm' gave me a tip."

"Well now. That *is* weird."

"And I found out something interesting — maybe I see this stuff because of family history."

"You're an adept, that's what. And Charter isn't the only scholar to note how these talents run in families. What's your background?"

"Genealogy? I have no idea."

"Sarzo — how to say this? — it's an unusual name, don't you think?"

"I guess. It was unique in high school and up at Butte College, that's for sure."

"We should track it down."

"How would we do that? I'm not in touch with any living relatives."

A cloud passed across Lorraine's face. "Oh dear. No mother? No father?"

Mary Ann was about to describe her family woes when they were interrupted by the young editor of the *County Courier*, who burst in without bothering to knock.

"Hey, take a look at this!" He held up the front page of his latest edition. The headline screamed:

HILLTOP BAND BUYS LOCAL HOTEL

Mary Ann gave him a sour look. "I thought you'd be leading with the latest murder."

His attention shifted from his journalistic triumph long enough to register her presence. "You. So you do have a uniform, and you really are a cop, like you said."

Mary Ann resented the casual intrusion. "Hey, we're having a conversation here, in case you didn't notice."

Lorraine looked from one to the other and back. "You two know each other?"

"Not really." The denials were simultaneous.

Lorraine laughed at their mutual discomfort. "Mary Ann, this is my son, Tom. He's taking me to lunch. Come on along. I'll make him apologize — I don't want you to think he's a jerk."

▼

They drove to Rossi's on the outskirts of Tarvolo in Tom Wagstaff's big yellow Toyota, where, at a table on the wisteria-covered patio, the conversation centered on Billy Rainwater's stunning real estate acquisition.

Lorraine Wagstaff was enthusiastic. "I like your sub-headline — 'Casino Speculation Rampant.' Might be good for business. That damn Kindle is killing me." She dispatched a consoling forkful of pesto pasta.

Tom Wagstaff was less sure. "I dunno. I talked to Rainwater, and he's pretty cagey, but I sense something else going on. I think he's got his sights on Auburn. You know, up there, he'd be right off I-80."

"Then why Brannan's hotel?"

"He traded, quote, 'ancestral land' for it. So it's tribal property now. I think he's hoping he can swing another trade, this time with Mayor Teasdale, who owns some undeveloped property in Auburn."

Mary Ann put down her glass of sparkling water. Suddenly she understood what he was talking about. "I overheard the mayor at her party — she thinks her son-in-law would like to run a bed-and-breakfast up here in the foothills. How about a hotel?"

Wagstaff waggled a finger. "Aha, not bad, not bad. Holmes, is that your name? I bet you nailed it."

Mary Ann remembered Ibañez' evaluation of Salvador Cruz. "I was at Bobby's memorial service. The Hilltop Band live way out in the tulies. I can't believe anyone would trade for their land even up. Where's the money come from?"

The Wagstaffs both wondered the same thing. Tom shook his head. "Good question."

Mary Ann was hoping for some gossip she could piece into Bobby's murder, and concealed her disappointment with a change of subject. "All right then, Tom. Where does your money come from? Is the *Courier* making you rich?"

Wagstaff welcomed the chance to be nice. He was starting to take an interest in the new police officer. "Don't I wish. But it's really just one of my hobbies. I teach cabinet-making at the community college down in Lodi. And, on a slow news day, I pan for gold up on the Whiskeyjack."

"You're kidding. Gold? In them thar hills?"

"You bet. The gold rush pulled out ten, fifteen percent at most. I find some color now and then. You just need the right rig and know where to look."

Lorraine watched the two of them sizing each other up and judged that the new police officer might be in a mood to forgive her son. "Mary Ann is curious about her family name. Maybe you can help her do a search."

"Lorraine — !" Mary Ann felt her cheeks get hot.

"Now, if anyone can find it, Tom's the one. And you two ought to get to know each other better."

"Mom — !" Wagstaff blushed to the roots of his shaggy blond hair.

▼

Back in the Book Nook after lunch, a subdued Wagstaff led Mary Ann to one of the half-dozen computers set up for customers. He popped open a browser.

"So, go to Google, yup, click there, okay, type in "genealogy" and your name, you'll get a million hits."

"Thanks."

"No prob. What *is* your name, anyway, if you don't mind my asking?"

She tapped the little engraved plastic badge pinned above her right breast. "Sarzo, like it says here."

"Oh, right, I should have noticed. Sorry about the Holmes joke. Look, keep digging. Some of these sites charge money, but if you hunt around, you'll find lots of free info. Just don't, ah, buy anything from Amazon on

Mom's machine, she'll really hate that, okay?"

"Right. Don't worry."

"Well then, see you."

"Hey, thanks for lunch."

"*De nada.*" He waved awkwardly and departed.

Mary Ann felt her nerves unwind. Hmm, why nerves, anyway? She bent toward the computer screen and dug through one website after another, searching for some sign of her history. After an hour of this, Lorraine walked over to watch.

"So, what do you think, you and Tom patch up your differences?"

Mary Ann colored. "Lorraine, you are a shameless woman. You're matchmaking!"

"What if I am?"

Mary Ann ignored her. "Look at this. Sarzo is a Cuban name. There's some rock star down in Miami. I don't remember anyone ever saying the family was Cuban. And then, now get this, the name is also Cajun, but down in Louisiana they spell it, S-A-R-Z-E-A-U."

Lorraine leaned forward and donned her glasses to read the screen. "What's your father's name?"

"Um, Emile."

"Not Emilio? That would be the Cuban version."

"No, Emile for sure. And when Mom remarried, she moved to New Orleans. Maybe that's where she started out."

"Why not ask her?"

"I would, but — Katrina."

"Oh my."

"She was in the hospital, and . . . it flooded."

"You poor girl." Lorraine pulled up a chair and sat down to watch as Mary Ann continued to plow through the web pages.

"Here's a picture." She clicked on a thumbnail to open up a blurry black-and-white snapshot of a rail-thin old man wearing a quaint aloha shirt over rolled-up trousers. He was standing on a little dock in a bayou somewhere, with one foot in a small skiff tied up there. It looked like the dock might lead to the cottage up on stilts in the background. He was holding a snake in one hand. His wide eyes burned into the camera.

"According to this, here we have Remi Toussaint Sarzeau. He married somebody named Justine Perrault in 1946, and one of their kids was named Emile! Lorraine — this could be my grandfather."

"You're not sure?"

"Dad's parents were never discussed in our family. I never heard of these people."

"Click over there, print the page." Mary Ann dutifully clicked on a button, and a nearby ink-jet printer went to work. Lorraine hustled away and came back with the hard copy. She examined it through her red-framed glasses.

"So that's what a warlock looks like."

19

ON SUNDAY MORNING Mary Ann arose early, put on a nice blouse over her jeans, and appeared for mass in Placerville's Saint Patrick's Catholic Church, an observance she hadn't made in all her adult life. Two days later, having decided that the experience wasn't utterly intolerable, she returned to make a confession.

She vaguely remembered the procedure from adolescent years when Sergeant Sarzo was still around to enforce good behavior. Stepping into the confessional booth with great trepidation, she knelt at the screen and made the sign of the cross.

"Forgive me, father, for I have sinned."

A mild voice replied quietly from concealment. "Welcome, my child."

Mary Ann struggled to remember the right words. "In the name of the Father, and of the Son, and of the Holy Spirit, my last confession was, oh boy, more than ten years ago."

"It's never too long to be reconciled with God," came the voice. "Are you truly sorry for your sins?"

"You know, I'm not even sure I'm still Catholic."

"Were you confirmed?"

"Oh yeah, a long time ago."

"Well then, you are in the fold. What's troubling you?"

"I saw a ghost. At least, I think so. Is that a sin?"

There was a slight hesitation. Then the voice continued, "If you take pride in it, I suppose so, yes . . . and if you're lying, of course. Otherwise . . . you really saw this?"

"No doubt. Several times."

"Ah. Do you believe this . . . ghost . . . was real?"

"I don't know what to think. It was like a reflection in the mirror, but really creepy. It had arms and hands. It made a lot of gestures." She failed to mention that she often understood those gestures.

"Anything else?"

"I took the Lord's name in vain. I've had unclean thoughts about a man I just met."

"I don't know about the ghost. God manifests himself in many ways, as does Satan. I will consider the matter. Let's leave it aside for today, with this admonition — be wary. For the rest, venial sins, ten Hail Marys. May God give you pardon and peace, and I absolve you . . . "

Outside, Mary Ann breathed a big sigh of relief, slipped into her car, and drove to work.

Part THREE

20

IN THE POLICE STATION, Ibañez stood up from his desk to hear Mary Ann read the latest weather and traffic report.

"Snow is not expected to accumulate today anywhere below the orbit of Pluto. For those of you down on the ground in Amador County, that means all roads are clear and traffic is flowing smoothly. It's hot out there, folks. So keep yourselves hydrated at any of our fine restaurants, fast-food joints, and markets. And remember to drink responsibly out on the road — lots of water and *no* alcohol."

Ibañez rolled his eyes and shook his head. "That was good, as usual, if just a tad informal."

"Yes sir, thank you."

"How do you dare?"

Mary Ann was pleased with herself. "Boredom makes me crazy."

"If the FCC ever checks, they'll have your ass."

"I'm not worried. Day like today, no one except the mayor will give us a thought."

The chief flapped his arms helplessly and started back toward his desk.

Mary Ann stopped him with a question. "Hear anything from Gardner on Mike Russell's murder?"

"Deputy Gardner does not confide in me."

"What about Bobby? Think the crimes are related?"

"Maybe, maybe not. I'm guessing Mr. Russell was up to no good, and someone didn't like that. Bobby was as clean as a whistle."

"What about his brother?"

Ibañez' brow darkened. "Who knows? If Billy Rainwater was a lot less ambitious, then I'd sleep better. But it doesn't matter what I think, we're out of this." He pointed a warning finger at her. "Especially you."

Mary Ann watched him return to his desk, sit down, and angrily attack a stack of paper.

After lunch Wade Gawley came off duty, and Mary Ann rotated out on patrol in her usual ride, the department's old black & white Jeep Cherokee. As she sat in the parking lot adjusting the rear-view mirror, she accidentally triggered the night-view lever. Lurking in the dimmed reflection was an otherworldly shadow.

"Damn. You again. I reported you to the authorities, I want you to know. The ones upstairs. You'll be hearing from them, I bet."

The shadowy image sharpened into a head and shoulder silhouette. It held up a hand with fingers cupped and waved it gently back and forth. Then, with the other hand, it seemed to pluck at the first.

"I don't get it. Repeat, please."

Obediently, the apparition repeated its performance, waving a cupped hand and plucking at it.

"Okay, it's a flower."

Affirmative nod.

"And somebody is picking it."

Another nod.

"Hey, I'm getting good at this."

The apparition pointed a forefinger at her.

"Me? What, I'm picking?"

The apparition faded away.

21

MARY ANN rolled her Jeep to a stop just outside the Hilltop Band property and parked, billowing a cloud of road dust through the gate. She waited a long moment for the air to clear, and for anyone to show up if they noticed her arrival. But everything was quiet.

She exited the vehicle holding a bouquet of daisies and yarrow, hand-picked from the roadside a few miles down the hill, and trudged up the drive. After fifty yards she crossed into open woodland, entered the Hilltop Band's tribal burial ground, hiked its length, and came to a halt at Bobby Rainwater's new grave. A few blades of grass were starting to poke through the fresh soil that marked the location. In a matter of months, unless a stone was placed, the grave would be lost in the landscape.

Mary Ann bent down and laid her bouquet on the dirt.

"Hello, Bobby. Here are some flowers. I picked them myself. Ha ha, maybe you watched me." Her eyes traveled over the area as she composed her thoughts. "I guess you haven't started on that long journey to wherever we go when we're dead, right? I'm not sure why I can see you, but I found out my grandfather was into this stuff, and maybe it's just" — she shrugged — "a genetic accident, you know, like musical ability. And I appreciate you helping me. It would help even more if you could talk. Want to work on that? Then maybe you could tell me what this is all about."

She paused to let her message do — what? Cross into the spirit world? Then she pulled a small compact mirror out of a side pocket and flipped it open, looking for the telltale shadowy presence. "Hey listen, is there something you want from me? What is it? You're giving me the creeps." But the mirror only showed her own face against a background of stunted oak trees.

"Bobby? This would work so much better if you just came when I called. It *is* you floating around out there, right? Some kind of Native American mojo? If not . . . then who?" She stared into the mirror for a long time, but nothing uncanny deigned to darken the glass.

The roar of a small internal combustion engine revving up interrupted her séance. She snapped the mirror shut. The noise seemed to issue from behind a nearby ridge, and it sounded muffled, like a chain saw under water. "Bobby? Is that you?"

She followed the noise up the ridge. On the far side the land pitched steeply downward. Through the trees she could make out the silvery surface of the Whiskeyjack River. She took a few careful steps down the slope for a better look, stopping at the tree line. Fifty feet below her, standing knee-deep in an eddy, Billy Rainwater was nursing a Husqvarna-powered placer mining rig into operation. After tinkering with the throttle for a while, he seemed satisfied that it worked. He started wading upriver, towing the rig behind him like a little catamaran.

Mary Ann watched him go, puzzled by the engine, the pontoons, and the purpose. She started back up the slope, but the dry grass was slick under her shoes. She slipped and fell hard, knocking the air out of her lungs.

"Whuhh!"

She caught her breath, and tried again. Planting each foot with care, she regained a few yards, then fell again and tobogganed down the embankment. She would have dropped right into the river, but she got one hand around a huckleberry bush just in time.

"Ouch."

Looking up, she could see that climbing out was hopeless. Instead she worked her way sideways on her belly, clumsily toeing the gravelly incline, using grass and small bushes as handholds. It took her fifteen minutes to traverse the riverbank to an area gentle enough to scramble up in relative safety.

She emerged into a flat expanse of alders and laurels. After brushing herself off, hoping she hadn't picked up a dozen ticks or a dose of poison oak, she looked around to get her bearings. Manzanita bushes, sticky monkey flowers, and trees blocked her view in every direction. She was lost in a labyrinth of foothill flora. She touched the walkie-talkie on her hip and briefly considered using it. But the police station was probably out of range, and she shuddered to think how Chief Ibañez would yell at her. She looked up to get the sun's position, calculating compass points. Away from the river, which she guessed was southward, the brush seemed thinner, so she headed in that direction. The laurels gave way to oaks, then brush, and she found herself on the edge of an open meadow. The sight she beheld stopped her cold.

Stretching across the meadow was a spectacular field of red poppies, nodding in a light breeze. It was as if she had been transported to the Land of Oz. She imagined that, like the Cowardly Lion, she might actually fall into a coma if she dared to walk any farther.

"Holy crap," she said.

Her cop radar started to pulse. She peered around for signs of a human presence. Nothing. She took a tentative step into the field and stopped. Still nothing. A couple more steps and she was surrounded by cultivated flowers. She bent down and pulled an entire plant out of the ground. Just below the beautiful blossom, the seed capsule was beginning to bulge. On the adjacent plant the blossom was gone, and the capsule was greatly enlarged. A neat dried-up incision showed where someone had already extracted a few grams of opium gum as some kind of test.

"Hey, Tom, bro, you've never had a headline like this."

Mary Ann hauled out her mobile phone, fumbled with the controls, and was about to take a photograph when she heard a metallic click and a challenge from the trees on the far side of the field. Someone yelling and cursing in Spanish. She withdrew her Beretta from its holster, held it up with her finger against the trigger guard, and yelled back: "You there, step into the open with your hands empty and up where I can see 'em."

Ka-twang!

A rifle bullet kicked up pebbles five yards to her right. Unfazed, locked in righteous cop mode, she yelled again: "Come on out, mister, you're under arrest!"

Zing!

Another shot sprayed dirt in her face. Then the adrenaline kicked in.

"What the fuck am I doing?" Suddenly panic stricken, she turned and darted back into the woods.

Zow! Pa-twee!

Bullets ricocheted off the rocks and peeled bark from the branches. Mary Ann ducked and dodged, running for her life. A quarter of a mile down the hill she crested a ridge and stumbled back into the Hilltop Band's burial ground. Keeping it to her left, she raced through open woodland to within fifty yards of the Band's main gate. There, breathing in gasps, she hunkered down and looked around, trying to spot signs of an impending ambush. She was trembling like a hunted animal. She wanted to bolt for her black & white Jeep, but she was too scared to move, so there she crouched for what seemed like an eternity. Slowly the fear turned to anger. After five minutes she couldn't sit still anymore.

"Godammit!" she yelled and sprinted for the truck. No one took a shot at her.

She hurtled down the gravel road for miles before she really knew what she was doing, skidding on the corners, leaving a gigantic rooster-tail of dust behind. When she finally hit pavement on County Road 520 she pulled over. She was so giddy she laughed aloud.

"Fucking opium!"

22

CHIEF IBAÑEZ stared gloomily at the tattered remains of a plant on his desk. Mary Ann stood before him, as much at attention as she could manage. Terry Gardner hovered in the background.

"This is — was — an opium poppy. So you claim." Ibañez prodded the limp stalk with a skeptical finger.

"That's right. I know the seed pod is gone along with the blossom. I saved what I could."

"There was a field full of these things, and someone shot at you."

"Yes sir. Multiple times. Scared the shit out of me, pardon me."

"A poppy field. Here in Amador County. Jesus, Mary, and Joseph, what next?"

"I know, sir."

"And when you found this field, you were trespassing on Native American land . . . why? For what purpose?"

"I, um, I was paying my respects to Bobby. I got lost."

"You got lost."

"Sorry, sir."

"Could you find your way back there?"

"Maybe. But why bother? Call in the DEA. Send a helicopter."

Ibañez sighed. "Federal law governing opium poppies is ambiguous, in case you didn't know. Opium is Schedule II on the DEA's drug list, but it's perfectly legal to grow poppies ornamentally and harvest seeds, just not what you call 'poppy straw.' So it would have to be determined that the activity wasn't a backyard farming operation."

"How many backyard farmers guard their crops with guns?"

Ibañez acknowledged this small problem by thumping his knuckles on the desk. "Okay. Terry's going to have a look, talk to Rainwater. Let's see how it goes."

Mary Ann scowled angrily, rebelling inwardly against the doubts. Gardner patted her on the shoulder and headed for the station door. "Take it easy, Sarzo. If there's anything up there, I'll find it."

Mary Ann slouched away toward her own desk, cheeks crimson.

"Come back here, Officer," ordered Ibañez.

She pivoted around.

"Now listen up, there's lots of ways to be a bad cop. You could be dumb — that's possible, I guess, based on what you're telling me. You could be careless — well were you? I'd say, guilty as charged. You could be physically unable to perform. You could be poorly trained, and you could be crooked. Aside from crooked, I guess you've got it covered. You make me wonder why I ever hired you. But I did, so from now on, catch me some LA speeders, do your radio broadcast, file papers, and that's all. *Comprende?*"

She nodded meekly.

"And take this damn plant and bag it up."

▼

An hour later Mary Ann was in the Book Nook, ready to cry on Lorraine Wagstaff's shoulder. But the proprietor wasn't on the floor or in her office. So, to pass the time, she sat down at one of the computers and plugged herself into the web.

Lorraine returned ten minutes later, burdened down with bags of coffee for her espresso service and a big box of day-old doughnuts.

"Hi, Lorraine, you left the place unlocked. As a cop I have to advise you to be more careful. I could have stolen everything."

"Ha. No one steals books."

Mary Ann beckoned her over to the computer display. "Look at this — Wraiths-Of-America-dot-com has a long article about the varieties of ghosts. I had no idea. There must be fifty different kinds. At least. Some types are only seen in mirrors. They're called 'virtual visitors' and, this is the weirdest part, it looks like these things have the ability to travel through time."

"Time travel? Like those crazy episodes on Star Trek?"

"I guess. The site here says that these things are, quote, 'disconnected from the time stream as we know it.' "

"What do you think? Is granddad your visitor?"

"I hope not. He looked like a scary old dude."

Lorraine was munching on an éclair. "I just refilled my snack tray. Want something?"

"You're tempting a cop with doughnuts? Shame on you." She turned off the computer. A cheerfully whimsical notion was chasing away her somber mood.

"What I really want is Bobby Rainwater's car. And now that Mike Russell is gone, so is that beautiful automobile. The question is, where?"

Lorraine picked up a copy of the *County Courier*, put on her glasses, and squinted at the classifieds. "Here it is, in Monday's edition. It's being advertised by Red's Hot Wheels, down in Ione."

"How much?"

"$11,500."

"I could sell my Honda, get a loan. I've got good credit."

"Don't go crazy on me, Mary Ann."

"I want that car, Lorraine."

▼

Mary Ann headed back uphill to Applefield, happily trying to anticipate the curveballs a car dealer would likely throw at her. As she rolled onto Main Street, she spotted Tom Wagstaff leaving the Golden Hills Hardware store with a bag of goods. She stopped and leaned out the window.

"Hey, Tom, afternoon."

He stopped, squinted at the black & white police vehicle, then ambled over. "Yo, M. Am I under arrest?"

"Depends. Whatcha got there?"

He held up the bag, opened it, pulled out a brass valve. "Maintenance project."

"Looks like you're innocent. Listen, as soon as I pick up my Honda, I'm driving down to Ione to buy a car."

"Cool. Something new?"

"On my pay? Be serious. Of course I'll get screwed by the dealer, being a helpless young woman and all. How would you like to ride along for moral support?"

He considered for a moment, looked up and down the street. "Is this, like, a date?"

"Whoa. Do people date anymore? Hop in. Just don't touch my riot gun."

Wagstaff slid into the passenger seat.

"I have to change into my civvies, and we're off."

"Heh, don't do that."

"What?"

"Stay in uniform. You want a deal, it won't hurt to look like a cop."

A few minutes later they were rolling down Route 88 in Mary Ann's Honda.

"What are you going to do with this car?"

"Trade it, what else?"

Wagstaff surveyed the interior. "Don't you want to wash it first? You know, and get rid of the gum wrappers?"

"There are no gum wrappers."

"Last week's TV Guide, then. And a Subway lunch."

"Think that's necessary?"

"God, yes."

On the outskirts of Jackson they found the Sierra Vista U-Wash just off the highway. Mary Ann changed five dollars for quarters in the adjoining Sierra Vista Quick Mart, and they lathered and sprayed, one on each side of the vehicle. Wagstaff turned the wand in Mary Ann's direction, sending a brief rain shower over the roof. She ducked.

"Hey, watch it, mister! How official am I going to look all wet?"

"Sorry, purely an accident. Won't happen again, ma'am."

He directed the water stream over the roof again. She ducked again. They both laughed.

When they were done the little car looked a lot more respectable. Mary Ann felt briefly nostalgic. "I'd forgotten — underneath the grime, the thing is actually painted. Look, it's all silver now."

Back on the road, Wagstaff was plotting tactics. "Ever buy a car before?"

"No, this was Dad's."

"How are you going to handle it?"

"I'll say, 'I'm a cop, no tricks.' "

"No, no, no. Go with the flow. Then, when the dealer finally tells you the price, and he wants to put pen to paper, you say, "I like the car. But, eleven-five. Is that the best you can do?"

This idea made Mary Ann very nervous. "And if he says yes, then what? I can't walk away."

"Say you saw lower prices online. That always works."

"You're kidding."

"Worst case scenario, you pay. But try it: 'Is that the best you can do?'

▼

Red's Hot Wheels announced itself with a huge sign painted like a checkered racing flag. It was rotating slowly on a tall pole above a glass-fronted office. The asphalt lot was filled with a random assortment of respectable used cars, glittering under flood lights. Flags and balloons strung between light poles fluttered in a light evening breeze. No customers roamed the premises. The dealer, a round little fifty-year-old man in a short-sleeved shirt and bright red tie, spotted Mary Ann the moment she got out of her Honda and waited to greet her as she threaded her way between the cars. Wagstaff trailed along behind, wondering about the lot's name. Except for a white Corvette near the curb, and the metallic blue 1969 Mustang two cars over, none of the machines on view seemed particularly hot.

"Evening, ma'am. I'm Del. What can I do for you?"

"I want to buy a car."

"Good, that's what I sell. For a moment I thought you might be chasing down a stolen vehicle. Believe me, that's not what 'Hot' in our name stands for. Everything you see here has a good title. We've got all the papers."

"Glad to hear it."

"What can I show you? How about that Subaru Forester over there? Or maybe our little Mini Cooper. It's in real good shape for a first-gen '05 model."

"I'm thinking about that Mustang out in front."

"Blue '69?"

"Yup."

Wagstaff was startled by her choice. "Are you sure, Mary Ann? That's a helluva car, but it's . . . old. No fuel injection, no airbags, no ABS. You'll have to get it tuned up every time you turn around. That's a car for car lovers who know cars."

The dealer drooped. "Uh-oh, flag on the play."

Mary Ann was undaunted. "How much?"

The dealer brightened. "But wait, upon further review — it says in the paper, eleven-five. Looks good on our lot, but I won't lie, it's been sitting here for almost a month, and you're the first to notice. So, I can let you have it for ten-nine."

"What about a trade?"

"That little Civic you drove up in?"

"Yeah, over there. Want to take a look?"

"Don't have to. I can give you Blue Book minus $500. Say, $2100."

"And I need a loan."

"We work through CarSpot, no problem. You are employed as a policewoman, right?"

"Golden Hills Tri-Town, up in Applefield."

"Let's go in the office here and do some paperwork."

Mary Ann was floored by all the little decisions she had to make and the disclaimers she had to sign. No rust treatment, thank you. No aftermarket emergency warranty either. Was she aware that she was buying this vehicle As-Is? Yes, it's okay. Finally the dealer got ready for the bill of sale. His pen was poised over the final document.

Mary Ann was sitting bolt upright like a statue, frozen by negotiation anxiety. Wagstaff nudged her in the back. She flinched and swallowed hard. "Oh, wait — you know, I like the car, even if no one else does. But, ten-nine. It just seems . . . steep."

The dealer's pen lifted away from the paper. He gave her a sharp look.

"Steep? I brought it down $600."

"Um, is that the best you can do?" She mouthed the words like a robot.

The dealer scowled, put down his pen. "What did you have in mind?"

Mary Ann thought about her tiny bank account and rookie salary. "It's a helluva car, but I'll have to get it tuned up every time I turn around. And, and . . . I've seen lower prices online." She took a deep breath.

"Nine-nine."

The dealer smiled at her shaky bravado. "You are a tough cop, young lady. Tell you what — I'd like to see that Mustang in good hands. Any hands, actually, except ours. Nine-nine it is."

As they drove away, with 302 cubic inches of V-8 thundering under the metallic blue hood, Mary Ann let out a whoop. She held up a fist. Wagstaff did likewise. They bumped. "All right! You just saved me one thousand dollaros, so dinner is on me."

Wagstaff grinned. "I know just the place."

Twenty minutes later they were sitting in Gordo's Mexican Grill, a funky little tavern a mile up the hill from Jackson, sipping margaritas.

"I'm not giving up, you know. No matter what Ibañez says."

"Be careful, Mary Ann. Two murders, that's unheard of around here."

She ran a wedge of lime around the rim of her glass and licked the salt off it. "I know. The chief is worried too."

"Then what's the point? You already told me the sheriff's department is running the investigation."

"I just can't . . . I dunno . . . file papers all day long."

Wagstaff raised his eyebrows. "Something in the mirror?"

Mary Ann almost choked on her drink. "Look, here come the fajitas."

They ate in silence for a while. Wagstaff fidgeted with his rice and beans, then leaned forward conspiratorially. "Mom told me."

"God damn Lorraine. She promised not to."

"Doesn't matter. I don't think you're crazy or anything."

"That's nice of you."

"So don't get all pissed off. I'm not judging."

"You mean, 'I don't believe a word, but I'm going to be polite.' "

"Mom's kind of into this stuff, but it's all new to me. I don't think too many people have your abilities. Faces in the mirror. Brr."

"Don't forget the time travel part."

"Oh, man. What do these things look like, anyway?"

"You really want to know? Or is this just your way of humoring me?"

"Honestly? You could be delusional, I guess. But — don't get mad — you seem normal."

"Seem normal. Wow." Mary Ann considered the appraisal. "All right, first you have to understand, I'm not a witch. I don't ride a broomstick. I don't mix potions. I don't cast spells."

"Not a witch. Agreed."

"Then here's the story: I don't see a lot of different ghosts, just one, and it's always the same, a flickering shadow in a mirror. I can't summon it or anything, it just shows up on its own. It never makes a sound, just a lot of gestures."

"Like the Ghost of Christmas Future?"

"Maybe. The spook books call it a 'virtual visitor,' if you want to know."

"Who is it?"

"Good question. At first I thought, Bobby Rainwater. But that's just a theory."

Wagstaff pursed his lips. He struggled to formulate his thoughts. "Were you and Bobby . . . close?"

"You mean, like, an item? I hardly knew him. We never hooked up."

"In that case, what does this — this visitor — want?"

"Who knows? Something to do with these murders."

"So . . . that's how you were on the scene when Mike Russell got slit open."

"Bingo."

"And that's why you aren't giving up."

She grimaced. "It won't let me."

23

IN THE LATE AFTERNOON of a glorious autumn day, Billy Rainwater, shirtless, with a kerchief tied around his head like a ninja headband, was sweating abundantly as he pushed and shoved a Sears rototiller across an open field on the Hilltop Band's property, grinding up the remains of one crop and preparing the field for another. As he reached the southernmost corner, he loosened his grip on the dead man's switch, and the engine shuddered to a stop. He freed a water bottle from its holder on the tiller's handle and was slugging down a mouthful when Deputy Terry Gardner appeared from among the oak trees.

"Sheriff Gardner." Rainwater nodded his greeting without much surprise. He wiped his mouth and held out the water bottle.

"Don't mind if I do. October now, still hot." Gardner tipped back a swig, handed the bottle back.

Rainwater drank another slug, then poured the rest of the bottle over his head. "What brings you up onto Hilltop land?"

Gardner leaned down, pushed some loose dirt around, found a chewed-up plant stem, picked it up, and examined the pitiful thing. He gave Rainwater a hard and unsympathetic look. "Got a report of opium poppies being grown up here. Is this, or more accurately, *was* this one of them?"

Rainwater laughed and shook his head. "That's just a weed."

"I hear shots were fired."

"That's possible. We don't take kindly to trespassers."

"You might want to rethink your defense tactics, bring them into compliance with twenty-first century standards. What are you growing up here, anyway?"

"A little corn, a lot of tomatoes and potatoes. Got a small apple orchard behind the ridge there."

"Unh-huh. Sure it's not medicinal marijuana?"

"Now, Sheriff, who do you think I am?"

"Leader of an impoverished Native American sub-tribe who needs money."

"Don't we all, Sheriff, don't we all?"

"Listen, Chief —"

"Friends call me Billy."

"Okay, friend it is. How about some friendly advice?"

Rainwater folded his arms. "Go ahead."

Gardner gazed out across the field. An acre or so, he judged. He was impressed to find a reasonably level expanse in the middle of the area's steep hillsides. He thought farming the place was probably hard work.

"Think about your situation, Billy — this field, a lot of plowed ground — to the wrong eye it could look like you're concealing evidence. And, if certain people got overly suspicious, they might consider calling in the DEA. That would mean search warrants, helicopters, tear your place apart."

"This isn't some backwoods state park or BLM turf, it's Native heritage territory," said Rainwater, temper fraying. "Fuck the DEA."

"I hear you and your group are dreaming of a casino. I want to help you realize that dream," said Gardner, maintaining his calm.

"It's not a dream. We've got plans. A strategy. It's all mapped out, we're on our way."

"Mice and men, Billy. The map is not the territory. If the Feds get excited about your crops, you can kiss your dreams, your plans, your maps goodbye. You know the rule, don't shit where you eat."

"That's right. We don't."

"Good. I'm sure your tribe members and outside supporters will be relieved to hear the news. We're all walking the same street, right?"

"Same street, unh-huh. I'm with you on that."

"Appearances can be damaging, my friend. Make your investors wonder if they're backing the right horse, know what I mean? To say nothing about attracting curious law enforcement personnel." Gardner gave Rainwater an encouraging slap on the back.

Rainwater winced. "Amen." He pulled off his gloves and pointed toward the trees. "Seeing how we're on the subject, sheriff, there's another field I think you ought to take a look at."

"What?"

Rainwater started walking toward the trees. He swept his arm forward in a come-along gesture. "It's not far. Over this way."

24

"PUMPKINS?" Ibañez was sitting in the Golden Hills Tri-Town Police station staring unhappily at the pleated orange globe on his desk, placed there in evidence by Deputy Terry Gardner.

"A half-acre at least."

"Pumpkins . . ." repeated Ibañez, shaking his head. "You saw the crop in the ground?"

"Oh yes. Also corn, tomatoes, and plenty of these . . ." Gardner reached into a paper bag and added a couple of dirt-encrusted potatoes to the desktop display.

"Officer Sarzo. Get in here," commanded Ibañez. Dutifully responding, Mary Ann rose from behind her own desk and hurried into the chief's presence. She was mildly surprised to see Gardner lounging in a chair beside him.

"Hello, Terry."

"Nice to see you, Officer Sarzo."

Ibañez cleared his throat, gestured toward the vegetables on his desk, waved an arm expansively. "Deputy Gardner paid a visit to Billy Rainwater today."

"Oh?"

Gardner produced an ear of corn and a tomato from his paper bag. "The field you described is plowed under. This is what they're growing up on Hilltop land."

Mary Ann slumped. "I saw poppies."

Gardner's blue eyes were hard and cold. "So you say. But there's absolutely no evidence to back up your claim. And, from an official sheriff's department point of view, you appear to be defaming a solid citizen and an upstanding community of our Native population."

"There must be more than one field, and you missed the one I saw."

Gardner nodded. "I thought of that, but Mr. Rainwater guided me all around the property. Nowhere did I observe any poppies."

"Shit — ! Oops, sorry, Chief."

Ibañez folded his hands into a church and steeple. His long-faced expression radiated deep disappointment. "Mary Ann, you're new and all, but what the fuck? Had we called in the DEA we'd be tagged as the dumbest crime fighters in all of California."

Mary Ann raised her arms, then brought them downward, slapping her thighs in frustration. She bit her lip. "I know what I saw. Pumpkins and potatoes are bullshit. This is all about drugs and money."

Gardner cocked his head. "Could be you're right. I'm looking into it. The investigation continues."

"And when can we expect some results?" she asked.

"These things take time. This case isn't a one-hour episode on TV."

25

ON HER WAY HOME that night, Mary Ann realized that she had no cash on hand, so she circled back into Applefield and rolled up to the Bank of America ATM. She stuck her debit card into the slot and was punching in her PIN when the now-familiar outline of a human figure shadowed the screen.

"Oh great, you again."

The figure rippled in and out of sight, gesticulating with its hands.

"What? I can't read you."

More gestures, all of them incomprehensible.

"Look, I'm really tired, I've had a really bad day, and I just want enough cash to buy some beer and go home, okay? So get out of my way."

The shadowy figure did not acknowledge her plight and continued to wave its hands. Suddenly a horn sounded, startling her. She turned around in her seat to see where it came from. A Toyota Camry had pulled in behind her Mustang, and the driver was impatient.

"Okay, okay, give me a second." Mary Ann touched the $40 button, collected two twenties, withdrew her card, waved to the Toyota, and pulled away. "Hey, mister, you deal with the damn ghost."

Later, in her trailer, she kicked off her shoes, pulled the tails of her blouse out of her pants, opened a beer, and poured it into a glass. As she was taking her first sip, the shadow reappeared on the bubbly surface of the golden liquid. She jerked the glass away from her lips. Then she had a better thought.

"I'll show you, Mr. Ghost."

She chugged the beer, then examined the foamy glass interior. The ghostly shadow was gone.

▼

Next morning she rose at ten, groggy with too much sleep. She had the late shift at work, and had set her alarm accordingly. Ten minutes after she had showered and dressed she was in the confession booth in Saint Patrick's Catholic Church.

"Forgive me Father, for I have sinned. In the name of the Father, and of the Son, and of the Holy Spirit, my last confession was a month ago."

"Yes," came the mild voice behind the scrollwork, "I remember. You thought you saw an apparition."

"That's me. The ghost girl."

"Any more, ah, episodes, sightings, or whatever you call them?"

"Oh yeah. Several. Whenever I'm not ready, bip, there he is."

"I see. Do you want to describe these encounters?"

"I dunno. Isn't this irregular, talking like this in confession?"

"Seeing a ghost doesn't happen very often, child."

"Not to you, maybe."

Mary Ann thought she heard the faintest hint of a chuckle, quickly stifled. After a moment, the mild voice resumed.

"Ten Hail Marys, for whatever venial sins you may have committed. Now, this is important — when you leave, go to the rectory. Find Sister Bianca, tell her who you are. May God give you pardon and peace, and I absolve you . . . "

Mary Ann left the booth, squinted in the bright sunshine outside the church, crossed the paved grounds to the rectory, and stepped inside. A trim older nun with greying blond hair was sitting behind the reception desk.

"Sister Bianca?"

"Yes?"

Mary Ann hesitated. "I'm, uh, the woman with the ghost problem. I was told to come see you."

Sister Bianca laughed lightly, hitting a musical note. "Father Eisen told me to keep an eye out for you. Ghosts were mentioned."

"Whoa there, I thought confession was a sacred trust."

"Don't worry, none of your sins were ever discussed. But that was weeks ago. Now where is it?"

"Where's what?"

"He left something for you. Aha, here we are." Sister Bianca pulled an envelope from a desk drawer and opened it. Inside were a folded sheet of paper and a small wooden crucifix.

"Father Eisen has a plan for your apparition. The next time you see it, read this prayer of exorcism." She handed Mary Ann the sheet of paper. "And show the ghost this cross. Father Eisen has blessed it." She handed over the crucifix.

"Okay . . ." Mary Ann had no idea what to think.

"Father Eisen is concerned that your ghost may harbor malicious intent. If it is evil, if it comes from Satan, the prayer or the cross will repel it."

"Let's see . . ." Mary Ann held up the paper. "Read him the riot act," — she held up the crucifix — "show him the cross."

"That's right. There you go."

"If he is repelled, he's bad medicine. But, what if he still hangs around?"

Sister Bianca shrugged. "No one can be sure. Look on the bright side. Maybe he's an angel."

"Wouldn't that be nice." Mary Ann stuffed the items in a side pocket of her uniform and headed for the door. "I'll let you know how it goes."

Sister Bianca waved goodbye. "Oh yes, please. We're very curious."

26

IN THE BOOK NOOK, Lorraine Wagstaff scanned the exorcism prayer. ". . . and do thou . . . hum, hum . . . cast into hell Satan, and all the evil spirits who prowl about the world seeking the ruin of souls."

"What do you think?" asked Mary Ann.

"Amen, honey. Sounds pretty emphatic to me. If I were an evil spirit, I'd be slinking off to hell and gone."

"No kidding, Lorraine, this is important." Now that she had Father Eisen's materials in hand, Mary Ann was troubled by them. Somehow, the very existence of tools to deal with ghosts amplified the seriousness of her odd situation.

Lorraine frowned. "Let me see that cross again."

Mary Ann handed her the little wooden crucifix.

"It's pretty small."

"Does size matter?"

"And it's made out of wood. I would have thought it had to be silver, like, you know, with vampires."

"I don't think my ghost is a vampire." Mary Ann screwed her face up. "Tell you what, let's check it out on the web."

She walked across the store to the bank of computers, flipped the switch on a monitor, sat down at the keyboard, and launched a browser as the screen brightened up. She was in the middle of typing in the URL for Wraiths-Of-America-dot-com when the Book Nook's home page clouded over with a moving shadow.

"Oh my God, Lorraine, here he is!"

"No!"

"Yes — look!"

Lorraine squinted at the screen. All she saw was a dramatic photograph of Mount Whitney, one of the many California views she had assembled into a slideshow to advertise her store.

"Are you sure?"

"He's right here. He's holding up his hand, telling me to 'hang on.' " Mary Ann mimicked the gesture. "Last time I kind of cut him off. He wants me to stay tuned."

"And — ?"

"And, well, now he's bringing his hands together in a circle. Okay, looks like a Frisbee, or pie plate . . . or something."

"Pie plate?" Lorraine was fascinated and frustrated in equal measure.

"Now he's moving the Frisbee, rocking it around. Now half is gone, and he's reaching into where the whole Frisbee was with his other hand. He's holding something up between his thumb and forefinger."

"This is absurd. Read the prayer," Lorraine shoved the sheet of paper from Father Eisen in front of Mary Ann.

"Oh, right, good idea." She snapped the paper to unfold it. "Listen up, Mr. Ghost." She cleared her throat and, trying for dignity, read the handwritten lines with a raised voice:

> Saint Michael the archangel, defend us in battle. Be our defense against the wickedness and snares of the devil. May God rebuke him, we humbly pray, and do thou, O Prince of the Heavenly Host, by the power of God, cast into hell Satan, and all the evil spirits, who prowl about the world seeking the ruin of souls. Amen.

"Is he gone?" Lorraine studied the apparently ghost-free screen, trying to see through the collection of images slowly cycling on the display.

"No, still here. Now he's wiggling the fingers of his other hand around the imaginary thing he's holding between his fingers. Now he's spreading his hands, palms up, and shrugging his shoulders — that's how he wonders if I get it. Well, I don't."

The hairs on Lorraine's arms were rising. She felt a peculiar mixture of unease and jealousy wash over her. "Show him the cross."

"Okay, cross." Mary Ann dug into her pocket and raised the cross to the monitor. "Father Eisen blessed this cross, Buster. Show some respect."

Lorraine thought the cross looked rather puny up against the images of Amador County foothills sliding through the screen. "Tell him, 'get thee gone, Satan.' "

"What?"

"I think you should be forceful."

"All right then, get thee gone, Satan!"

"Did it work?" Lorraine was breathless with suspense.

"He flickered there for a moment. Little flicker, I think. But no — here he goes again, repeating the whole show. The Frisbee, or pie plate, the rocking motion, picking something out, holding it up, fingers wiggling. I still don't get it." Mary Ann shoved her chair back from the computer and cocked her head. "Why can't he just talk to me?"

"Maybe we should turn this off." Lorraine reached for the monitor switch, but Mary Ann shot out a hand and grabbed her arm.

"Hang on, he's trying something else. Now he's moving his hand across the screen, up and down. I dunno, indicating water maybe. Now he dips a hand in, brings it up, holding something. Now he's walking his fingers back and forth, back and forth. Sort of a scissor motion. Dammit, what is he saying?"

Lorraine was starting to doubt the sanity of her young friend. "You're scaring me, Mary Ann."

"Oh crap, he threw up his hands. Now he's gone." Mary Ann sagged in her chair. Then she sprang to her feet. "But we saw him — you're my witness!"

Lorraine shook her head. She was pouting with disappointment. "Nope. Not me. I didn't see a thing."

"He was right there on the monitor."

"Unh-huh."

"And he wasn't repelled. Not by the prayer. Not by the cross. So, now we know something — my ghost isn't evil."

"I'm worried about you, kiddo. Either you're crazy, or you're a witch."

"Oh, Lorraine. Don't say that. Do you really think I'm crazy?"

"No."

"Or a witch?"

"I guess not. You're weird, though, you know that."

Mary Ann stood and paced the area in front of the bank of computers. "The question is, what was our so-called visitor trying to tell me?"

Lorraine reached again for the monitor switch and froze. The slideshow was just cycling from a photograph of the Book Nook itself to a shot of the downtown park in Applefield, centered on Mayor Teasdale's sentimental bronze statue of a gold rush miner caught in the moment of his big strike.

"Whoa! Mary Ann! Look!"

Mary Ann stopped pacing. "What?"

Lorraine pointed at the statue onscreen. "It wasn't a Frisbee or a pie plate. It was a gold pan. He was panning for gold.

"And, and, I think the walking fingers mean —"
Mary Ann finished her thought: "— follow the gold."

27

THE OFFICES of the *County Courier* in Applefield were housed in a small concrete block building that might once have been a warehouse. The doors were locked on a Saturday afternoon, but Mary Ann could see lights inside. A small crisply printed sign informed her of the paper's business telephone number. She punched it into her mobile phone, and heard the voice of Tom Wagstaff, sounding apologetic.

"We can't answer our telephone at the moment. For information about our publication, to advertise in our pages, or to report any news, please leave a message . . . "

"Damn." She ended the call, rang the bell beside the little sign, then beat on the door with her fist.

"Hey! Wait a minute!" It was Wagstaff, calling out from somewhere behind the building. Mary Ann started around the corner just as he stuck his head into view. "Oh, hi, M. Come on back."

Mary Ann rounded the rear of the building. Parked at the loading dock was Wagstaff's big FJ Cruiser, and attached to it was a little trailer. Sitting on the trailer was a placer mining rig, about nine feet long. Mary Ann recognized it as the same kind of thing she had seen Billy Rainwater towing up the Whiskeyjack. Wagstaff was lying underneath the Styrofoam pontoons, working on the unit's pump.

"What on Earth?"

"Damn thing doesn't want to prime up. The valve is clogged. I should have bought a good one."

Wagstaff rolled out from under, stood up, rubbed his hands on his pants to clean off the oil and grime. He gestured toward the rig.

"This is my suction dredge. Hand built. Great piece of equipment — when it works."

Mary Ann regarded the rig with a dubious eye. "Lorraine told me you pan for gold with this thing."

"I do. I'm just getting ready to head on up the Whiskeyjack. Want to see it in action?"

"Will I get rich if I do?"

"All I can promise is, you're going to get wet." He indicated her uniform. "Got a bathing suit?"

"Damn, I don't own one."

After a side trip to the Miners Market, where Mary Ann selected a skimpy T-shirt with "I ♥ Gold Country," stenciled on the front and a pair of cheap khaki shorts meant for fishermen, Wagstaff pointed his four-by-four up County Road 520. Mary Ann sat in the back while she struggled out of her police attire and into her new river outfit.

In a few miles the pavement turned into gravel. Five miles beyond that they passed the entrance to the Hilltop Band rancheria. The FJ slipped into a lower gear as the road pitched up and the turns tightened. Three miles later Wagstaff pulled over.

"Hey, you. Up front."

Mary Ann squeezed forward and dropped into the passenger seat. "It's the new me. What do you think?"

Wagstaff eyed the stupid T-shirt with appreciation. "On you it looks good." He handed her his smartphone. "Now take this. I've got my GPS running, and see, here's the map. You're navigating."

"I've never done this before."

"All you have to do is keep me on this squiggle — Forest Route 3N75. That will take us to the put-in I want to try. There's a million little turnoffs. A logging outfit down in Chinese Camp cleared this place out thirty years ago. Now it's all overgrown again. Hard to see what we're doing."

Wagstaff pivoted the FJ to his left, and they started bouncing down Forest Route 3N75, little more than a double trail in a jungle of Douglas-fir saplings.

"Hey slow down. Bear right up ahead." Mary Ann was amazed to see an actual sign noting where 3N09 diverged from 3N75. "Okay, now, next left." Two hundred yards later they veered onto the left fork. Branches scraped the mirrors on both sides of the FJ. A few car lengths beyond, the track angled steeply downward. Wagstaff stopped, shifted into low range, and proceeded slowly down into the trees with the engine whining at an unnervingly high RPM.

"Left again coming up," called out Mary Ann. Wagstaff swerved left through a curtain of conifer branches. Magically, they found they were still on something like a road, although the forest was closing in.

After jolting through a long series of forks and turnoffs that left her dazzled, Mary Ann noted the middle fork of the Whiskeyjack River crawling onto the smartphone display. There were no more signs to confirm her choices, so she hoped for the best.

"How will we ever turn around in here?" she wondered.

Wagstaff grinned. "When we get to Hansel & Gretel's house."

"Come on."

"You'll see."

After another quarter mile the trees opened up, giving way to a more familiar California oak savanna. Green turned to brown, underbrush thinned out, the road widened into a broad open area, and there before them was the Whiskeyjack, lapping at the shore.

Wagstaff groaned. There also was an old military-style Jeep hooked up to a small trailer, not unlike his own. The driver was nowhere in sight.

"Thought you had this all to yourself, right?" asked Mary Ann.

"Yes I did. Well, hell, we can always hope the dude is relying on some trash pump that won't hose up a single stone."

Mary Ann jumped out of the FJ and watched as Wagstaff backed it down to the water, stopping him, as instructed, when the trailer was completely submerged. At that point the mining rig lifted away, buoyed up by its Styrofoam pontoons.

Wagstaff waded into the shallows and unhooked the tie downs. "Here we go, M. Get your feet on, the river stones are murder."

Mary Ann kicked off her police shoes, slid her feet into a pair of pink flip-flops, and splashed into the water behind Wagstaff.

"Okay — the current isn't much this time of year, so we jump on and paddle, like so." Wagstaff flopped down on top of one of the pontoons. Mary Ann did the same on the other one. Together they dog-paddled the rig out into the river, dodging the many boulders protruding above the surface. Mary Ann found the bright sun and smooth water intoxicating. Her mood was as buoyant as the pontoons.

A half-mile upstream the river widened, and the current, already slow, became lazy. Wagstaff pointed to a little sheltered pool on the inside of a long bend, and they paddled over. When they eased off the pontoons, they were standing waist-deep in surprisingly cold water. Mary Ann gasped as it invaded her pants and splashed over her sunbaked skin.

Wagstaff threw a zinc-plated boat anchor overboard and bent down to secure it to the river bottom. "Okay, here's the drill. We're going to pump a lot of sand and gravel off the bottom here, where the current eddies around, and send the slurry through this sluice box. With a little luck, we'll haul some flakes. Maybe even a small nugget."

Wagstaff grasped the handle of the starter cord on his Honda pump engine and gave it a yank. It sputtered and died. He was about to yank again when Mary Ann shouted. She was pointing upriver.

"Hey, look, here comes another miner. The Jeep owner, I bet."

Sure enough, floating downriver was another mining rig, and straddling the starboard pontoon was a leathery old man with a long grey beard and white hair poking out from under a canvas sun hat. He was guiding his craft around the bend with a canoe paddle.

"Ho, there, folks," he called out as he drew abeam. "Any luck?"

Wagstaff stood up straight. "Yo, Slim. We just got here. Who knows?"

"How about you?" asked Mary Ann.

"Ha ha, nothing but mud. But who cares? A beer on the river goes down well on a hot day. Got me a rainbow too." He dangled a large fish aloft on a length of monofilament.

"I think it's catch-and-release up here on the Whiskeyjack, sir," said Mary Ann, unable to restrain her police mentality.

"Oh, don't worry, I'll release it. Soon as I get home. Right into the pan. Trout almondine tonight!" The old man saluted them and floated on past.

"Slim? You know him?" she inquired.

"Yeah, fraternity brother. Order of Hopeless Gold Dredgers, Amador County chapter."

"Does anyone ever make any real money with these rigs?" She was doubtful. "I mean, could Billy Rainwater be financing his casino ambitions this way?"

"Let's find out." Wagstaff yanked the Honda starter cord, and this time the little engine fired right up, loud and smoky. He attached a long handle to the end of his four-inch suction hose, and shoved it down into the gravel overburden on the riverbed. Soon a pile of gloopy muck started accumulating in the sluice box. Wagstaff directed the nozzle around and between the larger rocks while Mary Ann steadied the rig. It felt good to make herself useful.

After ten minutes, he pulled the suction hose free and started working the sluice box. Pretty soon the mud and gravel had been washed overboard, leaving behind a residue of fine particles caught behind a series of ridges along the bottom. Wagstaff bent over the box, examining the results of their efforts.

"Aha!" He pointed into the sandy material. "Here's your answer."

Mary Ann stared at the granules. One tiny grain sparkled in the sunlight. She pressed a finger down on it, turned her hand over, and held it up for close inspection. "Is this what I think it is?"

"Yup. A gold flake. What panners call pennyweight."

"One flake. How much is it worth?"

"A dollar or two, I guess."

Mary Ann shook her head. "So the answer is, no, Billy Rainwater can't get rich doing this."

Wagstaff sat down on a pontoon. He pulled on a little strap, and a section of the top opened up, revealing a built-in ice chest. He reached inside, extracted two bottles of Corona Extra, popped the tops off, and handed one to Mary Ann.

"Who cares? A beer on the river goes down well on a hot day." She nodded agreement. They clinked bottle necks together in a toast to futility.

28

FIRST THING on Monday morning, Gordon Hollinsworth knocked on the glass-paneled door of Vera Teasdale's mayoral office in downtown Applefield. She looked up from a pile of documents and waved him in. She stood when she saw Billy Rainwater tagging along behind.

"Hello, Gordon. Morning, Mr. Rainwater." She indicated chairs near her desk. "Coffee?"

"Yes, please."

The mayor turned to a credenza behind her desk and filled three cups from a tall thermos jug. "I just made this. Please sit."

"You need an assistant, Vera," said Hollinsworth, easing down.

"Can't afford one. When I need help, I turn to you, Gordon."

"Well, I can't even boil water. What I can do is bring you together with a man who will make you an interesting proposition. Billy?"

Rainwater squirmed around in his chair, placed his coffee cup on the desk, rubbed his hands on his pants. "Mayor, as you know, the Hilltop Band has purchased Bob Brannan's hotel here in Applefield."

"Yes, I read about it in the *Courier*. Congratulations — you've accomplished more than I could ever manage. I don't think Brannan liked me very well, especially after I drove through the visitor tax."

"It's a solid piece of property. I believe it will produce real revenue. I believe it is also known that the Hilltop Band wants to operate a casino."

"That's no secret, Mr. Rainwater."

"But not here in the Golden Hills."

"No? Why not?" She probably knew the reason, but evidently wanted to hear it spelled out.

Hollinsworth waved a hand. "They need business, Vera. Now, we all know you like tourists. God bless their disposable income. But Rainwater and his group — they need heavy traffic. The kind of traffic that moves up and down I-80."

"And Mr. Hollinsworth has informed us that you own a piece of undeveloped land in Auburn, right beside the freeway," said Rainwater.

"Yes, that's true."

"Next to the Lincoln Way off-ramp," he added.

"Yes. And . . . ?"

Hollinsworth smoothly took over. "Here's the picture, Vera. Your land is undeveloped. Nobody's building condos these days, not in this economy. So we see years going by, with taxes unmatched by revenue. On the other hand, you might consider trading that property" — he let the idea hang for an instant, then punched the idea home — "for Bob Brannan's hotel, right here under your eyes, all built and open for guests."

"Possibly run by your son-in-law, eh?" blurted Rainwater.

Mayor Teasdale fiddled with a pencil while she appeared to consider the idea for the first time. "I believe I mentioned that Douglas might be persuaded to give up his ridiculous fascination with bio-technology under the right circumstances."

Rainwater's eyes lit up. "Hallelujah."

"However, that property in Auburn is very valuable land in a unique location. Unbuilt? Yes, but that means no teardown to accommodate a casino, which surely must be bigger than Brannan's establishment."

Rainwater started to object, and Hollinsworth placed a restraining hand on his arm. "What are you saying, Vera?"

"I'm willing to trade, but I will need a cash payment to make it fair to both parties."

"How much are we talking about?" asked Rainwater, his mood swinging downward.

"A hundred thousand dollars."

Hollinsworth shook his head. "Now, Vera, be reasonable. Brannan's hotel is a going concern. It has cachet among previous guests who return every year. It's in all the travel books. Bob kept it in good shape, and it just about runs itself."

"Twenty-five," said Rainwater.

Mayor Teasdale leaned forward with both elbows on her desk. "I see your point, Gordon." She cast a steely glance at Rainwater and folded her hands. "Settle at fifty, then, shall we?"

Rainwater slumped visibly and turned to Hollinsworth for help. The lawyer only nodded his head slowly and deliberately. Rainwater got the message. He swallowed. "Fifty it is, Mayor."

"Will you be taking out a mortgage?"

"No ma'am. The money will arrive in cash."

Hollinsworth clapped his hands together in happy anticipation. "I'll draw up the papers. When do you want to close?"

Rainwater made a calculation in his head. "Two weeks."

The mayor rose from her chair. "More coffee, gentlemen?"

Rainwater shook his head. "Thanks, but no, ma'am. I'll be on my way."

Hollinsworth watched him depart, then lifted his cup. "Don't mind if I do."

Mayor Teasdale poured. "I would have taken twenty-five, you know."

"Unh-huh. Don't worry about it."

"Your client, what a peculiar fellow. He doesn't strike me as the sharpest knife in the drawer."

"Don't fool yourself, Vera, Billy is smart as a whip. Problem is, he's ruled by his heart, not his head."

"Rainwater. Is that even his real name?" she sniffed.

"I believe there are several family names associated with the Hilltop Band — Araujo, Donnelly, Valentine, among others." He sipped his coffee. "Billy wants to emphasize his tribal heritage. That's tough when your father's name was actually 'Robinson.' "

She rolled her eyes. "That's the sort of thing I'd expect to see on TV, the stage name for an actor. Will he ever get that casino approved?"

Hollinsworth grunted. "Stranger things have happened."

She raised her cup. "Here's to optimism."

29

TWENTY-FOUR HOURS later Mary Ann was in Ellen's Foothill Fashions, not far from the mayor's office, checking out various combinations of halter tops and shorts, shopping for something a little more stylish than the garb she had been wearing on the river. She was torn between a black O-ring bikini and a molded sports bra with cargo hikers. Keeping young Mr. Wagstaff in mind, she decided that the blue sports bra was ever-so-slightly more modest and businesslike, the sort of thing she thought appropriate for an off-duty police officer. She was in the process of admiring herself in the fitting room mirror when a ghostly shadow slipped into view.

Instinctively she grabbed her blouse and held it up over her breasts. "You! Are you stalking me? Get out of here, I'm dressing."

The shadow thrust up a hand, palm out, emphatically cutting her off. Then, using a finger, it started to draw letters in the air.

"All right, wiseguy. That's an *N*."

Then an *A*, followed by a *P*, and finally another *A*. The shadow made a clearing motion, then repeated the sequence.

"N-A-P-A — Napa? As in Valley?"

The shadow shook his head, pointed to one side of the mirror.

"Wine? From the Napa Valley?"

Another shake of the head. More pointing.

"You got me this time, pal. I give up."

She threw on her blouse, buttoned up, and fled the fitting room. She paid for the bra and shorts with her debit card and stepped outside. Then it hit her. Two stores down on the other side of Main Street was a blue-fronted building with a big black-and-yellow sign announcing: *NAPA Auto Parts*. What in the world?

She slinked into the store and looked around. What was she doing there? A middle-aged salesperson looked up from the shelves where he was rearranging touch-up paint cans. "Help you, ma'am?"

"I, uh, need some wax. For, um, an older Mustang."

"Wax is right over there — Turtle, Mother's, whatever you want. Is your finish all oxidized?"

"Well, no, I don't know. It looks pretty good, I just want to keep it that way."

"May I recommend Klasse? That's your best bet." He hooked a thumb. "One aisle over."

"Thanks."

She rounded the endcap and started down the next aisle, wondering why her ghost had sent her into an auto parts store. As she reached the wax display she overheard a Spanish-accented voice rising in impatience at the service counter. She pretended to do some comparison shopping while she listened.

"This is my car, what is the problem?"

"Sorry, sir. We're not supposed to make car keys without a valid registration," came the reply from a voice she took to be a store employee.

"But I have the VIN number here, on this paper. I show you. Look, it is 5J6YH286 —"

"Sorry, sir, it's in our insurance policy."

"But the VIN —"

"I Just need your registration. It should be in your car, wherever you parked."

"My car is at home. I am in my truck today."

"We're here whenever you come back, always ready to help."

Mary Ann inched forward until she could get an eye on the conversation. Now she understood her ghost's intentions, because the frustrated customer was Salvador Cruz.

"I live many miles away, on a ranch. It is inconvenient to return. What can I do to expedite this matter?"

"Sorry, sir . . ." the counterman was young and stressed. Mary Ann thought he was probably dividing his time between NAPA and a stint at the community college down in Lodi.

Cruz reached into his pocket and withdrew a fifty-dollar bill. He placed it on the counter. "Perhaps this will substitute for the registration I have left behind."

The young man eyed the money. "Gee, I don't know . . ."

Cruz added another fifty. "The gratuity is worth it to me for service today." He smiled. "What it costs to forget such an important document."

The young man nodded, swept the money into his pocket, and took the VIN number from Cruz. "I can groove a blank, but not the electronics."

Mary Ann tiptoed away down the aisle. The salesperson looked up as she passed.

"Find what you want?" he asked.

"Close enough . . ."

Outside she hurried across the street and jumped into her Mustang. There she waited until Cruz emerged. She guessed that he was going to get into the fancy green Range Rover she could see parked a block away, and was surprised when he walked right past it. As he turned a corner and disappeared, she started her car and rolled slowly along in his direction, wondering what he was up to.

She had never actually tailed anyone before and didn't know what to do, so she cruised right past the intersection where Cruz had turned. The man was nowhere in sight. She cursed inwardly and turned at the next corner, thinking to backtrack. Instead, as she motored down a narrow side street, she happened upon Applefield's municipal park. And there, in the center, was Cruz, lounging casually near the bronze prospector statue he helped pay for.

Mary Ann continued on for another block, then turned right, and right again, bringing her back along the other side of the square, where she found an open parking space near the children's jungle gym. She angled in and turned off the ignition.

"Now what are we waiting for?" she muttered.

As she watched, Cruz strolled slowly here and there among the park visitors, apparently content to enjoy the sunny warmth of an Indian summer day.

Mary Ann picked up her mobile phone and touched a button, dialing the Golden Hills Tri-Town Police number. "Hello, Wade? Mary Ann. I'm stuck — um, doctor appointment. He's backed up. Yup, right, our insurance plan sucks, I know. I'll be in when I can get there. Warn the troops."

She ended the call and noticed at the same time that something had caught Cruz' eye. Swiveling her attention to the far corner of the park she saw the reason: Billy Rainwater was sauntering his way.

"Well, look at you . . . "

She watched spellbound while Cruz stepped over to the statue, dropped a small metal item in the prospector's gold pan with a conspicuous flourish, and walked away. Rainwater nodded, picked up his pace, dodged through an unruly group of children playing in the water feature at the statue's base, reached into the gold pan, and collected whatever object Cruz had placed there.

Mary Ann had no doubts about the object's identity. "The key!"

Rainwater retreated a few paces, then stopped and examined his find. As he turned it this way and that it glinted in the sunlight. Apparently satisfied, he tossed it into the air, caught it one-handed, and ambled away with a spring in his step. Mary Ann fired up her Mustang and sat with the engine idling, waiting for him to exit the park. Then she swung around the perimeter and ducked into another parking place. Five slots up, she observed Rainwater back into the street in his decaying pickup truck and drive off.

She called the police station again. This time Officer Moss answered. "Hi, Rick. I'm still stuck. Gotta fill a prescription. Yes . . . no . . . none of your business. Cover for me."

She dropped the phone into her lap and searched for Rainwater's truck in the downtown morning traffic. She was afraid to move too quickly, because she was driving his dead brother's car, and he was sure to recognize it given half a chance. The truck disappeared behind a store. She rocked forward in her seat, anxious and uncertain. Then the truck reappeared in the middle distance beyond the downtown buildings, turning west onto County Road 520. Rainwater was heading downhill toward civilization.

"Got you!"

She pulled out of her parking space and followed Rainwater's path through traffic, hoping she could catch up out on the road, worried that she had already lost him.

A mile down the long hill she spotted his truck, winding through the switchbacks between Applefield and Ragtown.

She was so excited by her latest adventure she was talking to herself. "Now, brother, where art thou going? Placerville? Then hook a right. Jackson? Straight on till morning."

Rainwater arrived at old Red Hill Road, stopped at the sign, crossed over, and continued down County Road 520 toward Route 88.

"Jackson it is, my man."

Noting few other vehicles on the road to disguise her presence, she eased off the throttle, allowing the truck to pull away. She stopped at the

Red Hill Road crossing, looked in both directions with exaggerated caution, then gunned it down County Road 520. She had the pickup in sight again as it turned onto Route 88, but just to be safe she kept herself as far behind as possible.

The trip to Jackson had Mary Ann bouncing in her seat with anxiety, but Rainwater seemed oblivious to the blue Mustang trailing him. On the outskirts of town, however, he seemed to vanish. Mary Ann wasn't sure if she had been spotted or just wasn't paying attention.

"Damn it."

She cruised slowly north along Main Street, craning her neck at each intersection, but failed to reacquire her target. Soon the commercial buildings thinned out, the last gas station was in her rear view mirror, and she was back on the highway, sure that she had lost the tail. She pulled over at the entrance to the Forty-Niner Motel and backed into the driveway, preparing to turn for home. Just then the old Toyota pickup sailed on by.

"Whoa!"

She caught a glimpse of Billy Rainwater slurping a tall drink through a straw. Evidently he had stopped for a snack somewhere.

"Hey, we're already in Jackson. Where are you going, mister?"

She punched the gas pedal and re-entered the highway, determined to find out.

Rainwater drove north on combined Route 49 and Route 88, and stayed on Route 49 when they split. After ten miles he swung west onto Route 16, and two miles later turned north again onto Latrobe Road.

"Jesus, Billy, don't tell me you're going to haul my ass all the way into Sacramento?"

She gritted her teeth and slowed as the countryside opened up, leaving her Mustang fully exposed to view. What was she going to tell Chief Ibañez? Especially, what was she going to tell him if her escapade turned out to be, as she was beginning to suspect, a wild goose chase?

Up ahead, Rainwater drove on. After eighteen miles of farms, ranches, oak trees, dry grass, and cattle, the outlying suburbs of California's capital city came into view. The pickup truck eased into busy traffic, ducked through an overpass, shot up an on-ramp, and headed west on the El Dorado Freeway, U.S. Route 50.

Mary Ann followed through increasingly heavy traffic for six miles.

Then the truck abruptly circled down an off-ramp onto westbound Folsom Boulevard. There she was delayed by other cars, and by the time she got rolling, she had lost Rainwater again.

"Damn! Get the fuck out of my way!"

She swerved into the fast lane, roared past a dozen cars at twice the speed limit, then slowed again. There was no sign of her quarry. But her searching eye fastened on a stainless steel sign marking a business park entrance. Large metallic blue letters proclaimed: *Folsom Auto Mall*.

"That's it!"

She missed the turn and cursed herself, but a long block later she spotted a second identical sign. She hit her brakes just in time and turned into Auto Mall Circle.

Rainwater's machine was parked in plain sight in front of Capital City Motors, a spanking new Fiat "studio" recently spun off the Dodge dealer next door. Mary Ann drove on by and pulled over just beyond the Honda megastore. She adjusted her rear-view mirror for a good look at Rainwater, who was standing on the curb with a backpack held in one hand. He was staring at some two dozen little Fiat 500 automobiles arrayed around the lot.

She thought the cars were cute as lady bugs, but wondered how anyone who lived upcountry could ever consider owning one. After all, they were quintessentially urban machines, meant for traffic jams in the Big City and useless anywhere else. Apparently Rainwater was having similar thoughts, because he appeared very unsure of himself. He was soon rescued by a man wearing a white shirt and tie, who strolled out of the office to make a sales pitch. Rainwater listened politely for a few moments, then held up his key and waved a hand toward the collection of diminutive autos. The salesman looked unhappy and made a helpless gesture. Rainwater persisted. The salesman made a cutting motion. Rainwater leaned forward insistently. Both seemed to be getting hot under the collar.

"What is he up to? Shit, it's easier to figure out my ghost," Mary Ann muttered. She was talking to herself again.

The salesman abruptly returned to his office.

"Whoops, he's pissed. That's no way to sell a car, mister."

A minute later a genial older salesman dressed in a nicely tailored dark suit appeared.

"Aha, here comes the supervisor to smooth things over."

Indeed. The man smiled broadly, strode forward with arms outstretched as if greeting a long-lost relative, and clasped Rainwater in a warm embrace. Then the two shook hands enthusiastically.

"You two know each other?" Mary Ann raised her eyebrows.

Trailing behind came a mechanic dressed in coveralls. He was carrying a two-foot-long board under his arm. Mary Ann thought she could detect a number of car keys attached to the thing, dangling from little hooks. The mechanic took Rainwater's key and began comparing it to those on his board.

"And now the expert goes to work. What is he doing?"

It was slow going, checking one key at a time, and Rainwater began to pace. Finally the mechanic found a matching key with an electronic key fob attached. He turned toward the collection of stylish Italian autos and triumphantly pressed a button. Across the lot an olive green 500c distinguished itself from its lookalike siblings by winking its headlamps. Shouts of joy all around. Rainwater shook hands with both men, took the dealer's key, crossed the lot, tucked himself into the little car, and drove away with a cheerful wave.

"Rainwater, why in God's name do you want to test drive that roller skate?"

Mary Ann followed the little green machine to an empty lot behind a vacant building at the far end of Auto Mall Circle. She pulled over at the Chevy dealer next door and watched him get out, turn around, and lean into the back seat, which he appeared to be pulling apart. Then he dropped down behind the car and removed the spare tire tucked up underneath. He rolled it around to the far side and began doing something with it.

"Hey, work over here where I can see you, dammit."

Two minutes later he rolled the tire back under the car and reattached it. Finally he put the rear seat back together.

"Now what was that all about?" she wondered.

Rainwater whipped the car around and returned directly to Capital City Motors. He hopped out with backpack in hand, tossed the key to the waiting sales supervisor, expressed his appreciation of Fiat's innovative design, offered his thanks for the test drive, got into his truck, and drove away.

Mary Ann followed him all around Sacramento, where he made stops at a succession of banks. First at a Wells Fargo branch, then the Bank of

America, Union Bank, Merchants National Bank, River City Bank, and Chase.

Rainwater's final stop in the state capital was at a shop called Valley Gold Exchange on Fruitridge Road, down near the airport. Mary Ann watched him step inside and fought the urge to follow.

"What's with the gold, Rainwater? Something crooked, I know."

Twenty minutes later the man reappeared. Mary Ann thought his backpack looked heavier now.

She turned the key in her Mustang to continue her personal surveillance operation, but the starter motor failed to catch.

"No, no, horsey. Giddiyap."

She tried again. Something made a faint click somewhere under the hood, but the engine did not turn over.

"Come on, come on, gotta go!"

She waited a moment, then held her breath while she turned the key yet again. This time the Mustang fired right up.

"Whew, don't scare me like that."

She caught up with Rainwater on the outskirts of Jackson and tailed him into town. She was not surprised when he parked on the narrow Main Street and hauled his backpack into Millwood's Gold Rush Emporium.

"Well, well, well, look at your shopping habits." she murmured from her vantage point in a parking space a block away.

After ten minutes, Mary Ann got antsy. She left her car, found an ice cream shop, and treated herself to a scoop of raspberry gelato while she waited.

After another ten minutes the door to Millwood's opened and Rainwater emerged. She thought he looked happier, relaxed, somehow relieved. She watched him buy a newspaper from a sidewalk kiosk and idly scan the headlines on the way back to his truck.

"Mission accomplished, I guess, huh?"

She returned to her Mustang, strapped herself in, and turned the key. Once again the mighty 302 V8 failed to start.

"Christ."

She tried again and again, to no avail. Finally she had to face the awful truth — she was stuck in a broken-down antique. She picked up her mobile phone and dialed Tom Wagstaff's number. After four rings, the message machine answered.

"We can't answer our telephone at the moment. For information about our publication, to advertise in our pages —"

She ended the call and brooded over her unkind fate. Then, very reluctantly, she dialed the Golden Hills Tri-Town Police Department, hoping Wade would pick up.

"Tri-Town Police, Wade Gawley here."

Whew, he did.

"Hi, Wade. I'm down in Jackson."

"What kind of disease have you got, anyway?"

"Beg pardon?"

"Your prescription, it's taken all day."

Mary Ann had almost forgotten her ruse. "Oh yeah, they had to send out. Listen, my car broke down. I need a jump or something."

"Battery? Heh, Bobby had to replace it every year or so."

"I hope so, but it sounds worse."

"Man, that Mustang. Did you call triple-A?"

"I'm not a member."

"All right. Let me see what I can do."

▼

Half an hour later a tow truck and a Golden Hills Tri-Town Police Explorer SUV arrived almost simultaneously. The tow truck pulled in ahead of the Mustang, the police vehicle a couple of spaces behind. Mary Ann was cooling her heels on a nearby bench when the SUV's door opened and Chief Ibañez stepped onto the sidewalk. She cringed at the thought of the tongue-lashing she was about to receive.

"Officer Sarzo, what in the hell are you doing down here?"

"Hello, Chief. I'm sick. So's my car."

Ibañez regarded the young cop and her improbable ride. He seemed about to explode, then caught himself. "You both look okay to me. Let's open her up."

Mary Ann popped the hood of the Mustang and joined Ibañez and the tow truck operator at the front bumper. All three stared into the engine compartment as if peering into a coffin.

The tow truck operator hooked up jumper cables and twirled his hand around in the air. "Give her a try now."

Mary Ann reseated herself behind the wheel and turned the key, but aside from a faint click, got no response. The tow truck operator adjusted the cable clamps and signaled her to try again, which she did. Same result. After several more attempts, the tow truck operator sighed and removed the jumper cables.

"I'm not sure, but I'd guess the voltage regulator went south, and you fried your starter motor. Happens all the time with these older ponies."

"Oh boy," said Mary Ann, turning pale.

"What do you want to do?" asked Ibañez.

"God, I don't know. Tow it to a repair shop, I guess. A cheap repair shop."

"We've got one of those here in town, but I recommend our own garage. We're not cheap, but we know what we're doing," said the tow truck operator.

Mary Ann thought long and hard about the situation.

"Well?" prompted Ibañez.

"Okay, it's just — I've got to be careful with money."

"Once we take a good look we can have the parts in forty-eight hours," said the tow truck operator, attempting to reassure her.

"All right, take her away. Be careful. Don't scratch the paint."

"Don't you worry, young lady."

As the tow truck operator went about hooking the Mustang to his truck, Ibañez beckoned Mary Ann to follow and led the way back to his patrol vehicle. They buckled up. He inserted the key, but did not start the engine.

"Now, Officer Sarzo, what's the problem? You look terrible, but you're not sick."

Mary Ann's eyes welled up. "I'm going to lose my car. They're going to repossess it. I can hardly handle the payments as it is, and now this . . ." She sniffled. "I never should have bought it."

"Oh, for God's sake, grow up. You can't cry, you're in uniform."

This ridiculous remark had its intended effect. Mary Ann snorted and managed a crooked grin. "Sorry."

"So, while you're waiting for the car you shouldn't have bought, you can drive the Cherokee to work. Take it easy on the personal use, and no one will squawk."

"Thanks."

Ibañez gripped the wheel in his left hand, turned in his seat to face her, and took a deep breath, working hard to stay calm. "You missed your shift today."

"Yes I did."

"And I could fire your ass for dereliction, since you're still on probation."

"Yes you could."

"And for lying to conceal your unauthorized activities."

"Um . . ."

"Don't insult me. I don't believe it takes all day and a thirty mile drive to fill a prescription."

"Okay, I lied . . . shit."

"Jesus Jehoshaphat. What the ding-dong, Mary-have-mercy have you been up to?"

Mary Ann stared at her feet. She rocked back and forth indecisively, trying to figure out how to begin. Finally she blurted, "I don't think Terry Gardner is such a great detective."

"No? We're not here to talk about sheriff's deputies, be that as it may."

"Billy Rainwater is up to his neck in some kind of — what do you call it? — criminal conspiracy. Gardner should have spotted it."

"The pro didn't, but the rookie did, is that it?"

She wiped her nose and gave him a rebellious look. "Want to hear how I know?"

"It better be good, Miss Crime Theory."

"This morning in Applefield I observed Salvador Cruz pay one hundred dollars to have a car key made without presenting a valid registration, which is against the store's insurance policy. I then observed him to transfer that key to Billy Rainwater. I followed Rainwater to Sacramento, where he used the key to test drive one of those teeny little Fiat 500s."

Ibañez leaned forward. He was starting to pay attention. "And . . . ?"

"He drove it about a quarter of a mile and parked out behind some out-of-business garage. He pulled out the back seat, removed the spare tire, then replaced both, and returned the car to Capital City Whatever, the Fiat dealership."

"Did you get any photos?"

She turned on her not-so-smartphone, thumbed a button, and handed it over. Ibañez stared at the image. In the middle of a vast unused parking lot a tiny person was standing beside a tiny Fiat 500. Who he was or what he was doing was unidentifiable.

"Too far away for details. I was scared I'd get spotted."

Ibañez handed the phone back. "And what makes this enthusiasm for a dinky Italian fad criminal, may I ask?"

"You may. First of all, why did he want to drive that particular car? Those things are like peas in a pod."

Ibañez shrugged. "You got me."

"And where do you suppose Fiat 500s are made?"

Ibañez had no idea. "Italy?"

She pointed out the window. "There's a coffee shop across the street. While I was waiting for the tow truck I went over, borrowed somebody's laptop, and looked it up on the internet."

She paused for effect. Ibañez rolled his eyes and impatiently waved his hand. "What's the punch line?"

"Toluca, Mexico. The old Chrysler factory."

Ibañez resettled himself in the driver's seat. He drummed his fingers on the steering wheel. "You don't say."

"Yes. Rainwater then visited no fewer than six different banks in Sacramento, plus two different gold stores, one down there and one here in Jackson. Oh, and he was carrying a backpack in and out of all these places."

Ibañez scowled. "Good Christ. I don't suppose you tailed him right inside one of these pit stops."

"In uniform?"

"No, of course not." A cloud of doubt was descending on the chief. He waved his hand. "Okay, so wrap it up. What's going on here?"

"Rainwater is laundering money supplied by Salvador Cruz through some kind of cartel network drug deal thing."

"Hmm."

"As we both know, as they taught me in school, you can only move cash in amounts below ten thousand dollars without reporting to the Feds, right? So, I think he found at least sixty thousand dollars in that Mexican Fiat. He put ten each into six different bank accounts."

"And the gold?" Ibañez was mulling the implications of Mary Ann's story.

"Yeah, that's weird. Here's my guess — maybe he found more than sixty thousand, why not? He bought gold from the first store — another ten thou — then sold it to the second. Now he can claim his fortune comes from prospecting on the river, which I know he does."

Chief Ibañez was agitated. He was struggling to absorb the idea that his youngest and greenest officer was giving him a clinic in crime investigation. "Tell me, Sarzo, have you ever, *ever,* caught a speeder?"

"No, sir, I haven't."

"Didn't think so. That's what local cops are supposed to do, you know. That, and prevent drunken brawls in the local bars. Sort out car accidents. Maybe help an old lady cross a street now and then. What you're telling me — *this!* — this is deep shit. And you never actually saw a single dollar. We don't have a shred of proof."

"No, but it's supporting evidence." She was defiant. "It adds up."

"Write a report. Put in as much detail as you can remember." He sighed and started the engine. "Now, let's get on up the hill."

Part FOUR

30

ON THE FIRST STORMY DAY of the fall season, rain drops and dead oak leaves were rattling against the windows of the Golden Hills Tri-Town Police Department. Mary Ann was hunkered down at her desk, recording her morning travel advisory.

"Tri-Town travel update for ten AM. Expect rain today on all local roads, heavy at times, turning to showers after three PM. Listen up, motorists, and especially you bikers out there. You won't melt, but first wet weather frees up all that summertime dirt and oil on the pavement, and you can skid your way into an expensive insurance claim. Drive with caution."

Ricky Moss walked by her desk as she was finishing up. "Where'd you get that dirt-and-oil gag?

"Wade taught me. Am I wrong?"

"No, keep it up. It's good stuff."

Mary Ann blushed with pride. Someone appreciated her and wasn't shy about saying so. "Hey, Rick, take the phones for a second, okay?"

"Sure."

She left her desk and disappeared into the ladies' room. Five minutes went by, and then the door slammed open, and she burst forth, running for the station exit.

Moss raised a hand. "Yo, I can't fly your desk all day. Where are you going?"

She screeched to a stop and stared vacantly at him. Her mind was a million miles away. "Um, early lunch. I'm starved." She headed for the exit again, then thought of something and backtracked to her desk.

"Whoa, before I forget." She grabbed a pen and wrote five numbers on her notepad — *6, 21, 29, 12, 35.* She tore off the page and stuffed it in her uniform.

"I owe you," she called out over her shoulder as she raced away.

Moss watched her go. "Babe, you are one strange cop."

Mary Ann drove down Applefield's Main Street in her Golden Hills Tri-Town Jeep Cherokee, trying to decide what to do. Nearing the Miners Market she wrestled with a powerful urge to park and run inside.

"No, no, they'll know who I am," she muttered.

So she drove on, turning down County Road 520, then in and out of the Whiskeyjack River canyon, and on into Placerville, windshield wipers flapping all the way. There she cruised through downtown and stopped at the Placerville Maxi Mart.

Behind the counter was a thin and greying Asian man, apparently somewhat deaf, because she found herself impatiently announcing her presence several times before he abandoned his efforts to refill the coffee machine and shuffled arthritically over to the cash register. His English wasn't perfect.

"Help you?"

"Hi. I need to buy a lottery ticket, and I've never done this before. I don't know what to do."

"What game play?"

"What do you mean? I just want to play the lottery."

"Scratchers? Mega Millions? Fantasy Five? Many games here."

"Oh. I don't know. I have five numbers I need to use. I thought I read about six. Should I buy sixty tickets and write in every possibility to guarantee that sixth number?"

"What say? You wait." The old man fished around in a shirt pocket, pulled out a tiny hearing aid that looked like a pink earplug, and awkwardly twisted it into his right ear. He smiled. "Now I hear. Talk."

"I need to buy a ticket, but I only know five numbers."

"What problem?"

"Don't I need six?"

"Five enough. You play Fantasy Five. Five numbers, you bet."

Mary Ann was dubious and wondered if this old codger actually knew what he was talking about, but decided to let destiny take its course. "Okay, five it is. I'll buy a ticket."

"One dollar please."

Mary Ann handed over four quarters.

"First time play?"

"Yeah. I've never bought a ticket before."

"Mark numbers, sign back. Wait for drawing."

"Okay, I think. The numbers I see in the little brackets?"

"One to forty-one. Like you see. Want me pick?"

"No, no. I've got a plan here."

"Lucky numbers? Ha ha, good. We have plenty winners here in store. Plenty winners play here."

Mary Ann placed the page torn from her notebook on the counter and flattened it out. Very slowly and carefully she marked numbers on her ticket exactly as she had written them down back in the police station — *6, 21, 29, 12, 35.*

"Aha. Very lucky numbers. How pick? See fortune cookie?"

Mary Ann was having trouble decoding the old man's conversation. "How did I decide on these numbers, you mean?"

"Yes. How pick?"

"Someone told me to play and suggested the numbers. A friend, I guess."

"Trust friend?"

"Not sure about that. He's a ghost."

31

THAT EVENING found Mary Ann loitering in the Book Nook, pretending to study up on supernatural lore using one of Lorraine Wagstaff's computers.

"Enough with your ghosts, Mary Ann. I've got to close up."

"I know, I know. Be right with you, I'm onto something."

"Something hot?"

"Maybe. I read somewhere that 'Sarzeau' is the name of a town in Normandy, I think. France, anyway."

While Lorraine busied herself emptying the cash register and battening down the hatches, Mary Ann stealthily opened a new tab in the browser and, heart pounding, stole a look at the California Lottery website, where, with another click, she pulled up the results of the day's Fantasy Five game. She read the numbers several times — *6, 21, 29, 12, 35.* It took a dozen heartbeats for the realization to sink in. She had won!

"Woohoo!" she yelped.

"Good Lord, kiddo, what has gotten into you?" Lorraine crossed the room to investigate. Mary Ann was euphoric, and she was just about to explain it all to her good friend when she thought better of the idea and closed the browser.

"What's new in Ghostville?"

"Oh, nothing, really. I got a reference — Sarzeau is in Brittany, that's all. Not Normandy. They have those standing stones there, like Stonehenge." Mary Ann felt guilty dissembling about her real discovery.

"Menhirs," said Lorraine, frowning.

"Yeah, menhirs." Mary Ann stood up from the computer. "Gotta head out. Thanks for staying open for me." She clicked on the *Shut Down* icon to turn the computer off and started out of the shop.

"Night, Mary Ann."

"*Hasta mañana.*"

The day's storm was moving out, but ragged clouds were still drizzling. Mary Ann tucked her head down and jogged to the Cherokee. Once inside she locked the doors. She thought about her amazing good fortune and mulled her hasty decision to conceal everything from Lorraine Wagstaff, tipping her forehead onto the steering wheel in morose self-loathing.

Then she snapped upright.

"But if I told her, I'd be the golden goose. Damn."

32

IN THE MORNING, Mary Ann drove into Sacramento to deliver her lottery ticket in person to the California State Lottery Commission, which was located in a gleaming high-rise office building on North 10th Street. There she picked up a claim form. She was so nervous filling in the blanks that she ruined it and had to start over. Then she was told that she should make copies of both her ticket and the completed form. There was no working copier in the building, so she had to run around the city looking for one. After driving for half an hour she discovered a FedEx Office store, made the necessary duplicates, and drove back. Finally she handed in the properly prepared documents and learned that a check for $53,000, minus withholding taxes, would soon appear in her mailbox.

"Looks like I get to keep my car," said Mary Ann.

"You are a lucky lady," said the clerk.

Mary Ann was scheduled for a late shift and wasn't due at the station until mid-afternoon, so her next stop was Saint Patrick's Catholic Church, back in Placerville. She parked in the uphill lot, crossed the paved quadrangle, and entered the rectory. The nun behind the reception desk was chatting with a slender middle-aged priest who retreated a step as Mary Ann came forward.

"Sister Bianca?"

"Yes?"

"Mary Ann Sarzo, remember me?"

"Yes. Yes, of course. Goodness, how are you? How can I help you?"

"I wonder if Father Eisen is around somewhere. I need to talk to him."

"Let me guess — ghost business?"

Mary Ann gave her a sour nod.

Sister Bianca raised her eyebrows to the priest standing nearby. He shrugged agreeably. "As it happens, your timing couldn't be better. This is Father Eisen."

They shook hands. "Nice to see who goes with that nice voice," he said, in the same mild tones she remembered from the confessional booth.

"Um, yeah, same here."

"Let's take a walk, shall we?" Father Eisen smiled and gestured toward a rear door. As they slowly toured the church grounds, he listened attentively to Mary Ann's latest news.

"The main thing is, he didn't respond to the prayer when I read it."

"You showed him the cross?"

"Oh yeah, told him you blessed it and everything. This is funny, I even said, 'get thee gone, Satan.' "

"Really?"

"I was nervous."

"Understandable, no harm done."

"Since he wasn't repelled, that means he's not evil, right?"

"I don't think so, but it's unwise to be too sure. We know so little."

"Then yesterday, I won the lottery."

"You what?" He stopped walking and stared at her.

"Well, the Fantasy Five game. And who do you suppose told me what numbers to pick?"

"Your ghost." Father Eisen was dumbfounded. "Are you serious?"

"Absolutely."

"How could a ghost predict the future? Unless you're personally dealing with the Lord Himself, which I doubt."

"I read online that virtual visitors can travel through time. He didn't predict the future — he comes from the future," said Mary Ann. It all made perfect sense to her.

"How do you mean?" The priest was slow to grasp the idea.

"Well, I don't think my ghost is especially smart or lucky — he's dead, right? — but I think somewhere in the future he saw the lottery results, traveled back to yesterday, and showed me the winning numbers."

Father Eisen clasped his hands behind his back. They strolled along in silence for a while.

"I guess it's possible," he finally conceded. "Who knows?"

"At first I thought the ghost was Bobby Rainwater. But he was dead long before this lottery business, so I'm wrong about that," said Mary Ann.

More silence, more walking. Then Father Eisen stopped again and faced her. "This apparition of yours. It — he — whoever he is — troubles me."

"Me too."

"He challenges my faith."

"Father?"

"I thought I was a believer, and it has been amusing to help you cope with a ghost I thought was a figment of your imagination." He wrung his hands, interrupting himself. "You really won the lottery?"

"I turned in my claim this morning. They'll be sending me a check for almost fifty thousand dollars any day now." She handed him a photocopy of the ticket and claim form.

"Astonishing. Evidence like this makes it hard to take your 'visitor' lightly. If I accept your account, then I realize I hardly used to believe at all."

"That can't be true," said Mary Ann, coloring.

He straightened up and handed back the sheet of paper. "You know, your 'visitor' has given me quite a jolt. Believe it or not, that's good. Nothing like a reminder of the mystery of life to reinforce one's faith."

Mary Ann fidgeted. "There's something else that bothers me. I haven't told my friends about the lottery."

"Why not?"

"I don't dare. They'll be after me. They won't be able to help it, they'll want to win too, and they'll think I have magic powers or something."

He thought for a moment, then slowly nodded approval. "I think you did the right thing. The less temptation, the better. Just be tactful — don't let your secrets poison a friendship."

"Thanks. It would be so much easier if I could talk to the mirror man, like we are now. Or figure out how to summon him for some straight answers."

"Perhaps there is a way. Just as we Catholics use holy relics and rituals to focus our thoughts and draw closer to the Almighty, maybe there's some object associated with the ghost that will strengthen your ties."

Their walk had brought them to Mary Ann's Jeep. She got in, and Father Eisen politely closed her door.

"Think about this: if your visitor comes from the future, he or she might still be alive at this moment in time, even as we speak."

33

EARLY THE FOLLOWING morning officers Sarzo, Gawley, and Moss were all mustered in the Applefield station, but their chief was absent, causing bafflement and consternation.

"Where the hell is he? Something's up," said Moss.

"He's never around. Used to be tied to that desk and his telephone, and I don't think I've seen him all week," added Gawley. "Got any ideas, Mary Ann?"

She shrugged. "Nope. Every now and then he shows up, and I hide so he won't chew me out, which is his favorite pastime."

Gawley cracked a smile. "As you deserve, no doubt."

"No doubt," Mary Ann acknowledged grimly.

Moss chuckled, then grew serious. "You know, we all wonder what's going on with Bobby's investigation. And we've all heard the rumors about drug money. That worries me. Money is a powerful drug, and anybody can get addicted."

This idea shocked Mary Ann. "Are you saying the chief is on the take?" She had never imagined such a thing.

"Jesus, Rick," said Gawley.

Moss gave his fellow officers a sheepish look. "No? Then how about Gardner, our straight-and-narrow deputy? I sub for Alton Brothers on my days off — the contractors? — and a while back we were building this fancy restaurant over in Tarvolo. Class-A construction, I must say. We heard Gardner was behind it, got himself a big loan. He was going to get rich feeding the rich over there. But he knew zip about *foie gras* and it folded. Lost a ton of money before Rossi took over."

"I had lunch there. It's nice," said Mary Ann.

"So you never know. Not for sure. Money does funny things to people."

"Yeah, and you could use a chunk with your alimony payments," said Gawley.

"That's my business, Wade. And I've got it covered without any outside help, thanks, so fuck you."

"I told you not to marry that woman. Should have listened."

"Hey now, boys — time to go to work," said Mary Ann, stepping between the two.

"Right," said Gawley and headed for his patrol vehicle.

"I think Wade had a thing for Faye, my ex, is what I think," said Moss in self-defense.

Mary Ann spread her arms. "Whatever. No fights, okay? Get out of here. Go catch some lawbreakers."

When she was alone, she started to worry about Chief Ibañez. She realized she didn't really know him very well. Did he live in a house that was too big and too expensive? Did he gamble? Did he have a wife who wanted to be supported in fancy style? Was he having trouble sending his kids through college? How old would the kids of a man of sixty be, anyway? Come to think of it, did he have a wife or kids at all? What about an aged mother soaking up his salary in one of those assisted living places? They cost a fortune, right? She had no idea about any of it. So, yes, police corruption, it was possible. Ibañez' fiery outrage at her many missteps was burned into her brain, however, and it told against any improprieties. On the other hand, as Moss pointed out, you never know. Not for sure.

While she was thinking, she wandered idly around the station. It took her a while to understand why she was restless — she wanted to find something to connect her with the ghost. She believed that whoever he might be must know her, know her troubles, and that meant someone in the Golden Hills Tri-Town Police Department. So maybe some sort of important talisman was sitting in the station, just waiting to be found. But if so, it was well out of sight. As her eyes traveled around the desks, filing cabinets, lockers, tables, bookcases, and kitchenette, she also began to consider the ghost's impending demise. If indeed he did know her on a day-to-day basis, as indicated by her lottery triumph, someone on the force might soon be dead. She shuddered at the thought.

34

AFTER HER SHIFT, Mary Ann dialed the *County Courier* on her mobile phone and got a familiar message: "We can't answer our telephone at the moment. For information about our publication, to advertise in our pages . . . "

She sighed and was just about to end the call when a live voice answered. "Hello, *County Courier*, this is Wagstaff."

"Tom. Mary Ann. I need to pick up my car down in Jackson, and I need a ride. What do you say?"

"Sure. Come on over. I'm out back with the rig."

Mary Ann left the Jeep in its parking space behind the station and hiked five blocks to Wagstaff's *County Courier* offices. She tramped through the weeds to the back of the building where Wagstaff was busy tweaking his placer mining rig.

"Hi, M. Give me a sec."

She watched as he replaced a hose on the suction dredge pump.

"Okay, back to normal. Ready to suck up the largest nuggets seen in a century. Where are we going?"

"Jackson. Abbott's Auto Repair. They called, and my Mustang is good as new."

"Until the next failure, anyway."

She grimaced.

"Sorry. It's just that, old cars, it's always something."

"Mmm. Let's go, it's almost closing."

They climbed into Wagstaff's FJ Cruiser, and off they went, down the hill, through Ragtown, across Red Hill Road, and down Route 88 to the county seat.

Mary Ann scowled. "Damn, I was towed. I don't actually know where Abbott's is located."

"Look it up." Wagstaff handed her his smartphone.

She fussed with the map app and discovered that Abbott's was out on the south side of town, on Route 49.

When they got there, Abbott's tow truck operator was the only employee present, and he was just closing up shop.

"Well, hello, young lady. That Mustang, what a car. And it's running like a top. You're going to love it."

"I already do."

"Unh-huh." He looked her over as he thumbed through a pile of work orders. After a considerable amount of shuffling, he found hers. He picked up the sheet and scrutinized the details. "Yeah, well, it turned out that it was the voltage regulator, as I think I mentioned on the phone, starter motor, and this is too bad, battery too. We replaced everything. Like I said, parts, two-fifty. Labor, three-fifty. Total, six. Plus tax."

Mary Ann winced. "Take a check?"

"Local?"

"Applefield B of A. Don't worry, I'm not going anywhere."

"You're a cop up there, right?" He looked doubtful.

"Hard to believe, huh? But it's true," she replied.

He squinted at her, trying to understand something beyond his experience. "You're small, and a girl, but you probably know judo and all that martial arts stuff."

"And I pack. Watch out, sir."

He smiled. "Check will be fine."

She pulled out her checkbook and wrote goodbye to six hundred dollars, plus tax, pretty much draining her entire bank account.

Wagstaff whistled. "Whew, that's steep. I warned you about that car, M."

"Don't rub it in."

They followed the tow truck operator out into the shop yard, and he handed her the keys. "Drive safely, young lady."

She nodded, unlocked the door, then turned to Wagstaff, who was waiting courteously to be sure the Mustang would actually start.

"Thanks for the lift." She glanced up at the sky and noticed that the sun was down. Stars would soon be twinkling in the deepening blue above the eastern hills. She pondered the two-car problem, which threatened to separate her from Wagstaff immediately, and considered her next step. She was reluctant to say goodnight, and she hoped Wagstaff might feel the same way. "What do you think? Dinner somewhere? Celebrate my working auto?"

Wagstaff hesitated. "Sure, I guess. Where?"

"How about Rossi's, up in Tarvolo? It's been a while."

He nodded agreement and headed for his FJ. Mary Ann hopped into her Mustang, fired it up on the first turn of the key, and led the way out of town.

The deck at Rossi's was closed, and the stylish steel chairs were stacked up in a corner. Leaves were blowing under the table legs. Mary Ann and Wagstaff sat down inside, close by a floor-to-ceiling glass wall framing the Tarvolo golf course. Someone was still out there, whacking balls off the practice tee.

A waiter appeared and lit a candle on their table. They ordered red wine and sat back to enjoy each other's company.

"Cool tonight," said Mary Ann.

"Halloween coming up," said Wagstaff.

They clinked glasses. After a moment, Wagstaff asked the burning question. "Anything new on Rainwater and Russell?"

"You mean, tips from my shadowy informant?"

"Yeah. What's on his mind these days?"

"Nothing new. I haven't seen him for almost a week."

"Ah."

"You know, I can't tell you how nice it is to be talking to a human being with a voice, instead of my silent visitor, and not getting yelled at in the process."

"Chief Ibañez, huh? Everyone knows he's a pain in the butt. Hang in there."

"You try it. I can't do anything right."

Wagstaff shrugged to acknowledge her complaint. "I did some research in the *Courier* archives. The last time we had a murder here was in the seventies. Some bar fight got out of hand, and a guy ran his car over another guy. The case was solved in forty-eight hours."

"You think we ought to know something by now."

"Yeah, where's my headline? What's holding everything up?"

"Your guess is as good as mine." Mary Ann toyed with her glass. "There's been talk of corruption. Rumors. Bad cop stuff. Do you think that's possible?"

"Drug money at work? On Ibañez?"

"That's the idea, I guess."

Wagstaff thought about this, then shook his head. "I don't believe it."

"Here's another thing. I just found out this restaurant was originally built by Deputy Sheriff Gardner, but it folded and became" — she waved a hand — "what we have here, Rossi's Fine Italian Dining."

Wagstaff looked around. "He didn't count his pennies, that's for sure. The place is beautiful. Cost a fortune."

"Yeah, and maybe he's looking for an easy way to get his fortune back."

"I doubt that. The whole story was in the *Courier*. He was incorporated. If he did the paperwork right, it was a bankruptcy, and he's personally in the clear."

"But you never know, right? Not for sure."

"No, you don't. Good God."

Steaks arrived, and they paused to eat. Mary Ann told herself to drop the shop talk or lose the evening. So, after a decent interval of knife and fork action, she changed the subject. "How about you? What's life for normal people like? I haven't seen you since we were out on the river."

"Classes have started. I'm teaching kids how to rout out dovetail joints. We're making side tables with little drawers this term," said Wagstaff between mouthfuls.

"How do you do that? Hammers and chisels?"

He shook his head. "More like fifty thousand dollars of the State's money in DeWalt power tools."

"Oh. I'd like to watch that. See you all covered with sawdust." Significant pause. "That was fun, panning for gold. We should do it again."

Wagstaff looked up to find her gazing at him warmly, candlelight flickering in her dark eyes.

"You okay?" he asked.

Not what she wanted to hear. "Yes. Fine. If you can call our waiter over, I'll chance another glass of wine."

"You got it." He signaled the waiter.

Mary Ann ruminated on the moment. Wagstaff seemed oblivious to what she thought was a loud-and-clear advertisement of romantic interest. Maybe she was wrong about him.

Wagstaff finished his steak. "Mom told me you were worried your car might get repossessed."

"We did talk about it. Rookie salary, and all. It's a stretch."

"Too bad. In spite of its faults, it's a nice piece of machinery."

"But something amazing happened and —" She stopped herself from mentioning the lottery.

"And — what?" He seemed to expect her to confirm something he already suspected.

"Oh, nothing really. I, uh, came into an inheritance."

"Inheritance."

"Out of the blue. I'll be paying off the car and be debt free. Well, except for my credit card."

He munched on a french fry. "Wow, that's great. Wonderful."

The waiter glided over and inquired about coffee and something from the dessert menu. They decided not to indulge, split the check on their credit cards, and found themselves outside on a gravel path, strolling to the parking lot under a cool canopy of stars. Mary Ann was feeling bleak. Wagstaff made no attempt to take her hand, and now they were facing the two-car problem again. Before she could think of a workable tactic to prolong the moment, Wagstaff held up his car keys apologetically, as if they were to blame for an urgent departure, and headed for his FJ Cruiser.

"See you later, M. Nice dinner. Sorry to run, but I've got a publishing deadline, and I've got to put the *Courier* to bed."

Mary Ann watched the big four-by-four motor away down the road and waved as its taillights vanished around an oak-bound curve.

"What's the matter, Tom? Why can't you put *me* to bed?"

35

POW! POW! *Pow! Pow! Pow! Pow!*

Mary Ann was up early and on station in the Foothill Shooting Center, emptying her 9-millimeter Beretta into a target ten yards out. Without examining the results she inserted a second clip into the gun and —

Pow! Pow! Pow! Pow! Pow! Pow!

— ripped right through it, firing as rapidly as she could pull the trigger. Then she dropped that clip, slammed in a third one, and —

Pow! Pow! Pow! Pow! Pow! Pow!

— emptied that as well. The pistol was hot in her hands as she eased up, raised her goggles, and reeled the target in. As expected, it was well-ventilated by a number of hits, although only three made it within the seven ring. Her best shot just grazed the line bordering the eight ring. If the silhouette had been a real live criminal, he might have been lightly wounded by her fusillade. She should have been greatly annoyed, but the sheer exhilaration of blasting away without a care brightened her otherwise foul mood.

She attached another target, ran it out fifteen yards, reloaded, and had at it all over again — *Pow!* — *Pow!* — *Pow!* — squeezing off the shots a little more carefully, but not by much. Upon inspection, she found the usual erratic spread, but one shot had penetrated the nine ring. Good enough, she thought, tore off her ear protectors and goggles, packed her gear, and headed out the door.

In the parking lot she popped open the trunk of her Mustang and was dropping her bag inside when a voice called out, "Hey, Sarzo!"

She closed the trunk lid, and there was Terry Gardner just getting out of his truck, which she noticed was a spiffy Honda Ridgeline.

"Morning, Terry."

"Going home? How'd you do?"

"Tight patterns right on the X, as always."

"At least you're practicing."

"That I am. Just in case I spot an attempted murder while I'm there to do my duty."

"Let's hope that never happens."

"Second the motion. So, anyway, how are we doing on Rainwater and

Russell? What's the heads-up?"

He gave her an appraising look. "Not so good. We're having trouble developing solid evidence in both cases."

Mary Ann threw up her hands. "A few days ago I tracked that Rainwater dude to Sacramento, where he appeared to deposit cash smuggled in from Mexico in six different banks. I'm new, but it looks like money laundering to me. I think he's buying and selling gold too."

"The Fiat 500 escapade, right? I'm aware of Rainwater's activities. Ibañez sent your report over. We'll keep an eye on him."

Mary Ann wasn't satisfied with this explanation. And she wanted to dispel her sense of unease about the entire situation. "There are rumors kicking around out there. Drug money. Cops on the take."

"I've heard them all," said Gardner.

"What do you think?" asked Mary Ann.

"Why cops? It could be anybody." He paused. "If — that is, *if* — drug money actually plays into the scenario."

"If . . ." said Mary Ann, disappointment showing.

"Don't worry, Sarzo. Leave it to Beaver, we'll get our man."

"Yeah, well then, good shooting." She made a little finger wave and, stung by the patronizing dismissal, dropped into her Mustang without another word and headed off to work.

36

MARY ANN drove up and down Applefield's Main Street twice before she found a parking spot. Even in October the tourists were an overwhelming presence, delighting Mayor Teasdale and the Chamber of Commerce and irritating the hell out of local residents.

Her check from the California Lottery had arrived in yesterday's mail, and she was heading for the local branch of the Bank of America to deposit the thing before it turned into a pumpkin.

On her way she noticed the Tri-Town Police Explorer SUV stopped in the street. Chief Ibañez was leaning out the driver's window chatting with a slender man in a cowboy-style straw hat. The man was gesticulating unhappily, and Chief Ibañez was attempting to calm him down. She caught a word or two as she passed by.

"The dead don't give a damn, Hector, but the rest of us have to make a living. This thing has festered for two months. What in the name of God and country are you doing about it?"

She couldn't hear Chief Ibañez' reply, but she could imagine it, and anyway, in another few steps she was inside the bank, multiplying her personal worth by an unheard-of amount. Watching the teller routinely accept her check without hesitation or apparent curiosity brought home the fact that she was now a genuine member of the mythical middle class. She was walking on air as she made her exit.

Ten paces down the street the man in the straw hat stepped out of the Pick & Shovel Coffee Shop, a tall latte in each hand, and blocked her way.

"Hello, officer. It's Sarzo, am I right?" He held out one of the lattes and aimed an elbow at a sidewalk bench. "Got a moment? Let's talk."

Mary Ann allowed herself to accept the coffee and take a seat. "Have we met?"

"I don't think so. Howard Turnbow."

"Now I remember, I saw you at the mayor's garden party."

"I was there. Mmm, that ridiculous statue." He removed a pair of expensive sunglasses and pinched his nose to chase away bad thoughts. "I'll get right to the point. In addition to this little shop and the Miners Market over there" — he pointed down the street — "I own the local FM radio station. K-V-I-G. That's the call letters I got stuck with, — man, you'd think those bureaucrats would add a letter or two to make things easier — but we have a jingle, and we're *The Vig*, purveyors of whatever kind of pop music our listeners want to hear."

"Pardon me," said Mary Ann, sipping her coffee, "I didn't even know we had a radio station. I've never listened."

"Doesn't matter. We're very popular, and not just locally. We're on the internet. My aunt Rose and her card-playing friends listen to us all the way down in Visalia."

"Wow."

"Now here's the thing. My Sunday night disc jockey took off for Reno with one of my baristas. I'm told they're eloping, then moving on up to Boise. I guess she's pregnant." He paused to brood. "The help these days. So, my problem is, I need a replacement."

"Me?" Mary Ann was astonished.

"I've heard a couple of your weather reports. Very creative."

"I thought Mayor Teasdale was my entire audience."

"No, no. You've got a good voice. You could do it."

"I don't know a thing about radio. Well, not real radio."

"We subscribe to a playlist service down in Dallas. It's easy. You press a few buttons, talk about the weather or whatever strikes your fancy, I don't care, say our name once in a while, and Spin-O-Matic, Inc., does the rest. What do you say?"

"Are you serious? This is coming at me from way, way out of left field."

Turnbow removed his hat and twirled it around on a finger. "Come on, Sarzo. Like they say, this is show biz. I'm not asking you to swamp out the elephants or work full time — hell, your boss would run me out of town. You can still be a cop."

"And get paid?"

"Of course. Four hours a week, at most. It's a good opportunity. You can practice up your patter, learn the ropes. For someone with your talent, It'll be falling off a log."

Mary Ann took a big gulp of coffee and thought it over, thought about Tom Wagstaff's advice on negotiating for her Mustang. "You know, I'm not sure about taking on a second job. I recently came into an inheritance, so I don't really need any money. Just this minute I was in the bank depositing a big check."

Turnbow bestowed a canny smile. "Tell you what, I can go as high as thirty an hour. That's my limit."

Mary Ann thought some more. Then she nodded.

"All right, Mr. Turnbow —"

"Howard."

"Okay, Howard, then. When do I start?"

"You can reach me here." He handed her a business card. "Let's go over everything at the station on Saturday."

They shook hands. Turnbow put his hat back on, excused himself, and walked away toward the Miners Market, leaving Mary Ann with her coffee cooling and her head spinning.

▼

Billy Rainwater was coming out of the Miners Market with a brand new pay-as-you-go mobile telephone just as Turnbow entered. They exchanged nods of vague familiarity in passing. He hiked up the street, smiled respectfully at the young policewoman sipping a latte in front of the Pick & Shovel, and took a seat on a bench in the Applefield town park. There he tore the packaging off his new phone and keyed in a number. After several rings a pleasant recorded voice announced:

"The party you have dialed is not answering. Stand by, and the party will return your call."

After a few minutes cooling his heels, the phone rang.

"Hello, this is Rainwater."

"Are you alone?" asked a precise male voice.

Rainwater looked around. Over near the prospector statue tourists were taking family pictures. Otherwise the park was empty. "Pretty much."

"Listen to me: the local police know that you have been laundering money."

"That's impossible." Rainwater was stunned.

"Yet it is true. I have a source that knows all about these things. There is a young police officer, a woman. She followed you. She watched you go in and out of all the banks, the gold shops."

Rainwater stood up and peered back down Main Street. "Hey, I think I see her right now, she's standing on the sidewalk here in Applefield."

"She could be dangerous. You must find a way to put her off the scent. Turn her aside. Convince her not to pursue our activities any further."

"Are you saying, get rid of her . . . ?"

"Only if all else fails. We see what the tragic death of one police officer can do. Another will awaken the department, cause scrutiny. We must not kick over the hill of ants."

"What, then?"

"I leave the method to you. Bring in your allies. I am sure you will find a way."

"Thanks for the pep talk. A lot of help you are."

"We do what we can," said the voice and — *Click!* — ended the call.

Billy Rainwater took a deep breath, retraced his steps down Main Street, deposited the brand new phone in the nearest trash receptacle, and jaywalked to his pickup truck in a thoughtful mood. The young policewoman was nowhere in sight.

37

IN A RARE MOMENT these days, Chief Ibañez happened to be at his desk when the call came in. "Tri-Town Police. Yes? When did this happen? All right, then, when did you discover the broken lock?" He listened for a moment, sighed, and intoned his standard response: "We'll send someone to investigate and take a statement as soon as personnel become available."

He stood up from his desk and peered out into the main station area. No one was there except Mary Ann, with bills spread out all over her desk while she verified maintenance expenses for the department's vehicle fleet.

"Sarzo. Burglary downtown at the Apple Ranch Restaurant. You're up, see the woman, find out what's going on."

"This is a first for me. Do we ever solve these things?" asked Mary Ann, strapping on her duty belt.

"Once in a while we do get lucky," said the chief.

"Sounds iffy. What should I tell her?"

"We're on it, we'll investigate, we'll let you know. Take a fingerprint kit, that always impresses the hapless victims. Now go on, get out of here, git."

Mary Ann left the department's bills in a disorderly heap, picked up a small black case from one of the lockers, and headed for the door.

The Apple Ranch Restaurant, favored by tourists and shunned by locals, was an easy walk from the station, but she jumped into her assigned Jeep Cherokee anyway, having learned the concept of total readiness from her often ill-tempered boss.

So she drove three blocks down Main Street, parked in the yellow zone beside a fire hydrant, and entered the slickly-appointed eatery, where the host, a well-mannered man twice her age, automatically presented a menu and asked to seat her.

"Can I speak with the manager, please? We got a call," said Mary Ann.

"Oh? Pardon me, sure, I'll get her, just a moment." He started away, thought about it, stopped, and gestured for Mary Ann to follow. "I guess you two should discuss things in her office."

The manager, one Bessy Strathwaite, was roughly Lorraine's age. Considering the small population of the Golden Hills Tri-Town Area, they probably knew each other. She wagged her head in sad regard for the venality of the world. "Sometime last night our rear door was forced. The alarm was deactivated, and quite a lot of stock was taken."

"Can you show me, please?"

Strathwaite led Mary Ann through the gathering crowd in the dining room, through the bustle of the kitchen, where quick hands were assembling orders of flame-broiled burgers and fries, and on into the storeroom beyond. Mary Ann hauled out her digital camera and shot pictures of the back door where the bolt had been torn loose.

Strathwaite indicated empty steel shelving. "Here's where we store our stuff."

"What's missing, do you think?" Mary Ann pulled a small notebook out of a pocket and was poised to take notes.

"Sort of funny — we keep whole-grain Oroweat buns and bread for our famous apple burgers and equally renowned meatloaf sandwiches here. Retail product, wrapped just like for Safeway. They grabbed twenty loaves or more, give or take. We've got cheap Franzia boxed wine here, maybe fifteen liters. The cooks use it when grilling up our continental steaks — we'd never serve that to customers, you understand — and it's all gone. Fifty jars of Grey Poupon mustard. A case of nice Ravenswood merlot, a case of Mondavi cab, our house pour, and a case of Foxglove chardonnay. All gone. Looks like three cases of Pepsi are missing, and six cases of Arrowhead bubbly water as well. Sheesh."

Mary Ann pointed to several gallon jugs of Heinz yellow mustard. "But not these."

"That's what I mean. The stuff packaged in bulk is still sitting here. Look at those tortillas, a hundred to a bag."

"Can you put a value on the theft?"

"I know it's not like we're a bank that got robbed. Seven-fifty, I suppose. Wholesale, of course."

"Of course," agreed Mary Ann, trying to sound like the seasoned pro she hoped to become.

She doodled on her notepad, opened her little black case and, relying on the memory of her forensics class at Butte College, made a clumsy attempt to capture some fingerprints. Amazing herself, it appeared she might have something from the alarm controller. She took a picture.

"Well, Ms. Strathwaite. We're on it, we'll investigate, we'll let you know."

"I hope you catch those bastards. We look busy here, and we are, but we've got a lease, a payroll, and restaurants work on slim margins. In this economy, we're on the edge."

"Yeah, tough times." Mary Ann hesitated. "I, um, probably shouldn't say this, but we might need another hit before we can put the facts together. Call your insurance company. Your stolen goods aren't coming back. Recovery is rare, especially with a sell-by date. Yuck — somebody out there is eating bread and mustard sandwiches."

"Thanks for your candor. Appreciate it."

"We'll be in touch."

Mary Ann left the restaurant in a morbid frame of mind. Somehow, small town crime depressed her as much as Murder One. It all seemed so stupid.

▼

Back in the station, Chief Ibañez paused on his way out the door to examine her fingerprint photo. "That's good, I'll be damned, a good print."

"Thanks. I'm stunned it actually showed up. You think the burglar knew all about the alarm code?"

"Hmm? Probably. Doesn't matter. We don't really know if that's the perp's print, do we?"

"No, I guess not. But it's a clue, right? Maybe, if the dude has a record, we'll get a match, and then we'll have our man."

"Forget about clues. What we need is a *tip*. That's how it always works," growled Ibañez.

"Mmm," said Mary Ann, completely deflated.

"Of course, we might be able to use the print as evidence he was at the scene."

"Right on," she said, brightening.

"Still, it wouldn't be enough to convict at trial."

"Mmm," again.

"But it might get him to plead, if his public defender is dumb enough, or overloaded with enough cases. So, there you have it — crime in the countryside."

He handed back her camera, strode outside, lifted himself into his Explorer, and drove off, leaving Mary Ann to her vehicle fleet maintenance bills.

Half an hour later, officers Gawley and Moss checked in. Their curiosity was mildly aroused by the criminal action of the day, petty as it cer-tainly was.

"Hey, Mary Ann — heard you got a call, nailed a print at the crime scene," said Gawley.

"What did they get? All that tourist trade — how much cash does the Apple Ranch keep in the till, anyway?" wondered Moss.

"Money's in a safe overnight. They didn't touch the register. Instead they stole food supplies," explained Mary Ann.

"You're kidding."

"Funny, huh? Who would do that?"

"Some dumb bastard running a camp?"

"Yeah, Scout's Honor, heh heh."

"Who knows? The chief says we need a tip."

"That we do, that we do."

And they left it at that.

38

AFTER WORK Mary Ann drove to the Book Nook, where she pretended to be interested in the latest issue of People Magazine and more internet research on her family history. But all she really wanted was a chance to chat with Lorraine Wagstaff.

Happily for the Book Nook's financial health, this was not immediately possible, because several customers were in the store, drinking coffee, surfing the net, thumbing through the self-help guides and bestsellers on display, assisted at every turn by the friendly advice of the well-read owner.

As a result, Mary Ann had plenty of time to sit down at a computer, open a browser, and click through dozens of search pages pointing toward her grandfather. She already had a short description of the old man on her monitor when the customers drifted away and Lorraine drifted over.

"Hello, kiddo, what's new?"

"Oh, not much, checking out granddad again."

Lorraine pointed at the article onscreen. "That piece ain't the half of it, my dear. I've been hunting around, and it looks like your grandfather was some sort of black belt voodoo king."

"Voodoo," murmured Mary Ann with a shiver.

"Well, look, don't be too concerned. Maybe it's just an urban legend — or bayou legend, as the case may be."

"Oh boy."

"So, how's your ghost these days?"

"Haven't seen him for a while." Mary Ann scowled. "Listen, Lorraine, I don't want to talk about my virtual stalker."

"Who can blame you?"

"I want to talk about your son, Tom."

Lorraine tugged at an earring. "Uh-oh."

"Why hasn't he called me?"

Lorraine sat down and removed her glasses. "I'm just his mother, Mary Ann. He's an adult, like you. He does what he thinks best."

"You mean, he hates me."

"No he doesn't. He's just very busy."

"Shit. Worse than I thought."

Lorraine looked up at the ceiling for advice from above. "This feels very strange, a mother advising her son's girlfriend. Don't you agree?"

"I'm not his girlfriend."

"Oh, sorry, advising a casual acquaintance."

Mary Ann pouted. "Who else could I talk to?"

"Got me there. He does like you, by the way. He said so."

"Likes me — !"

"You two have had a lot of fun together. He thinks you're . . . unique."

"Okay, okay. What's the problem?"

Lorraine squirmed around in her chair.

"Come on, out with it," demanded Mary Ann, crossing her arms.

"All right. He's shy about your 'visitor.' I'm only interpreting, mind you, but I guess that when he's alone with you, he thinks there's still three people in the room."

"Oh my God. Is he seeing someone else?"

"Not to my knowledge. Last year, if I remember correctly, there was Paula. She taught journalism down in Lodi. But then she moved to the Big City. We heard she married the weatherman on Channel Four."

Rebelling against her will, Mary Ann's eyes moistened. Lorraine noticed the limpid look. "Want me to say something to him?"

Mary Ann's expression hardened. "Don't you dare. I will handle this myself."

39

IT WAS A SLOW NIGHT at the Palomino. Mary Ann was sitting alone at the bar, nursing her second beer. In a vague way she was staking out the joint in hopes young Mr. Wagstaff would sashay in. What she might say to him she did not know, but she imagined it would be something bright and charming, something perfectly phrased to advance their relationship.

To pass the time she bought a postcard from a rack by the door. It depicted a gold pan filled with shiny nuggets set against a rushing hillside creek. The caption read, *Hello From Gold Country*.

"Well, hello, Dad," she said.

Borrowing a pen from the barmaid, she wrote the address she used for her father in the right hand side, being careful to include what she hoped were the magic words — 75th Ranger Regiment, Fort Benning, GA, APO 31905 — then sat back to formulate a short note. What could she tell him that might attract his serious attention? Probably nothing. She thought about the matter for a while, then gave up and wrote:

Hey, Dad — did you ever see a ghost?

— love, M.A.

Suddenly the evening calm was shattered by the machine-gun popping sound of Harley-Davidson motorcycles arriving outside. A moment later three knights of the road clad in black leather swaggered in, plopped their gloves and little Nazi helmets on the bar, and took up seats on either side of Mary Ann. Their leader, not too tall, but broad and well-muscled, motioned to the barmaid, who hastened over.

"Three Buds, babe," said he.

She hurried to comply. As she was opening and pouring, he turned his attention to Mary Ann. He had a pock-marked face suggesting severe acne during his long-gone teenage years.

"Get you something, miss?"

Mary Ann shrank on her stool. "I'm good, thanks."

Beers arrived. The leader gestured for another to be delivered to Mary Ann in spite of her indifference. It was on the bar in a flash. He pushed it toward her.

"Here you go."

"Um, no thanks. I've had my quota, and, you know, gotta work tomorrow."

The biker casually waved a hand and knocked the beer over. Pale yellow liquid splashed in Mary Ann's direction.

"Oops. Say, you're the new bitch cop, right? Where's your tiny little pussy gun, huh?"

Mary Ann straightened up. "Ankle holster. Where's *your* tiny little pussy gun?"

"You're a cute cunt, know that?" he opined.

Mary Ann felt a hot flush of anger boil up. She was about to lay down the law when she noticed a shadow in the wet slick on the bar. Her ghost was there, barely visible among the bubbles, waving his hands in a time-out gesture. The barmaid was quick with a sponge, but Mary Ann held her off. Without realizing it, she spoke to the apparition:

"Don't get into it, right?"

More frantic gestures. Then, the ghost's hand traced a *B* in the air.

" B for biker? B for boob? B for what?"

The ghost faded away.

Mary Ann dropped some bills on the bar and slid off her stool.

"Have a nice night, Hitler," she said, and ran for the exit.

She hurried down the block to her Mustang, unlocked it with shaking fingers, jumped in, and relocked the doors. She sank down into the driver's seat with her eyes on the entrance of the Palomino, trying to regain her composure.

"What is it with these letters, anyway, Mr. G?" she mumbled. "I had your gestures knocked. No, I didn't. I barely understand a thing you do . . . but . . . wait a minute — the letter B. Oh my God, B is for butcher."

When no one had appeared after a couple of minutes, she started the engine, threw the car in gear, and drove back to the station, where she rummaged through her desk for a stamp. Then she stopped at the Applefield post office and, assuring herself that no one was lurking anywhere nearby, dropped her postcard in the streetside collection box.

No motorcycles claimed the winding road as she drove out of town, but when she turned north toward Placerville and home she began to have second thoughts. She had stopped to perform an errand. By now the bikers might be ahead of her. Not much traffic on Route 49 late at night. What if they ran her into a ditch? What if she led them right to her trailer in

Placerville?

After a mile of fretting, she imagined she could hear the distant roar of a Harley. After another mile she decided it was just her nerves vibrating and forced herself to relax. But then, coming out of a curve, she glimpsed a real Harley waiting under the trees, chrome parts glinting in her headlights. As she passed she heard it snarl to life. She downshifted and stomped on the gas pedal.

She drove as fast as she could for five minutes or more, images in her head bouncing between the danger posed by bikers and the consequences of hitting a deer.

"Where the hell is Wade? I'd love a speeding ticket right now."

Rounding a tight bend, the sign for Sandbar Road suddenly appeared in her headlights. She jerked the wheel and swiveled onto the narrow byway, tires squealing. She eyed the rear-view mirror. Sure enough, before she had traveled a quarter of a mile, a Harley zipped by, heading north. Whew, missed me. Then she remembered — Sandbar Road was a dead end. She screeched to a stop beside a lonely barn, backed into the drive for a one-point turnaround, stopped, killed the engine, turned out the lights, took her foot off the brake.

She fumbled in the darkness for her mobile phone, pressed a button to turn on the screen. In place of the little signal strength bars she saw *No Service*.

"Damn." Allowing herself to get trapped in the middle of nowhere was idiotic, and, too late, she knew it.

She turned the phone screen off. Gradually her eyes became accustomed to the profound darkness of the countryside. Stars were sparkling overhead. She decided to sit tight for a while, let the trail go cold.

She didn't have long to wait. Pretty soon she could hear the unmistakable *potato-potato-potato* cadence of a Harley motorcycle, in no particular hurry, but growing louder. In another moment a headlight appeared. The bastard had found her.

She was momentarily paralyzed. Then she remembered Bobby Rainwater's emergency light. She fumbled under the dash, found it, rolled the window down, and stuck it on the roof.

The bike cruised slowly up Sandbar Road. When its lights fell on Mary Ann's blue Mustang, it pulled to the shoulder and stopped. The rider dismounted and walked forward. Mary Ann recognized her chief tormentor from the Palomino. She could see something metallic hanging from his right hand. Jack handle? Gun?

She hit the power switch. A hot red LED light rotated and flashed, reflecting off the biker's black leather garb, causing him to hesitate. In that moment she started the car, jammed it into gear and roared back down Sandbar Road with her heart racing as fast as her engine.

When she reached the T-junction at Route 49 she halted, considering the best course of action. The biker was closing in again. Making a snap decision, she turned left and accelerated south, back toward Ragtown. Soon the bike was pacing her, threatening mayhem and what the newspapers always call a "fatality."

As she climbed back up the hill separating Ragtown from Applefield two other motorcycles joined the chase. At last buildings and streetlights came into view, and the bikers backed off, apparently more interested in simple intimidation than actual harm.

She slowed and punched a number into her mobile phone — service at last, thank God.

"Officer Moss here. Help you?"

"Rick, where are you? I've got an ugly biker parade on my tail out here on Main Street."

"Over in Tarvolo. Be brave, I'll swing by."

She slammed on the brakes and parked in front of Mayor Teasdale's modest City Hall. The bikers halted near the Miners Market a few blocks behind, engines idling with casual menace. Three minutes later Moss arrived, flashing the emergency lights on his black-and-white Crown Vic. The motorcycles evaporated.

Mary Ann leaped from her Mustang. Moss stepped out as well, watching the Harleys' taillights diminish into the distance. She almost hugged him.

"Did you get a plate?"

"Shit, no. Did you?"

"No. Damn."

"I'm a moron."

"Who are those guys? I thought I knew all the local boys."

Mary Ann grimaced. "They were in the Palomino. I think the leader, whoever he is, might be our prime suspect to cut up Mike Russell. He could have got me."

Moss gave her a worried look. "Geez, Mary Ann, that's a big jump in the conclusion department."

"I know, I know."

Mary Ann spent the night in the station, head down on her desk. When morning light finally penetrated the high eastside windows, her mouth felt like cotton wool, and her hair was as flat as a tortilla. She tottered off to the ladies room in a fog.

When she emerged, Chief Ibañez was waiting for her. "Rick tells me you've got a suspect in Mike Russell's murder."

Mary Ann blinked. "Um, no name. No evidence. Typical rookie mistake."

"Hmm," he grunted, and disappeared into his office.

40

ON SATURDAY AFTERNOON Mary Ann drove out of Applefield toward Tarvolo and turned onto a long narrow asphalt drive on the edge of town. Down at the end was a tall mast painted red and white, held upright by long guy wires. Beside it was a small rectangular building with a flat roof, built from cinder blocks. It looked how she imagined a World War II bunker might appear. And she wasn't far wrong. It had, in fact, been constructed as a secure storage facility for a general contractor in 1948. Now it wore a coat of pale grey paint and an identifying metal sign with neon letters spelling *K-V-I-G*. A Mercedes SUV was parked near the small red door.

Howard Turnbow was waiting for her as she pulled alongside the Merc.

"Mary Ann Sarzo. Welcome to *The Vig*. Let me show you around."

He sorted through a dozen keys on a large metal hoop and unlocked the door. Inside it was almost dark. Small LEDs indicated the various states of electronic gear racked up against every wall. A microphone was suspended over a mixing board covered with a forest of little yellow knobs, but no one was present to use it.

"All these lights. It's like being inside a Christmas tree," said Mary Ann.

"That's one way to look at it, I guess." Turnbow consulted a laptop computer open beside the mixing board, logging operations. He seemed satisfied with his inspection.

"Now, during the day, this place runs itself. We transmit a playlist from Spin-O-Matic, and our station ID calls are threaded right in. I receive text messages from Dallas on my phone if something goes wrong, but practically speaking, nothing ever does. Well, we did have that one storm a couple of winters back, and lost power overnight. Our generator froze. FCC was on us, what a mess.

"We're a Class A station, so we only pump out six thousand watts, but so what — we're also on the net, you can hear us anywhere, like I think I mentioned before."

"Then what do you need me for?"

"Why, personality. A little rough yet, maybe, but hey, this isn't the Big City, now is it?"

"I guess not."

"The point is, at night we change. We accept requests, so we need a live disc jockey."

"Uh-oh. How will I find the songs? I don't see any CDs around. I don't really listen to a lot of music."

"That's the beauty part, my girl. See this laptop? It's connected to Spin-O-Matic twenty-four-seven. You type in the requested title, and bingo, it plays, next track up. Digital, all the way from some damn server farm somewhere."

Mary Ann looked closely at the laptop screen. Incomprehensible numbers and song titles were slowly scrolling upward in little jumps. She caught Lady Antebellum's name on the list, a country band she actually recognized. "Unh-huh, if you say so," she said doubtfully.

"See, I don't have any musical taste. I'm just a local businessman. But I don't need any, and neither do you. As each request comes in, it tweaks the playlist, so we're always adjusting to what people want to hear. That's why we go live at night. It keeps us fresh."

"You mean, like Pandora."

"Exactamundo. You're quick, I like that. But you won't just be twiddling your thumbs. While you're monitoring the action, you'll also be recording a series of weather reports, call sign IDs, and — this is the important part: local advertisements — and feed them back to Dallas."

"How do I do that?"

"This mike right here. Controls on the panel over there." He pointed a finger. "It's not live. Play back in your headphones, and if you don't like what you hear, don't send it."

"It's that simple."

"Yes, well, don't let that get around."

"I'll never tell."

"Any questions?"

"Can I call someone if I get in trouble?"

"Use the numbers posted there on the desk. You'll reach me or one of my regulars."

"I'm thinking of calling myself, 'the Golden Girl of the Golden Hills.' Is that all right?"

"Perfect. Anything else?" He handed her a key to the station.

"Let me get my feet wet, but, uh, keep your phone handy."

Turnbow looked uncomfortable. "Okay then, here's a question

for *you*."

"Shoot."

He hesitated, then gestured toward the wide world outside. "It's these damn murders. Not a hint they'll ever be solved. Going to wreck the tourist trade here . . . "

"We're not involved. I'm sure you know that — it all sits with the sheriff's department."

"But the local force can't be blind . . . can it? You're a cop, so tell me, what's taking so long?"

"Not a clue. But you're right, it seems like forever," she allowed, attempting to agree without betraying her fellow officers.

Turnbow spread his hands out to make room for a big idea. "Well, I have a theory."

"Really. And that is — ?"

"Corruption."

Mary Ann's skin prickled. Her very worst fears, rumored among her colleagues, and now surfaced by an outsider. She took a deep breath.

"Who?"

"I don't know. But this whole thing smells of drug money. How else do you explain the lax investigation?"

"You suspect it's a police officer."

"Not necessarily. It could be anyone in authority."

"I don't think you can just up and buy a cop."

"Sure about that? I just bought you for thirty an hour. Enough money, honey, can buy anyone and anything."

▼

With that exchange Turnbow and Mary Ann went their separate ways. But on the following evening, Sunday, she returned to the station, fumbled with the lock, stumbled inside, hooked her jacket on a hangar by the entrance, and sat down on a stool under the microphone. It was set up on casters so she could roll around and reach every switch in the room. Her stint didn't begin until 7:00 PM, so she had a few minutes to play. First she tried the stool, just to get the hang of it and calm her nerves, zipping from wall to wall. Then, feeling a little more comfortable, she put on her headphones, found a red record button on the previously identified panel, pressed it, and tried speaking into the microphone.

"Hello, foothill folks. This is your Golden Girl, calling all music lovers out there in the Golden Hills to phone in your favorites to *The Vig*."

She rattled off a phone number, stopped the recording, hit the play button, and listened. Hmm, not great, not bad, okay for starters. Then she noticed the laptop screen. A timeline was ticking upward, and in the middle, on the *7:00 PM* row, rising higher and higher, was a blank slot labeled *Station ID — Select File To Upload*.

"Oh shit."

She scrutinized the control panel. Under the record button was another marked *Save*. She pushed it, and a little LCD screen lit up with a number: *101017-KVIG-1SUN*. She pressed the button again, and the LCD screen displayed *File Saved*.

"Station ID, station ID. Oh my God, that's not what I want." She pushed the record button again.

"This is K-V-I-G, coming to you from the Golden Hills Tri-Town Area in Applefield California at ninety-three-point-one on your FM dial. It's seven o'clock."

This was a slight variation on IDs she had heard on every radio station she had ever listened to. She saved the file, automatically named *101017-KVIG-2SUN*, and then turned back to the laptop screen. She clicked her mouse pointer on the empty *7:00 PM* slot. A dialog box opened with a list of filenames. She selected *101017-KVIG-2SUN*, hoping for the best, and clicked again. The screen slot now contained the file number. It ticked upward until it moved in between a pair of arrows labeled *NOW*. She desperately searched the control panel for a switch to route the transmitted signal into her phones. Nothing, but she found a worn push button built into the desktop labeled *MONITOR*. She punched it and caught the tail end of her spiel, ". . . ninety-three-point-one on your FM dial. It's seven o'clock."

Whew, she was on the air.

The next item on the continuously rising list from Spin-O-Matic was a song title, Bonnie Raitt's cover of Gerry Rafferty's *Right Down the Line*. As the text moved up between the arrows, a drum beat pounded out the catchy groove, bass and guitars filled in, and the song began. Mary Ann let out a sigh of relief. She was barely competent, and although still half lost among all the electronic gadgets Howard Turnbow had failed to explain, and frantic with stage fright as well, she already knew with grim certainty that she would get over the hump. This was going to work.

While the tune was playing, she called Turnbow's phone number. "Hey, it's your new disc jockey. Listen, do I have to use that control panel? Isn't there a way to put it all on the computer?" Turnbow growled a suggestion. She scribbled a line on a notepad. "Okay, I'll find it. Thanks."

She ran her eyes over the panel and focused on a button labeled *AUTOSPIN*, which she pressed. A dialog box appeared on the laptop display. She clicked a screen button, and suddenly everything was there before her, in little window panes. She relaxed further as Bonnie Raitt finished up and Randy Travis took over.

While the country star warbled, she uploaded her blurb inviting requests, which played automatically the moment his song ended. Wow, she thought, the elves are hard at work here.

Next up, The Eagles' golden oldie, *Peaceful Easy Feeling*, revved up, radiating the lush production values of the seventies. Before her time, but what did she care?

As the chorus came on and the band was already standing on the ground, the phone rang.

"Hold on, please. I'll take your request live as soon as the Eagles finish."

A few moments later the final chords rang out. She pressed yet another button, and went live.

"Hello, this is your Golden Girl of the Golden Hills. Got a request? Your wish is my command."

A raspy voice, vaguely familiar, responded. "Yeah, lady, play *Born to Be Wild* for me, okay?"

"Got a dedication?"

"It's for you."

She typed in the name. "Coming right up, sir, and thanks. You have a good alternative hard rock country evening — on me."

"I surely will."

The text moved up the screen to *NOW*, and John Kay and Steppenwolf started howling out the great rock anthem. As the track progressed the phone rang again.

"Hey, bitch, thanks for playing my song."

"Beg your pardon?"

"You call yourself the Golden Girl, right? Ha ha, our little cop cunt is moonlighting to stay out of trouble, what do you know?"

Click — the phone went dead. Mary Ann's heart skipped a beat. The same raspy voice, now unmistakable. It belonged to the biker in the Palomino. She was shaken by his boldness.

Somehow she struggled through the rest of the evening. Requests as diverse as Ingrid Michaelson's *Be OK*, Rascal Flatts' *Changed*, and Paul Simon's *You Can Call Me Al* kept her busy. She read out some weather, some musical notes (not too many of these, since she had never heard of most of the songs that played), several station IDs, plus numerous local advertisements ranging from fast food to snow tires, and called it a night.

She was in a daze when at last she switched the station back on automatic pilot, locked the door, and started for her car. And it was only then that she remembered the ugly phone call from her biker pal. She stopped and surveyed the area, assessing places to hide and launch an attack. But the station was at least a hundred feet from the nearest rock or bush more than a foot high. There were no outbuildings on the property. The night was clear and chilly. A dewy haze coated her Mustang's windshield. No one was anywhere near the place.

When she was pretty sure the coast was clear she plodded over to her car, flopped in, and drove slowly up the drive. A few minutes later she was on the road to Placerville with the Mustang's defogger set on high to clear her view. She was beyond tired, and the songs she had been playing kept running through her head. Occupational hazard, she assumed. She sang as she drove to stay awake —

"I just want to be OK, be OK, be OK . . . "

Nary a motorcycle was seen or heard.

Part FIVE

41

ON MONDAY MORNING everyone was already out of the station patrolling some patch of the Golden Hills Tri-Town Area when Mary Ann arrived for her shift. Her new job had left her bleary-eyed with fatigue. She told herself she had better find a routine that minimized her stress levels, and secretly doubted she would ever be able to do so.

The empty office reminded her of Father Eisen's observation: if one of her fellow officers was destined to die, and the walls were destined to echo with his former presence, his ghost might well be hanging around at this very moment. She also remembered Father Eisen's idea about rituals and relics. She wanted to talk to her ghostly visitor very badly and find out who he was once and for all. Accordingly, to pass a solitary hour, she renewed her search for some sort of object that might strengthen her connection to the elusive spirit.

To that end she prowled the station from front to back, looking into lockers, opening drawers, scanning the various shelves, hoping for something to suggest itself among the workaday books, manuals, files, and knick-knacks.

But nothing presented itself as a likely candidate. She briefly considered the stapler on her desk and held it up in one hand while she peered into her folding pocket mirror with the other.

"Show yourself, Mr. Ghost. Right here where I'm looking."

Well, that didn't work.

Next, mindful that her car once belonged to the late Bobby Rainwater, she went outside, unscrewed the shift knob from its shaft, and held it aloft while again peering into her pocket mirror.

"Hey, Bobby? Where are you? Let's talk."

That was short and to the point, but no Bobby, no ghost.

After wasting half the morning toying around with several other equally far-fetched ideas, she gave up. She had risen late; she had barely squeezed in a too-quick shower; her hair was still damp when she arrived at work; and breakfast had been out of the question. Now she was hungry.

Wedged into a corner at the back of the station was the department's tiny kitchenette. There, positioned beside a small industrial-style sink, a half-size office refrigerator supported a one-burner hotplate, a toaster, and a drip coffee maker. A small tray held packets of sugar and wooden stirring sticks. She pulled an English muffin from the refrigerator, popped it into the toaster, and hunted around for a knife that might not be too dirty. Instead of a knife, however, her hand came to rest on a white ceramic salt shaker in the form of a peculiar statuette. It was hiding between the hotplate and the coffee maker.

She picked it up and examined the thing, vaguely aware that it was inspired by Mexican traditions of the Day of the Dead. Staring back at her with painted eyes and a ferocious lipless grin was a skeletal girl holding a bouquet of red flowers. There was a hole in her skull where salt could pour out. A plastic insert under her full-length skirt indicated where the supply could be replenished. From top to bottom, the figurine measured around three inches tall.

"What do they call these things? I know I've seen them in every stupid gift store."

She hefted it, tipped it over to dispense some salt. But no, a brown powder emerged in little puffs. She tasted it — chocolate. Meant for coffee, probably.

"It's a cava-something. Cavalier? Cavatappi? Wait, I know — *calavera!*" She paused for a moment, turning the little figurine in her hand. "It's a calavera, all right. Spooky little chick." She paused again. "Whoa . . . could it be . . . ?"

Grasping the calavera firmly, she marched into the ladies' restroom, snapped on the light, and held it up to the mirror.

"Okay, ghost, visitor, nameless person, come here, I want some answers."

She waited a moment. Nothing but her impatient face showed in the reflection.

She thought she knew what Lorraine Wagstaff might suggest and made an attempt at supernatural formality: "Ghost, I summon thee to appear before me." That sounded pretty official, but she felt it lacked oomph, so she added "make that forthwith" for good measure.

That ought to do it. But her ghost, if he heard her command, must have had other ideas.

Gripping the little statuette even tighter, she shouted, "Hey you!"

A small blur appeared in the center of the mirror, as if far away in some unfathomable depth of the universe. It expanded rapidly, and suddenly her ghostly visitor was flying into close-up view. He looked irritated.

"Ahh!" Mary Ann was so startled she nearly dropped the calavera.

The ghost held his hands out in a what's-up gesture.

"Okay, you're here. That's good, because we need to talk."

The ghost waggled his head indifferently.

"First, and this is the most important thing — I want you to stay away from Tom and me when we're together. Leave us alone, let us live our lives. Got it?"

The ghost hesitated, then nodded.

"All right then. Next up — thanks for the lottery tip. That saved my ass."

The ghost brought a hand to his brow in a little salute and bowed his head.

"I just wanted to get that out of the way. Now, here's what worries me — well, aside from the fact that I'm having this weird conversation with a ghost — what do you know about Tri-Town people on the take?"

The ghost held up his hands. He made the sign of a *C* in the air. Then he moved one hand with fingers scissoring to simulate walking.

"What?"

The ghost repeated his performance.

"C — walk — walk C. Wait, wait a damn minute, I'm thinking. Man, this sign language of yours . . . why can't you just talk to me, anyway?"

The ghost ignored her question and reprised his little sequence of gestures.

Finally the light went on in Mary Ann's head. She clapped her hands together. "Ha! That's it! Follow Cruz!"

The ghost nodded. He placed a hand beside his head with thumb and little finger extended, as if making a telephone call. Then he pointed at Mary Ann and waved both hands back and forth, signaling negativity. Once again he made the telephone gesture, pointed at himself, then at her.

"Now what?"

The ghostly apparition blurred and vanished.

"Hey, come back here. I still don't know your name! Oh, I get it, 'Don't call me, I'll call you.' That's just great."

She exited the bathroom, placed the calavera on her desk, and would have headed out the door in immediate pursuit of Señor Cruz, but the telephone rang.

"Golden Hills Tri-Town Police. Officer Sarzo here. How can we help you?"

The voice at the other end was breathless and confused.

"Slow down there, Mr. Hoggins. Where are you? Terra Linda Market. Outside Tarvolo. All right, I'm copying the address." She remembered the standard mantra: "We'll send someone to investigate and take a statement as soon as personnel become available."

She was on the verge of radioing Moss or Gawley to drive over and have a look when she realized that the Terra Linda Market was on the way to Cruz' alpaca ranch. Two birds with her own stone — why not?

She was reluctant to leave the station unattended, however, fearing Chief Ibañez' justified wrath. But Officer Gawley saved her by arriving at the station with a sheaf of speeding tickets in hand.

"Hold the fort, Wade, got a call out in Tarvolo."

Before Gawley could object she was out the door, into her black & white Jeep and on the road.

The Terra Linda Market, Mary Ann discovered, was a convenience store for Tarvolo's affluent golfers when they didn't want to venture far from their locked community gates. As she walked through the aisles looking over the merchandise, she concluded that the regular customers were inclined toward gluten-free living. Many of them also appeared to favor foods made of soy and hemp. She had never heard of most of the brands on display in their brightly-colored packages. She was feeling distinctly out of place as Albert Hoggins, a rotund man in his middle years, appeared from behind the fancy deli counter and strode forward to greet her.

"Hello, hello. Thanks for popping over so quickly." He radiated charm, and she guessed that his light British accent was carefully maintained as part of the upscale ambience.

"No problem. What happened here?"

"Let's have a look, shall we?"

He led the way to the back of the store and into his stock room. The rear door had been forced, a padlock hasp had been ripped from the frame, and empty shelves were evident.

"Would you look at that? Not only did they break in, but they knew how to turn off my alarm."

"You did set it?" asked Mary Ann.

"Oh yes, every night when I close." He wrung his hands.

"What did you have on these shelves?"

"Well now, not much, really. Some cheap boxed wine, three cases of rather drinkable wine, several cases of beer, loaves of bread, and, ah, three boxes of beef jerky."

"You sell beef jerky?" Mary Ann was surprised.

"My customers don't all have the sort of taste you might imagine."

"Let me guess — the boxed wine was Franzia. The good wine was Ravenswood. The bread was Oroweat."

Hoggins' stared at her. "Quite right. You're a wizard."

"Not exactly. There's a pattern. Cheap food, packaged for retail. I've seen this before."

"Have you now?"

"Notice that none of your ultra-pasteurized soy milk is gone. And none of those funky amaranth cookies either."

"Now that you mention it . . . "

"What's the dollar damage?"

"Oh dear, not quite sure. Five hundred dollars, probably."

"Mind if I check for prints?"

"By all means."

Mary Ann felt clumsy, as if she were back in police school, but managed to lift a partial print from the rear door frame. She photographed it.

Hoggins watched her work. "Do you think you'll catch whoever did this?"

"Honestly?"

"Always the best policy, I'm told."

"Maybe not right away. Call your insurance company, even if it's just to register the facts. Meanwhile, we're on it, we'll let you know."

Back in the Jeep, Mary Ann turned south on Copper King Road, passed the Tarvolo golf course and Rossi's Fine Italian Dining, worked her way through the turns to Upper Bar Lake, the local reservoir where the Whiskeyjack River was impounded to irrigate Big Valley crops, then onward through loosely spaced oaks, the occasional volcanic outcrop, and little else; winding for miles until at last she arrived at a heavy steel gate. It was situated on the downhill side of the road under a wooden archway supporting an elegantly carved sign that read, *Golden Fleece Ranch*.

Salvador Cruz' alpaca operation.

Mary Ann parked, got out to open the gate, and found it locked. There was a weatherproof intercom fastened to the archway, but she didn't think it would be a good idea to try it out. She leaned against the gate and peered down the long gravel drive to an impressive collection of stucco buildings with red tile roofs. Well-kept barns and garages were set back among tall cottonwoods. Shaggy animals were grazing in the distance. Alpacas? Hard to tell. A dozen automobiles were parked near an immense two-story house. She thought she could also see at least one motorcycle. If this was a working ranch, it functioned with invisible labor. No one was wrangling the livestock, anyway. Aside from a tractor churning up dust way out near a remote line of trees, the place seemed lifeless.

She hauled out her digital camera to see if she could capture any license plate numbers, but the zoom was only 3x, and the cars were too far away. Damn.

Mary Ann watched for five minutes or more, as much enthralled by the ranch's handsome and expensive appearance as anything else, but saw no activity whatsoever. Feeling very disappointed, she returned to the Jeep and started back toward Applefield.

On the way she paused at an inlet on Upper Bar Lake. She had never been there before. A ten-foot-tall stripe of bare ground ringing the shore indicated the difference between the high water mark and the present lake level, attesting to the enormous volumes of liquid gold that had poured forth over the summer to grow fruits and nuts.

Even at low water, she marveled at the reservoir's vastness. Docks in the local marina were set up on floats to rise and fall with the seasons, and a swarm of jet skis, ski boats, aluminum fishing boats, and houseboats were either buzzing around or tied up there.

She was wondering what it might be like to tour this inland sea with Tom Wagstaff when she noticed a truck coming along Copper King Road from the direction of Salvador Cruz' ranch. Some life out there after all, apparently. As it flashed past she noticed it was a Honda Ridgeline pickup — and hey! — wasn't that Terry Gardner at the wheel?

42

DARK OF THE MOON. Midweek early shift.

Mary Ann arrived for work under indigo skies with dawn still an hour away. She scared a deer and a bobcat on the commute and counted herself lucky not to have hit either one. She turned on all the station lights, hung her jacket up, started the coffee maker, and sat down to take care of the day's mundane housekeeping chores. First up was the telephone message queue: a flashing red light on her handset summarized a night's worth of crime in this rural corner of California. She pressed a button to play back the bad news.

"Police? Hello? This is Rosarita Crespo at the Miners Market in Applefield. I have just arrived to open the store — it is five forty-five, early, I am looking at a clock — but where I come in, the back door, it has been almost torn off the hinges. We have been stolen by burglars. Please help now."

Mary Ann picked up the phone to return the call. "Ms. Crespo? Golden Hills Tri-Town Police. Officer Sarzo here, how can I help you?" She tapped a pencil on the desk while she listened. "Now calm down, take it easy. Are you safe where you are? Yes? Okay, then, you've got a big store there, and I'm sure other employees will be joining you soon. We'll send someone to investigate and take a statement as soon as personnel become available."

An hour and three cups of coffee later, Chief Ibañez arrived. She briefed him on the overnight developments.

"I'll be here for a while. Go on, get over there and find out what's eating the lady Crespo. And watch out, Howard may be on the scene, kicking up a ruckus."

"Turnbow? Oh, right, he owns the place. He told me."

"Told you?"

"I work for him at the radio station on weekends. I guess I should have mentioned that."

"Hmm. Don't get carried away with visions of stardom, Little Miss Amateur Hour. Don't quit your day job. Who knows? You might get good at it."

Mary Ann was touched by the sentiment. "You mean it?"

"Someday, maybe," he growled. "Far in the future."

Mary Ann drove down Main Street to the Miners Market. At this hour no one was on the street, so parking was a breeze. The store was open for business, but still awaiting its first customer of the day. She looked for someone matching her mental picture of Rosarita Crespo, but found Howard Turnbow waiting for her instead.

"Mary Ann, what are you doing here?"

"Morning, Howard. I'm a cop today. What's up?"

"Wait till you see the mess out back."

He led the way to the Miners Market stock room. The scene was familiar — broken lock, disabled alarm, empty shelves. This time, in addition, several liquids had spilled. The floor was swimming in olive oil and mayonnaise.

"Can you believe this shit? What kind of a moron steals Bud Light and six cases of bathroom tissue?"

"How about beef jerky?"

"Yes, that too. Good Lord, the thieves broke in right here on Main Street. Couldn't be more than a couple of hours ago."

"How do you know that?"

"My closer left at two AM. All was dandy. I already talked to the security company, and the alarm was still on at four AM, when they last checked."

"Three hours, plus."

"Well, if you split hairs. What are you going to do about it?"

"First I'm going to photograph the scene, take some fingerprints. While I'm doing that, you're going to figure out the value of the theft."

"I already know — six hundred bucks, give or take. Impossible to make a claim, it's below the deductible."

Mary Ann wrote the information down in her notebook.

"It can't be for the money. Somebody must really hate me."

Mary Ann touched his shoulder. "Come on, Howard. It's just a burglary. We're on it, we'll investigate, we'll let you know."

"I'm not holding my breath."

Three men with mops and buckets appeared. Mary Ann left Turnbow to supervise the cleanup and made her way through the aisles toward the front of the store.

Turnbow called after her. "Hey, not a bad debut on Sunday night. If you ever want to trade in that uniform for a mike, let me know."

"Thanks, but in spite of all the crap I just walked through, I love this job."

As she reached the exit she was intercepted by a nervous Latina woman wearing a Miners Market apron.

"*Hola.* You are police I call? *Por favor,* I must talk to you."

"Rosarita Crespo?"

"Yes. *Aquí.*" She ducked into the kitchen gadget aisle and motioned Mary Ann to follow.

"What's the matter?"

"I know who commit this crime," whispered the woman.

"Excuse me — ?" Mary Ann's cop radar switched on.

"The same one who commit other crimes."

"You mean stealing from stores, this string of burglaries?"

"Yes. That's it. You must stop him."

"Um, love to. Who is this person?"

The woman fretted with her apron, hesitating. Then, showing some courage, she said, "My husband, Miguel."

"His name is Miguel Crespo?"

"Yes."

"Where can I find him?"

The woman's expression conveyed woeful misery. "He, I mean we together, own a small store on the road to Ragtown. Chevron mini mart. We cannot pay the payments. Miguel fights, he stocks the store with stealing, but it is not a fair fight, he cannot win."

"No he can't. Whatever the reason, these are crimes."

"Miguel knows. He gives up. He wants to work for Señor Cruz."

"I don't understand. Why the burglaries?"

"To show Señor Cruz his *cojones.* He hopes to join Big League with Señor Cruz."

"Now that is interesting. That is *very* interesting. Your husband will be arrested, you know that?"

"No, we will sell Chevron, we will pay. You, you have powers, you can make him change."

"Yes, I'm a cop, I can arrest him. I'm sorry, but I have to do my duty."

"But you have many other powers. You must use them."

"What are you talking about? What powers?"

"You are a witch. Witches know many things, have many tricks."

Mary Ann was shocked to learn that her secret life, however much distorted, was common property. "Whoa there, sister, wait a minute. Me. A witch. Where'd you get that idea?"

The woman shrank away. "I know. Many know. Please don't hurt me."

Mary Ann felt her face reddening. "I might! You better tell me who fed you this crock."

"It is in the air," said the woman, certain of her position.

"Jesus Christ, what a load." Mary Ann was now tingling with anger.

"Listen to me, Ms. Crespo. Call your husband right away, tell him what you told me, and you both can run if you want. The honest thing to do is stay and wait to get arrested. We've got his prints at the scene. That probably means he'll do time in county jail. Is he undocumented? He'll get deported. Maybe you too. Think it over."

"He is not illegal. He was born in El Centro. I am here by marriage."

"All right then, you want change? The very best thing would be, your husband drives up to our station and voluntarily turns himself in."

"I will tell him."

"Will he beat you up?"

"No, he is a good man."

"Contact a lawyer."

Mary Ann stood out on the sidewalk and telephoned the department.

"What do you want me to do about this?"

Chief Ibañez was thoughtful. "We'll have to arrest the guy. But why don't we wait a while? He owns a gas station? He's not going far."

"Yeah, I was thinking the same thing. Will he turn himself in?"

"Your guess is as good as mine. If he's more worried about Cruz than your faithful public servants, maybe not. Worth the wait to find out."

"Unh-huh. Look, if it's okay with you, why don't I do some rolling and patrolling, seeing as I'm already out here."

"Balancing our books too tame now that you've actually solved a crime?"

"Yes sir. I guess so."

43

THE BOOK NOOK'S doors opened for business at ten o'clock on weekdays, and Mary Ann made sure she was down in Ragtown at 10:00 AM on the dot. She parked her Jeep, took a deep breath, and marched inside. Lorraine Wagstaff was in the back at her coffee counter loading the snack trays. She looked up as Mary Ann advanced toward her, brows furrowed, mouth set in a grim line.

"Morning, Mary Ann. Uh-oh, you look unhappy. What's the problem?" Lorraine had no trouble sensing the black cloud over her young friend's head.

"I need a doughnut. Make that an apple fritter."

"You got it." Lorraine handed over the fat-rich snack. "Unusual for you, yes?"

"Very. How about an espresso to go with it?"

"Sure. Coming right up. Tell me, are you pissed or something?"

"How can you tell?" grouched Mary Ann.

"Oh my, really pissed."

Lorraine swiftly composed a double espresso, added a hint of milk, and handed it over. "At me?"

"I don't know. Should I be?"

"Hmm, unstated accusations in the air. Chilly, these October mornings."

"Look, I just solved a burglary —"

"Good for you."

"— and in the process I found out people think I'm a witch with supernatural powers."

"Oh no."

"Oh yes. A witch!" Mary Ann groaned under the weight of the humiliation. "It's all over town. Everyone thinks I can cast magic spells. I bet they're wondering where I keep my broomstick."

"And, let me see here, you think I might have told a tale or two?"

Mary Ann put down her fritter. Her eyebrows crinkled. "Oh Lorraine, did you?"

"Nope. Not a word. Not guilty."

"Then I apologize. I'm sorry, I'm really upset. What about Tom? Do you think —"

"— Not a chance. Don't be silly."

"Then how?"

"I can guess. Is there something you forgot to tell me?"

"What do you mean?"

"Your, ah, 'inheritance.' I must say, it has been the subject of some speculation around here," said Lorraine, trying for tact.

"My inheritance."

"That's what you called it."

"Oh shit."

"Exactly."

"I don't think Tom believed me, now that I think back."

"He didn't, because you were already a big hero at the Placerville Maxi Mart."

Mary Ann grimaced. "You're talking about the lottery, right? He already knew."

"Like they say, news travels fast, kiddo. Especially when there's a ghost involved."

"Oh my God, how did that get out?"

"No idea, but it did."

Mary Ann moaned and downed her espresso.

"Now it's my turn," said Lorraine. "I'm your friend. Don't you owe me an explanation?"

Mary Ann thought for a long moment, eyes downcast. At last she met Lorraine's gaze. "It's true. I won the lottery. And yes, with numbers supplied by you-know-who."

"I thought so!" Lorraine slapped her thigh in triumph.

"Well, I had nothing to do with it. My visitor guy motioned some numbers, I wrote them down, bought a ticket."

"Just one ticket?"

"That's all. And it was only the Fantasy Five game."

"How much?" pressed Lorraine.

"Just under fifty thousand. Enough to pay off my car, and a little nest egg."

"Lucky you." Lorraine's face betrayed her bitter loss of faith in the universal American right to good fortune.

Mary Ann was dismayed. "See? Look at you — you know what happened, and you still blame me."

Lorraine pulled herself together. "Yes, I see. You were worried I would be after you to help me win too."

"You and everybody else." Mary Ann bit her lip, determined not to cry. "I can't do it."

They fell together in a hug.

"I'm so sorry . . ." Their words came out together.

▼

Later that morning Mary Ann paid a visit to the Placerville Maxi Mart. As she entered, the old Asian gentleman who ran the place shuffled forward, a big smile on his lips.

"Ah, winner here! We say, plenty winners, we tell it like so!"

"You ought to be ashamed of yourself, old man."

"What? Big winner, very proud."

Mary Ann looked around the store. Behind the counter was a large and crudely printed poster. The black & white photo was a shot of Mary Ann as recorded by the store's surveillance camera. It was contrasty and blurry, but she was clearly recognizable. The caption read:

Ghost Of A Chance? WITCH WINS!"

Mary Ann rounded the counter and ripped the poster from the wall.

"Stop! Can't do that!" protested the man.

"Where'd you get this? Some wiseguy son of yours? Did he print it for you?"

"No son." The man drew himself up. "I have Photoshop. Print at Costco. Pretty good, huh? Good poster."

"Listen here, you — try anything like this again, I'll . . . I'll sue your ass." She ripped the poster into strips, then tore the strips into confetti. "Got that?"

The man was shocked. "Ruin poster!"

"That's not all I'm going to ruin."

The man screwed his hearing aid into his ear. "You are wrong in my store. Commission say publicity OK. Store publicity good for lottery."

"Oh really?"

"Most absolutely."

"All right then, try this — if I see any reference to me or my winnings here again, I'm going to cast a spell on you. How's that?"

"Cast spell?"

"You heard me." She held up a finger, twirled it around like a magic wand.

"Witch spell?"

"A very bad luck spell! Understand me?" She pointed her finger at him, an imaginary pistol cocked and ready to fire.

"No bad luck. No more posters. Go away now."

"I'll be checking on you. Stay clean, maybe you'll be okay."

The proprietor bobbed his head deferentially, mortally afraid of this terrifying young monster. "No more posters. Good luck only."

Mary Ann was still furious as she stalked out the door. "You better damn well hope to God."

44

CHIEF IBAÑEZ was waiting for Mary Ann as she pulled into the department parking lot. She stopped, and he heaved himself aboard.

"Sure about this? I just found out this morning," she asked.

"He's had plenty of time. Any more and we're derelict. Let's go."

Mary Ann drove out onto the highway leading toward Ragtown.

"Ever done this before?" Ibañez asked, eyeing her tense grip on the steering wheel.

"No sir."

"They taught you, though, right?"

"Yes, of course."

"Always a first. You'll be fine."

It was late afternoon, and Mary Ann was grateful to be included in what promised to be her first criminal arrest, so she didn't argue her misgivings.

Ibañez briefed her as they motored down the hill from Applefield. "When we get there I'll take the lead. Got your service weapon handy?"

She nodded, patted her holster.

"Right. Stand behind me and just to one side. Make sure our suspect sees you with your hand on the grip. Got it?"

"Yes sir."

"There's no telling what might happen. It's just a burglary, economic crime, nothing sociopathic, but I've seen lesser situations turn into tragedies."

"Yes sir."

"If he resists, we may have to wrestle. I'll do the heavy work, but you be quick with the cuffs, okay?"

"Yes sir."

"We're the authorities, he's the bad guy. Always remember. No matter what, he must be subdued."

She gripped the wheel even tighter. "I'm ready."

Midway between Applefield and Ragtown, coming out of a tight curve, a Chevron gas station and mini mart revealed themselves on a tiny plot of land within a narrow canyon. It offered a welcome chance for tourists to fill an empty gas tank and for busy locals to stock up on milk, bread, butter, and beer in an emergency. Mary Ann had driven by a hundred times and, knowing of better bargains in the nearby towns, had never stopped.

She pulled up to the pumps. A quick glance at the meters told her that gas prices had recently dropped. They both got out. Ibañez walked quickly over to the store entrance, but the door was locked. A hand-lettered sign was posted on the glass:

No Attendant "Credit Only" Today

"Look at that, will you?" He motioned Mary Ann to follow and led the way around back, where a decrepit trailer was parked, evidently the owner's residence. Ibañez carefully stood to one side of the door, reached around, and knocked sharply.

"Miguel Crespo?"

No answer. Mary Ann freed up the handcuffs on her duty belt.

"Mr. Crespo, this is the police. Open up."

Still no response. He pointed to a small window. Lights were on inside. Mary Ann nodded. Then he motioned her to check around the other side of the trailer. With an eye out for snakes she did so. No exit there. Crawling out of a window would be hard work. She returned to the door, shook her head.

"Miguel Crespo, police. You've got five seconds. Then we're going to break this door down and haul your ass out of there. You won't enjoy the experience."

Mary Ann put her hand on the butt of her Beretta, fingertips poised on the holster snap.

Suddenly the door cracked open. Rosarita Crespo, shaking with fear, poked her head around the edge. Here eyes were brimming with tears.

"Where is my husband?" she asked.

Chief Ibañez and Mary Ann looked at each other.

"We'd like you to tell us."

But she had no idea. She invited them in, proving that her husband was not hiding on the property. They decided not to arrest her for receiving stolen goods, at least not right away. But they did force her to open up the store. Mary Ann photographed the stock and recorded a representative selection of lot numbers from some of the toilet paper, boxed wine, and mustard jars she found.

Driving back to Applefield, Ibañez was philosophic. "Well, we're fucked, but at least we answered the big question."

"We did? What was the question?"

"Our thief is more afraid of Sally Cruz than he is of us."

Mary Ann's mind was elsewhere. She was worried that Ibañez had heard about the lottery and was wondering what to say if he brought it up. "Not good, huh?"

"It's a dot. It's connected to another dot. Where it leads us . . ." His voice trailed off as he brooded upon the possibilities.

"More dots out there?"

"Lots of dots."

Mary Ann considered this and Rosarita Crespo's bleak anticipation of a shattered future. "Shouldn't we have taken his wife into custody? She's terrified, and she'll run too."

"Maybe not. She has a decent job. She's not involved, unless someone wants to silence her, which I doubt." He stretched his arms. "Better if she did, though, for everybody."

"What about the crime? Bringing the perps to justice and all that?"

"Justice?" He laughed. "That's a rare beast, like unicorns."

45

THE RUMORS about Mary Ann, vague, puzzling, and outlandish as they were, found their way to Billy Rainwater. His cousin Elizabeth overheard staffers gossiping in the Miners Market. The attendant at the Ragtown gas station mentioned something when Rainwater stopped by to fill up. He found it impossible to credit the crazy stories, but an idea took shape in his head, and he decided to pay another visit to Hannah Crowfoot.

Her door in Angels Camp was open, and the foyer was empty when he stepped inside. He rang the bell on the table, and waited for shuffling feet to bring the old lady out of hiding. Soon a tapping cane approached, and Mrs. Crowfoot pushed a curtain aside and stood before him.

"William, my boy."

"Hello, Mrs. Crowfoot. Look, I brought you something." He hefted a large paper bag covered in frost and held it out to her. "Tom turkey, shot by me, dressed and frozen by Grandmother Rainwater."

"How kind."

"Probably best to keep it frozen until the day."

"Are the organs in there? That's important." She licked her lips.

"Yes. Grandmother knew to keep them."

"Good. How can I help you today? Come along." She led the way into her consulting room.

"Sit. Tell me."

Rainwater sat on the wooden seat, and Mrs. Crowfoot began to prepare her spiritual paraphernalia.

"Don't bother with that stuff, Mrs. Crowfoot. It's okay, I don't really need spiritual advice today."

"No? Then what are you doing here?"

She sank into her upholstered easy chair and sat back to find out.

Rainwater struggled to explain. "It's like this . . . there's a new young cop up in the Tri-Town Area, a woman. She's been annoying the Hilltop Band for some time, and now there are these . . . rumors."

"What, is she a lesbian?"

"I don't think so. I have no idea about that."

"What then? Come on."

"They say she's a witch. They say she can see ghosts."

Mrs. Crowfoot slowly digested the idea. It raised an interesting question. "Can she see Bobby?"

"Sweet Jesus. You think his spirit is still nearby?" Rainwater shuddered at the thought.

"I doubt it. I'm not sure he had a spirit, going white and all."

"Now, Mrs. Crowfoot, we're all God's children."

"So you say. Why are you telling me this tale?" Her eyes bored into Rainwater.

"I thought, you know a lot about the spirit world. You might be interested in a professional sort of way."

"And — ?"

"And, I was hoping you might have some idea of using spiritual tricks to put her off our trail."

"Spiritual *tricks?*" Her lip curled. "I don't know any tricks. There aren't any tricks."

"Maybe there's a spell . . . "

"You want her to leave the tribe — our people — alone, is that it?"

"Yeah."

"If she really is an adept — someone *you* might call a witch — then I doubt any spell I know would do any good." She pondered the matter for a long time. "Do you think the rumors are actually true?"

"Something's up. Gossip has it that some ghost gave her a winning lottery ticket."

"I need to meet her."

"I'll run you up to Applefield any time you like."

"Never mind, I'll manage. I'm not supposed to drive with these cataracts, but I still do."

46

ON SUNDAY EVENING Mary Ann motored slowly down the long driveway to her gig at the radio station, considering whether or not to change her on-air persona. Maybe she should forget her fears, be bold, and wholeheartedly embrace the ugly rumors out there. Why not? She could start each show with a chorus of *Witchy Woman*, call herself the Whiskeyjack Witch. Or, maybe just adopt the Eagles' song title as her handle. Sure, I'm the Witchy Woman, coming to you blah blah blah.

By the time she was inside and prepping for her session, however, she had retreated from the idea. Too weird. Insane, really. Maybe the news was spreading, but maybe it hadn't reached everyone. And even if it had, a little mystery seemed in order. Let listeners wonder. With that in mind, she fired up her show.

"This is the Golden Girl of the Golden Hills at K-V-I-G, coming to you from the Tri-Town Area in Applefield California at ninety-three-point-one on your FM dial. I'm pulling levers and pressing buttons to bring you the best listening experience you'll get anywhere this side of the Sierra crest. It's seven o'clock."

The playlist racked upward on her laptop screen, and *Need You Now*, Lady Antebellum's big hit, jumped up between the arrows. While Hilary Scott's vocal rose in romantic yearning, Mary Ann's first request call came in. She picked up as the song ended.

"You've got the Golden Girl. What can I play for you?"

"Have you got *Run* over there? I'd like to hear that."

Mary Ann's fingers raced over the keyboard, and the laptop screen revealed the artist. "You mean the Sugarland hit?" She mentioned the name like she knew what she was talking about, when in fact she had never heard of the group.

"That's right. Great song."

"Dedication?"

"I just want to hear it."

"Well, I'm sure you're not alone. Your wish is my command. Here it comes . . . "

Mary Ann was relieved that no mention was made of the lottery or her alleged supernatural powers. But, on the third request, it happened.

"Yo, Golden Girl here. What's your pleasure tonight?"

"How about *Season of the Witch*?"

Startled, Mary Ann involuntarily took a quick breath., then, knowing dead air was anathema, grimly plunged right in. "I guess we're in it, Halloween coming up and all, they're out there somewhere."

"And dedicate it to the best DJ K-Vig ever had."

Mary Ann chuckled theatrically. "I will. Whoever that might be. Thanks for thinking of the crew here at *The Vig*."

Uh-oh, she thought. It's out there. The rumor has spread like oil on water. And sure enough, forty five minutes later, it happened again.

"*Buenas noches*, K-Vig?" An unknown woman's voice on the phone.

"Good evening from the Golden Girl, what's on your Golden Hills wish list tonight?"

"Please play *Black Magic Woman*."

"Getting to that spooky time of year, huh?" asked Mary Ann, hoping to deflect attention.

"I pray for you," said the woman and hung up.

Mary Ann hesitated. What to do? She felt completely lame. "Hey, there, good to know I've got someone watching my back. And requesting some great Golden Oldies up here in the Golden Hills."

She typed in the request and fixed herself a cup of coffee while it played. She was unacquainted with Carlos Santana's music and surprised herself by humming along to the laid-back guitar riffs. Her mind was whirling, trying to figure out some sort of adroit repartee for the next caller, but came up blank. Either the rumor was going to die down or get much worse. She felt like she had been thrust back into the middle ages, being pilloried in the village square. She looked at the clock, willing the hands to move faster so she could escape from her audio prison.

An hour passed with no further hints about witches or ghosts. She was starting to relax, when the phone rang with another pointed request.

"Hiya, sugar. How's tricks in the sticks?" The raspy voice was familiar, a little more cheery than she remembered. She shuddered.

"Well hello, there. From what I hear in the background, your place must be jumping tonight. Got a song for me? We play what our listeners want to hear, old, new, borrowed, blue."

"*Bad to the Bone*. I can't find it on the jukebox here."

"Glad to help out." No doubt about it, this was Mary Ann's badass bully from the Palomino. Her discomfort instantly turned into loathing, which she concealed under the sweetest possible tone. "How about a dedication for your main squeeze?"

"Yeah, she knows who she is. Who I am."

"I'll bet she does. Okay, this one goes out to all my biker buddies, I'm sure they know who *they* are . . . "

George Thorogood's oddly transgressive hit stuttered into her headphones and out through the transmitter — *b-b-b-bad to the bone* — blasting a weird vibe over the countryside with six thousand watts of power.

Mary Ann still felt jumpy an hour later when it was time to put the station back on autopilot and drag herself home to bed, even though none of her last dozen requests had conveyed the least suggestion of strange abilities or lottery luck.

As she turned out the lights and grasped the doorknob to leave the station building she halted. Her hand was trembling. She was alone in the dark, a mile out of town, and someone out there hated her for reasons unknown. What if that someone was right outside?

"Dammit, I'm letting myself get rattled."

She bent down and pulled her little Beretta from her ankle holster and tucked it into her belt. Then she yanked the door open and stepped outside.

The night was cool and crisp. Stars by the thousands were glittering all across the sky. The red light on top of the KVIG transmitter tower pulsed confidently. She looked around. No motorcycles were on the scene, and bare ground in every direction prevented concealment. She exhaled slowly, and her breath formed a dewy cloud.

She stood on the doorstep for a long time, taking in the night air and the majestic spectacle of the Milky Way blazing overhead. At last, sensing no danger, she advanced to her car.

As she inserted the key into the door lock, a ghostly image appeared in the driver's side window.

"Whoa! You! What the hell — !"

The ghost held up both hands in an emphatic stop gesture. So she did.

"All right, what do you want? No more requests tonight, pal."

The ghost put his hands together, then flung them apart.

"Here we go again."

The ghost appeared to sigh. He then repeated the gesture. Mary Ann sighed too. Both of them were frustrated by the always uncertain communication channel.

"Something wrong, but what? Where?"

The ghost pointed downward, indicating the car itself. Mary Ann took a quick step backward and froze. Her keys were dangling from the door lock. After a moment she reached out and jerked them free.

"Jesus, what now?"

The ghost shrugged and disappeared.

Mary Ann pulled her gun out and held it at her side while she took another look around. All was calm. She walked slowly up the drive, searching for identifiable tire tracks, but the hard gravel revealed nothing. She put her hands on her hips and muttered softly to herself.

"B-b-b-bad to the bone . . . "

She jammed her gun back in her pants and pulled out her mobile phone. She started to dial the police line, then stopped. She paced around in a little circle twice, made a decision, dialed a different number.

"*County Courier*, hello?" Wagstaff picked up on the third ring.

"Tom? Mary Ann. Got a moment?"

"Oh, hi, M. Sure. Geez, it's late."

"I'm out at the station —"

"— Still? I thought you signed off."

"You were listening?" She smiled in spite of her jitters.

"Yeah, well, I'm working on the *Courier* layout. It passes the time."

"Aren't you nice." She was flattered and also flustered.

"What were all those weird requests about, anyway?"

"So you heard. You, of all people, already know the answer."

"Right. So what's up?"

"I'm standing in front of my car, ready to drive home, but a certain someone doesn't want me to start it. You know who I'm talking about."

"Hmm. What's the problem?"

"He thinks there might be . . . I don't know . . . something wrong with it."

Wagstaff chuckled. "That Mustang, what a machine. And it just came back from the shop."

"I don't know what to do. If I call in the troops, I'll have to explain everything, and I'd rather not."

"Hang on, I'll be right out there."

The constellation Orion was rising into view and Mary Ann was chilled to the bone when, twenty minutes later, Wagstaff arrived in his FJ Cruiser.

"Okay, let's have a look."

Mary Ann followed as Wagstaff performed a walkaround inspection of the Mustang.

"Got a flashlight?"

"Sure, in my trunk."

"What about in the station there?"

"I dunno. I'll look."

She re-entered the station, rummaged through all the drawers and cabinets, and came up empty. Back outside, she threw up her hands.

"No go. If there is one in there, it's hard to find."

"Okay, then, give me your keys."

She handed them over, and Wagstaff approached the Mustang's trunk.

"Better stand back, just in case," he said.

"Ha, ha," she replied, but retreated anyway.

Wagstaff inserted the key, turned it, and the trunk popped open. He picked up Mary Ann's Maglite and dropped the lid back down.

They looked at each other. "Hey, we're still here," he noted.

He turned on the flashlight, got down on the ground, and scooted under the car just behind the left front wheel.

"All right, I'm looking, I don't see any wires or anything unusual. Just a little oil or brake fluid. There's a puddle in the drive here. And I do smell gas, so something's leaking. You should have it checked." He rolled back out and scrambled to his feet.

"Car is locked, right?"

She nodded. She felt as useless as a baby.

"Can you open the hood without yanking on the lever inside?"

She shrugged. "Not sure, probably not, I've never tried."

"Well, I think you're okay. Let me start her up."

"Be careful."

Wagstaff nodded uncertainly, unlocked the driver's side door, and started to slide behind the wheel. Mary Ann watched passively as he fumbled with her keys, searching for the right one. Then something clicked in her head, and with a little shriek she sprang to the car and grabbed the key ring out of his hand.

"Let me do it!"

He started to protest. She jerked a thumb. "My problem. Get out of there."

"Okay, if you're sure."

"I'm not. Get out anyway."

They traded places. She inserted the key into the ignition.

"Better stand back, just in case," she said, with an ironic grin.

He nodded and backed away. She gave him a here-goes-nothing look and, leaving the door open, turned the key.

Varrroooom. The Mustang started right up. They both breathed big sighs of relief. Mary Ann closed the door. She was determined not to let herself be seen angling for a romantic encounter and wanted to leave before everything went awry. She gave Wagstaff a little wave.

"Thanks for coming over — see you around the town." She shoved the shift lever into first gear.

Wagstaff took a step toward her to say goodnight, then stopped in his tracks. Smoke was emerging from the grille. A moment later visible flames licked up around the windshield wipers. In another few seconds — *Bang!* — the hood flew up at an angle. The engine compartment was a roaring bonfire.

"Wait!" Wagstaff snatched the door open, grabbed Mary Ann under her arms, and wrestled her out of the car. She dropped to the ground on her butt, and Wagstaff dragged her halfway across the station property. When he was pretty sure they were safe, he helped her stand up.

"Holy crap," she declared.

He smacked her clothes, dusting her off. "Say that again."

"Holy crap again."

The Mustang was completely engulfed in flames. They staggered back from the heat.

"Whoa, M, somebody doesn't like your style."

"At least I'm alive. No more repair worries."

"Yeah, I told you not to buy that thing, remember?"

"I remember."

"Want to know what I think?"

"Do I?"

"One of your fans poured about a gallon of gas into the drain on the hood there. It must have trickled onto the engine block, and then — *whoom!*"

"I smelled it, but that car always smelled funny."

"Better call the fire department."

Mary Ann dialed 9-1-1 on her mobile phone. "Hello, there. Mary Ann Sarzo, Tri-Town Police on this end. Got a car fire out at K-V-I-G, outskirts of Applefield on Copper King Road. Pretty big. Can you send someone to put it out? Yes, thanks, that would be awesome."

They watched the Mustang burn for a while.

"Think the fire will reach my gas tank?"

"Maybe. It's a total anyway, so what if it does?"

"Man, it's cold out here. At least this warms me up."

"Attaway, stay positive."

"It was a beautiful car."

"But you have your 'inheritance.' You can buy a new one."

She twitched visibly. "Ouch. I'm so sorry, I should have told you about the lottery."

"You're a tough chick."

He slid his arm around her waist. She nestled her head on his shoulder. Firelight flickered on their faces.

By the time the Tri-Town Volunteer Fire Department arrived to quench the blaze it had very nearly extinguished itself. The flames never did reach the gas tank.

Wagstaff opened the passenger door of his FJ Cruiser. "Where to?"

Mary Ann hesitated. Now or never. "I don't dare go home." She spread her arms to indicate she was too weary to offer an alternative.

"My place then."

▼

Wagstaff lived in the *County Courier* office building, in a large open area that might as well have been a Big City loft. They slouched on a sofa in front of a fire (a tame one this time) crackling away inside a stone fireplace he had built himself. They were nursing tumblers of tequila. After a half hour of staring, he leaned over and kissed her on the cheek. She responded by moving her fingers into his long hair, running a hand down his chest.

He rubbed his nose against hers. She rubbed back. They kissed; a long, slow, exploratory kiss that gradually shifted from playfulness to passion. Then Mary Ann fell asleep, utterly exhausted by the day's events. So much for romance.

When she woke up the sofa had been opened to form a lumpy cot. She was lying under a rough wool blanket, and Tom Wagstaff was still there beside her. The faint light of a cloudy morning was slicing in between the window blinds.

She nudged him. "Hey, I thought you said you had an extra bed."

He opened his eyes, rolled around to face her, scratched his head. "I did. And I do. It's right over there." He pointed across the open space to the opposite wall.

"But here we are."

"Yup."

"What are you going to do about it?"

He nuzzled her neck.

"Everything."

An hour later they were still on the sofa, but the blanket was rumpled up in the corner, and their clothes were all over the floor.

Then they were in the shower together, soaping, rinsing, kissing. After all the false starts, Mary Ann felt completely at ease and happily judged that he did too.

As they were toweling off, Mary Ann's mobile phone rang. She ran to grab the call.

"Yes sir, good morning. That's right — *whoosh!* At the radio station. I received a threat, and what do you know, it wasn't idle." She listened for a moment, moving the phone away from her ear to soften the caller's voice. "I'll be right in, but I spent the night in town, I don't have my uniform. Yes sir, give me five minutes."

Wagstaff came up behind her, cradled a breast in each hand. "What was that?"

"Gotta run. Chief Ibañez is on the warpath."

47

WADE GAWLEY was sitting behind Mary Ann's desk when she hurried into the Tri-Town Police station. He smiled.

"Heh, Mary Ann, I warned you about that Mustang."

She ignored him.

Ricky Moss was idling nearby.

"You know, Sarzo, that's what you get for moonlighting."

She glared at him in passing. "Is that so?"

Moss put a finger to his lips. "Take it easy — our usually mellow chief is ready to explode. Don't give him a hernia."

Mary Ann rolled her eyes and tiptoed into the corner office, where Chief Ibañez was pacing back and forth and around his desk. He was so hot Mary Ann thought he might levitate.

"Tell me again. You got a request for a song. You thought it was a threat, you figured your car might be booby-trapped. And yet — you didn't call the department. You started it anyway, with help from our local gossip-in-chief."

"That's about it. Tom thinks someone poured gasoline on the engine block."

"Maybe. Probably. Something happened. And you recognized the voice. How?"

"Not long ago I was drowning my sorrows in the Palomino when three biker dudes got in my face. The leader — same guy."

"Who is he?"

"I don't know. They chased me home, but I never did clock a plate. I should have."

"Damn right you should have. Bikers are all over the foothills. Our back roads are their favorite recreation, and we can't begin to track them all."

"I was so scared I turned around and spent the night in the station."

"You should have told me right away."

"I thought you'd think I was Chicken Little."

"Christ. Officers of the law cannot be stampeded by a bunch of hicks on Harleys. Or whoever they are working for."

"I'm okay."

"Fuck. You could be dead." He slammed a fist into his palm. "This can't go on. It can't be permitted. It is *in-TOL-erable.*"

He dropped into his chair, spun himself around.

"Go home. Get dressed, for Christ's sake. Until you get some transportation, drive the Jeep." He waved her away, audience over.

"Now let me think."

Gawley and Moss were lounging a little too close, ostensibly finishing their morning coffee, when she came back around the corner. She realized they had heard the whole scene and blushed.

Gawley piped up first. "He never yells at us."

Moss joined in. "We never fuck up."

Mary Ann whirled around to face them, hands knotted into fists. "You two morons."

They chuckled amiably.

She was halfway to Placerville when it dawned on her that the mild hazing she had just received might be meant to welcome her into a little club. A few miles later she remembered that the ghost had fingered her stalker as a butcher. She had failed to mention that fact.

"When will I ever learn?"

An hour later she was back in the station in full uniform. Gawley and Moss were out on patrol. She was relieved she wouldn't have to figure out a way to show she was part of the team. She started toward her desk, but then paused. Coming through his office door, Chief Ibañez' voice could be heard, running at full volume. She moved closer. It sounded like an angry telephone call.

". . . somebody was threatening one of my officers. Now I don't know where this comes from. Granted, business is business. Maybe you don't think so, but this puts pressure on your operation. That's right. Money talks, but it doesn't walk, *comprende?* Your activities must not involve my force in any way. Think it over. Talk to Gardner, he'll tell you the same thing." There was a long pause, then Ibañez' voice resumed in a markedly less confrontational tone. ". . .what's to discuss? Ranch security? Well, I'm a reasonable man, of course I'll listen. All right, then. Your place."

Mary Ann retreated to the kitchenette. A moment later Chief Ibañez emerged, throwing on his hat and jacket. He stalked out the door without the least acknowledgement.

She made herself a cup of coffee and considered what she had just heard. It sounded compromising. It sounded tricky. It sounded suspicious, as if back room deals were being made. She put down her coffee untasted, picked up the little white calavera statuette from her desk, and stepped into the women's restroom.

She held the figurine up before the mirror and sang out, "Hey, ghost! Come here, you."

The center of the mirror blurred slightly, like a ripple on a pond. The ripple spread outward, and suddenly her shadowy visitor was there, frowning and wagging his finger.

"Whoa!" she gasped. By now she'd seen him appear dozens of times, but it always seemed dreamlike afterwards, and the impact of the real thing always threw her.

"I know. You call me, I don't call you. But we've got a situation. The chief is acting weird. He's on the take or something, I don't know. What should I do?"

The ghost's image wavered uncertainly, then steadied. He traced the letter C in the air. Then the mirror blurred again, and he was gone.

Mary Ann stared at herself. "Cruz," she said aloud.

When she opened the restroom door Wade Gawley had returned from patrol and was working at his desk. Without missing a beat she said, "Hi, Wade. I'm rolling now," and was outside, running for the black & white Cherokee.

She drove the winding road between Applefield and Cruz' alpaca ranch at high speed, fighting to groove the unwieldy Jeep through curves that her Mustang would have taken with ease.

When she rounded the final corner, she could see a dust trail boiling up behind a black & white Explorer traveling down the long ranch drive-way — clearly Chief Ibañez' vehicle. She stopped at the gate, rolled down her window, and pressed the button on the intercom.

"Hello?" came a buzzy metallic voice.

"Ah, police here. Let me in, I'm with Chief Ibañez."

"I am sorry, but this entry is not authorized."

"I'm his, his, what do you call it? Lieutenant. I'm here to take notes."

"No notes. No entry. Very sorry."

She pressed the button again. Dead. No answer.

"God damn it."

She sat in the Jeep, thinking hard. What on Earth was the chief doing here, in enemy territory? Then she made a decision, backed the car around and re-parked on the far side of the road. She grabbed her camera, hopped out, and climbed over the gate. About halfway down the drive she got cold feet and stopped. Far ahead she could see the chief's SUV, parked by the main house. A quick look around revealed that she was visible to anyone on the ranch who cared to cast a glance in her direction. But no one was anywhere to see or be seen. So she resumed hiking toward the ranch buildings. After all, she thought, echoing Chief Ibañez, she was an officer of the law and not to be stampeded.

She got as far as the first barn and stopped again. The door was open. She stuck her head inside, hoping to see an illegal drug lab, or a bench covered with poppies, or at least large quantities of opium packaged up in plastic bags. But no, there was some hay on the floor, and empty animal stalls.

She continued down the drive. The main house was getting closer. All at once she heard a small engine firing up. A moment later a ranch hand was motoring toward her on a little all-terrain quad cycle, kicking up dust.

"Uh-oh."

Lying across the driver's lap was a long slender object, possibly a rifle or shotgun. She could feel panic hyperventilating toward her. She held total terror at bay long enough to aim her camera, zoom in as far as possible, and take a few snapshots. Then, with adrenaline flooding her system, she sprinted back toward the gate, hoping to outrun the man on the quad. With each step, the noise of the engine got louder. She reached the gate with the machine on her heels, clambered up, and fell to the ground on the roadside.

"Don't shoot!"

She scrambled upright, thrusting her hands over her head to stave off the attack. But wait. The quad cycle wasn't quite as close as she had imagined. It had come to a halt around a hundred feet back. The ranch hand was bent over on the edge of the drive, paying no attention. The rifle or shotgun was in reality a shovel, and he was using it to coax a section of culvert into better shape.

She laughed self-consciously and waved. He paused in his work, gave her an indifferent glance.

"*Hasta*."

She jumped into the Jeep and fled the scene.

▼

An hour later she was sitting at her desk, examining the photos on her little camera. There were five of them. Three were so blurry they were outright rejects, but two contained hints of detail. She could see a motorcycle parked a few cars over from Ibañez' SUV, but she couldn't read any plate numbers.

She picked up the phone and dialed.

"*County Courier*, Wagstaff here."

"Tom, it's me. I've got a couple of photos of suspicious vehicles, but I was a long way away, and I need help."

"Try PixelPolish."

"What?"

"It's online."

"What?"

"Never mind. Come on over, I've got Photoshop."

Mary Ann drove the short distance to the *Courier* office, parked in back, and rapped on the door. Wagstaff opened it. She handed over her camera, then leaned forward, head tilted upward for a kiss. Wagstaff obliged with enthusiasm.

"This is business, bub. We're working here." She stepped past him.

"If you say so."

He removed the SD memory card from her camera, copied the pictures onto the hard drive of his work computer, started up Photoshop Elements 10, and opened the first photo.

"Whew, did you grease the lens?"

"I was under duress. Shaky me."

"Well, that one's useless. Next — ooh, even worse."

"I can't shoot a gun straight either."

But the third photo was more promising.

"Let's resize." He clicked on a menu item.

The image went blank, the little cursor flashed its busy signal, and they waited. Then the picture reappeared much enlarged, with a small detail filling the entire frame. It showed part of an automobile. Wagstaff slewed the image around, clumsily looking for anything intelligible.

"Let me."

Wagstaff backed away. "Press spacebar to grab the thing."

Mary Ann took the mouse, held down the spacebar to activate the grabbing hand, and moved the image upward, revealing the rear end of Chief Ibañez' SUV.

"Look at that, it worked." Wagstaff was surprised at the detail.

"But I don't see the motorcycle."

Wagstaff leaned over her shoulder and pressed a key combination to zoom out. The photo did not include her intended target.

"Next."

The next photo was too blurry.

"Damn."

"One more."

But the final one appeared to show a motorcycle near the left edge.

"Resize."

The photo ballooned up. Mary Ann scrolled over to the motorcycle.

The license plate was visible. Wagstaff zoomed in. The letters and numbers were unreadable.

"Oh no," moaned Mary Ann.

"Now, let's autosharpen." Wagstaff clicked on another menu item. A couple of seconds later the picture looked like a fog had lifted. The motorcycle seemed to be etched in stone. But the plate numbers were stubbornly obscure.

"Ahhhh, dammit."

"Wait, wait. Don't give up. We've still got some headroom. Let's up the contrast and sharpen some more. He pulled down menus, dragged sliders, clicked on little dialog boxes. The image disappeared, then reappeared.

"That's better."

"Is that a three or an eight?"

"Looks like a five."

"Are you sure?"

"This is getting us nowhere."

"Hang on. It's the color fringes. Your camera lens sucks." Wagstaff pulled down the image menu, clicked on mode, clicked on grayscale. All the color drained away. What was left of the photo was in stark black and white. The numbers were unambiguous.

Mary Ann read them off: "37-V-9-8-7-5."

She wrote them down, then threw her arms around Wagstaff.

"Woohoo!" she shouted.

"Hey, take it easy. Let's get to the important stuff. Are you staying over?"

"I might be persuaded. Call you."

▼

Back at the station Mary Ann ran the numbers through the California Department of Motor Vehicles database on her office computer, privileging herself by assigning a fictitious case number to her requests. She sucked in her breath when the results appeared.

"Well hello, hello, if it isn't my radio fan."

48

MARY ANN ended her shift and was getting ready to drive home for a change of clothes and a toothbrush when Wade Gawley, who had just arrived back from patrol, fielded a phone call.

"Hey, Mary Ann, got a motorist-in-distress down on 88. Woman out of gas."

"Hey, yourself, Wade. I'm atmosphere." She was planning on a quick trip to Placerville and an overnight with Tom Wagstaff. She picked up her keys from the desk, collected her hat, and started for the door.

"Now hang on, you're headed for 88 anyway. You've got the company Jeep, full gas can tucked in the wayback, and I've got to write up my tags."

Mary Ann stopped short. "Shit, all right, where is she?"

"About a mile west of the 520 crossing. Take you five minutes. You'll feel good about yourself."

Grumbling and griping, Mary Ann rolled down County Road 520, winding around the curves at speeds that worried her Jeep Cherokee, crossed Red Hill Road, and turned west on Route 88. Only then did she slow to a respectable pace, keeping an eye peeled for her chance to be a good Samaritan.

Sure enough, after a mile or so she spotted an ancient Hyundai in a paved turnout. Once upon a time it might have been dark green, but the paint was so oxidized and patchy you'd never know. The driver's door was open. The motorist-in-distress turned out to be a heavy old woman who was sitting sideways in the driver's seat with her legs on the ground, waiting patiently. She was leaning on a white cane for support.

Mary Ann pulled over at some distance from the car and studied the woman. She couldn't put her finger on the problem, but something was not quite right about the situation. She checked her holster, felt the encouraging heel of her little Beretta, and slowly climbed out. She lifted the two-gallon gas tank from the rear of the Jeep and warily approached the Hyundai.

"Hello, there. You called in to Tri-Town? Out of gas?"

"Good evening, young lady," came the calm reply.

"I've got a couple of gallons here, get you as far as Jackson." Mary Ann raised the gas can as evidence.

The old woman waved her cane. "I don't need any gas."

"No? I thought . . . "

"I might someday. But not tonight. I came because we need to talk."

"Me?"

The old woman adjusted a pair of glasses with lenses a quarter-inch thick and peered through them at the helpful young policewoman. "Mary Ann Sarzo, isn't that your name?"

Mary Ann lowered the gas can. "You think dragging me down here on a pretext is a good way to meet me?"

"It worked."

"Yes, and I will kick Wade Gawley's butt."

"He had nothing to do with it. I *summoned* you."

"You did what — ?"

"I'm an adept. I have heard the stories that are all over the foothills, and I understand you are too."

"God Almighty." Mary Ann took a step backward, keeping her distance. The woman stood up and shuffled toward her.

"I'm Hannah Crowfoot." She held out a pudgy hand. Mary Ann stretched for a guarded shake.

"Adepts are vulnerable to others who prey on us. Some of them are people we meet every day, and some come from . . . the spirit world."

She gestured toward Mary Ann's SUV. "Do you mind? I can't spend a lot of time on my feet."

Mary Ann opened the rear door for the woman, then walked around the car and, being careful with her tactics, got in the front seat.

"I can see you're suspicious of me," observed the woman, touching the clear acrylic panel that separated front from rear. "That's understandable. Have you ever met another adept before?"

"No. How do I know you are what you say?"

"Look in the driver's side window there."

Mary Ann turned her head. "Oh my God."

Lurching this way and that, turning around and around as if trying to orient himself, a faintly visible figure was competing with the reflections from the Jeep's dash — Mary Ann's visitor.

"How did you do that?"

The old woman seemed to be short of breath. She waved dismissively, and the visitor vanished. Then, to recover, she put a hand over her heart and desperately wheezed in a slug of air. "You notice, I can't get your visitor's attention."

"You see him, though. Nobody else does."

"Yes. Adepts have unusual talents. How are people treating you, those who hear the stories, but see and know nothing?"

"So far so good, I guess."

"That may change. The day may come when you will need spiritual assistance to fend off the unbelievers."

"Fend them off?"

"Your ghost is no help. He is a little wisp, a mite, a confused and helpless shadow."

"He can't talk, that's for sure," said Mary Ann.

"You need a power spirit at your side."

"Hell yes. Got one handy?"

"Not now, not at the moment, not casually. And never for the fun of it, my dear." She wheezed some more.

"Too bad for me."

"But that's why I've come to see you. Here . . . "

She brought forth a clear plastic bag from a voluminous purse. Mary Ann stared at the contents. There were three large trumpet-like flowers inside, yellow and dried.

"What are they?"

"Datura blossoms."

"Aren't these things poisonous?"

"Oh yes. But you aren't going to eat them. And we also have this . . . "

Another plastic bag. This one contained a snarl of grey hair.

Mary Ann smiled. "This is like an evidence bag. The victim's hair. Who was it?"

"The cat who made the donation is still alive and well at my house, thank you very much. It will work, but you'd do better with a cat of your own."

"I don't have a cat. There's an old neutered tom that hangs around my trailer when he's hungry."

"Ever feed it?"

"Now and then. He's not a black cat."

Mrs. Crowfoot laughed a wheezy laugh. "Color means nothing. Pull some hairs from its tail.”

“Datura, cat hair, what am I supposed to do with this stuff?”

“Why, make a *bonfire*, throw it on, and conjure a *power spirit*, of course.”

“Bonfire. Do I have to say a spell?”

“Use your own words. Your purpose is a *summoning*.”

“My own words? I really don’t know anything about this stuff. I wouldn’t know what to say.”

“Whatever you think will cause the power spirit to appear will work, if your mind is focused.”

“And I do this . . . why?”

“To have a guardian when trouble starts.”

Mary Ann nodded, humoring the old woman. “Hmm.” She was beginning to wonder how she was going to get this strange person out of her Jeep. Then a thought struck her. “Have you ever conjured one of these . . . power ghosts?”

“Long ago, when I was a younger woman. But no more.”

“Why not — are they scary?”

“Very scary if you’re careless about your work. But that’s not the reason I don’t do it anymore. To conjure a power spirit one must also sacrifice a small supply of blood.” She paused for effect. “And sadly for me, but not for you, it must be . . . menstrual blood.”

“Eww.”

“I know, it’s disgusting. But it is absolutely essential. Datura, cat hair, menstrual blood — throw them into the fire, and out comes a power spirit, to protect and guide you.”

Mary Ann was inwardly frozen in horror, but she maintained a perky surface. “Telling me this, it’s very kind of you . . . ”

The old woman’s lips curled upward in an eerie smile. “We adepts must look after each other. We’re an endangered species.”

Mary Ann nodded absently, committing the old woman’s instructions to memory. “Datura . . . cat hair . . . menstrual blood . . . bonfire.”

Mrs. Crowfoot pushed on the door handle at her elbow.

Mary Ann was apologetic. “Oh, wait, rear doors are always locked on police vehicles. I’ll come around and let you out . . . ”

But somehow the door opened before she could move. Leaving her gifts behind on the seat cushion, Mrs. Crowfoot shuffled away.

"Power spirit. That's the ticket. Punch it, and control your destiny."

Mary Ann watched the woman's rattletrap Hyundai move away down Route 88. Then she checked to be sure the rear door locks were in working order. They were. She shivered involuntarily.

"What a creepy old crone."

49

THE NEXT DAY dawned cool and damp. Mayor Teasdale was staring out her office window, unhappily contemplating the sharp drop in tourism bad weather would surely cause, crimping her already inadequate town budget. Gordon Hollinsworth was there to share her low spirits, but for other reasons.

"There may be some difficulties with the Auburn property, Vera."

She looked over, smiled a wan smile. "Do you know, I thought the Tri-Town redevelopment program would guarantee prosperity. Now I'm not so sure."

"Everything slows down in the fall. We've still had a record year. But I didn't drop in to cheer you up."

"What is it?"

"As I said, the Auburn property."

"Something wrong?" She refocused in an eyeblink.

"Your title's good. Zoning is favorable."

"Get to the point, Gordon."

"What I hear is, some of the local businesses are going to oppose a casino."

"Will it matter?"

"I don't know. All laws are open to interpretation, or I wouldn't have a job. They'll complain about sightlines, traffic, the wrong clientele, unsavory business partners, you name it."

"I don't see the problem."

"Well, Rainwater will be making his payment soon to transfer title. This is going to throw sand in the gears, slow him down once he takes over, maybe wreck his whole grand scheme. Do we want to warn him?"

"Is that your advice?" Her eyes narrowed to flinty points.

"Just wondering. Politically, you have a record as a friend of the Hilltop Band. He's sure to kick up a fuss when he finds out just how rocky the road is going to be."

"Are the papers bulletproof?"

"Of course."

"Am I legally required to make further disclosures?"

"No, you're fine. He'll have the standard five days to reneg."

"Then no, politics be damned, I don't want to warn him." She was glowering.

Hollinsworth held up his hands. "Okay, we won't."

An ironic smile creased her lips. "I think we should look at the upside. We're doing our level best to give the Hilltop Band a decent future."

"I guess that's a good way to frame the picture."

"That hotel is mine, Gordon."

"Understood."

At that moment Chief Ibañez arrived at the mayor's door. Following a polite knock, he took half a step into the office. "Whoops, excuse me, I didn't know you were busy." He checked his watch.

"Hello, Hector. Come in, we're just finishing up," said Hollinsworth, rising out of his chair.

They shook hands; Hollinsworth gave the chief a pat on the back, a little wave to the mayor, and closed the door behind him on his way out.

"You wanted to see me?" asked Ibañez.

"Have a seat." The mayor indicated the chair Hollinsworth had just vacated. Ibañez took a step forward, but remained standing.

"What's the problem?"

"The violence here. There was a segment on *Channel Four News* last night, the anchor mentioned it while he was talking about the end of the fire season. But look — it's all over the Big City. We're infamous! Tourists will shun the Golden Hills for fear of being murdered in their sleep."

"Vera, for God's sake. As you know very well, the investigation is in the hands of the sheriff's department. I don't have the resources or the personnel or the authority to get in their way."

"Well, do it anyway, or prod them into action. Something, anything." She waved her hand in a royal sweep that took in all outdoors. "Put those beautiful new cars and trucks I wangled for you from the CHP to work."

"You're worried Howard will use this against you next November."

"I've whipped that man three times, but he never quits. Of course he will."

Ibañez suppressed a chuckle. "I wouldn't lose any sleep. The election is a year away. His views are, how would you put it? Polarizing, right?"

She softened momentarily. "I suppose."

He thought the interview was over, but he was wrong.

"Nevertheless, I want you to get on this, and stay away from my guy."

"Your guy?"

"Our guy. The town's guy. Sally Cruz. I hear you've been harassing him, you and that young woman you hired, the one who does the traffic reports. How unfair."

"We talked, but" — he paused, wondering how far to take this, and decided to be careful — "I'm unaware of any harassment."

"He's a concerned citizen, a supporter — with money! — of our community," she insisted.

"And where does that money come from, don't you wonder?"

"His family runs a factory."

"Oh really, where? Sinaloa? Michoacan?"

"Um, Monterrey, I think that's what he told me."

"Hmm. Maybe. Listen, may I speak freely?"

She snorted. "You always do."

"Well, this may ruffle your feathers, but I've got to say it — our connection to this guy bothers me. It doesn't look good. We can't trust him."

"Just because his origins are in Mexico."

"Vera, in case you hadn't noticed, *my* origins are in Mexico."

▼

Mary Ann was waiting with checks to be countersigned when the chief returned to the station. His face was red, and he was muttering to himself.

"Morning, sir."

"Stay out of politics, Sarzo. That's my wise word of the day."

"Yes sir. The mayor, huh? I noticed your appointment."

"She's worried about our murders wrecking the tourist trade, for Christ's sake."

"I'd worry more about the tickets Wade writes — he's going to do the job without killing a soul."

He laughed. "You're probably right. What's up? What's that in your hand?"

"Bills, checks. I need your signature." She handed him her pen.

He sighed and dropped into the chair at her desk. While he was scribbling away, Mary Ann worked up her courage to tell him something.

"Want to hear the news?"

He looked up. "Uh-oh, what now?"

She summarized the story as she had practiced it. "Two days ago you drove to Cruz' ranch. I was out on patrol" — a little lie — "and I followed you."

"Jesus. At least I'm sitting down. Don't give me a heart attack."

"While you were there I photographed some of the vehicles on the premises."

"Trespassing, were you?"

"One of them was a motorcycle. After some photo processing I was able to read the license plate. I ran it through the DMV, and what do you know?"

"I don't have the foggiest. How did you get access to the DMV?"

"I made up a case number."

"Good God."

"Bad idea?"

"That depends. Go on."

"So, the plate belongs to the motorcycle owned by one Dale Bremer."

"The guy in your beer at the Palomino."

"One of them, anyway. Remember way back when Mike Russell got himself sliced open? You asked, butcher, baker, candlestick maker, and I picked butcher."

"Yeah?" He couldn't recall the moment.

"I was right."

"How in hell do you know that?"

"Once I had the name, I then spent thirty-five of the department's dollars — on our petty cash credit card — to perform a background check."

"Christ. Again, how?"

"Online — Backgrounder-Pro-dot-com. We already had an account, so you must have used it before."

"Now and then. You better hope we've got probable cause."

"Okay. Today this guy works for Golden Fleece Exotics LLC — that's the Cruz ranch — but get this, until two months ago he was employed at the Albertson's market down in Lodi. As the meat manager."

"Your stalker is the butcher."

"He's the butcher."

Ibañez got up from Mary Ann's chair and paced the room while he thought things over.

"Suppose it's all true. Good story, anyway, points for that. But we can't be sure we've found a murder suspect just because some Neanderthal has it in for a cute young cop. I see the dots, but I don't see them connecting yet."

"Bremer's occupation, Russell's manner of death," she emphasized. That was enough for her, case closed. But the chief did not appear to be persuaded.

"I think Russell was a sideshow. My guys, to a man, were convinced he was running a meth lab somewhere, and maybe retailing drugs he got from, yes, some other operation. So it could be he was just in somebody's way. Maybe he was annoying the big boys, or maybe some local rival. Your man Bremer, for example. Or maybe, even, somebody just thought he had been overcharged at Russell's garage."

"Do you really believe that? Sir?" Mary Ann was crestfallen.

"It doesn't matter what I believe. How often do I have to tell you — we need evidence. Evidence strong enough to make an arrest."

He pointed the pen at her. She snatched it back. Somewhere in there she had hoped for a word of praise for her hard work. It was not forthcoming.

50

THAT EVENING the Book Nook was open late. Lorraine had mounted a Scrabble tournament, and she had several players, all of them chatting and agonizing over the dangerous Qs and Zs.

Mary Ann found her friend wandering among the card tables she had set up, marveling at the wordage.

Somebody played "QUARION" off somebody else's U, right on the triple word score. She raised a fist.

"Good one, Penny," sang Lorraine.

Her opponent reached for her dictionary.

"It's a candle, Jane, perfectly legal," pronounced Lorraine with authority. Then she waved to Mary Ann, beckoning her toward the bank of computers in the rear of the store.

"I was wondering where you were. Tom dropped by. He told me about your car. Will insurance pay?"

"Good news, bad news. I had a high deductible, but I'll get some tiny Blue Book settlement."

"That's bad. What could be good?"

"Tom and me," Said Mary Ann. "But . . . I can't talk about it." Her cheeks turned red.

"Why not? Something wrong?"

"Um, you're his mother. That makes it very awkward."

Lorraine's eyebrows shot up into space. "You didn't!"

"Yeah, we did." Mary Ann grinned sheepishly, willing to risk parental disapproval.

Lorraine threw her arms around her. "No wonder you look so cheerful. Bless you both!"

Mary Ann hugged her back, then pulled away. "Thanks. Somehow, I'm not as cheerful as I should be, considering."

Lorraine's face fell. "No? Why not?"

"Last night some really strange old Native woman tracked me down, said she was an adept."

"An adept? So she's heard the rumors too?"

Mary Ann heaved a big sigh. "Like everyone else."

"Is she the real thing, do you think?"

"She can see my ghost."

"O-ho. That is a piece of news. Wish I could." Lorraine's envy was palpable.

"She gave me some tips on conjuring up a power spirit."

"What's that?"

"I have no idea. Gotta check."

They started up one of Lorraine's computers and, while the Scrabble tournament raged on behind them, got down to business @ Wraiths-Of-America-dot-com.

"See here, power spirit. 'Rare and dangerous ectoplasmic manifestation. Engage with extreme caution,' " noted Lorraine.

"Let's find out if you can call one up with datura blossoms and cat hair."

Lorraine typed some terms into the search box. "I don't see anything, except, watch out for datura, babe."

"What about menstrual blood?"

"You're kidding."

"Wish I were."

"Hmm, menstrual blood — I'll be damned — here's something. 'Thought to be an important ingredient of witches' brews in medieval times. Possible source of ancient prejudice against witches. Sometimes used in love potions.' "

"Love potions — ?"

"Wait, here's the disclaimer. 'Obsolete in modern wiccan practice.' " Lorraine sniffed. "Oh sure. As if witches wore white lab coats now."

"Hmm," said Mary Ann, visibly disappointed.

"What's wrong? Hey, don't even think about conjuring any power whatzis."

Mary Ann shrugged. "I was hoping for help getting my ghost to talk."

Lorraine regarded her young friend with a stern expression. "I can see you're tempted."

"I'm all right."

Listen to me, kiddo, you don't want to take chances with this stuff."

"Don't worry, I hear you."

"You better. Take a look at these printouts. I've been doing some research."

She brought out a sheaf of papers. Each one, in a different way, laid out some uncomfortable facts pertaining to grandfather Sarzeau.

Mary Ann looked them over. "Where'd you get this stuff?"

"I found a website that does photo-matching. You upload a picture — I scanned the one we found weeks ago — and they come back with the most amazing news and information.

"Check this out" — she shuffled through the pages — "Remi Toussaint Sarzeau, a resident of Terrebonne Parish, is accused of using voodoo on his neighbors. It's right there in the local newspaper! In, let me see, 1951." Lorraine pointed to another page. "And here we are again, also 1951, arrested for poaching animals, snakes I think, for use in, whoa, 'so-called black magic spells.' Paid a fine and was released."

She paused and pushed her glasses higher on her nose. "Now we have this, are you with me? In 1954 he was arrested again, convicted of arson, and sentenced to ten years for burning down someone's house. The judge later complained that he was cursed by him and lost his wife to another man as a result."

"Oh my God." The color was draining from Mary Ann's face.

"If your dad changed his name, well, who can blame him?"

▼

Mary Ann left the Book Nook in a dismal mood. She sagged into the Jeep and made a call to Tom Wagstaff. He didn't pick up, so she left a message.

"Hi, Tom. I'm exhausted, and I've got an errand in the morning. Call me when you get this, okay? *Hasta* Luigi."

She then drove home to Placerville with her thoughts in a jumble.

When she got out of the Jeep at her trailer, she noticed a familiar orange tabby cat sitting on the step. She delicately stepped past him, unlocked her door, and went inside. A moment later she was back with some shreds of chicken leftovers in a little dish.

"Here you go, fella."

As the cat eagerly started in on the meal, she whipped out a pair of scissors.

"Hold still, I've got to try something. It's the price you pay."

She snipped a tuft of hair from his tail and deposited it in a plastic bag. Then she re-entered her trailer and, lip curling with disgust, rescued a used tampon from the rubbish in her bathroom. This she deposited in another bag.

Mary Ann kept an old Weber grill out behind her trailer. She filled it with charcoal, poured a cup of white gas over the pile, and lit it.

Whomp!

The flames leaped up. In spite of Lorraine's warnings, she was bent on learning how far her powers might extend. Itching with anticipation, she watched until the fire was burning steadily and then returned to the trailer for the datura blossoms the Crowfoot woman had given her.

But when she came back outside she was carrying a hamburger patty and bun instead. A brief meditation on her grandfather's crimes cautioned her to cook some food and not to experiment with witchcraft until she knew a lot more about it.

She ate a lonely supper and was already in bed when the phone rang. She was too tired to pick up, and the caller, Tom probably, didn't leave a message.

▼

By nine o'clock next morning she was out on her errand — patrolling the quadrangle of Saint Patrick's Catholic Church, hoping to buttonhole Father Eisen. She was ragged with fatigue, having tossed and turned all night. Not long into her vigil he came striding out from the rectory.

"Father!"

He turned, smiled in recognition, and waited patiently for her to hurry over.

"Mary Ann, how are you?"

"Okay, I guess."

"You look tired. How's your visitor?"

"He's okay too. You were right about finding an object. I learned how to summon him. Well, sometimes. He doesn't like being bossed around."

"Hmm. Not surprised. Nothing surprises me anymore. So, what brings you here this morning? Confession?"

Mary Ann winced, remembering her recent and technically sinful deeds. "I'd rather not."

"What, then?"

"I've been studying up on my grandfather. He was a convicted criminal, and people thought he cursed them."

"I take it this is keeping you awake at night."

"Have you ever heard of adepts? People who inherit magical powers?"

"You mean witches and warlocks?"

"Yeah, or voodoo dudes, I'm not sure. I met a woman who claims to be one."

"Theoretically, it's all just folklore. But then, so are ghosts, right?" He allowed himself a small ironic smile.

"Could someone like me start out okay and then, you know, do terrible things? Geez, I don't want to wind up as a nasty old lady with a wart on my nose."

He almost laughed. "Knowing you, I doubt it. Don't trouble yourself."

She nodded vaguely, not entirely satisfied with his answer.

"Look, I'm on my way to mass. Want to join us?"

"Um, not today. Late for work."

"Excuse me, then . . . the flock awaits." He touched her shoulder, made a little bow, and strode away toward the church.

She watched him go, lost in thought.

On her way through Ragtown she pulled over at the Book Nook. While Lorraine made her a jolt of espresso she addressed a postcard and wrote a brief message:

Dad — does the name "Sarzeau" ring a bell?

— xoxo, M.A.

Part SIX

51

AT THE END of a long and boring shift, Mary Ann drove down to the Foothill Shooting Center. Ever since her Mustang went up in flames she was taking her practice sessions a little more seriously.

She ran the target out ten yards. She adjusted her goggles and ear protectors. She spread her feet, braced her arms, locked her hands around her Beretta 9-millimeter. She started to squeeze off a carefully aimed round, then relaxed. The Beretta drooped toward the floor.

"Who am I kidding?" She shook her head. Then she brought the pistol up again and —

Pow! Pow! Pow! Pow! Pow! Pow!

— blasted merrily away, emptying the clip.

She inserted a second clip and repeated the action —

Pow! Pow! Pow! Pow! Pow! Pow!

Other cops on the line leaned backward to get a glimpse of the maniac in station number five.

"Whoa, Sarzo, you'll melt that thing."

It was Deputy Gardner, pushing up his goggles, pulling off his ear protectors, ambling her way.

"Evening, Terry." She removed her own ear protectors.

"What in the name of some agreed-upon sacred deity are you doing?"

She grinned at him. "I heard a saying once. 'If you can't tie good knots, tie plenty of 'em.' "

"So, blind fire, hope for the best?"

"That's my theory."

"Remind me to stay the hell out of your way." He held up his hands in mock surrender and swung back toward his own station.

"Hang on there, sheriff."

He stopped, turned back to face her.

"Mike Russell case," she said.

"Yes? What about it?"

"That man was sliced open from his burp to his blow. It looked to me like the work of a professional knife-wielder."

"You saw the corpse?"

"Oh yeah, I'm the one who found it. And I've got a suspect for you."

"Let's hear it," he said doubtfully.

"Recently I was harassed by a biker named Dale Bremer. He issued a threat, and then my car burned up. He works for Salvador Cruz now, but he was formerly employed by Albertson's."

"Beg pardon?"

"He was the meat manager in the Lodi market. He's a butcher."

Gardner took a step forward. He was on full alert.

"What's the name again?"

"Dale Bremer."

"Bremer, Bremer. And he came after you? I'll look into this."

He turned away, brows knitted in consternation. When he reached his own station he raised his weapon in a little salute and called out, "Thanks," over his shoulder.

She turned back to her well-perforated target, inserted a third clip into her Beretta, pulled her ear protectors back into position, braced herself, and let fly again —

Pow! Pow! Pow! Pow! Pow! Pow!

52

IT WAS JUST AFTER NOON on Halloween when the electrifying word came in. Ricky Moss was returning from patrol and stopped Wade Gawley at the door.

"Hear the news? On the intersquad loop. Sheriff's department just arrested some guy for the murder of Mike Russell."

"No shit," said Gawley.

Chief Ibañez and Mary Ann, overhearing, left their desks in a hurry and joined the gathering. An arrest! — it sent their law enforcement spirits soaring. They all looked like kids on Christmas morning.

Moss turned up the volume on the station's police scanner. "*Khsszzk* . . . yeah, we had cars up and down 520 waiting . . . *bzhrrp* . . . 8:25 . . . on the road up to Ragtown . . . *sshhhssszzz* . . . "

"Who is it?" asked the chief.

"Some guy named Bremer. Works out at that fancy alpaca ranch."

"Bremer!" yelped Mary Ann, hanging her jaw open to emphasize her astonishment.

The chief turned her way. "Your stalker?"

She nodded.

"I'll be damned. You called it." The chief raised his hand, she did the same. They slapped a businesslike high five.

"Think he's the one who torched your car?" asked Gawley.

"I sure do," she affirmed.

"Maybe this guy also did Bobby," suggested Moss.

"Wouldn't that be nice?" said the chief.

Mary Ann shook her head. "I bet he didn't."

"Uh-oh, another lesson in police work coming up," growled the chief. He folded his arms. "But I'll bite. Why not?"

"Bobby was shot, Mike was cut wide open."

"But who's to say Mr. Bremer doesn't own a small caliber handgun or have one available?"

"And maybe Russell was shot, but the bullet was removed when he was cut up," added Moss.

Before the discussion could really get rolling, the chief's phone rang on his desk. He went to pick it up. When he came back he confirmed the news.

"That was Gardner. Their theory is, the guy is a local dealer who employed Russell as a go-between, and maybe Russell was keeping a little too much for himself."

"Where the hell was Russell getting his stuff?"

"Who knows?"

"Gardner says they discovered a ruptured balloon in the remains," said the chief.

Mary Ann frowned. "I didn't spot that. Did you?"

The chief shook his head. "Nope. But I didn't look too closely."

Another phone call. Ibañez scurried off again. Mary Ann went to the files, hauled out an SD flash memory card from the department's own case folder, shoved it into her computer, and scanned through the pictures. Gawley leaned over her shoulder.

"Jesus, Mary Ann, I still can't look at this stuff."

"Then don't. Hey Chief, I don't see anything in the pictures we took that night . . . Chief?"

Ibañez came back into the room rubbing his hands. "That was our honorable mayor. Is she excited! Tourism is saved!"

"Chief, come over here. I can't find any damn balloon," called Mary Ann, standing up.

The chief took her seat and stepped through the documentation photos slowly and methodically. "Wait, here's a possibility." He pointed toward a close shot of Russell's horrendous wound, where a ragged shred of blue was barely visible among the organic coils. "Patch of rubber? What do you think?"

Mary Ann nodded. "Yeah, I missed that. Hard to be sure, though. See, there's blue in the shirt fabric."

"Could be the ME used a scope, you know, worked some forensic magic," said Moss.

Ibañez closed the computer's image viewer and stood up straight. "Doesn't mean much either way. Our victim was practically sausage. He was doing something wrong for sure, and somebody settled his hash. Bremer, so it seems."

"Who's betting they'll find a handgun when they search the Bremer household?" asked Gawley.

"How much?" asked Mary Ann.

"Make it twenty bucks."

"Too rich for me. But I'll bring you a latte every morning for a week if they do. Anyone else?"

None of the others wanted to bet either way.

Eventually the excitement wound down. Chief Ibañez returned to his office to answer a dozen phone calls. Gawley went out on patrol. Moss signed off for the day. Mary Ann returned to the mountain of paperwork waiting for her. Then, when all was quiet, Ibañez re-emerged. He strolled across the station's open interior and perched himself on a corner of Mary Ann's desk.

"You were right about Bremer. I was skeptical, like any good cop, but you were right. I'm impressed."

"Thank you, sir."

"You've been right about a number of things."

"I try to keep my eyes open," said Mary Ann, affecting modesty.

"What I'm wondering is, how do you do it?"

"Sir?" a little chill ran through her.

"You're the one who found Bobby's gun. You're the one who found Mike Russell's body. You seem to have found evidence of Rainwater laundering money, and now Bremer."

Mary Ann wasn't sure what was coming, but she detected a long slow curve and decided to stand tall. "Not too bad for a rookie, huh?" she said.

"That is the point. The point exactly. You're a rookie cop. I guess you're smart, and you're plenty aggressive." She started to protest, and Ibañez held up a hand. "Those are good qualities. But experience, you've got none at all, *nada*. Your theories make sense, but you don't."

"I don't understand."

"You can't be digging all this stuff up on your own. I couldn't do it either. Somebody's helping you. Who's your source? Wagstaff? Who does he know? Somebody who's in on all these shenanigans?"

"Tom has nothing to do with it."

"Who then?"

Mary Ann propped her head between her hands and stared at her desk. "I, um, I can't tell you."

"Of all the people in the world, I'm the very one you absolutely must tell," said Ibañez. "You owe it to me, to the department."

She kept her head down and shook it. Her hair flew out of its clip and lashed out every which way. "I have to protect my source."

"No you don't. You're a cop, not a reporter," Ibañez was using his sternest tones.

She looked up at him. Her eyes were moist. "How do I know . . ." She faltered, swallowed, then sat back and folded her arms. "How do I know you're not involved?"

"Me? In bed with drug runners?" Ibañez reddened.

"Money does funny things to people. The rumors are out there."

"You're right." He forced himself to remain calm. "You never know. But" — he pointed a finger — "you work for me. You have to trust me. You have to tell me."

"I just can't," she wailed.

"Look at this from my point of view. Your source could be citizen Cruz. You could be working for the man himself. A naïve young woman, caught in the snare of a charming rogue. Why not? That would answer a lot of questions. Maybe you've been set up as a spy to keep an eye on the law, just in case. How does that sound?"

"Why would I implicate Cruz and Rainwater then? Or accuse Bremer?"

"No idea. You tell me."

He plucked a tissue out of the box on her desk and handed it over. She blew her nose. Then she sat rigidly upright for a long minute while her mind sifted the possibilities. At length she breathed a weary sigh.

"When I tell you what I'm going to tell you, you'll think I'm insane or worse. So get ready."

He nodded.

"Every now and then I see a ghost in the mirror."

Ibañez regarded her sympathetically. "So it's true."

She angled her head to one side. "You already heard."

"As you said, the rumors are out there. Is that how you found Mike Russell's body?"

"Yes. He was the tip."

"Who is this . . . ghost?"

"I don't have a name. For a long time I thought it was Bobby."

"But then you won the lottery."

"I know — shit — that's out there too. It sounds like science fiction, but the kind of ghost I see is called a 'virtual visitor.' They only appear on reflecting surfaces, and the books and websites I've checked claim they can travel through time. So Bobby was killed beforehand, and maybe it was somebody else who saw the lottery results and later came back to help me."

"This thing, this 'visitor,' whatever it is, does it seem familiar?"

"He's a shadow, he comes and goes. Hard to see details. No, he doesn't."

Chief Ibañez paced the station, thinking hard. On his fifth lap he paused.

"Show me," he said.

Mary Ann stood up. She grabbed the little calavera statuette she was using as a paperweight and held it up before the chief.

"What is that?"

"It helps make contact. Father Eisen's idea. Come with me."

She led the way to the ladies' restroom, pushed the door open. She held out her hand to invite him in. Mumbling under his breath, he stepped past her. The two of them squeezed into the narrow space in front of the mirror.

She brandished the calavera in a tight grip. "Okay, ghost, come here. I really need to see you — and right now."

They waited. Ibañez fidgeted with his tie.

"Sometimes it takes a while. I don't have any control. Ghost, can you hear me? Come in, ghost! Save my ass, will you?"

Ibañez watched her performance with detachment.

"Hey, ghost! Hey you!" she yelled.

"Is that how you call him, 'hey you?' "

"You thought it would be a lot more mystical. Candles and black cats, right?"

"I don't know what to think."

"Well, he's not here."

She led the way back into the station's main open area, her eyes traveling around to take in all the mirror-like possibilities. She crossed to the kitchenette and peered at the stainless steel coffeepot, bubbling quietly. Any telltale shape in the reflections? No. Next she examined the glass window in the chief's office door. Completely transparent. Then she angled a look at her computer screen. An innocent screensaver undulated slowly across it. Nothing else. She opened her pocket mirror. Nothing there either.

At wit's end, she turned to a large sepia-toned photo reproduction hanging on the wall, an image of proud men with shovels stoically posed before a tunnel entrance. It commemorated the Headwall Mine Bonanza that brought the first settlers to Ragtown. Other copies, large and small, were on view in establishments all over the Tri-Town Area, reminding tourists they were traveling through history. Here it was nicely matted and framed under glass. And in that glass Mary Ann saw a shadowy shape twisting and writhing. She jumped back.

"Oh my God. Here he is!"

"Where?" Ibañez could see nothing.

"Right here." She pointed at the photo. "Okay, what say? Time? Time for what? Okay, not much time. Right. And yes, here's the chief. Say hello, Chief."

Ibañez remained silent, watching Mary Ann's performance, if not the ghost himself. To his eye, she seemed hypnotized.

But she wasn't. Abruptly she turned toward him. "Take a good look — he won't hang around forever."

Ibañez strained to see something in the photo, and after a few seconds he did: a sudden flash, a flicker of movement. Was that the ghost? His stomach lurched. Then the rumble of tires on rough pavement caught his ear. He glanced out the window. A FedEx truck was just passing by outside. Afternoon sunlight was glinting off the white sides and reflecting from the photograph. He wiped his brow.

"He still there?"

"Yes. He doesn't talk, just makes a lot of gestures. Sometimes I get his drift, sometimes not."

"Ask him why Bremer would want to kill Russell."

Mary Ann turned back to the photo. "Hear that? Want to tell me? Wait, stick around for a goddamned minute, will you please?" I still don't know your name." But the shadow receded and vanished. She slammed the calavera down on her desk in frustration.

"Did you see him?" she demanded.

Ibañez made a long face. "Sorry."

He picked up the calavera. The girlish grinning skull seemed to mock him. "You did go to cop school, right, Sarzo? You weren't a theater major?"

Mary Ann took the calavera out of his hand, plopped it back down on her desk. "When you asked about Bremer, Mr. Ghost made a sign with his finger. He traced a *C* in the air."

"What does that mean, if anything?"

"Cruz, I guess, who else? What if Bremer was already working with the cartel, or maybe the drug guys knew him at least, and they got him to slice up Russell, their own guy who was skimming, to recover some drug balloons he swallowed."

Ibanez rolled his eyes. "God Almighty, Mary Ann, have you got a satellite dish or something tuned in to ten channels of *CSI* all day long? Because this is great fiction."

"I think he acted on orders. And maybe that's why he came after me."

Ibañez appeared to give this idea some credence. His eyes narrowed. "Yeah, I see what you mean." He marched back to his office. "I'll talk to Gardner." Once inside he closed the door, stood at his desk, picked up the telephone.

Then he put it back down. His attention was drawn to a small ceramic figurine standing guard over his papers, pens, and business cards. He picked it up and looked it over. Like Mary Ann's statuette, it was a calavera. This one stood about four inches tall. Black spots for eyes, a monstrous grin, black jacket, top hat. Maybe it was a bridegroom ready to take some afterlife marriage vows. Or possibly a wealthy businessman hoping to cut a deal with the devil. Hard to tell. He wondered why he had never thought about it before. Casual inspection revealed a hole in the top of the hat and a rubber seal on the bottom. He turned it upside down and shook some reddish powder into his open palm. He sniffed, then tasted it.

"Huh. Cinnamon."

53

BILLY RAINWATER received a phone message later that day while he was down in Jackson. He bought the cheapest pay-as-you-go mobile phone he could find at the Safeway, and was soon treated to a dose of bitter irritation on the part of his caller. In spite of every effort, that *chica maldita* on the Tri-Town police force was a still big headache, and why hadn't Señor Rainwater done what he promised to do about it?

Rainwater kept his angry reaction to himself, disposed of the telephone in a public trash bin according to protocol, and aimed his pickup truck toward Angels Camp for some answers to this burning question.

Hannah Crowfoot was sitting on a little wheeled stool in her garden, weeding out the squash plants, when Rainwater arrived.

"Afternoon, Mrs. Crowfoot." Now that he was in her presence, he found it difficult to vent his frustration.

"Hello, William. How are you? How's that casino project coming along?"

"That's why I'm here, ma'am." A pained look passed over his face.

"Ahh, I see. Come inside. We can talk freely there."

She led him into her consulting room, thick as always with foul and smoky odors. Rainwater wrinkled his nose as he sat down.

She eased into her upholstered chair with a sigh. "Now, I know why you're here. You think I haven't been doing much to deter that young policewoman."

Rainwater was startled by the mental quickness within the old lady's shapeless body. She sure was something. "Uh, yes, that's about it, I guess. I suppose you're trying, right?"

The spirit woman leaned forward, folded her hands on the table. She gave him a glimpse of her eerie smile. "Better than that. I have done it."

"Then why is she still after us? She's causing a lot of trouble."

"Not for long, she won't. I showed her how to conjure a power spirit."

"What's that?"

"A demon."

"Won't that make her even more of a threat?"

"Here's a lesson for you, William. When you conjure a power spirit in water, it is as meek as a goat. It will do your bidding, obey your commands, fulfill your wishes."

"Uh-oh, that doesn't sound good."

"On the other hand, when you conjure a power spirit in *fire*, it is untamable. This is what I told her to do."

"But she's got to chant a spell, or whatever you do, right?"

"Be patient. She is alone. She needs an ally, and soon she will seek one. She will perform the ritual. When the power spirit appears, it will surely kill her."

54

LATE ON THE FIRST of November, All Saints Day, Gawley
returned from investigating half a dozen Halloween pranks and sat down
to write up his reports. He was working his way through a complaint
involving trees and toilet paper when he noticed a military Humvee pull
up and park in front of the station. It was painted in radical camouflage,
giving the impression that the Golden Hills Tri-Town Area was a battle
front.

"What the —"

He stood up for a better look. The driver, a tall young man in an army
combat uniform, got out, opened the station door, and came inside.

"Hello?"

Gawley found the man's presence so surreal that he nearly saluted.
"Hello yourself. What can we do for you," — he noted the stripes —
"corporal?"

The young man removed his patrol cap. "Delivery for Officer Sarzo."

Gawley looked around. No Mary Ann. But just then the back door flew
open, and in she came lugging bags of milk and muffins to stock up the
kitchenette.

"That's her, over there. Hey, Mary Ann, someone to see you." He
wiggled his eyebrows and pointed at the soldier. She put down her
groceries, wiped her hands on a towel, and walked over.

"Geez, Wade, at the market I had to scrape pumpkin rinds and dogshit
off the windows," she remarked. "Can you believe?"

"Officer Sarzo?" The young man sounded unsure. He studied her name
tag suspiciously. Whoever sent him apparently hadn't bothered to
mention his target's sex.

"That's me."

"Sarzo? The cop?" He wanted to be certain.

"Yup, you found me." She reached out to shake his hand. Instead he
handed her a sealed white envelope. No postmark. No return address. It
was labeled simply:

Sarzo, Police, Applefield, CA

"What's this?" she inquired.

"None of my business, ma'am. It's from Master Sergeant Sarzo, ma'am. Perhaps you know him?"

She felt slightly dazed. "Unh-huh, I do, sort of. Where you from, soldier?"

"Entrance Processing Station, Sacramento. Sign here, please."

Mary Ann signed a receipt and handed it back.

"You have a nice day, ma'am." The young man saluted her, pivoted, and marched back to his Humvee.

Chief Ibañez came out of his office in time to see the Humvee drive away. "What was that all about?" he wanted to know.

Mary Ann held up the envelope. "Letter from Dad, I think."

"Does this happen often — soldiers deliver your mail personally?" asked Gawley in amazement.

She was pleased by the commotion. "Never before. This is my first actual letter from the old man since I was fifteen."

"Well, open it."

"Oh no! I'm going home, sit on the couch with a glass of wine, and read it three times." Just receiving the letter at all, to say nothing of its extraordinary manner of delivery, lifted her mood.

"*Hasta* banana, guys."

She drove to the end of town, parked and called Tom Wagstaff, regretfully declining yet another evening together. Then she wound up the Jeep and lit out for Placerville.

▼

As promised, once inside her trailer she opened a bottle of red wine from the convenience store, poured herself a generous glassful, kicked off her shoes, and made herself comfortable on the sofa. She took a sip and ran a kitchen knife along the edge of the envelope. Inside was a single page, composed in blue ink. The handwriting looked like her father's. The signature was convincing. She sipped again and slowly read through the text, starting from the top, savoring every thought:

Angel —

Looks like you've got the makings of a fine detective, if you ask me. You're right: SARZEAU is the family name. Since you found out, maybe you already know why I don't use it.

We're all different. You are what you are, and must discover what that means for yourself. But you are not your grandfather.

Remember how your seizures went away when you were thirteen? A good sign. Ghosts? Don't worry. All I can tell you is, you're not crazy. And you're not in league with the devil.

I'd love to be with you and help you through your troubles, but I'm heading overseas again. Can't tell you where, that's against the rules of the game I play for our country.

Take care of yourself.

    — love, Dad

As she told her colleagues she would, she read the letter a second time and then a third. Although the words were somber, when her eyes welled up they leaked tears of joy.

55

MAYOR TEASDALE stopped at the Pick & Shovel on her way to work and ordered up some sugary snacks for an important meeting scheduled to begin within the hour. She wanted it to make sure it would go well. The counter girl complimented her excellent political leadership with gushing praise and a discount. The mayor waved away the praise with a gracious smile and refused the discount on principle. Humming to herself, she walked a block to City Hall where Gordon Hollinsworth was waiting. She took his arm, and they strolled into her office together.

While Hollinsworth seated himself and sorted the papers in his briefcase, she made a pot of strong coffee.

"Today's the day, Gordon. All our ducks lined up?"

"Everything's set. Who's going to notarize?"

"The fire department dispatcher doubles up. A widow in midlife, like me. Just got her license. She's a wonderful find."

"Can she leave her desk?"

"She forwards calls to her cell. Don't worry."

Hollinsworth chuckled. "I'm not. Nervous anticipation, I suppose. You too, I notice."

"I can't wait to tell my daughter. She and Douglas will have a big decision to make. How lucky they don't have kids in school down there, and friends and all."

A knock on the door announced Billy Rainwater. The leader of the Hilltop Band looked around the office and warily stepped inside. He was carrying his backpack and a set of documents.

"Morning, Mayor. Mr. Hollinsworth." He stood at attention, waiting for a word of welcome.

"Come in, come in, Mr. Rainwater. Good to see you, what a lovely day," trilled the mayor.

Rainwater took the chair beside Hollinsworth, placed his documents on the desk.

"Coffee?"

"Yes, please. Cream and sugar."

Mayor Teasdale poured three cups. They all stirred and sipped.

"Is that the acreage parcel?" asked Hollinsworth.

Rainwater pushed the documents toward the attorney. "Grandmother Rainwater and my cousin Elizabeth have both signed on behalf of the Band. Liz doesn't live on the land, but she's the other governor."

Mayor Teasdale made a quick call, and the Tri-Town Fire Department dispatcher appeared in a wink with her notary's seal and record book.

"I'm sitting in for the title company today, Billy. Let's add your name, shall we?" Hollinsworth handed Rainwater a silver pen. "All three copies, please."

Rainwater signed. "There you go."

The notary stamped and signed and recorded the title transfer.

"Care for a scone, anyone?" asked the mayor, already munching on one.

"Now the Hotel," said Hollinsworth.

This time Rainwater and Mayor Teasdale signed. The notary verified the purchase contract.

"And finally, the Auburn property."

More papers shuffled back and forth, more signatures, more stamps, more names and dates recorded.

"Worse than a three-way basketball trade, huh, ma'am?" said Rainwater with a wry smile.

"All that remains now, Billy, is payment to finalize the whole transaction. I believe you said you would present this sum in cash," intoned Hollinsworth.

"Yes."

"And the agreed-upon amount was fifty thousand dollars, is that right?"

"Yes it is."

"Do you have the money with you, Mr. Rainwater?" asked the mayor.

"I do, ma'am."

Rainwater lifted his backpack to the desk, removed a pile of greenbacks and placed them in front of the mayor.

"My goodness, look at that," she goggled.

"Better count, easy to miss a hundred here and there," said the notary.

So Mayor Teasdale, Hollinsworth, and the notary each picked up a stack of bills and did the count. Hollinsworth fumbled and mumbled through his while the two women whizzed through the rest.

"We're good," said the attorney after several minutes, when the total was finally reached. He laid a receipt in multiple copies on the mayor's desk. They all signed. The notary stamped and booked each copy, nodded to the group, and returned to the fire department.

The mayor rose from her chair, took Rainwater's hand in both of hers, and squeezed it in her best campaign manner. "Good luck on your enterprise, Mr. Rainwater. We're all hoping to see our Native Americans secure the prosperity they deserve."

Rainwater replied with equal formality. "The Hilltop Band thanks you. We're grateful for this opportunity."

Hollinsworth stood up as well. "Vera, I think we're done here. The hotel is yours."

He also shook Rainwater's hand and used the gesture to guide them both to the exit.

"So long, ma'am," called out Rainwater, and the two men left the premises.

Mayor Teasdale allowed herself another scone.

On the sidewalk outside, the leader of the Hilltop Band was triumphant. "Finally, at last, hallelujah. Now that we've got the location, my investors will be falling all over themselves. Pour the concrete — right, Mr. Hollinsworth?"

"That's right, Billy."

"We're going to call it, *The Feather Mountain Casino & Spa,* what do you think?"

"Sounds catchy. Catchy name, I like that."

"You don't seem all that excited. I guess it's just a lot of paperwork to you."

"Nonsense, this is going to be something else."

Rainwater slapped his hands together. "Yes it is! Nothing between us now and those gamblers' bad habits."

"Nothing except a sea of permits, Billy. They'll be expensive. Be sure to warn your investors."

Hollinsworth thumped his client on the shoulder in a genial sort of way and sauntered off down the street.

56

THAT SAME MORNING, Chief Ibañez interrupted his routine patrol of Ragtown for a reconnaissance stop at the Book Nook. Lorraine was surprised to see him. To her knowledge he had only entered her store once previously, and that was five years ago, back when he introduced himself to the Tri-Town Area's shopkeepers on a goodwill tour. A tour, she remembered, that was ordered by Mayor Teasdale, who was nervous about hiring him.

"Good morning, Lorraine."

"Morning, Chief. Haven't seen you for a while. Coffee?"

"Please."

She poured a cup and watched as he browsed the racks, sipping slowly, reading the little signs, and gravitating at last to the Non-Fiction section. He was staring at the occult offerings when she glided over to assist.

"Can I help you find something?"

"I'm lost. I need to get up to speed on ghosts."

She smiled. "Did you see one?"

He gave her a peculiar look. "No. But I've got a young rookie on the force who says she did. Officer Sarzo. Maybe you know her?"

Lorraine nodded. "We've met."

"Really?"

"Right here in this aisle, actually."

This got the chief's attention. "What was your impression? Think she's crazy?"

"No more than most of us. Why? Does she seem crazy to you?" Lorraine couldn't help fishing.

"I can't really discuss personnel. But — this is a close call — no, she doesn't."

"Oddball, though?" she prompted.

"Oh boy." The chief rolled his eyes and shook his head. "So, what should I look at?" He gestured toward the perplexing line of occult volumes.

"If you had the time, well, *Charter* is the definitive text for Supernatural 101. But if you just want the executive summary, I'd suggest this little item — *Ghastly, Ghostly & Grim*. Behind that vivid title, it's the straight scoop.

"Unh-huh, if you say so."

"And online, try Wraiths-Of-America-dot-com. It's the Wikipedia of weirdness."

▼

Later at the station, Ibanez closed his office door and opened up his laptop. He registered at Backgrounder-Pro-dot-com and typed in a name: *Mary Ann Sarzo.*

"Who are you, anyway, little Miss Why Did I Hire You?"

He retrieved her basic personal data — name, past addresses, employment history — and plugged the information into a series of Google searches. After much digging he came up with references to her high school days in Sacramento, where she sang in the a cappella choir, to her college career at Chico State, where she earned a business degree, and where, he was surprised to discover, she was a star athlete. He marveled at a photo of her as a soccer goddess, racing toward the goal, hair flying, dribbling the ball with authority while fending off the knees and elbows of an interfering defender.

"Whoa, who knew you could move like that?"

He noted her stint running a Dairy Queen and her POST courses at Butte College.

"Look at that, you really did go to cop school."

After a lot more digging, he also discovered that her mother had died in the Katrina disaster, and that her father was a master sergeant in the U.S. Army Special Forces, whereabouts unknown. Finally, he found a medical report detailing treatment for pre-adolescent seizures.

"Good God."

He sighed and closed his laptop.

"So . . . where did the ghost come from?" he muttered.

57

FORTY-EIGHT HOURS after his arrest, Dale Bremer was released from custody for lack of evidence.

The news hit hard in the Golden Hills Tri-Town Police Department, where all four officers gathered around the coffee maker to discuss the situation.

"I've tried to reach the mayor, but she's not picking up," said Chief Ibañez.

Moss sighed. "We're back where we were in August, for Christ's sake."

"You'd think they could hold him on a threat charge at least," said Gawley.

"Maybe they didn't even file a threat charge. Gardner knew it was made on the radio. It was subtle if you didn't listen too hard. So maybe the judge didn't believe it," said Mary Ann.

"Who the hell is the judge, anyway?" asked Moss.

Mary Ann stepped away from the group and dialed information on her mobile phone. She listened briefly, ended the call, punched another number.

"Terry Gardner, please. Officer Sarzo." She tapped her foot while she waited for him to pick up, wondering if he would. After an agonizing minute, he did.

"Terry? Hi. We just heard the news up here in hicksville. What's the story on Bremer? Unh-huh. Sure. Right, but I'm directly involved. Makes me nervous to see him back on the street. Yup. Well, we have the headline, but not the story." Long pause. "Okay, got it. Thanks. See you on the firing line."

The rest of the crew looked at Mary Ann in surprise.

"Didn't know you were tight with the man," said Gawley.

She shrugged. "I'm not. Just worried."

"What's he got to say for himself?" asked the chief.

"They found a knife at Bremer's house, some organic material on it, possibly blood. Traces of heroin in a CD jewel box. Also fibers at the scene."

"But the judge didn't buy it?"

"The organic material was tested. Get this — it came back deer blood.

Probably a year old."

"I guess our boy is a hunter."

"The heroin, the fibers?"

"No idea. And no, they didn't file a threat charge."

"So he walks."

Ibañez' phone rang, and he returned to his office to answer. A few minutes later he came back, looking grim.

"That was the mayor. She called down to Jackson. Release was authorized by Judge Avery O. Parnell of the Superior Court. She knows the guy pretty well. He tells her the blood thing was a fiasco, thinks it reflects badly on the sheriff, who should know better."

"Damn."

"Didn't say he didn't believe Bremer is the perp . . ." he threw up his hands in disgust.

"I know," said Mary Ann. "We just need evidence."

"Attagirl."

▼

Later on, Mary Ann drove down to Ragtown and met Lorraine Wagstaff for lunch at the Fire In The Hole Café, where they both ordered Claimjumper omelets.

"You better take to sleeping with your gun in your hand, kiddo," advised Lorraine.

"Hey, I'm scared enough, don't make it worse."

"Okay, just saying. Your stalker is going to be very annoyed after his false arrest."

Mary Ann leaned over the table and stopped eating long enough to hiss, "He did it, Lorraine. He killed Mike Russell."

"You don't really know that for sure. Maybe he was an accomplice. Maybe someone was trying to set him up."

"You're right, I can't prove anything. But for all I know, he was in on Bobby's death too. Him or his friends or all of them together."

"Call Tom. Don't be alone."

"Unh-huh."

"How is Tom, anyway?"

Mary Ann arched an eyebrow. "Hey, you're his mother . . . "

"What I meant was, how are Tom and *you* ?"

"Um, we haven't seen each other for a few days. Very busy. But we might be pairing up. At least I hope so." She smiled a conspiratorial smile. "If he asks, tell him you think that's how I look at it."

"I'll deliver the message."

"Make me look interested, but not taken for granted."

"I know what to do."

"I am interested, you know."

Lorraine laughed. "I can tell."

Mary Ann polished off her omelet and changed the subject. "I sent a postcard to my father."

Lorraine was working through her hash browns. She pushed them aside. "Aha. Did you ask about your name?"

"Of course. And this is amazing — he actually sent me a letter. Sealed envelope, a whole page."

"Yes? I'm terrible at suspense."

"We were right, the name is Sarz-E-A-U. And he knew all about granddad."

"Eureka."

Mary Ann unfolded the letter and placed it on the table in front of Lorraine, who adjusted her glasses and looked it over.

"Your father is in the military?"

"Some sort of spy, from what I read."

"So, he's a spook. Does he actually see spooks?"

"Who knows? But something's going on. I think that's why he never tells me anything."

Lorraine shivered and passed the letter back. "At least he's on our side. That's a comfort."

Mary Ann sipped her iced tea. "I'm thinking of changing my name."

Lorraine's jaw dropped. "You can't be serious."

"Yes I am."

"Change to what — Shirley Holmes?"

"Lorraine, geez . . ." She tapped the little plastic name tag on her uniform. "Back to the original. French spelling and all."

"Don't you need a judge's order or something?"

"I suppose. I haven't figured everything out yet."

"And won't that upset your partners in crime prevention, who already think you're a nutball?"

"Probably."

"Hey now, don't be hasty. If Dad doesn't think it's a good idea, I don't either. It sounds like you're sliding toward the dark side."

"Never — that's a promise. Look here." Mary Ann reached into her blouse and extracted the small wooden cross Father Eisen had given her, now strung on a beaded loop around her neck.

Lorraine pinched her lips together and rolled her eyes. "Does this prove you're right with the saints?" She was still skeptical.

Mary Ann nodded emphatically. "I believe it does. You read Dad's letter . . . I am who I am." She tucked the cross back under her blouse. "And I kind of like the heritage factor, no matter what Dad said. I'd spell 'Mary Ann' as one word if I did it. Pretty cool, huh?"

"Exotic, anyway. You could wear purple eye shadow and Victoria's Secret bras. Tom might go for that."

▼

Mary Ann was planning to spend the night with Mr. Wagstaff, but he was tied up with the next issue of the *Courier*, and called it off. So she retreated home to the Placerville Gardens RV Park & Resort, where she spent a restless night imagining Dale Bremer on the prowl.

On Sunday morning she paced her trailer liked a caged lioness, waiting for the phone to ring. When eleven o'clock rolled around and Wagstaff hadn't called, she swallowed her pride and punched in his number. He answered on the first ring.

"*County Courier*, Wagstaff here."

"Hi, Tom. It's me. What's up?"

"I'm organizing all the little pieces for this week's paper. You?"

"Sleeping late. That's about it," she said in an offhand manner, trying to sound casual.

"Any word about your pal Bremer?"

She sucked in a deep breath. "Just that he's out there somewhere. Plotting my demise, no doubt."

"Let's hope not. Let's hope his close call shows him the error of his ways."

"Let's hope."

"Where's your optimism?"

"He's scary. And I have to do my radio show tonight."

"Yeah, I forgot."

Long pause.

"Tell you what," he said at last. "I'll drive you down there and stand watch."

Mary Ann expelled a huge sigh of relief. "Would you?"

"Sure."

"You'll be bored out of your mind. Bring your laptop, you can edit your news items."

"Sounds wonderful."

"Meet you in Applefield."

Night was upon them when Wagstaff pulled up in front of the police department in his FJ Cruiser. Mary Ann was standing under a streetlamp, carefully maintaining high visibility, just in case. She flagged him down and hopped aboard.

At the entrance to the KVIG property, he slowed and crawled down the drive to the little grey cinder block building.

"Leave your lights on."

Mary Ann reached down and removed her Beretta from its ankle holster. She chambered a round, flicked the safety off. Then she handed him her key ring, pushing the correct one for the station between his fingers.

Wagstaff was confused. He reached for the gun.

"No, no. I actually know how to handle this thing. You open the door, I'll cover you."

He eyed her doubtfully. "You sure you know what you're doing?"

"More or less."

"Hmm . . . "

They both got out of the SUV. She put her back to the passenger door while he fitted the key into the station's lock. Click. It opened.

Mary Ann darted forward, reached around on the inside station wall and flicked a switch. Dim light filled the little room.

"After you, ma'am," chimed Wagstaff.

"Here we go."

She stepped inside, Beretta at the ready, and quickly searched through every dark corner.

"We're all right," she said, putting her weapon away.

"Oh good," said Wagstaff.

She removed her jacket and began flipping switches, preparing for the night's gig. Wagstaff took the moment to have a look around. Unless someone was hiding in the little bathroom, the place was clean. He checked, just to be sure.

"Look, M. There's no one here. Why don't I go sit in the car, keep an eye out?"

"You'll freeze."

"I'll be fine. I can write up the big news about Mr. Bremer."

Mary Ann considered the matter. "If something funny happens, blow your horn. Short beeps. Keep blowing. I'll bring the artillery."

"And save me?"

"Count on it."

It was a slow night. Mary Ann surmised that everyone was recovering from Halloween, or if not, then watching Sunday Night Football. The Oakland Raiders were making a rare appearance.

She only received a single request all evening. It happened in the last half of her show, in the midst of a string of hits from yesteryear. *Harden My Heart,* Quarterflash's only known song, was winding down, its signature saxophone honking away.

"Hello, this is *The Vig,* and tonight we're spinning a stack of golden oldies. Who's calling the Golden Girl?"

"This is Sleepy in the Sierra." The connection was noisy, but Mary Ann thought she recognized the voice.

"And what is your pleasure on this nippy evening, sir?"

"You're playing a lot of negativity down there. Lost loves, betrayals, broken hearts." No doubt about the voice. She smiled and covered her mouth to silence a giggle.

"A lot of love songs are like that," she managed to get out without laughing aloud.

"So I'd like to hear something a little more cheerful."

"How about *Love Me Tender*, the Elvis classic?" she teased.

"Too sentimental," judged the voice.

"I suppose so. Tenderness is so last century. It was already prehistoric when I was in diapers."

"I need something upbeat. Sweet, but not too sweet."

Mary Ann checked the playlist on the station's laptop screen. Something slightly more recent and apt was moving up between the arrows. She vaguely recognized it from a video she once saw on YouTube.

"Well, then, Mr. Sleepy, wake up to *Take On Me,* from the eighties."

"Aha. Perfect."

"A-ha, indeed." She closed her mike, and the Norwegian group's famous 1985 synthpop smash filled the air.

While it played, she pre-recorded two station IDs, lined up several advertisements for snow tires, antifreeze, and pellet heaters, then filed them all on the server and returned KVIG to the care of trusty Spin-O-Matic, Inc.

She was cautious opening the station door, but quickly holstered her Beretta. The night was quiet and the only soul stirring was a coyote, which poked its head around the corner of the building before loping away across the field. She could see Wagstaff sitting in the FJ, illuminated by his laptop screen. He looked over at her, waved his mobile phone, and grinned. She threw on her jacket and jumped in beside him.

"Hello, Sleepy. That was cute."

"I like that song." He leaned over and kissed her lightly.

"Me too." She kissed him back.

He put away his laptop and started the engine. "Where are we going?"

"My place is twenty miles away, and it's a mess."

"Right. In case you're wondering, I'm not sleepy."

"Let's go find out if that's really true."

And off they went. If Dale Bremer and his gang were out looking for trouble, they didn't find it.

58

BILLY RAINWATER drove his pickup truck north on Route 49 past Placerville all the way to the American River, crossed it, and followed El Dorado Street up the hill into Auburn. Consulting notes on a scrap of paper, he turned onto Lincoln Way, drove a half mile to the eastern outskirts of the city, and parked in the Target lot at the intersection of Lincoln and Old Spanish Road.

Inside the megastore he purchased yet another pay-as-you-go mobile telephone for cash.

Then, leaving his car in the lot, he crossed the street to survey the lay of the land. Stretching before him along several hundred feet of Old Spanish Road was the Hilltop Band's newly acquired property. It amounted to twenty or so acres of open ground, a couple of tumbledown sheds, the gnarly remains of an old apple orchard, and behind that a dense thicket of brush and timber trees. It backed onto a housing development on one side and a CalTrans maintenance yard on the other.

Rainwater opened the telephone and keyed in a number. After two rings the recorded voice recited the usual mantra:

"The party you have dialed is not answering. Stand by, and the party will return your call."

Rainwater stepped over a ditch and a decaying rail fence, walked out into the open glade. He tilted his head back, thrust out his arms and murmured, "Yes! Thank you, God."

His phone rang.

"Are you on the property?" asked the familiar male voice in his always formal manner.

"That I am."

"And what is your impression?"

"It's perfect. Some clearing will be required, there are trees. Demolition of two small buildings that look like they're going to fall over on their own. And listen —" Rainwater held the telephone above his head with the microphone aimed toward Interstate 80, where the hum of traffic was clearly audible.

"Yes. What is that sound?" asked the voice.

"That's I-80. That's our customer base whizzing by not a quarter of a mile away. On their way to Reno today, stopping here soon."

"Yes, soon." The voice agreed.

"And how about this — the Lincoln Way off-ramp is just a few blocks south of here. Talk about easy access!"

"I am told the final permits will not be issued until we have plans drawn. Is this Hollinsworth's view?"

"Probably. There's always something in the way in that man's mind."

"We will need an architect. I have contacts, they have given me the name of someone who has designed other casinos. This we must do, for the credibility," said the voice.

"Yes, let's get this project rolling," echoed Rainwater. He turned in a circle, taking in the broad expanse of his domain. "You know, this is going to be our money-maker in the future. We should abandon the farming operation, don't you think? It's small potatoes now, if you know what I mean, ha ha."

"We must do both. It is my partners' wish. We are obligated."

"But Mr. C., it's a big risk. We already had a close call."

"Do not refer to me on the telephone," warned the voice.

"Sorry."

"And do not worry. We have protection, we are protected."

Rainwater frowned. "Are you sure? Who's our man?"

"That cannot be revealed. Just do your job, and I will do mine," said the voice — *Click* — and hung up.

On the way back to his truck, Rainwater noticed a cardboard sign on the side of the road. It read:

NO CASINOS HERE

He stared at it briefly, then brought up a leg and kicked it flat. Then he picked it up and hurled it into the Target parking lot. He looked around for more, and sure enough, another sign was set up over toward the highway:

DON'T GAMBLE WITH OUR FUTURE

He trudged along the fence line, smashed it flat as well. Then he found two more just around the corner:

CASINOS ARE BAD BUSINESS

GAMBLING IS IMMORAL

He ripped them to pieces. "Fuck you. Fuck you all . . . "

There was a trash bin near his parking place. He dropped the mobile phone inside, climbed into his truck, and drove away.

59

IN THE SECOND WEEK of November, Wednesday was Mary Ann's day off. The weatherman predicted sparkling sunshine and unusually warm temperatures before the fog and chill of real autumn settled in, and Wagstaff's first thought on waking up was to go prospecting. Mary Ann, on the other hand, wanted to speed around Upper Bar Lake and catch some rays. Guided by mutual affection, they compromised on prospecting Water Cannon Creek, which flowed into the lake.

Wagstaff's pontoon-equipped suction dredge was torn down and lying in pieces outside the *County Courier* office, awaiting routine maintenance. While Wagstaff put it back together, Mary Ann drove home and changed into her sporting clothes. When she returned, he was still working. It took them the rest of the morning to get everything organized. But finally, huffing and puffing, they mounted the restored rig on its little trailer, hooked that to the FJ Cruiser, gathered up their gear, and set off south on Copper King Road, stopping at the Terra Linda Market in Tarvolo for sandwiches and beer. There, as Mary Ann half expected, the proprietor recognized her.

"Well, hello there, Miss. Under that drab uniform there's a woman, I see."

"Hello, Mr. Hoggins. We found out who got into your store."

"Hanged him, did you? Locked him up and threw away the key at least."

"No such luck. He has left the area. We've got bulletins and warrants out, but he might be over the border."

"Too bad. I was hoping I'd get to stone the sod."

"Don't want to be a vigilante, sir."

"I guess not. Look at me — amazing how crime brings out the worst in people, don't you think?"

She nodded politely.

"Let's bring back the stocks in the town square," he said in a not entirely self-mocking tone. "I'll start the petition."

"That might work with enough votes."

Wagstaff paid for their picnic. They waved goodbye, hopped back into the FJ Cruiser, and drove on to the Dwight Parker Memorial Launch

Facility on the north arm of the lake. Mary Ann had seen it from a distance on her trips to the Cruz ranch. Now she was down on the shore, hip deep in water that still held a surprising store of summer heat. Wagstaff was backing the four-by-four down the launch ramp. She held up her hand to halt him when the little trailer was completely submerged and the mining rig was tugging at its tie down straps.

With minimal fussing, grumbling, and cursing, they stowed their gear and food aboard and wrestled the mining rig free of the trailer. Mary Ann was loathe to leave her service weapon behind, so she bagged it up and wedged it in with the beer. Wagstaff handed her a canoe paddle, picked one up for himself, and climbed onto the starboard pontoon. She took his hand and wriggled up onto the port side.

"Here we go. The creek is across the lake beyond that point of land."

The sun was bright, the day was calm, and the lake surface was flat. They dipped their paddles and propelled the little catamaran through the water with ease. In less than half an hour they were in sight of a canyon leading back into the northeastern hills with a wide body of water flowing out. In another few minutes they were well up the stream. The noise of high-powered watercraft faded away. Now, as the canyon narrowed up, they could hear the chatter of jays in the oaks and brambles along the shore. At last Wagstaff called a halt and dropped the anchor overboard, giving it a sharp tug to make sure it would hold fast.

"This looks good. It's shallow enough, we're on the inside of a bend, lots of gravel on the creek bed. Dredge first, or lunch?"

"Dredge, I guess. I don't see anything like a beach," said Mary Ann.

So dredge they did. Wagstaff fired up his little Honda pump, lowered himself into the water, and began sucking up mud, sand, and gravel. When the sluice box was full, Mary Ann held the rig in place while he switched to washing it down. Within five minutes they had uncovered half a dozen tiny gold specks.

"Not quite a 'eureka' moment, I guess, but not bad, not bad," Wagstaff mused as he picked out the flakes and deposited them in a little plastic vial.

They towed the rig twenty yards upstream, re-anchored, and went through the same procedure all over again. This time Mary Ann handled the nozzle, directing it around the rocks on the streambed according to Wagstaff's detailed instructions. Fifteen minutes later they had another dozen flakes.

"This is work. How do we know we're not raking in fool's gold?" she puffed.

"Pyrites will float away when we sluice. Gold is much heavier."

"Ahh."

They towed the rig another twenty yards upstream, revealing a previously hidden grassy area on the farther shore. They dredged and sluiced again, found three more flakes.

"Okay, I'm ready for some food," said Mary Ann, pointing at the grass. "That looks like our spot."

They removed their supplies from the built-in cooler on the rig, waded across the stream, spread a checkered tablecloth on the grass, and arranged a modestly elegant picnic for themselves.

"We're rich," said Wagstaff, cracking open a beer and leaning back.

"We are?" asked Mary Ann, doing the same.

"Not the gold — this." He waved his beer toward the placid water, the rocks, the dry hillsides, the oaks, the deep blue sky.

"Amen," murmured Mary Ann.

After sandwiches, more beer, and a shared bunch of grapes, they were ready to tackle the river again. But they didn't.

Instead, supported by an outstretched arm, Wagstaff ducked his head and planted a kiss in the small of Mary Ann's back. She swiveled around, yanked his arm, dumping him on the tablecloth. She rolled over on top. They gazed at each other in happy appreciation for a few seconds. Then he reached up and undid her hair clip. Fair locks fell around both their faces as she bent forward to kiss him.

They held each other closely for a while, kissing and nuzzling. Then he pulled at her bra. She hunched her shoulders, and he lifted it over her head. He rolled her off, tugging at her shorts. She lifted her butt and wiggled them down around her ankles. He tossed them across the grass. She removed his T-shirt, undid his belt, pushed his pants down. He slid a hand between her thighs. She responded by throwing a leg over his hip.

Much later, sweaty and spent, they sat up and looked around. The sun was moving west. Long shadows were reaching into the canyon. It took them a while to gather up the remains of the picnic and their clothes, stuff everything back into the mining rig, and launch themselves back toward civilization.

Out on the lake the ski boats were still roaring around. Wagstaff was paddling hard while Mary Ann lay sprawled out on the other pontoon, face up, hands behind her head, topless, humming to herself.

"What if someone sees us?" asked Wagstaff.

"What do I care? I am a brazen hussy."

"You're also a cop, remember?"

"I suppose. But right now I just feel lighter than air. An officer of fairyland or something."

"If you don't pick up a paddle, it will be dark before we reach the marina."

"Then my shame will be concealed, so there."

But she sat up, grasped the other paddle and dug in. They were nearing a heavily wooded point of land when she noticed a shadowy form in the ripples made by the pontoon. She lifted her paddle from the water and stared down at her visitor. He pointed two fingers at his eyes, then swiveled them around this way and that.

"Yes, I see you, you see me. What's up?"

"Come on, Mary Ann, help me steer," called Wagstaff, trying to keep their little craft aimed toward home.

"I am," she said, feeling flustered. "But my secret pal just turned up in the water."

"You're kidding."

"Nope."

The visitor put his hands to his head, mimicking alarm. Then he was gone, swirled away in their wake.

"Something's up."

"What?"

"No idea."

Mary Ann looked around. The lake was calm, and the other boats were far away. Then she spotted a big jet ski heading toward them at high speed. It flashed by within twenty yards, kicking up a huge wake that rocked their little craft.

"Whoa, dude!"

"What a jerk!"

Mary Ann dropped her paddle. They had to circle around to retrieve it. She almost fell overboard in the process, but managed to get her fingers on the handle and drag it back.

"Here it comes again!" she yelled before they had gone fifty yards.

"Let's get closer to shore, M." said Wagstaff, looking over his shoulder at the jet ski bearing down.

"Shouldn't we be wearing life jackets?" asked Mary Ann.

"Yeah, they're in the pontoon. Under your seat."

This time the jet ski sped by within ten feet, soaking them both with its wake, and spinning the mining rig sideways.

"Jesus Christ!"

As it roared off into the distance Mary Ann shifted her position, tore the Styrofoam lid off the built-in locker. She pushed aside the picnic remains and got her hands on a pair of life jackets. She threw one to Wagstaff and was buckling on her own when the jet ski roared down upon them again.

"Watch out!"

Wagstaff paddled desperately to shift direction, but the mining rig was a clumsy boat, and it had just started to turn when the jet ski sideswiped Mary Ann's pontoon.

Wham!

Chips of Styrofoam exploded in every direction. Sheets of water blew into the air. The impact threw both of them ass over teakettle into the lake.

Mary Ann bobbed to the surface, saw Wagstaff's life jacket floating by, and swam over to grab it. The man himself was nowhere in sight.

"Tom!"

She got no response.

"Tom! Hey, Tom!"

Bits of Styrofoam were floating all around her. She batted them out of her way. With her eyes just inches above the surface, she couldn't see very far across the lake. She could still hear the jet ski, though, racing away, the roar of its engine already faint and getting fainter.

"Tom! Where are you?"

"Yo, M, over here."

His voice came from the far side of the still intact starboard pontoon. She swam around the stern and there he was, clinging to the thing with both hands. She handed him the life jacket.

"Here, put this on."

He loosened his grip and got one arm in, then the other. He looked a little dazed.

"Turn this way," she ordered. She threaded the jacket ties through their buckles and snugged them down. "There. You're good."

"We can't stay in the water very long. It doesn't feel cold, but it will sap our strength," he said, his mind clearing. "Help me right this thing."

She looked at the rig, slowly becoming aware that their boat had capsized. The center section of the shattered pontoon was still attached to the cross members, which were twisted at a sharp angle. The pump and sluice box were upside down in the water.

They hauled themselves up on the good hull and leaned over to grab the cross members. Then together they shifted their weight backwards, lifting for all they were worth. Very slowly the rig tilted upward. They were grunting and groaning. Suddenly it flipped over and splashed down right side up, dropping them back into the lake.

Mary Ann swam away and returned with the paddles.

The rig was listing to port, and riding the ruined pontoon was out of the question, so they both clambered aboard the starboard one. Their combined weight pushed it down to the waterline.

They dipped their paddles on one side and then the other to hold course for the marina, a long slow slog away.

"Did you see the guy?" asked Mary Ann.

"No, did you?"

"No. He had a hat on, an orange baseball cap I think. What color was the jet ski?"

"Yellow over white. Big, powerful. Looked like a Sea-Doo."

"Maybe we can track it down."

"Still the cop."

"Damn right, mister."

When they arrived at the launch ramp in the marina they were exhausted. Wagstaff backed the FJ Cruiser down to the water, submerging the trailer. Mary Ann guided the battered remains of the mining rig over the frame and tied it down. Wagstaff hauled it up into the parking lot and got out to survey the damage.

The port pontoon was missing both bow and stern. The forward section had been severed by the collision, and the wrenching twist in the water had separated the rear. Unnoticed while they were still on the lake, the starboard pontoon showed a long ugly crack. The steel cross members were bent and bowed. Oily water was draining from the pump engine.

"Ai yi yi. It might as well be a total . . . like your car," he lamented.

"I'm so sorry. Unless you just published some scandal you haven't told me about, I'm sure this was meant for me." She put her arm around his waist and hugged.

"We should probably have a look at the jet ski docks. Maybe we'll find paint scratches on one of the rentals," he suggested.

"The hell with it. I can't do everything. I'll write it up and —"

Over by the marina's general store some movement caught her eye. A man in a DayGlo orange baseball cap was loping along the docks toward the parking lot.

"Hey, look!"

The man jogged across the asphalt and slowed to a walk upon reaching a fancy pickup truck. A second man was leaning against a heavily chromed up motorcycle parked nearby. Mary Ann thought she could see them exchange a greeting.

"What?" Tom was still occupied with the mining rig.

"There, see? What do you think? Our guy?"

Tom squinted. "He should have been gone an hour ago."

"Maybe not. Maybe he doesn't think we could ever make an ID and doesn't give a damn."

The motorcycle and the pickup truck started rolling and exited the parking lot in close order drill. A dark Chrysler 300 they hadn't noticed before fell into line, making a procession of three.

"Let's get after them!" cried Mary Ann. She ran to the rear of the FJ, and rummaged through the partially smashed locker on the port pontoon.

"What are you doing?"

"Looking for my gun. It was in the cooler with the beer. Shit, it's gone!"

"But, hey, the good news is, we're still here."

"You don't understand. Policemen don't lose their weapons. That should never happen. Ever." A cauldron of anger boiled up and overflowed. "Son of a bitch. Fuck!"

"Nice talk."

She ignored him and unhooked the safety chain from the trailer. She lifted the coupler, pushed backwards, and let the hitch tilt down onto the pavement.

"Mary Ann —"

"We need to drive fast. Screw the trailer."

He looked at her as if eyeing a stranger. "Are you nuts?"

She was running for the passenger door. "Come on, come on!"

He got behind the wheel and started the engine. "Look, we don't know if these cars have anything to do with us."

She laughed grimly. "No, but we're going to find out. It's called investigating!"

They drove out of the parking lot and up the access drive. The trio of vehicles ahead of them were coming to the intersection with Copper King Road. The motorcycle turned left, heading south. The car and truck turned right.

"Okay, sleuth. They're splitting. What do you want to do?"

She scowled. "I'm thinking."

"Let's have it. Here comes the stop sign."

"All right, I bet the motorcycle is heading for Cruz' ranch. We know what that means. The others, I don't know what they're up to. Follow them!"

They turned right, heading for Tarvolo. While they were still a quarter of a mile away, they saw both vehicles slow and turn into the resort town's main entrance. By the time they arrived, their targets had already passed through, and the gate had already closed again. Wagstaff drove right up the metal bars to see if that would trigger the barrier to reopen. It did not.

"Damn. Locked out. I don't see an intercom, do you?"

"No."

"Ever been here before?"

"Not inside the compound."

"Me neither. Shit, Wade's car has the clicker. Back up."

Wagstaff backed away from the gate.

"Park over there."

"Yes ma'am." He maneuvered the FJ into a position well away from the gate, but facing it.

"Now we wait."

Five minutes went by before another car approached. Mary Ann was frantic. Then the local mail truck came slowly down the road and turned in. Magically, the gate swung wide. The mail truck drove on through.

"Go! Go! Gun it!" she demanded, pounding the dashboard.

"Take it easy. Don't yell." He punched the accelerator and the FJ shot up between the gateposts. The gate itself had already started to close, but it stopped moving instantly. After bouncing on its hinges for a few seconds, it decided to be polite and cautiously reopened.

"Ha! We're in!" whooped Mary Ann.

Wagstaff guided the FJ across the boundary and onto private turf. A few yards beyond the gate the drive ended in a T-junction.

"Which way?"

"Doesn't matter, we'll circle around."

"Always turn right in a maze," said Wagstaff.

"What? Is that how it works?"

"Geometry class."

They drove along a broad avenue edged with granite curbing and decorated every few yards with newly-planted trees. Six-bedroom houses with ridiculous rooftops sprouting dormers, gables, turrets, and huge chimneys were set back on either side behind walls and fences. The unifying style theme seemed to be grandiose contemporary, with vast windows fronting two-story atriums, and plain beige stucco walls attempting, but failing, to suggest modest good taste.

"See anything?"

"Not yet. Keep going. Slowwwwly."

At the north end of the street they came to another intersection.

"Uh-oh. This place is bigger than I thought," moaned Mary Ann.

They took the right-hand street, and motored slowly along. Some of the houses they passed had blue aluminum roofs, like ski chalets, instead of the preferred Spanish tiles. Otherwise they seemed to be much the same.

They were heading back toward the exit when Mary Ann grabbed Wagstaff's arm.

"Pull over."

He did so. Mary Ann jumped out of the car and walked fifty feet to a driveway leading back toward the largest house they had yet observed. A veritable McMansion. She waved to Wagstaff, climbed over a low fence, and marched purposefully down the drive toward a charcoal-colored Honda Ridgeline pickup truck parked behind a green Range Rover.

"No no, M, what are you doing?" muttered Wagstaff.

She looked in the driver's window, then walked back to the rear bumper, kneeled down, and put her hand around the exhaust pipe.

Then she returned to the FJ.

"Still warm. Been driven recently. I think that's our truck."

"Who lives here?"

"The address is 5591 Summerview Place. We'll find out. Let's move on."

They continued their tour, always turning right at intersections. Presently they came upon another palatial residence whose driveway was host to several late model luxury cars and SUVs. Among them was a dark red Chrysler 300.

Again Mary Ann left the FJ, climbed a gate for access, and checked the temperature of the 300's exhaust pipe. It was still warm. She checked the others — all cool.

"That's our boy. He's got friends, look at all those cars."

"I thought the 300 we saw was, like, dark grey."

"Looks are deceiving. We were a long way away back there."

"Are you sure it was red?"

"No. But eyewitness accounts are always unreliable."

"They teach you that in cop school?"

"Yes they do."

As they were watching and questioning each other's perceptions, another vehicle joined the rest. A black and white Ford Explorer of the Golden Hills Tri-Town Police Department. It parked, and none other than Chief Ibañez emerged. He casually looked around and entered the house by the side door.

"Did you see that?" Mary Ann's eye were popping.

"The chief?"

"Shit, who lives here?" She hopped out of the FJ again, walked across the street to the mailbox, looking for a name. Nothing there. She threw up her hands for Wagstaff's benefit, opened up her not-so-smartphone for a photo, and discovered to her dismay that it was waterlogged.

Back in the FJ she threw the phone on the floor mat. "Damn thing got fried in the lake. And I can't quite read the plaque beside the door — 2335 something, Hollin-something."

Wagstaff picked up the phone to double check Mary Ann's diagnosis. "Hollinsworth," he said.

"Who's he?" She wasn't sure if she had ever heard the name.

"Gordon Hollinsworth, Esquire. He's the Tri-Town attorney. Thick as thieves with the mayor and that guy Rainwater. Cruz too, probably. I heard he arranged Cruz' citizenship with Congress."

"Now that you mention it, I think I met him at Bobby's service."

"Can we go now?"

They drove back to the Upper Bar Lake marina and hitched up the trailer. While Wagstaff dropped the coupler over the ball and attached the safety chain, Mary Ann was muttering to herself, "DZH 513, OPD914, DZH513, OPD914, DZH513, OPD914 . . . "

"Have you lost your mind? What are you mumbling?"

"Hail Marys."

"Huh?"

"License numbers on those cars. I didn't bring my notebook." Her eyes went blank. "Damn, you threw me off. OPD, ODP? 5-what? Or was it 9-something? 13 or 14? Arrrrgh."

On the way back to Applefield silence prevailed. They were both worn out.

"Where's your car?" asked Wagstaff when they arrived in town.

"At the station. Keep things discreet, right?"

"Better that way."

He drove to the station and parked.

"Here you are, M. I'm beat. Talk to you tomorrow." He gestured toward the door without looking at her.

She brushed his cheek with a light kiss and stumbled onto the pavement. The FJ backed up and moved off toward the *Courier* offices. She waved goodbye.

"Now what did I do wrong?"

60

"RAIN TODAY in the Tri-Town Area and on Route 49. Snow expected above 7,000 feet. First big storm of the season, folks. The Carson Pass over the Sierra remains open, but if you're traveling east on Route 88, be sure to carry chains, and expect delays while the plows do their work. Stay tuned to 1610 for further developments."

Mary Ann finished her gloomy weather report in a gloomy mood. She put away her microphone and closed the radio control program on her PC. When she looked up, Officers Gawley and Moss were standing silently in front of her desk. They looked inquisitive. They looked embarrassed.

"What?" she inquired.

"Morning, Mary Ann."

"What's the matter — bad forecast?"

The two older cops looked at each other.

"You ask her," said Gawley.

"Ask me what?"

Moss fidgeted with his hat. "Mary Ann . . . are you a witch?"

"Oh my God. You guys."

"Well — ?"

She realized they weren't just teasing her. "No, I am not a witch," she said sharply, irritated by her blossoming reputation. "I have no special powers of any kind. I'm just a rookie cop. There, you heard it from me."

"We understand you can see ghosts too. Is that right?" said Gawley.

"Good God, it's that bastard down in Placerville." She smacked a fist down. "Here's the straight scoop. I won a prize in the lottery, okay? Enough to pay off my car — lucky me. That senile old bastard who sold me the ticket misunderstood something I said and put up a poster claiming I was a ghost-watching witch."

They didn't seem convinced; the gossip was just too good.

"It's all over town, Mary Ann," said Gawley, as if no further proof were needed.

"Lemme say it again— *ot-nay oo-tray*. Got it?"

The two of them just stood there.

She waved her arms in frustration. "Believe what you want. You'll never catch me speeding on my broomstick, Wade, 'cause it can outrun your stupid Crown Vic."

At that moment Chief Ibañez entered the station. He took in the standoff, seemed to understand its context, and barked at them all. "What are you all hanging around for? Aren't you two guys supposed to be out there keeping our streets safe?"

"On my way, sir," said Gawley.

Moss nodded, donned his hat, and bowed out too.

When the coast was clear Mary Ann stopped messing with the papers all over her desk and looked up at her boss, who was pouring himself a cup of coffee.

"Thanks for the rescue, Chief."

"Don't mention it. My advice — don't get into your weird shit with anyone. It doesn't help." He gave her an uncharacteristic smile. "Unless, of course, you happen to solve the Kennedy assassination once and for all."

"Understood." She resumed her paperwork, shuffling bills while she thought about how to proceed. Then she looked up again.

"Uh, Chief. Question: what were you doing out at Mr. Hollinsworth's house yesterday afternoon?"

He snapped around to face her, spilling coffee. "You were in Tarvolo?"

"Tom and I were out on Upper Bar Lake and got run over by a jet ski. We followed cars to Tarvolo. One of them parked at Hollinsworth's."

"Who?"

"Don't know. The car was a Chrysler 300."

"Doesn't ring a bell. Did you check the registration?"

"I didn't have my notebook, and I didn't memorize it properly. I tried several of the letters and numbers in various combinations. As far as I can tell, it belongs to a car dealership down in Ione. Victor J. Redstone LLC, doing business as Red's Hot Wheels."

"Hmm. Probably sold recently. DMV hasn't updated yet."

"So, what were you doing there . . . ?" she asked again.

"You are one nosy cop, Sarzo."

"Maybe I am. But, um, we're talking about you."

"I was investigating the Rainwater & Russell mess, if you must know."

"How so?"

"I don't owe you an account of my doings, Miss Busybody."

"No, of course not."

"But I can see you're worried. All that talk about drug money floating around."

"Yes sir, that's it."

"Well . . ." He sat down on the chair by her desk. "You might be right about Gardner not being such a great detective. He's not getting anywhere. Maybe he's just loafing, or maybe . . ." He let the thought hang.

"Or maybe you're just trying to put me off the scent."

"That would be clever of me, I'll grant you. But think — Moss has an alimony problem. He barely gets by. Gawley's got a hefty mortgage. Maybe he's underwater. And who knows about our respected town attorney, Mr. Gordon Hollinsworth? He's a smooth old guy, rolling in dough, and God knows he's not getting rich working for the local government."

"Yeah . . . ?"

"So which is it? Which one of us is up to no good, if anyone?"

"Someone who can influence the investigation," she said.

"Then don't forget our mayor. She knows everyone in the county. She's got her own axe to grind, she thinks the world of Señor Cruz. And, in case you're wondering, Vera has insisted that I put our resources to work on this, even though the sheriff has jurisdiction. Influence? She could be in that category. I could be in that category. So could poor little you."

Mary Ann slumped in defeat. "You're right." She stood up, cracked a wan smile. "You know what? I hate driving around in that damned Jeep. Time to buy a car."

61

IT WAS DRIZZLING when Mary Ann left the station. Her first thought was the knotty problem of transportation. She needed a ride down to Red's Hot Wheels. She sat in the Cherokee to stay dry and punched a number on her mobile phone.

"*County Courier*, Wagstaff here."

"Hi, it's me."

"Oh, hi, M. I was going to call you."

"I need a favor. My insurance check came through, I'm off to buy a car, and I need a ride again. Can do?"

"Oh man. I'm really busy. Classes, the paper, I can't."

"No?" She felt her ego deflating like yesterday's party balloon.

"Really sorry."

She thought back to the end of their day on the lake together, the chill that developed. She should have paid more attention.

"I understand."

"Good. That's good."

"Look, Tom. I'll be glad to help pay to replace your rig. That was no accident we were in. I was the target, I'm sure. Bremer or someone wants me to cease and desist."

"No, no. Don't even think about it. I'm a big boy. I'll take care of it."

That mysterious chill was still in the air.

"If that's how you feel," she said.

There was a long silence.

"Tom?"

"Ah, what the hell. Give me ten. Where are you?"

"At the station."

"I'll pick you up."

▼

They arrived at Red's Hot Wheels down in Ione after a silent trip. The rain had stopped.

"Here we are. Go get 'em."

She nodded, exited the FJ, and walked through the cars on display, hoping something would grab her attention. But nothing did.

Smelling a sale, Del was already out of his office under a precautionary umbrella, ready to spring. "Well, hello, young lady. Still the cop, I see. How's that Mustang treating you?"

"It burned up."

Del scratched his head apologetically. "I believe I might have heard something about that. Nice car. What a shame." He grinned. "But we've got a lot of nice cars. What's your pleasure? Over here, a Mazda 3, almost new, zoom-zoom, your kind of wheels, am I right?"

She looked it over and shook her head. "I know it's supposed to be sporty, but it looks so ordinary." She cast her eye around the lot. "I was thinking more along the lines of a Chrysler 300."

"Really. A young woman like you."

"No accounting for taste, right?"

"Well, can't help you, I'm afraid. We did have a very sharp 300 on the lot, but I sold it last week."

Her eyes narrowed. "My bad luck. Was it red?"

"Not plain old red — Deep Cherry Red Crystal Pearl."

"Unh-huh. Remember who bought it?"

Del furrowed his brow. "Someone in the sheriff's department, I think he said. Gardner, I believe."

"Okay, thanks, that helps. How much did it cost him?"

"Thirty, minus the trade."

Mary Ann whistled.

Del's shoulders sagged. "Listen, if you're thinking about buying that 300 from the current owner, I'd say don't. Either he won't sell, or he'll see you coming and nick you on the price. We'll have more 300s. They show up now and then." He cocked an eye at Mary Ann's uniform. "Are you actually looking for a car or is this some kind of police investigation?"

"Oh, I need a car. But the truth is, thirty is way out of my price range. What else have you got?"

Del perked back up. "Come this way and have a look at my Subaru Forester. It's a 2010, in real good condition. Four wheel drive, you will never get stuck when the weather hits. And," he confided, lifting his umbrella for emphasis, "from what I understand, it's about to hit."

She gave it a once-over.

"Want to drive it?"

"Too practical. I'll feel like a school teacher in that thing. Anyway, I'm not on the ski patrol anymore."

"Unh-huh. Not too ordinary, not too practical." He thought for a moment. "Well, you turned me down before, but I've still got a little Mini Cooper on the lot. Oh-five, first gen, but solid, all the bugs worked out. I'd give you a warranty."

"Where is it? What color?"

"That little blue and white job over beside your friend there." Indeed, Wagstaff was out of his FJ and inspecting the Mini on his own. Mary Ann walked over.

"What do you think?" she asked.

Wagstaff shrugged. "Not bad. It's blue. It's got racing stripes. On our roads it will out-corner that old Mustang. Better gas mileage too."

"I like it, but that makes me nervous."

Wagstaff looked at her fondly. "It's you, Mary Ann. You all over."

Del stood by with a fatherly smile on his face. "Ninety-six hundred."

She touched the moonroof, peered into the front seat. She glanced at Wagstaff, then looked Del right in the eye. "Is that the best you can do?"

Del's smile widened. "I've seen this movie before. What are we talking about?"

"Nine even."

"Cash?"

"That will take a couple of days. Debit card."

"Done. But As-Is. At that price I can't offer the warranty."

"Screw the warranty."

"Then let's write her up."

Del led the way back across the lot to his office, a happy salesman humming a little tune. On the way they squeezed between a Dodge Caliber and an older Toyota pickup truck. Something about the truck stirred Mary Ann's memory. She stopped to look it over.

"Excuse me, hang on a sec," said Mary Ann.

Del turned around.

"This truck. Where did you get it?"

Del walked back to the pickup. "Well now, funny story. Last week the guy who bought your Chrysler 300 traded a clean Honda Ridgeline to seal the deal. And not twenty-four hours later another Joe drove up in this truck and traded for the Ridgeline. Native fellow."

"Rainwater."

"Why, that's the name. Friend of yours?"

"No, everyone up in Applefield has heard of him. Hilltop Band."

Del arched an eyebrow. "Oh-ho. What did he do?"

"Nothing that I know of. I'm just curious."

It took almost an hour, but Mary Ann's debit card went through, papers were signed, and she had the keys to a little blue rocket ship. She jingled them together to show Wagstaff, who was sitting patiently at a vacant desk, working with his laptop on Del's company Wi-Fi. He stood up, closed the computer.

They stepped outside. It was drizzling again. Wagstaff pulled the hood of his jacket over his head.

"Thanks for the ride," she said, leaning close and stretching for a kiss. Wagstaff rubbed her uptilted nose.

"Mary Ann. Can I talk to you?"

The tone, cool and deliberate. She knew what was coming.

"What's wrong?"

"Nothing. It's just that . . ." He hesitated, looking for the right words. ". . . you're a cop."

"So what?"

"You're adventurous, fearless it seems, tough, and uh, very aggressive."

"And I see ghosts and I'm a witch, is that it?"

"Hey, this has nothing to do with how weird you are. You're smart too, so you know that."

"Okay. What is it?"

"It's me. I'm not much for adventure. I'm not fearless or tough or aggressive. I'm a woodworker, a teacher, a would-be journalist. I'm happiest sitting at a desk running markup software in my cozy office."

"I know that. It doesn't matter."

"Yes it does. Your way of living scares the shit out of me."

She was about to protest further, but a thought struck her. The ghost! Alive now, dead tomorrow. The idea had never occurred to her before — her nameless visitor could easily be Tom. He knew her as well as anyone, knew all her hopes and fears. In spite of everything, she knew he felt affection. And damn, his association with her might have put him in grave danger. Her face went pale.

"Too bad," she managed.

"You going to be okay?" he asked.

She nodded bleakly. "I'm tough, remember?"

"Right. I'll be on my way."

He gave her a little peck on the cheek, ruffled her hair, and drove away, leaving her standing under the wet used car banners.

On her way back up the hill she turned on the windshield wipers and put her new machine to the test, plunging into the corners, flying through the straight stretches.

"I love this car!" She shouted.

Part SEVEN

62

NEXT MORNING Mary Ann was fighting traffic on Applefield's Main Street when she spotted Chief Ibañez rolling toward her in his big Explorer. As they came together she shot out an arm and flagged him down.

"Your new wheels, Sarzo?"

"Yes sir."

"Cute."

"Thanks. Listen to this — Chrysler 300, Deep cherry something, very expensive, just like the one I trailed from the lake, sold to Gardner. Then Rainwater shows up the next day and buys the fancy truck he traded in."

"Sounds like you bought this little item at the same dealership."

"Yes, I did."

"What do you make of all this?"

"Money. Money and dots and connections." She was proud of her sleuthing, but Ibañez barely nodded. Traffic was piling up behind them.

"Wade tells me you dropped your weapon in the lake. True?"

"Arrrgh, I shouldn't have said anything."

"You should be ashamed of yourself."

"I am." She could feel her ears burning.

"I don't know about you, but like a lot of cops, I'm superstitious about that sort of thing. Get yourself equipped, okay?"

She bobbed her head. "Already on it, sir."

Horns started honking. Ibañez waved the irritated tourists to silence and pulled away.

Mary Ann drove to the Miners Market and parked in the lot, even as she had intended before encountering the chief. She was on a mission. Inside she worked her way along the wall to the sporting goods section, where she pawed through the water toys until she found a cheap snorkel, a pair of swim fins, and goggles. At the end of the season they were all on sale for peanuts.

Twenty minutes later she was at Upper Bar Lake's Parker Launch Facility, renting a fifteen foot long aluminum boat at the marina. It had a high seat for fishing, and a tiny Mercury trawling motor clamped to the transom. She inspected the thing doubtfully.

"I don't see an anchor."

"Cement-filled paint can there in the bow. That'll hold it while you fish," said the rental operator.

"I'm not fishing."

"Or you can tie her up."

"What about a life preserver?"

"Under the seat."

"And how do I start this thing?"

"Small as it is, it's all electric. Press *start*."

"Oh. Thanks."

She was already dressed in what passed for swimwear. Sports bra and shorts, since she still didn't own an actual swim suit. Plus, to stay warm, she had purchased a neoprene water skier's jacket off the rack in the marina's general store. She threw her gear into the boat and climbed aboard.

"What's the weather going to do?" she asked, checking the puffy clouds visible in every direction.

"Gonna clear, they say. Hot this afternoon, then cold tonight. Frost on the pumpkins. You planning on taking a swim?"

"Got to. I'm a cop, and I lost my gun over the side last trip out."

"Going to be chilly," warned the man.

"Yeah, but I've got to find the thing. Call it superstition — my chief's, anyway. Cops aren't supposed to lose their weapons."

"Good luck. Better wear that." He pointed at her ski jacket.

She nodded and wrestled herself into the sticky neoprene. Then she put on her life vest and yanked the ties tight, just in case.

The rental operator stuck out a foot and shoved the little vessel away from the dock. She pressed *start*, heard the engine rev up, and after fumbling with the twist grip on the tiller, turned the boat and drove slowly out across the lake.

When she rounded the point of land where the jet ski had staged its attack she headed in toward shore, being careful not to ground the little outboard motor's prop. Pretty soon she could see what she was looking for — stray bits of white Styrofoam lapping against the brown gravel embankment. She continued on for a while and then cut the motor. A chunk of Styrofoam three feet long was beached on a little bar running out from the main shoreline. She glided in, felt the hull crunch onto the sand, and stepped out, pulling the anchor with her.

"So here we are. Found you." She dropped the anchor on the bar and picked up the Styrofoam. It had only been in the water a few days, and already it was filthy with oil and muck. She gazed back along the shore, trying to orient herself.

"There's that point we were heading for. I remember those trees. Gotta be close." She was talking to herself again.

She sealed her car keys in a plastic bag and stuffed them into a side pocket on her shorts. Then she discarded her life jacket, donned her swim fins, pulled the goggles over her head, adjusted the snorkel, and clomped into the water. As the lake reached her hips she shuddered and groaned. After the recent storm, the temperature was down. Cold work awaited.

She swam out into the lake until she could see the bottom falling away. She remembered the jet ski collision. They were close to the north shore when it happened, but she never touched bottom when she was thrown overboard. She forced herself to remain calm while breathing through the snorkel and patrolled slowly westward. Her view through the goggles was remarkably clear, if tinted blue, and nothing connected with the attack was visible. After a few minutes she pulled her head out of the water and pushed the goggles up onto her forehead in order to reacquire landmarks. Her little aluminum boat was fifty yards away.

While she was treading water she heard a sound wafting across the lake. She stiffened, shook the water out of her ears, and listened intently. A motorboat somewhere. One of few, she guessed, since the lake had seemed almost empty while she was driving across it. She adjusted her goggles, gripped the snorkel between her teeth, and resumed her patrol, moving back toward the boat. After a few strokes she splashed up into a water-treading posture and listened again. That sound. Was it louder? Without a doubt. She had heard it even while partially submerged. She pulled off her goggles and twirled frantically this way and that, trying to catch a glimpse. Uh-oh, over there, further west, coming her way, a jet ski.

"Jesus."

She headed for shore, arms flailing, fins kicking up a wake. Then she stopped, suddenly wary of attracting attention. She faced the lake instead and backpaddled, gently pulling herself into the shallows. Her feet touched bottom, then her butt.

The jet ski was yellow and white, and it motored by at a sedate pace a couple of hundred yards offshore, apparently attracted to the little aluminum rental boat. Then the driver throttled up, and the jet ski circled back to the west. Mary Ann stood up in the waist-deep water to watch it go. She was shivering.

Once the jet ski was out of sight she resumed her underwater patrol, swimming slowly back eastward. Her body heat had warmed the water under her neoprene jacket, and she was starting to get comfortable. Suddenly something winked at her from the lakebed. Partially embedded in bottom mud was an unopened bottle of beer. The bottle cap sparkled in sunlight filtered through seven or eight feet of water. She made an exclamation, causing a huge bubble to erupt from her mouth. It dislodged the snorkel. She pulled up, coughing and spluttering.

"Gahh. Pfluhh."

She shook out the snorkel tube, jammed it back in her mouth, blew out the remaining water, and submerged again. A few feet farther along she spotted another beer, and nearby a shiny opener. Taking in a big breath, she attempted to dive for a closer look, but stalled out less than two feet down. She kicked back up, blew more water out of the snorkel, took another deep breath and tried again. On her second attempt she kicked and paddled furiously, but was unable to propel herself any deeper. She felt like a balloon. She rose to the surface to think it over.

"What's wrong with me?"

Then it hit her. She might as well *be* a balloon. On the third try she took several deep breaths, then exhaled completely and kicked hard for the bottom. Without a chestful of air to buoy her up, she made it. Six, seven, eight feet deep. Her eardrums threatened to burst under the pressure. She touched the beer bottle, then pushed past it, hauling herself along the lake bed with her hands.

Ten feet away a partially open plastic bag was sticking up out of the ooze. Inside it the grip of a handgun was visible. With her lungs about to explode she reached out and grabbed it. Then, holding tight with both hands, she shot to the surface, gasping for air. She extracted the gun from the plastic bag. It was covered with mud and slimy bits of underwater plant growth, but it was definitely her Beretta, safely back in her possession. She ripped off her goggles and snorkel.

"Hah!"

Her triumphant cackle quickly turned into a coughing fit. When she calmed down she could hear the roar of a jet ski approaching again.

"Whoops."

She got her goggles back on, reseated the snorkel, and sank down, keeping her eyes just far enough above the surface to watch the little yellow watercraft pull right up and beach itself beside her rental boat, not a hundred feet away. The driver dismounted. He was wearing rubber boots and a DayGlo orange cap and was cradling a hunting rifle. He gave the boat a quick once over, then hiked up the exposed embankment to the high water mark and disappeared into the trees beyond.

Mary Ann was terrified. So she waited, half-paralyzed, timidly moving her hands and feet in slow arcs to hold her position.

Ten minutes later the driver reappeared. Mary Ann sank back underwater. He looked around, obviously hoping to spot the owner of the little boat. But he failed to notice Mary Ann's snorkel or her goggled eyes watching him from just under the surface. Apparently satisfied that nothing serious was amiss, he skidded down the embankment, pushed the jet ski back into the water, climbed aboard, and drove away up the lake and out of sight.

Mary Ann paddled into the shallows. When her feet touched, she pulled off her fins, dug in her toes, and worked her way up and out of the water. Her teeth were chattering. She was shivering uncontrollably. She dipped her Beretta back into the lake and shook it to clean off the goo. She attempted to open the chamber and discovered that her hands had no strength. She could hardly feel them anyway, so she sat down on the warm gravel and waited for the sun to warm her up and dry her out.

She was falling asleep when she picked up the sound of a powerful engine thrumming steadily not far away. She jerked upright and scanned the lake. What now? Just a ski boat cruising by, a quarter of a mile offshore. But the jolt was enough to get her juices flowing again.

Mary Ann couldn't decide if the jet ski driver was Billy Rainwater or not. But she wanted to know what the man was doing here, whoever he was. She hiked back to the rental boat in a speculative mood. She was starting to doubt that the attack on Wagstaff's mining rig had been specifically directed at her, but was instead part of a general effort to keep people away from the area.

She dropped her swim gear into the boat and flexed her fingers experimentally. The feeling was coming back, so she put on her shoes. She was able to tie the laces, so she worked the action of her gun and chambered a wet round. She wondered if the damn thing would fire if she pulled the trigger and hoped she wouldn't have to find out.

Thus equipped, Mary Ann climbed the embankment. Not far along the grassy overhang she found what looked like a well-worn path into the woods. She shoved the Beretta under her waistband and stepped in among the trees.

The path wound away through a dense stand of oaks and manzanita bushes. She ducked under the low branches and hopped over the tree roots, keeping her eyes on a patch of bright sunlight ahead, intermittently visible through the sparse fall foliage.

After a hundred feet or so the woods opened onto a wide field.

"Holy crap," she said.

Filling the sun-drenched area was a mature crop of opium poppies. Here and there a late blossom still clung to a plant, but for the most part all she could see were drying bulbs on slender stalks — poppy straw. She pulled her gun out of her pants and held it at the ready. She was no longer cold, but she was shivering again.

"And, damn, no camera."

She remained motionless for several seconds while she eyeballed the territory. The field tilted gently uphill away from the lake. A couple of acres, probably. Bigger than the other field she had stumbled upon for sure. The far side was hemmed in by another stand of oaks and underbrush. She strained to figure out if she was seeing a wooden platform tucked in among the higher branches of one of the trees over there. An observation post, maybe, apparently unmanned.

When she was pretty sure she had the field to herself she dashed into the crop and yanked one of the plants out of the ground.

Then she ran for the lake.

Ten minutes later she was heading for the marina at full throttle. Churning out all nine-point-nine horsepower, the little Mercury outboard managed to push her along at fifteen miles an hour. She hoped that was fast enough.

Mary Ann reached the dock without incident, and the operator chained the boat up. She gathered her gear, trudged across the parking lot to her car, and traded it all for an armful of police attire. Then she marched back toward the launch facility's restrooms.

On her way she observed a jet ski entering the marina. Sure enough, it was yellow. The driver wore a DayGlo orange cap. He slowed, puttered along near the rental craft, and stood to peer over the dock and into the parking lot beyond, checking the place out. Mary Ann continued walking, keeping an eye peeled while the jet ski floated the length of the harbor. She opened the restroom door just as the driver finally hit the throttle and roared away.

Mary Ann breathed a sigh of relief and closed the door firmly behind her. She was halfway into her work garb when her ethereal visitor loomed into focus in the mirror. As always when he made his appearances, her heart skipped a beat.

"Ahh! Hello there, thanks for scaring me again. What do you want?"

The ghostly shadow made a series of baffling gestures. She snorted.

"You've got to do better than that. I can't understand this little charade."

He tried again. Hands and fingers flipping and dipping.

"No idea what you're talking about. This is ridiculous."

More gestures, animated, almost frantic. She finished dressing.

"Whatever." She brandished her Beretta. "Hey look, I found my gun, aren't you proud of me?"

The ghost put his hands to the sides of his head and rocked back and forth in mock despair.

"That's your opinion, big guy. I think I scored."

The ghost vanished.

63

GUN OIL and gun rags and gun parts were strewn all over Mary Ann's desk when Wade Gawley burst into the station. She stopped wiping out the barrel of her little pistol and looked up to see what was goosing him. "Wade?"

He craned his neck to survey the whole station, then quickstepped over to the chief's office door and peered through the glass window.

"Seen the chief?"

"Not in the last half-hour. What's up?"

"Where's Rick?"

"I don't know. Patrolling, I guess. What's wrong?"

Gawley came to a deliberate stop and spread his arms.

"Bremer is dead."

"Say again?"

"Your guy Bremer. Down and out."

"Where? How?" Little hairs rose up on Mary Ann's forearms.

"Come on, I copied the scene location."

They piled into Gawley's Crown Vic and drove out of town at high speed. Gawley made it down to Red Hill Road in no time and turned north. A few miles later they were descending into the Whiskeyjack River canyon.

"Should be right along here above the river," he said.

They rounded a corner, and he hit the brakes. A fireman in a yellow-green vest was standing in the middle of the road. He held up a *STOP* sign.

"What's the problem?" asked Gawley.

"Got a little brush fire. It's under control, but our guys are all over the road. Be aware. Drive slow."

"Wilco."

They eased on down the grade to the Tri-Town Volunteer Fire Department's big pumper truck. Men in fire hats and the same yellow-green vests were staggering up the hillside hauling sections of rigid intake pipe. Others were rolling limp attack hose onto reels on the side of the truck.

Gawley parked. They got out and peered down over the safety rail into the canyon. Near the water a bent-up motorcycle was lying in a swath of blackened grass. The fire was out.

Other service vehicles were parked higgledy-piggledy up and down the road for a hundred yards. Maddening emergency lights were strobing on every machine.

Chief Ibañez and Officer Moss were standing near an ambulance, where a blanketed form was lashed to a gurney behind the tail lift. Gawley and Mary Ann joined them.

"That Bremer?" asked Gawley.

"There are burns." The chief indicated the shrouded figure. "We don't have an official identification yet, but we ran the plates on the bike down in the slot there. It's his."

"He ran off the road?" asked Mary Ann. She was confused.

"Eventually."

"What do you mean?" she persisted.

Moss pulled back the blanket covering the body. It was blackened, hair frazzled. He pointed to an indentation on the left temple.

Ibañez held up the victim's little Nazi helmet. There was a ding on the left side.

"What do you think, Chief?" asked Gawley.

Ibañez turned to Mary Ann. "This is your guy, what do *you* think, Miss Law & Order?"

Mary Ann rocked back on her heels. "Are there skid marks?"

"Just a spot on the rail." The chief pointed back up the hill.

"Okay, then, this guy — Bremer presumably — was riding along on his bike when somebody overtook him, rolled down a window or something, and shot him in the head." She paused for a thought to form. "Only he had his helmet on, so the bullet didn't penetrate. Instead it knocked him silly, and he ran off the road."

"Is that right, boys?" asked the chief.

They both nodded.

"And what does this mean?"

Gawley shrugged. Mary Ann looked blank.

"Murder. Small caliber weapon," said Moss.

"Yes," said the chief. "Murder, not an accident."

"The same gun that killed Bobby!" exclaimed Mary Ann with a shudder.

"Can't be sure about that," cautioned Gawley.

"No, Wade, but it's a plausible idea," mused the chief.

"So, what's the deal? Are we giving this to the sheriff to screw up another case?" Moss failed to keep the bitterness out of his voice.

"Have to, Rick. And speak of our local devil . . . "

Deputy Sheriff Gardner was walking down the hill toward them. He paused to view the twisted and burned motorcycle, then continued on to the ambulance.

"Victim deceased?" he asked.

Moss pointed at the gurney. Gardner strolled over, looked carefully at the burned corpse, and whistled.

"He's cooked. ID?"

"Not yet, Terry. But we think it's that guy Dale Bremer."

"The dude we arrested for Mike Russell's murder?"

"Looks that way."

"Rough justice, I guess, huh? He would have been a lot better off back in the can. Tell that to Judge Avery O-Fucking Parnell."

▼

When the excitement wound down, Chief Ibañez returned to his office. He was joined there by Gardner, starting his investigation with a few questions for the Golden Hills Tri-Town police chief.

"So who found the body, anyway?"

"Ricky Moss. He was out on patrol and came upon the fire. He called the local FD. It wasn't until they had the blaze under control that he realized there was a death involved."

"I heard the word 'murder' used at the scene. What I saw leads me to believe we're looking at a bad accident. Man moving a little too fast, skidding out of control, knocked out on impact, dies in the fire caused by his motorcycle in the dry grass."

"Is that how you're going to file this?" asked Ibañez in disbelief.

"What else could it be?"

"You saw his helmet, the depressed fracture on the skull."

"He took a real bad fall. Lots of rocks and gravel on that hillside."

"Show that helmet to your forensics guy. He'll tell you that the paint chip and the pointed dent are the result of gunfire. If he doesn't, then I'll retire."

Gardner moved to a chair and sat himself down. He massaged his temples with his hands. "Of course, it's possible. And if it's true, it wasn't some random thing. It was a hit."

"What was Bremer up to, aside from intimidating one of my cops? That would tell us a lot."

"Any photos I should have?"

Ibañez rose from his desk and stuck his head out into the station. "Mary Ann?"

She was just reassembling her Beretta. "Sir?"

"Did you get any photos of the Bremer scene?"

She appeared in the office doorway. "Yes, a few. I made copies." She held up a flash drive. Ibañez pointed to Gardner, and Mary Ann handed it over.

"Good work, Sarzo," said Gardner.

"What I don't understand, Terry, is why we're having a full-scale crime wave up here in the foothills," grumbled Ibañez. "That's why I left the Big City war zone, for Christ's sake. Peace and quiet in my old age."

"Now, Chief, this isn't much of a wave. Just the modern world leaking into the backwater we live in. Murder — it's du jour, it's the fashion these days."

"Do either one of you have the faintest idea why this crime was committed?" asked Mary Ann, letting some irritation show.

They looked at each other, looked at her. "Not really," sighed Gardner, "to tell you the truth."

"I didn't think so. And, as a target myself, it would be nice to know." She returned to her desk.

Gardner smiled. "Your new girl? She's something, Chief."

"You're telling me," agreed Ibañez with a weary nod.

Gardner put on his hat and excused himself.

"I'll be in touch. So long, Sarzo."

When he was gone Mary Ann reappeared in Ibañez' office. She held up her Beretta and demonstrated its readiness by dropping the clip out, reinserting it, pulling the slide to load a round.

"There. See? My gun, I got it back. Good as new."

"Don't shoot, I believe you. Where was it?"

"Bottom of the lake."

"And you found it underwater, in the mud?" He seemed genuinely impressed. He leaned forward, studying her.

"Just offshore," she said, withering under his gaze. What was going through his mind? She couldn't decide if he was flattering her, testing her, or marking her doom. She had planned to keep her poppy find a secret lest the field get plowed under before she could prove a thing. But the chief's reaction might tell her something. After weighing the problem for what seemed like an eternity she decided to take a chance and added, "that's not all I found."

She placed the opium plant, now stuffed into a plastic evidence bag, on his desk.

"Oh no, we've been through this already," he protested.

"Notice the size of the seed bulb."

"All right, tell me your story."

She did. The diving operation, the jet ski on patrol, the cultivated field.

"On Upper Bar Lake, you say. Where exactly?" Ibañez was becoming uneasy.

"North shore. I was checking maps, and it looks like Hilltop Band property. I know they own some of the lakefront."

"Photos?"

"My cell is dead. And anyway, I was spooked."

"So, another dot." Ibañez scowled. "You've collected quite a few."

"Yes sir."

"What does your supernatural partner think?"

"Nothing about the poppy field. I got lucky, if you look at it that way."

"Hmm."

She couldn't read his reaction, so she tried another tack.

"Want to hear my latest theory?"

Ibañez braced himself. "You and your theories . . . "

"I think Bremer did the dirty work for Cruz. And I think they killed him because coming after me brought the cartel unwanted attention."

His brows knitted into an angry frown. "It's possible. Is this you or your ghost talking?"

"Me. My ghost can't talk, remember?"

Ibañez abruptly stood up from his desk and began to pace.

"There's another possibility," he countered. "He worked for Cruz, and our favorite citizen was afraid the man would spill some beans while pleading to a murder charge. Now both their worries are over."

"You know, I thought Bremer was the Cruz enforcer. So who killed Bremer?" The unknowns of the case filled Mary Ann with mortal anxiety.

"No idea."

"Whoever it was, he's out there." She said, biting her lip.

"And that worries you."

She nodded. He picked up his hat.

"You should be worried. You know a lot of things, Sarzo, but in this business, take it from me, you never know enough."

He slapped his hat on the desk for emphasis and jammed it down on his head. "Cover the office."

He grabbed the bagged-up poppy, brushed by her, and strode to the station door.

"Where are you going?" she bleated.

"None of your business."

"Wait. Might get calls. The rest of us might want to get in touch. I might want to know if anyone is planning to murder me." She envisioned crosshairs already centering on her forehead.

He paused, waved the poppy at her. "I'm going to annoy Señor Cruz."

With that he was gone.

She stood in the office door for a while, musing over the chief's erratic behavior, noticed and commented upon by all members of his tiny force. She wanted to give him the benefit of any doubt, but she couldn't help it, paranoia was creeping into her heart.

She shrugged it off and returned to her desk and the pile of unfinished administrative crap that consumed most of her working hours on a daily basis. She paid the department's electric bill, the gasoline bill, the vehicle maintenance bill. She paid the petty cash credit card and Gawley's and Moss' expense reports. She filed the daily traffic citations. She forwarded notice of the moving violations to the Superior Court in accordance with the California Vehicle Code, so points could be recorded and insurance premiums increased for the lawbreakers nabbed by her colleagues. She filled in the mayor's weekly report form with a summary of the department's latest efforts. For an hour she managed to distract herself with these everyday tasks, but suspicions were bubbling. Finally they erupted, and she couldn't look at any more paperwork.

She pushed the forms and bills aside. She stood up. She rapped her fingers on her desk while she considered the situation. Then she marched into Chief Ibañez' empty office.

"So what do we have here?" she said to herself. She was looking for evidence of corruption, hoping not to find any, fearful that she would.

To start, she toured the office. It was sparsely furnished. A black umbrella was hanging from the coat tree, along with a pair of old nickel-plated handcuffs. A souvenir of some sort, she guessed.

A small frame on the wall displayed a scratched and tarnished badge from the Big City on a velvet background. Beside it was a photo of a couple of dozen policemen grouped into a graduation pose. Police Academy? She couldn't pick out the younger chief from all the others.

A third frame contained a scrap of yellowing newspaper torn from a larger story. The terse headline read, *Multiple Slayings (continued from page 3)*. Below it was a grainy photo of a pretty young woman and a few lines of text ending with the sentence, *Officer Ibañez is credited with the arrest*. There was no date. More souvenirs.

An upright gun cabinet in the corner contained a Remington shotgun with a nicely checkered walnut stock. An old skeet slinger was tucked in beside it.

She opened the credenza behind the chief's desk and was mildly surprised to discover a partially consumed bottle of Herradura reposado tequila there, along with a couple of shot glasses.

"Uh-oh, what's next, porno magazines?"

She turned to the desk itself. On the blotter was a scattering of letters, notes, and papers. She scanned them without much interest, but one attracted her attention, a note from Mayor Teasdale. It was brief:

> *As you know, police security is an issue at Salvador Cruz' ranch, where valuable property is exposed. Please discuss this matter with Cruz personally at your early convenience. Sincerely, etc.*

Innocent bureaucratic correspondence or coded message? Hmm . . .

Under the fluorescent desk lamp, where a family photo might be expected, was a metal calendar instead, with the months and days made out of little magnets. The chief had doodled the magnets into a crudely shaped face.

Mary Ann opened the top desk drawer. A small hardbound book was lying there: *Ghastly, Ghostly & Grim*. She lifted it. Several of the pages had turned-down corners.

"You've been studying, I see," she noted.

Underneath, amid pens and pencils, was a small statuette. Her eyes narrowed. Slowly her hand moved out, gripped the thing, and brought it up for inspection. It was a ceramic figurine in a black top hat and tails, about four inches tall. The face was skeletal, with the same black spots for eyes and the same rictus grin found on the female calavera she used, with occasional success, to summon her visitor. There was a hole in the top of the hat. She turned it over and sprinkled powder into her palm. She tasted it.

"Cinnamon . . . "

She turned the figurine this way and that. Funny how the left arm was extended to the side, the hand slightly cupped. A momentary chill formed between her shoulder blades and rippled through her body.

"What in the world . . ." she breathed.

She carried the statuette back to her desk and placed it beside her own little calavera. She nudged the figurines toward each other. When they clinked together she noticed that the left arm of the top-hatted gent fitted nicely around the waist of the smaller girl. They made a pair. The costumes, the flowers, the skeletal grins; suddenly she understood — they were grotesque wedding cake toppers.

"Good God," she exclaimed.

She hurried back into the chief's office, sat down in his chair, and opened the desk drawers, one after another, pawing through notebooks, files, and scraps of paper. In the third drawer on the right, behind an older model digital camera, she found a loose collection of paper receipts and ticket stubs. The receipts were for various small credit card purchases. The ticket stubs were from the California Lottery.

"So, you're a player too, are you?"

She thumbed through them. Some had sets of numbers, apparently the winners, penciled in over the chief's own wrong choices.

"You could use some of my ghost's help, I guess, huh?"

She looked through the pile and paused on one of the Fantasy Five stubs. The winning combination scribbled over the printed selection was the sequence: *6, 21, 29, 12, 35*.

"Ahhh . . . "

Her heart started pounding. Something funny here. It took a second, but then she recognized the sequence as her own set of winners. She checked the date to be sure — it matched.

"Holy crap."

She felt numb all over. The penciled numbers weren't proof of anything, but they were suggestive. Supporting evidence. Dots. She jumped to her feet, propelled by a crazy thought. It was so crazy she almost giggled.

"You — Chief Hector Ibañez — you are my ghost!"

She bounced out of the office, grabbed a calavera in each hand, and started for the women's restroom. Then she stopped.

"Oh no."

If Ibañez was the ghost, did that mean he was destined to die? Maybe, maybe not, she reasoned. Who knew how it all worked? Maybe the ghost came back a long way from a very distant future. Or maybe time meant nothing in the afterlife.

"We'll find out," she decided, and opened the restroom door.

Once inside she gripped the calaveras tightly and called out, "Hey, ghost! I need to talk to you. Calling Mr. ghost, come in ghost. Let's go, don't be shy . . . "

A tiny distortion in her reflection surged outward, a shadowy form emerged from the blur, and her visitor was glaring at her.

"Well, hello. Thanks for showing up."

The ghost made no motion. The quivering image just stared. She gritted her teeth.

"Good to see you too. Okay, um, listen up here, big question coming — are you — is your name — Hector Ibañez?"

The ghost shrugged.

"Yes or no? This is important."

The ghost splayed his hands in a neutral gesture.

"Well that's just great. Who, then? I've got to know."

Again the ghost made gestures of ambiguity, uncertainty, unhelpfulness.

"Don't tell me you don't know, because that is just bullshit."

The ghost's head wobbled from side to side to demonstrate unhappy ignorance.

Mary Ann sighed. "Then let's move on to more immediate worries, and

I've got plenty. Who killed Bremer? Who might still be after me?"

The ghostly image roiled and boiled. It wavered, steadied, disappeared, reappeared, blurred, sharpened, flickered wildly. Mary Ann squinted. She could hardly bear to look at the phantasmagoric display.

"Come on — who?"

The ghost pointed at Mary Ann, wiggled his fingers across the mirror in a walking motion.

"Yeah, move, do something. What? Who? Me or you?"

The ghost pointed at her with both hands and faded away.

"God damn it. Come back here," she commanded. But the ghost, whoever and wherever he was, paid no heed.

Mary Ann exited the restroom in an anxious mood. She placed Ibañez' top-hatted calavera back in the chief's desk drawer and tidied up the mess she had made.

On the way back to her own desk she became aware of the station's police scanner squawking feebly in little spurts. Puzzled, she crossed over to have a closer look. Somebody had turned the squelch way up, and almost nothing was coming through. She backed it off and heard what she thought was Gawley's voice.

"*Brrrpp* . . . need a wrecker . . . *squrrzt* . . . Copper King . . . *krrkk* . . . police vehicle down . . . Lake . . . *sssssss* . . . "

"What the hell — ?"

She was immediately on full alert. She picked up her desk phone and punched a contact number. No answer; leave a message. She tried a different number from the same list. Ricky Moss answered on the first ring.

"Rick, I just heard some static on the scanner. Sounded like Wade's in trouble. What do you know?"

"Where?" he asked.

"Not sure, Copper King Road, maybe. He's not answering."

"I'm hell and gone down at Spencer's Corners. Call the chief."

Mary Ann ended the call and punched in the chief's number. She let it ring several times, then got dumped into his voicemail service.

"Where are you, sir? I think Wade's got a problem. Call me."

But just as she put her phone down, it rang.

"Mary Ann?" It was Gawley.

"Wade, you okay? What's your twenty?"

"Copper King where it meets the lake, on that first sharp rise."

"I've been there. What's the problem? What's wrong with your radio?"

"Intersquad is always bad south of Tarvolo. You better get out here. Call Rick. Both of you, all hands on deck." His voice became garbled. She could hear him talking to someone on the scene, directing action away from the phone.

"Wade?"

But he had hung up.

She called Moss again. He was ready to roll. "Wade's not usually dramatic. Better go see what's biting his ass. Maybe that Crown Vic blew a gasket."

Mary Ann backed the squelch all the way off the scanner, but no voices again interrupted the grating hiss of the airways.

She weighed the situation. If she took off, the department would be unmanned. If she stayed, some unknown disaster might befall. Gawley had sounded strangely agitated, however, so she picked up her keys, set the station alarm, locked the door behind her, and hopped into the department's old Cherokee.

Mary Ann flipped on her emergency lights and sped south out of Applefield on Copper King Road, past the radio station and on through Tarvolo. Twilight was upon the land when she crested the lonely rise where Upper Bar Lake first came into view. Flares were sputtering all over the road. She jammed on her brakes. Gawley's Crown Vic was parked halfway across the highway there, red and blue emergency lights flashing. Gardner's patrol car was nearby, also strobing. A heavy-duty wrecker meant to haul big trucks was sitting behind them, and like the other response vehicles, its hazard lights were blinking. The scene pulsed like a corner of Las Vegas.

Mary Ann abandoned the Cherokee and hurried between the police cars, looking for Gawley. A siren whoop from behind made her jump. A boxy ambulance, with even more flashing lights, wanted to inch by her. She stepped to the edge of the traveled way to let it pass.

Gawley and Gardner were standing by the guardrail above the lake, peering down the steep hillside. Mary Ann joined them.

"What's going on, guys?"

Gawley pointed toward the lake. A long steel cable ran down from the wrecker to the operator who was standing below on the shore, lashing hooks around the undercarriage of a black and white SUV that was partially submerged.

Mary Ann gasped. "Ours?"

Gawley nodded.

"What happened?"

"Have a look —" said Gardner, with a gesture toward a green Range Rover sitting a few yards away. The left front fender was caved in, hood rumpled, headlight glass shattered. A puddle of fluids was still spreading underneath the engine compartment.

"Is there . . . ?"

". . . a body down there? Yes," said Gardner.

"Did anyone try to get him out?"

"Of course."

She looked at Gardner and noticed for the first time that his clothes were soaked.

"What stopped you?" she wanted every detail.

Gardner was irritated, and he was cold. He waved his arms in frustration. "The door was either locked or the water pressure held it shut, I don't really know."

"Who got here first?"

"Our alpaca rancher, Señor Cruz. That's his car."

"I recognize the car. Where's the man?"

"He made a statement to me and to Officer Gawley, and someone from his ranch drove up and took him home. He called in the accident when it happened, and that's how I turned up. So, to summarize, when I attempted to open the door of your vehicle there, it had probably been under water for twenty minutes or more. Understand what that means?"

Mary Ann nodded miserably.

They turned their attention to the SUV. The wrecker's engine was laboring, the winch was winding, and the Golden Hills Tri-Town Police Department's almost new Ford Explorer was slowly emerging from the lake, tail first. Once it was clear the winch stopped. A couple of emergency medical technicians descended the slope with an aluminum stretcher. One of them used the butt of a Maglite to shatter the driver's side window. He reached in and opened the door. A deluge of water cascaded out. Tugging and grunting, he and his partner pulled a beefy man out from under a deflated airbag. They laid him out on the stretcher and proceeded to check for breathing, for body temperature, for dilating pupils.

Once they were sure of themselves, the senior EMT looked up at his little audience and made a thumbs-down sign. He and his partner slipped a black bag over the figure, now officially deceased, zipped it shut and lashed it to the stretcher. They packed rocks under the rear wheels of the Explorer to make sure it wasn't going back into the lake, unfastened the cable, and hooked it to the stretcher instead. The wrecker operator threw a lever on his truck and hauled away. The stretcher skidded up the slope and bumped against the battered guardrail. The winch stopped.

Mary Ann climbed the barrier and bent down over the black bag.

"Hey, Mary Ann, you don't want to do that . . ." cautioned Gawley.

She ignored him and unzipped the bag. Lying there was Chief Ibañez, skin pale and waterlogged. There was a small bruise on his cheekbone. She placed the back of a hand against his forehead. He was already cool to the touch.

"Good God, it's him," came a voice. Mary Ann turned around. Officer Moss had finally arrived. She grimly re-zipped the bag.

"Yo, Rick, what do you say we get a lot of photos?"

He nodded, retreated to his patrol car, and came back with a digital camera. Gawley did the same. They methodically toured the entire scene, shooting everything in sight.

▼

Hours later the three local police officers were huddled in their station. Mayor Teasdale had arrived to comfort and instruct them.

"We will overcome this tragedy. Chief Ibañez made this department what it is, and I know you'll carry on his strong tradition."

"Thank you, ma'am," said Moss.

"Who is senior now? I don't even know," asked the mayor.

Gawley and Moss looked at each other.

"I guess I am," said Gawley, "by about three weeks."

"Is that right, Officer Moss?" She wanted to be sure.

"Yes, ma'am," Moss confirmed.

"All right, then, Wade, you're in charge. For now. We'll start a job search, and I have to say it will be my purpose to bring in another veteran officer to run the department, but meantime, do your best. All of you, for the good of the Golden Hills, do your best."

When she was gone they poured themselves strong cups of coffee and grouped themselves around Mary Ann's computer screen. They were going over all the photos they had taken for the third time.

"Look at this one. How the Range Rover is aimed. It's backward." said Mary Ann. Her instincts told her something was wrong, but she wasn't sure what.

"Yeah? Cruz was going south toward his ranch, and the car winds up facing north, so what?" Gawley objected. "That's what happens in a collision, things wind up like tails on a birthday donkey."

Mary Ann pointed at the road. "But, Wade, where are the skid marks? If the chief's ride got spun around, you'd expect to see rubber."

Moss shook his head. "Maybe, maybe not. I've tidied up a lot of car accidents, and the forensics don't always add up."

Mary Ann clicked to the next image, a shot of the interior of the Range Rover, taking in the driver's position and controls.

"Okay, what about the airbags?"

"What about them?"

"Ours inflated, but the Range Rover's did not, as you can clearly see. Don't you think that's damned odd?" she asked.

"Again, accidents are odd by nature. I don't see the problem," said Gawley.

Mary Ann sighed. Maybe she was spinning the facts because, sentimental as it seemed, she wanted to exonerate her overbearing boss.

"I didn't get to interview Señor Cruz, but you did. So, was he hurt at all?"

Gawley thought back. "Not really. No cuts. He seemed a little dazed, though."

"And the cause of the accident?"

"The Explorer was on the wrong side of the road."

Mary Ann pursed her lips. "Think about it, guys. Does that sound like our chief?"

She clicked, and another image popped up: Gawley and Gardner inspecting the beat-up Explorer after the wrecker had it in tow.

"So who got there first, Wade? You or Terry?"

"He beat me to it. I heard a report, but when I arrived Gardner had already made his rescue attempt. So we called in the response teams."

Moss was getting restless. "What's the point, Mary Ann?"

"What if this wasn't an accident? Cruz is up to no good. What if the chief had evidence on him and wound up like Bremer?"

Gawley chuckled. "And here I thought you hated the guy for pounding on your case all day long."

"Fair enough, but murder?"

Moss was more thoughtful. "I agree with you about Cruz. But this accident isn't going to bring him down."

Gawley stood up and issued his first tentative orders as acting chief: "How about I take the first patrol, then Rick, you next, and then our rookie here?"

They murmured assent, and the meeting broke up. Long after Officers Gawley and Moss had departed, Mary Ann was still going through the photos, examining each one over and over again.

64

LORRAINE WAGSTAFF was emerging from the Miners Market when she saw the front page of the *Sacramento Bee*. Just above the fold was a small story that stopped her in her tracks. As soon as she reached her shop in Ragtown she called Mary Ann.

"Have you seen the morning paper?" she inquired.

"Nope, should I?"

"Oh my yes. Get down here, espresso waiting."

There were no customers in the Book Nook when Mary Ann arrived. She wandered through the empty store and found Lorraine in her office. Her motherly friend was perusing the latest edition of her son's weekly newspaper.

"Here, read this. Down in the capital it's a sidebar, but up here, look, big headlines." She shoved the *Courier* into Mary Ann's hands and rose to make coffee.

Mary Ann sank into a chair and read the headline aloud:

POLICE CHIEF DIES IN
DRUG-INDUCED CRASH

She stared at the words. Then she poked around on Lorraine's desk, liberated the day's *Bee* from the pile of odds and ends there, and read its version of the same story:

> The Amador County medical examiner has disclosed a shocking scandal in the Golden Hills special district, where Police Chief Hector Ibañez recently died in a tragic automobile accident that plunged his vehicle into Upper Bar Lake. Autopsy has revealed the presence of heroin breakdown products in Ibañez' bloodstream. The cause of the fatal accident appears to be the result of impairment under the influence. Now the local police force is left with the task of explaining how a sworn officer of the law was himself in the addictive grip of an illegal substance.

Lorraine returned with a double espresso. Mary Ann looked up at her, a fierce glint in her eyes.

"Lorraine — *I — don't — believe it.*"

Lorraine resumed her seat and rested her elbows on her desk. "It explains a lot, kiddo, you've got to admit."

"What do you mean?"

"Why the investigation of all these killings has failed. Bad cop gets in the way, makes sure it all goes south."

"What a load!" Mary Ann was furious. "We aren't even investigating. Not officially, anyway."

"What does Tom say about this?" asked Lorraine. "Apart from the printed story, I mean."

"No idea." Mary Ann fidgeted with her coffee cup. "We haven't spoken."

Lorraine gave her a searching look over the rim of her glasses. "So I gathered. What's the problem?"

"Him — not me."

Lorraine nodded. "Remember the women's rule of thumb — if it's got tires or testicles, you're going to have trouble with it."

She dialed a number on her telephone.

"Hello, Tom? It's your mother. I've got someone here in the store who wants more info on the Ibañez accident you wrote about."

She handed the phone across the desk. Mary Ann flinched, took it, and clapped her hand over the mouthpiece.

"Lorraine! You are a terrible woman!" she hissed. Then she sat up straight, composed herself, and spoke.

"Hi, Tom . . . "

"M? That you? How are you?"

"Good, I'm good." She was bobbing her head around like a schoolgirl. Lorraine smiled.

"Glad to hear it. What's up?"

"Um, business. I'm checking into Chief Ibañez' accident. What's the detail on this heroin claim?"

"There's an official report from the coroner. They autopsied and discovered heroin. Or, at least, the results of heroin."

"How do they know it's not pain medication he was taking for something, like a toothache?"

"Sorry, M, I made a call down to Jackson. There was enough smack in there to anesthetize a horse. Basically an overdose. The doc wondered why that alone didn't kill the man."

Mary Ann's skin went cold. "Um, thanks, Tom. Big help."

"Sure. Take care."

"Unh-huh. You too." Mary Ann put the handset back in its cradle and stared out the office window toward the street.

"Hey, what's the verdict?" prompted Lorraine.

Mary Ann slowly refocused. "An hour before the accident I had a conversation with the chief. He was alert, spitting bullets, yelling at me. How he always was."

"Maybe the people who bought his services were paying him in product, and he didn't learn how to handle it."

"Never. There's not a shred of gossip about this heroin crap on the force either."

"Just a thought," shrugged Lorraine, looking to dodge a nasty dispute.

Mary Ann stood up and began counting on her fingers. "There was a twenty minute gap between the time of the accident and when the cops showed up — that's one. A head-on collision powerful enough to send the chief over a guardrail and into the drink barely bent that Range Rover's sheet metal — two. There were no skid marks — three. The airbags didn't fire — four. And now Tom tells me the chief was pumped too full of dope to stay awake, let alone drive a car — five!" She wiggled her outstretched fingers.

"So?" Lorraine was mystified.

"So, the whole thing could have been staged. Who says Cruz was alone out there?" She raised her hand to heaven. "This — this is a setup," she declared with finality.

"What are you going to do?"

"Little me? Miss Rookie of the Year?" She thought for a while, failed to reach a conclusion. "I don't know."

"You watch yourself, kiddo," warned Lorraine. "Four deaths in three months. It's an epidemic."

Mary Ann pushed her empty cup across the desk. "Thanks for the coffee." She squeezed Lorraine's hand. "And the call to Tom."

314

65

MARY ANN sat at her desk in an empty Golden Hills Tri-Town Police Department, plugged her microphone into her PC, opened up the audio control program, and clicked the mouse on a screen button.

"Tri-Town travel advisory for eleven AM. Snow above 6,000 feet accumulating in the higher elevations, turning to rain after noon. Exercise caution on all Amador County roads. Skies will clear after two PM, but expect to find plows working on 88 as you approach the Carson Pass. If this pattern holds, it looks like we'll be having a chilly Thanksgiving, folks. Stay warm, stay safe, and you'll have something to be thankful for. And, of course, stay tuned to 1610 for further updates."

She fed the traffic report into the local information radio station with another click of the mouse. Thanksgiving was still a week away, and she doubted she was going to be very thankful for much of anything.

She pushed her chair back and stood up. The scanner crackled briefly, so she bent an ear toward it, but no telltale police chatter followed. Not much crime, not many civil violations today.

"Let's go, Sarzo," she said aloud to motivate herself.

She walked across the station, let herself into the chief's office and opened the middle drawer on his desk. She reached down and wrapped her fingers around the little top-hatted calavera lying there. At her touch the head fell off.

"Oops . . . "

She lifted the damaged figurine out of the drawer to see what went wrong, and it shattered in her hand, raining ceramic chips and powdered cinnamon all over the floor.

"What the — ?"

She picked up the shards and examined the head. The top hat was still crowning the little skull with its black eyespots and monstrous grin. Then the hat fell off and rolled under the desk. She chased it around a chair leg and then, cringing with guilt, dropped all the pieces into the drawer and slammed it shut.

"So much for you."

She backtracked to her own desk, picked up the little female calavera sitting there and stood before the photo of the Headwall Mine in its glass-covered frame.

"Hello, ghost. You there?"

Her reflection blended with others from the station windows. No supernatural distortion disturbed the glass in any way. She held the little calavera above her head, imagining it as a radio transmitter that needed height for clear signals.

"Yo, ghost — this is the Golden Girl of the Golden Hills, calling her favorite visitor. Wondering about the weather? Got any requests?"

Nothing happened. So she marched into the women's restroom, stood before the mirror there, and tried again.

"Hey, ghost. Make yourself visible, will you? I need some help here."

The ghost failed to appear. She waited for a moment to give him a chance, then tightened her grip on the little calavera.

"All right, Mr. G. This is an emergency. Rookie cop needs expert help, how about it, partner?"

Still no reaction. She grasped the little figurine tighter still. Her fingertips were turning white.

"Ghost, I order you to appear before me, you no-good —"

Splink!

The calavera exploded into smithereens. Pieces flew everywhere. Mary Ann was shocked. She stared at herself in the mirror. Her face was white, her eyes wide. She brushed tiny bits of pottery and a dusting of powdered chocolate from her hair and blouse. Her hand, still clenched into a fist, hurt like hell. She opened her fingers. Blood was dripping where razor-sharp ceramic bits had cut into her palm.

"Holy crap."

▼

Wade Gawley arrived in the station just after the lunch hour.

"Your turn to tour the jungle, Sarzo. I'm supposed to review applications to become the new chief."

"We got any?" Mary Ann was amazed anyone would consider the job.

"Five so far. Those guys from the Valley, they think this is heaven on Earth up here."

"Yeah, don't we all," she said as she put on her jacket and headed for her Jeep.

She drove slowly along Main Street in Applefield trying to decide whether to arrest a few violators down near Spencer's Corners or have another chat with Lorraine.

She opted for Lorraine and was soon parked in Ragtown, picking her way through the best sellers and celebrity memoirs to the row of computers in the rear of the Book Nook. Lorraine was busy ringing up a stack of audio books for one of her infrequent customers. She waved to Mary Ann, who sat down, launched a web browser, and started cruising through the pages of Wraiths-Of-America-dot-com. When her sale was complete, Lorraine ambled over.

"What happened to you?" she asked, pointing to Mary Ann's hand, which was crudely swathed in overlapping band aids.

"Hazard of talking to ghosts, I guess. My little calavera relic shattered. I got cut."

"What's your visitor have to say for himself?"

"Nothing. Just when I really need some help, he's ignoring me. That's unusual, especially when I beg and plead and squeeze that thing real tight. But this time I squeezed too hard."

"So what do you need? First aid tips?"

"The last time I saw my pal, I was convinced it was Chief Ibañez. Coming back in time, like we read about. So I accused him directly. But you know, he wouldn't answer."

"You need to take a look at the *Spectral Identity* page," said Lorraine. She reached over Mary Ann's shoulder, clicked a few buttons and tabs on the computer screen, pointed a finger, and read aloud:

> Virtual visitors are often confused about their selfhood. The renowned ectoplasmic anthropologist, Dr. Ugo Damiano, explains this phenomenon as "supernatural surprise," the shock the recently deceased receive when they discover they have joined the ethereal plane and have become mere shadows of their former selves.

". . . mere shadows . . ." echoed Mary Ann wistfully.

"Hey, kiddo — I thought you hated Ibañez, the way he treated you." Mary Ann sniffled. "I did."

Suddenly, tears were flowing. She put her head down on the keyboard and sobbed convulsively, ambushed by previously submerged grief. This went on long enough to make Lorraine very uncomfortable.

"Mary Ann? Hey, there . . . "

Mary Ann raised her head, trying hard to swallow her anguish.

"You should talk to somebody," Lorraine advised.

"What's wrong with talking to you?"

"You know what I mean."

▼

Mary Ann drove her Mini slowly down through the Whiskeyjack River canyon. She was still miserable. In Placerville she turned up the hill to Saint Patrick's Catholic Church, parked, and hiked across the paved courtyard to the rectory. She was relieved to find Sister Bianca staffing the reception desk.

"Hello, sister . . . "

"Yes?" After a short pause Sister Bianca's face warmed in recognition. She took note of the grim mood and red eyes. "Officer Sarzo. You okay?"

"I'll live. Any chance Father Eisen is around here somewhere? I'd like to speak with him."

Sister Bianca frowned sympathetically. "My dear, I'm sorry. Father Eisen isn't with us anymore. He may be back, but not for months."

"What do you mean?"

"You haven't heard? It's in our newsletter. He's taken a posting in the Congo."

"The Congo," repeated Mary Ann, stunned by this development. "The Congo in Africa — ?"

"They're almost fifty percent Catholic over there, did you know that?"

"In the jungle? With diamond smugglers?"

"He'll be based in the capital. Kinshasa, I think it is. Yes, Kinshasa, that's what he said."

"Well then, that's that." Mary Ann looked around helplessly, flapped her arms in defeat.

Sister Bianca suddenly remembered a news item she had read. Her lips tightened. "Please accept my condolences on the loss of your police chief."

"Yeah, thanks. Tough few days."

Sister Bianca studied the young cop. "But . . . that doesn't seem to be the problem at the moment, does it?"

Mary Ann's thoughts were drifting. "No, actually, you're right. It's not."

"What, then?"

"Um, as you may remember, I see this ghost. Only not anymore. I was wondering how to get his attention again, and I need some advice."

"Whooo. I'm no help with that sort of thing, I'm sure. I doubt Father Eisen would know either."

"Probably not."

"I'm afraid you're on your own, my dear. That shouldn't be so bad — most of us are in the same boat."

"Alone in my boat . . ." Mary Ann tapped the reception desk and turned to go.

"I believe Father Eisen was inspired by you, if that helps."

"Huh?"

Sister Bianca touched her fingertips together. "I'm not sure how, shall we say, *devout* Father Eisen was. Modern man, you know? I shouldn't say this, but sometimes I wonder if he really believed in anything before you came along."

"Before I came along — ?"

"Your ghost, the lottery, all that. It made him reconsider everything."

Mary Ann managed a warped smile. "And look where he wound up."

66

MARY ANN got back in her Jeep and drove to her trailer in the Placerville Gardens RV Park & Resort. She thought she would change into civvies and call it a day, but when she saw the wall clock above her kitchen stove, she changed her mind. It was only three o'clock. Mid-afternoon. Even in November it wouldn't be dark for hours. She stood staring at the second hand circling the clock face. Suddenly she clapped her hands together.

"Wake up, Sarzo!"

A vague plan was taking shape in her head.

She threw open the door of her only closet and rummaged around until she dug up a ratty old polyester-filled winter parka and a pair of fleece gloves. She threw them on her sofa.

She filled a kettle with water and set it on the stove to boil. She dropped a paper filter into her coffee maker, filled it with Folger's best. She then pulled a little-used thermos bottle out of a cabinet and set it on the counter.

While waiting for the water to boil she ran out behind her trailer and picked up the small can of white gas sitting under her rusting Weber grill.

Back inside she plucked the plastic bag containing datura blossoms out of a kitchen drawer along with the bag of cat hair she cut from the roving tomcat and the bag holding one of her used tampons.

She poured the kettle of boiling water through the coffee filter. When the pot was full, she poured six cups of coffee into the thermos, adding a smidgen of non-fat milk.

She unlocked her tactical gun case, retrieved two extra clips for her Beretta, and loaded them up from a box of Winchester Ranger 127 grain rounds. Then, as an afterthought, she stuffed another dozen rounds into her jacket pocket.

She collected the parka, gloves, coffee, white gas, magical ingredients, and ammo in a well-worn backpack and returned to the Jeep. She was still in uniform.

▼

The Golden Hills Tri-Town Police Department was empty again when Mary Ann returned. Her first move was to check all the reflecting surfaces in the station for signs of a ghostly presence.

"Yo, Ghost," she said to the Headwall Mine photo.

"Little help here," she demanded of the shiny toaster.

"Where are you?" she asked the restroom mirror.

She got no answer. Everything was depressingly normal.

"On my own for sure," she sighed and braced herself. "So what?"

As she moved around the station she went over a mental list; necessary items for an expedition of entrapment. She had strong suspicions about Señor Cruz, but no proof, and was only certain about one thing — someone she already knew, one of two or three people, was in on the deaths associated with his phony operation. The question was, who? She thought she might know how to find out.

She rustled around in the kitchenette, found a leftover bagel. She shoved it into her backpack.

She plugged in her phone charger, connected the cheap mobile phone she bought after her good one sank in the lake, started topping off the battery.

She opened up the telephone white pages and scribbled down some numbers on a scrap of paper, which she shoved into a side pocket.

She opened all the lockers in the station, looking for a bulletproof vest. No such luck, but she did come up with a pair of bolt cutters and an old-fashioned five-cell Maglite big enough to double as a baton.

"Aha!"

She disconnected her phone, which now registered a respectable 70% charge, and headed for her Jeep, lugging her backpack in one hand and the bolt cutters in the other.

On the way out of town she stopped at the Miners Market. In the sporting goods section she browsed a locked glass counter containing several different optical devices. She wasn't sure what they were. The counterman strolled over.

"What are you looking for?"

"Night vision."

"For a rifle?"

"No, just seeing."

"I've got a few." He pointed. "ATN XT Nightvision goggles. Top of the line, new item, the best."

"How much?"

"Six hundred."

"Ooh, too steep. Anything else?"

"For the price-conscious shopper we do have this here Night Owl Nex Gen Nightscope. Hundred and fifty."

"I'll take it."

"Okay, but be aware, in total darkness you'll need the infrared spotlight. This button right here, see? When you turn it on, whatever you're hunting will see you."

Mary Ann gulped and nodded. "Thanks for the warning."

"Right, then, go bag a buck."

"Yeah, or something bigger."

▼

Mary Ann drove south out of Applefield on Copper King Road and slowed when she came to Chief Ibañez' crash site. The guardrail was still beat up. A year until CalTrans would get around to the repairs on such a rural road, she guessed. She continued on to the Parker Launch Facility on the north arm of Upper Bar Lake and parked in the marina lot.

The more she thought about her days-old bagel, the dryer it became in her mind, so she decided to stop at the marina's general store.

While she was browsing the candy aisle, a young woman flitted through her peripheral vision, sweeping the floor. Something familiar about her.

"Rosarita?"

The woman vanished through a door marked *Employees Only*. Mary Ann followed right after her into the room beyond.

"Rosarita Crespo, is that you?"

After a pause the door to a small closet creaked open, and the woman shyly emerged, hands clasped together, worry lines etching her forehead.

"The police lady," she said.

"That's me. What are you doing here? Where's your husband? He's a fugitive who missed his court dates, you know that, don't you? He knows it too, I bet."

"Miguel is not here."

"Obviously not. Where?"

"In . . . Mexicali. I don't have an address."

"And you're hiding out here. Turnbow fire you?"

"No, I feel too open in that big market, too many people, so I come here instead. And I am Rosarita Ortiz now."

"Maiden name? You got a divorce?"

"Maybe divorce, someday. If Miguel cannot return." She gave Mary Ann a sheepish shrug. "I just like Ortiz."

"You should talk to your husband, do the right thing."

"Miguel says to me he will come back to face justice when Señor Cruz goes away."

"Hmm. That . . . that could happen."

"Use your magic witch powers — make it happen."

"I told you, I don't do magic. I'm just a cop. But . . . I might have other powers. We'll see. Now sell me a couple of candy bars."

Back in the parking lot Mary Ann stuffed two Snickers bars into her backpack, hefted the bolt cutters, locked the Jeep, and set out for the rental dock. It was after five o'clock. The sun was already behind the low hills on the western horizon, and the rental operation was closed for the day.

She spotted the little aluminum fishing boat she had previously rented, but noticed with dismay that the gas tank was missing. Other boats in the lineup were in the same condition, apparently as a security measure.

She walked over to the rental hut. Beside it on a rack of shelves were a couple of dozen portable gas tanks, secured to the structure by chains threaded through their handles. She pushed and tugged until she found one that sloshed noisily, signaling plenty of fuel. She placed the blades of the bolt cutter over the chain, gripped the long arms, and pulled with all her might.

Snap!

The chain parted. The lower links rattled onto the asphalt.

"What do you know? Now I'm a lawbreaker too."

She pulled the tank off the rack and walked it back to the boats. After some consideration she selected a slightly larger craft than before, one with a much larger outboard motor. She nestled her backpack under the seat, got in, and attached the gas tank to the flexible fuel line. She squeezed the priming bulb multiple times, turned the tiller handle to switch on power, pressed the *start* button. The engine purred to life. Satisfied that her transportation was ready, she placed the bolt cutters around the chain fastening the boat to the dock. With a mighty squeeze the chain broke and the boat came free. She leaned forward and pushed hard on the nearest support pole. The boat slowly drifted out into the harbor. There she opened the throttle, pulled the tiller over, and curved smoothly away toward the open waters of the vast reservoir.

The lake surface was calm and grey under a grey sky. Not another craft of any kind was in sight. As she motored north her mind turned to thoughts of Chief Ibañez and his foul temper. It was hard to admit that he had taught her a thing or two about police work. But now he was gone, along with his ghost. No more on-the-job training. How would he want her to handle the situation? Follow established police procedures? Of course. Collect evidence? Sure, good luck with that. Listen for tips? Absolutely. And stay out of trouble. Or . . . maybe not. Maybe, at wit's end, try the crazy long shot she had in mind.

She consoled herself with the idea that his ego-shriveling outbursts concealed a hint of fatherly affection. And she had never thanked him. That made her sad, but her eyes stayed dry, because his death — a murder she was sure — also made her angry. Deeply angry. She was filled with anger, the cold kind that sharpens your senses, clears your head.

It was getting dark when she located the little sandbar near the poppy field. The fractured Styrofoam pontoon from Tom Wagstaff's suction dredge was still sitting there, a dirty white beacon in the half-light. She powered back the engine and aimed right for it. The boat beached itself and lurched to a halt with a wear-producing crunch.

Mary Ann pulled the anchor out of the bow and dropped it in the middle of the sandbar. She looked around. Lights from the marina across the lake were twinkling on the water. A waxing moon, rising behind the trees to her left, sparkled in the lake as well.

It was already chilly, so Mary Ann buttoned up her jacket. She took a deep breath and puffed it out.

"Whew. Here I am, ready or not."

Time to put her half-assed plan into action.

She walked up and down the beach composing her thoughts. Then she pulled out her mobile phone, consulted her hastily compiled list of numbers, checked her signal strength — three bars — and made some calls.

"Mayor Teasdale? This is Officer Sarzo. I found an opium poppy field on the north arm of Upper Bar Lake. I'm concerned that the people who planted this field and are already harvesting the crop are aware of my discovery, so I'm on scene guarding it until help arrives. If you pick up this message tonight, please notify someone."

There, just a message on the mayor's machine, but tight and to the point. She looked at her list again, punched in some more numbers . . .

"Wade? I just discovered an opium poppy field on the north arm of Upper Bar Lake. I'm worried that whoever planted it is onto my discovery, so if you get this message, send some backup."

She duplicated the call to Ricky Moss. As she half expected, they also went to voicemail.

Okay, next . . .

"Howard? It's me, your Golden Girl."

Turnbow answered his phone with a growl. "Sarzo? What do you want? It's not even your night to bark."

"Hey, I'm here on Upper Bar Lake, where, believe it or not, I came across an opium poppy field." Pause. "Yes, you heard me right. Listen, I'm afraid that whoever did this knows I found it, so I'm hanging around to preserve evidence. If you get a chance, call my guys, okay? Their message machines are working overtime. Thanks." Another pause. "Will do, bye."

She dialed a fifth number, was dumped into her fourth voicemail system. What the hell, is everyone at dinner?

"Terry — it's Sarzo. I'm out here on Upper Bar Lake. I stumbled on another poppy field. Believe me, I'm not looking at pumpkins. I'm worried the people behind this know I've been here and will destroy the evidence, so I'm guarding the place until someone can help me. Put out the word, okay? Thanks . . . "

And last but not least . . .

"Mr. Hollinsworth?"

"Yes, who am I speaking to?"

"It's Officer Sarzo calling."

"Who?"

"Tri-Town police. I'm on Upper Bar Lake, where I have located an illegal opium poppy field."

"Really. Here in California?" Hollinsworth sounded like he was into his third scotch and soda.

"Yes, sir. I'm concerned about preserving evidence, because I have reason to believe whoever planted this crop knows I found it. I'll be here all night if necessary. Please call someone who can provide backup."

"Who should I call?"

"Anyone who can help me keep a lid on out here."

"Hmm. Sarzo. Poppies. Does Vera know?"

"Yes, sir."

"Oh good, that's good. I'll call her."

"You might want to speak to Billy Rainwater as well."

"Oh, and why is that?"

"I understand he's a client."

"Yes, that's right — for certain matters — why?"

"Well, I'm pretty sure I'm standing on Hilltop Band property."

"Of all the . . . thanks for your call, officer."

He hung up.

That ought to do it. Mary Ann put her phone back in her pocket. Six calls, the word was out. She was betting that whoever was behind the money and the murders would be first on the scene. Or more probably, she reasoned, the bad guy's designated hitter.

If she knew for certain who that person was, she wouldn't dream of being out here alone. She'd have backup at least, and her fellow cops would doubtless insist on proper procedures instead of a lonely nighttime vigil. But she didn't know. She reminded herself of her visitor's early warning — don't trust anyone.

Now that she had set things in motion, however, she was having doubts. What if Wade Gawley showed up? She couldn't imagine him on the wrong side of the law, but if he arrived first, what then? She shook her head. No, the bad guys had a lot to lose. They were the ones in a hurry. And, she believed, as the main thorn in their side she made very good bait.

Night was falling. She turned on the heavy Maglite, shouldered her backpack, and scrambled up the steep embankment. She aimed the light into the trees and panned it around to see if it caused a stir, but there was no reaction.

She hauled out her Night Owl Nex Gen Nightscope and put it up to her eye. Every shadowy object within her field of view suddenly glowed brightly in stark high contrast, edged with a hazy green halo, like old-time TV. Guided by the imagery, she found the little trail she had used on her previous visit and turned into the woods. She moved quickly, avoiding the stumps and branches, anxious to end her suspense over the state of the crop. Had someone already plowed it under, like the first one? When at last she reached the field she was relieved to see the plants still in place and no one to guard them. She took a deep breath. So far so good.

Now she moved to the north side of the field and ducked back into the woods. After twenty yards she found a small open area. She shed her backpack and scraped a shallow hole into the grass with the tag end of the Maglite. She edged the hole with nearby stones, creating a circular fire pit. She gathered up some downed wood, cracked the longer pieces, and piled them into the pit. She opened her can of white gas and poured a liberal amount over the twigs and slash. Then she struck a match and dropped it on the pile.

Whooosh!

Within seconds she had a roaring bonfire.

That done, she grabbed her pack and advanced farther into the woods, working her way back toward the shore. When she had the lake in view again she stopped behind a little knoll, donned her parka and gloves, poured herself a cup of coffee, unwrapped a Snickers bar, and plunked herself down on a log.

Nothing to do now but wait and see.

An hour went by. Then another. On her third cup of coffee, an owl hooted. Quietly, a rapid succession of little beeps. She hardly knew one bird from the next, but guessed it wasn't one of those big horned ones. She took a look in her Night Owl Nightscope to test the thing, and there was the real bird, maybe twenty feet away, a little round ball of feathers on a low branch, glowing bright yellow. Its eyes blazed like headlights when she fingered the infrared illuminator, and it flew away. After a minute or two she could hear it calling faintly in the distance.

The moon was riding high in the sky, sending its beams down between the tree trunks, when she heard the soft purr of an outboard motor floating toward her from across the lake.

Uh-oh, company coming.

She made her way back to her campfire and piled on more wood.

In spite of all the warnings and her own misgivings, Mary Ann was gripped by an overpowering urge to test herself, to see if she could accomplish an actual spell, to find out once and for all if she qualified as an 'adept.' And, not incidentally, get some help nabbing a killer.

"All right, listen up, you ghosts and spirits prowling around — come here, I need some otherworldly help. A power spirit would be especially nice to see at this moment." She opened her pack, found the plastic bag containing the datura blossoms and threw them on the fire.

Hisss!

The flames leaped upward. Sparks flew. Smoke engulfed her, carrying with it a strange flowery aroma. She coughed. Her brow crinkled as she focused in on her goal.

"Show yourself, power spirit. I am *summoning* you, hear me?"

She took a step forward, squinting in the radiant heat, and threw the cat hair into the blaze.

Phooom!

Twigs and sticks crackled and popped. Flaming brands flew up like fireworks. She opened the bag containing her used tampon and delicately grasped its little string tail between a thumb and forefinger. She was about to toss it into the fire as well when something stirring in the flames made her hesitate. What was it? A shape seemed to be writhing around in there.

"Come on, let me see you."

Deep within the fire she saw an apparition taking form. Not her ghost, or anything like it. As she watched, what looked like flaming arms appeared. The impression of a blazing head flickered up out of what might be broad shoulders. White hot coals glowed where eyes should be.

"Well, hello, there," she said, pretending to be brave.

Tongues of flame loomed above her. Hands took shape on the ends of the arms. Claws appeared on the flaming fingers. The apparition, whatever it was, reached out toward Mary Ann, beckoning her.

"Take it easy, boy. We're not there yet."

The thing looked dangerous, but Mary Ann was desperate for an ally and excited by her amazing success. A power spirit! And she conjured it up! The tampon was still dangling from her fingers. She readied herself to throw it into the fire to complete the spell, but then, still nagged by doubts, she hesitated again.

The flaming apparition ballooned to a towering height. She thought she heard it exhale a smoky roar of command. *"Givvve to meee . . . "*

Mary Ann stumbled backward. She fought to keep her heart, which was thumping wildly, from rising into her throat. But she still held the tampon.

"Okay, now, calm down. When the bad guy shows up, you're going to nail him for me. Got that?"

The apparition reached out, cocked an arm. Mary Ann's eyes widened. "Don't you dare . . . "

Fiery claws tore the air in front of Mary Ann, lunging for the tampon. She leaped back from the fire and the monster within, but she was still game.

"Hey, that's no way to behave!"

The apparition lashed out with its other arm, singing her eyebrows. Small fires were starting in the leaves at her feet.

"Whoa there!"

She kicked them out and sprang away into the trees. When she thought she was out of reach she turned back. The monster was reeling around in the bonfire. Sparkling claws flailed in her direction, hungry for flesh and blood. A glowing leg appeared. A foot stepped into the grass outside the stone circle. Sparks and flames erupted where it touched the dead leaves. Then another leg, another step, another new fire. It looked like the entire forest would soon be ablaze.

Mary Ann began to understand, possibly too late, that she had fallen into a trap and was fighting for her sanity, if not her life. "That's enough!" she yelled. "Stop right there!" She jammed the tampon into a pocket.

The apparition hesitated. The fires under its feet sputtered.

"I made a mistake. You're not for me. Go back where you came from!"

"*Nooooo . . . *" she heard the apparition fume, "*. . . I have you . . . *"

"Oh no you don't." Mary Ann fumbled under her blouse and pulled out Father Eisen's cross. She held it on high and willed herself toward the thing, trying to remember the priest's prayer. If it came out wrong, too bad.

"And now, may I, heavenly princess, by the power of God, or whoever is in charge here, cast into hell this guy and all the evil spirits and ghosts, whatever, who prowl about the world seeking the ruin of souls!"

The apparition flickered and grudgingly backed away toward the fire. Mary Ann advanced a couple of steps. She recalled Lorraine's admonition to be forceful.

"Get thee gone, Satan, or whoever the hell you are!" She thrust the crucifix toward the thing with all her energy.

The apparition reached out to snatch the talisman away, but when its claws made contact it recoiled with a demonic howl of pain — "*Wahhhhh*"

— and shrank in among the flames. The secondary blazes that looked so dangerous were all extinguished.

"Looks like I'm on my own again," said Mary Ann, trying to pull herself together. She wasn't sure if she had actually conjured a monster or had only suffered a powerful hallucination, possibly induced by the smoke from those damned datura blossoms.

Her stomach was churning. She felt lightheaded. She reached into her backpack with unsteady hands, dug out the extra ammo clips, and pocketed them. Then she dropped the pack near the fire and hurried back to her lookout position.

The outboard motor was getting louder. She peered through her Nightscope to check it out, bracing herself against a tree trunk to stabilize the image. It was another small aluminum craft, a couple of hundred yards offshore, heading straight for the sandbar where she had run her own boat aground. One person on board, sitting in the stern at the tiller. Too far away for recognition.

She unholstered her Beretta and racked the slide, getting ready for . . . what? She didn't really know.

A few moments later she heard the distinctive scraping sound of an aluminum hull on rough sand. She took another look through her Nightscope. A man in dark clothes was dragging the boat up onto the shore. He had a watch cap on, pulled down over his ears. He was close, less than thirty yards away, but he was looking downward at his immediate surroundings, so she couldn't see a face.

"Oh boy . . . who are you?" she whispered.

Taking a big risk, she crouched low and punched the button on the Nightscope's infrared illuminator. The man sparkled in glowing high contrast, as bright as day. He turned his face up toward Mary Ann, apparently, like the owl, able to see the source of the IR beam. She sucked in her breath. The man's features were blurry, he was some distance away, but she had no doubt.

"Son of a bitch — *Gardner!* It's you . . . you utter fuck!" She wasn't really surprised, but her voice was filled with bitter disappointment.

She backed away from the shore and got herself under the trees, hardly daring to breathe. She could hear the aluminum boat hull clank as something was lifted free. Then, after a short pause, footsteps were crunching on gravel.

"Sarzo? That you?" Gardner shouted. "Listen — I'm here to relieve you! This is my investigation. Come on down here, you can go home now."

Here we go, she thought.

"I don't think so, Terry. I'm calling the DEA." She tried to inject some force into her bold words, but her voice sounded unsure, even in her own ears.

"Now, Mary Ann, you don't want to do that. We have to assess the situation before we go off crying wolf."

"I've already assessed it." She said, nerves fraying.

She was shivering all over. She touched her forehead, checking for fever. She glanced around at the forest understory in the dappled moonlight. Something was wrong with her vision. The tree branches were starting to glitter with jaggy edges. She tried to lift her gun arm and found she couldn't do it. Away toward the poppy field she could just glimpse the glow of her bonfire. The flames were sparkling in multiple colors, like costume jewelry, and all without any enhancement from a power spirit or her Nightscope.

"Buhhhhh . . ." she mumbled.

Saliva was dripping from her lower lip.

What was wrong? She was confused. Oh no. For the first time since middle school, fifteen years ago, she was having a seizure. She stood rooted in place, half paralyzed, wondering vaguely if her magical exertions had brought it on. Then, trying to take a step, she teetered backward and came down on her butt with a thump, cushioned only slightly by oak leaves and pine duff. Her gun went flying.

"Ow."

She sat there, senses spinning, mind whirling. Footsteps were ascending the embankment.

"Come on, Sarzo, off your ass," she gargled. Then, with more force: "Now!"

She willed herself into a kneeling position.

"I . . . am not . . . a witch," she insisted, cursing herself inwardly for listening to a single word old lady Crowfoot had ever said. Her mind was slowly starting to clear. The sparkles and colors were fading from the firelight. She flexed her fingers. The world was coming back into focus.

Mary Ann stared at the dying fire. Now she could make out Gardner moving up beside it. The flames blazed up at his approach, then dwindled again. Was the power spirit still hiding in there? She shuddered.

Gardner glanced at the embers, then picked up her backpack, examined it, dropped it. He squinted into the darkness.

"Sarzo? Don't do anything stupid. You are impeding a sheriff's department investigation. Glad to see you're taking an interest, showing initiative. Now come on over here, call it a day, so I don't have to file an administrative complaint with your mayor."

As her head cleared, Mary Ann felt herself toughen up. An unexpected cold resolve enveloped her, flowed into her limbs, steadied her hands, quieted her heart. She looked at Gardner through her Nightscope. In the light of the fire he was glowing like a second power spirit. And in his right hand, clearly visible, was a handgun. That big Glock of his, probably.

"Nice," she said.

Where oh where was her own little Beretta? She turned the Nightscope on her surroundings. There, over there in the weeds. She scrambled away on hands and knees, groped around where she thought the gun must be, but found nothing. She peeled off her fleece gloves and widened her search pattern. Then widened it again.

"Hey, Terry," she chirped, "I hear you and all, but I don't believe a word." She was trying her best to keep the conversation going until she found her hardware.

At the bonfire, Gardner peered toward her voice. "What are you talking about? Here's our chance to wind this up. But it's my job, not yours."

"What bullshit! I see that gun in your hand. And I also saw that slick car you just bought. You're in on the deal."

"Please, Mary Ann, stop this nonsense."

"Am I wrong?" she shouted. "I heard you lost your shirt on that restaurant in Tarvolo. Got your loan from the wrong people, didn't you? They wanted their money back, but you were broke, so they put you to work. Who cares if they're crooked? Who cares what the job might be!"

"Crazy talk from a crazy cop who believes in ghosts. Who do you think you're fooling?" Gardner's tone had changed. Gone was the smooth persuader whose tricks didn't work. Now he sounded more like a hunter trying to spook his prey.

"Everyone will be stunned when you turn out to be the perp. Offed Bobby for making improper advances, persuaded Bremer to do Russell, then popped Bremer because he was going to turn you in."

"That's a great story, Sheriff."

"And here's the convincer — they're going to find the murder weapon on you, covered with your cute little fingerprints." Gardner chambered a bullet in his Glock.

Mary Ann held the Nightscope up to one side at arm's length, aimed it toward the campfire, and pressed the IR button. A little red dot climbed up her arm — Gardner's laser sight zeroing in. She rolled away.

Blam!

The bullet nicked a tree limb right beside her and whined into the underbrush. Close. But also proof. Proof that the senior man in Amador County's Investigations Bureau had crossed the line.

Damn.

Gardner kicked at the fire, sending sparks in all directions. Now he too was in darkness. What was he doing? Mary Ann became aware that she had dropped the Nightscope as well as her gun. What a dope. She was creeping back toward her lookout position to grab it when she accidentally bumped into cold steel instead. Her Beretta! She breathed a sigh of relief.

Now footsteps were whisking through the leaves, circling around to her right. Trying to cut her off from the lake, probably. She raised herself up on her knees, grasped her little 9-millimeter with both hands, aimed toward the faint sound, and —

Pow! Pow! Pow! Pow! Pow! Pow!

— let fly a half dozen shots.

"Fuck you, Sarzo!" piped Gardner and hustled away.

Mary Ann dropped to her belly and crawled further into the trees. Moonbeams lit small patches of open ground here and there, just enough to reveal some of the roots and branches, so she jumped to her feet, ran up a low rise, and dove to the ground on the other side. Gardner's red laser dot followed on her heels.

Blam!   Blam!

Big bullets smacked off rocks and punched through leaves just behind her. She rolled downhill and crawled behind a gnarly old stump. Pretty soon she could hear movement again. She tightened her grip on her pistol.

"Hey, Sarzo, you can't hit a thing in broad daylight. How can you expect —"

Pow! Pow! Pow! Pow! Pow! Pow!

"— shit!"

His voice had come from her right. A feint, probably. She crawled away from the sound and collided with a good-sized rock protruding from the ground. It was tall and cold, and it reminded her of a gravestone. She shivered. Where was that guy? Faking right, going left, she thought.

Pow! Pow! Pow!

The brief burst brought no reaction, and, damn, she had already expended fifteen rounds. She extracted the empty clip, dug around in her parka and shoved a loaded one into place. A minute went by in total silence. Maybe he was pulling a double fake — right, then right. How to find out? Gotta say something, that's the only way.

"Still on your feet over there?" she yelled.

Blam!

He was waiting for that. The bullet zinged off the rock and almost took her head off. And sure enough, the blast came from her right, toward the lake.

She crawled several yards, angling around him. She was still out in the open when she heard rapid footfalls, coming toward her. The red laser dot was zipping back and forth. She rolled over and took aim.

Pow! Pow! Pow! Pow! Pow! Pow!

"Whoa!"

Gardner hit the dirt and thrashed away through the underbrush. Now it was Mary Ann's turn to move. She stood up and danced through the trees, using the little pools of moonlight to guide her.

Blam!

Another near miss. She dropped to the ground, crawled into a low swale, turned herself around on her elbows. She raised her head just enough to see over the lip of the swale. What she saw made her heart sink — the bright orange glow from an infrared illuminator. Somehow he had found her Nightscope. She ducked back down, flipped over sideways and brought her head up again. The orange glow was panning this way and that. She leveled her Beretta.

Pow! Pow! Pow! Pow! Pow! Pow!

"Holy shit!" The glow vanished. She heard Gardner hit the dirt and then heard him tearing through the bushes, heading back toward the poppy field. She jumped up and did the same, paralleling his track.

Blam!

Gardner fired off a round on the run, but this one was way off target.

Out of the corner of her eye Mary Ann could see the embers of her fire. She stopped, crouched, and waited. Gardner was still moving fast. Then he stopped too. Suddenly his laser sight found her, flicked across her eyes. Dazzling fireworks filled her vision.

Blam!

She heard the shot whiz past her ear. But she couldn't see a thing. She might as well be having another seizure. She aimed in Gardner's general direction.

Pow! Pow! Pow! Click! Click! Click!

"Son of a bitch," he yelled.

He started moving again, shuffling a few steps, then running, then shuffling again. Mary Ann dropped her second clip and slammed in her last one.

Pow! Pow! Pow! Pow! Pow! Pow!

She took a breath.

Pow! Pow! Pow! Pow! Pow! Pow!

"Jesus Christ!" Gardner squawked.

More running, then —

Thwack!

Mary Ann heard a low moan, heard Gardner's body crash to the ground.

She dropped to her belly again. What's he up to? What's the trick? She waited for what seemed like forever, listening intently for the faintest movement of grass or leaves or twigs. She imagined her ears getting bigger and bigger, becoming elephant-size under the strain.

But the only thing she could hear was the muted roar of a jetliner far overhead, carrying sleepy travelers south to the Big City. Streaks of light still seared her vision, but they were fading. Pretty soon she could make out the shape of things, so she cautiously raised herself up and crept through the trees to the smoldering remains of her bonfire.

"Yo, Terry?"

There was no reply. Maybe she nailed the bastard. After a minute cowering in doubt, she jumped up and grabbed her backpack. She reached inside for the baton-like Maglite. Holding it well away from her body, she switched it on and panned the beam around the area. Where was that guy?

The flashlight revealed nothing except twisted branches and bushes. She switched it off.

Suddenly the embers of her fire blazed up. A column of smoky flame rose behind her, seemed to bend over her. She jerked around and found herself staring into what looked like a pair of white hot eyes. They fixed her with a fierce inhuman gaze. Flaming arms seemed to reach out to seize her.

"Go back to hell, you!" She windmilled her backpack through the air and brought it down on the base of the fire.

Foof!

An explosion of sparks and smoke enveloped the little glade. When the air cleared, the fire was out. The apparition was gone, and revealed in its place was a human figure, not five feet away, hobbling toward her with gimpy steps.

"Unnnnhhh . . . "

The watch cap was gone. The hair was matted with blood. Bloody streaks ran down half the face, and one eye was swollen closed. It was Gardner. He looked dazed. His Glock was gone, lost in the woods when, as it appeared, he had collided hard with a tree.

"Ahhh — !"

Mary Ann jerked backward and brought her Beretta up to bear. Gardner swung an arm and slapped it away into the darkness.

"Sarzzz . . . "

He reached out to grab her. She backpedaled. He tottered after. She turned and ran, skipping over rocks and roots. He followed slowly, stumbling, recovering, shambling implacably forward, growling with rage.

After thirty yards Mary Ann emerged from the trees above the lakeshore. Her heel slipped on the edge of the steep embankment. She flailed the air with her arms to hold her balance.

Gardner kept coming, moving faster. He was regaining some of his wits.

"Got you now, bitch!" he snarled.

She watched him come, gauging the distance, assessing the situation with perfect clarity — she was trapped. In two seconds she would be dead.

Go, girl!

She threw herself aside and dove back under the trees. Gardner barely missed snatching a lock of hair. His momentum carried him to the precipice. A foot stepped into thin air, and he pitched over.

Mary Ann heard the impact, heard the clatter of gravel avalanching down the slope, heard a soft splash. She crawled back to the edge of the embankment and peered downward.

Ten feet below, outlined by moonlight, was a figure, head and shoulders in the water, legs still on dry ground. It wasn't moving.

"Holy crap."

Back at the site of her bonfire, she switched on the Maglite and swept the beam around in a broad search pattern. She was furious with herself for losing her weapon three times in a week, but after a few passes she spotted metal glinting in the bushes and snatched it up.

Then she picked her way down to the shoreline and warily approached the body lying there, pistol at the ready. It was Gardner, all right. She focused the Maglite on him. Unconscious? No, the man was face down in the water. Dead for sure. Mary Ann leaned over for a close inspection. There was no sign of gunshot wounds, just that ugly bruise on the side of his head.

She looked back up the slope. He must have panicked while she was firing away, hit his head on a low branch, and got knocked cross-eyed. She tucked the Beretta back into its holster.

"If you can't tie good knots, tie plenty of 'em," she said.

Suddenly all Mary Ann's adrenaline drained away. She wobbled over to a boulder and collapsed with her back against it. She was exhausted. Her eyelids fluttered. Before she knew it she was sound asleep.

▼

She woke up hours later. The moon was setting. The sky was grey now instead of black. She was cold and groggy. It took some thought to remember where she was. When the pieces came together she jumped up and looked around, working hard to orient herself. Gardner's body was still there, still half in, half out of the lake. It startled her.

"Oh God."

She braced her mobile phone against her chest and punched in some numbers with trembling fingers.

"Golden Hills Tri-Town Police. Gawley here. Help you?"

Mary Ann let out a grateful sigh. "Hi, Wade. Come on up and get me, will you?"

"Where the hell?" he grumbled. He sounded as sleepy as she was.

"Upper Bar Lake, like on my message."

"What message?"

"You didn't pick up?"

"No, I was — am — entertaining someone. Sorry."

"Don't be sorry. Just get up here, I'm freezing. Northeastern shore of the north arm. You can launch from Parker, but all the rentals will be chained up."

"I'll get the patrol boat. Did you clock the time? This might take a while."

"It's important. Bring witnesses. Preferably someone from the sheriff's department."

"What's the fuss?"

"You'll see. I'm not touching a thing till you get here."

The sun was rising when Gawley arrived in the sheriff's department patrol boat, a twenty foot inboard-outboard with a canvas canopy over the occupants. Moss was with him, plus an unfamiliar deputy sheriff. Mary Ann was squatting on top of a boulder, huddled in her parka, cold as hell. She gave them all a weak wave as they dropped anchor and waded ashore.

"Mary Ann? You look terrible," said Gawley. He handed her a blanket, and she wrapped it around herself. She pointed along the shore.

"God almighty. Who's that?" wondered Moss.

"Take a look."

They walked along the embankment for a closer inspection.

"What in the hell —" said Gawley, leaning down to get a purchase on the body's left leg.

"Hey, troopers, photos first," cautioned Mary Ann.

The sheriff's deputy went back to the boat for his camera. Gawley looked at the body, looked at Mary Ann.

"Gardner?" he asked.

She nodded.

"That superior asshole," said Moss.

"You shot him? You? How is that possible?" Gawley could hardly imagine the idea.

"I shot *at* him, but I doubt I actually hit him. We'll know for sure when we turn him over. I think he hit his head on a branch."

"And drowned," Gawley concluded.

"Unless the coroner contradicts me, yeah, that's it."

The sheriff's deputy came back with his camera and a body bag. He took a dozen pictures from every angle he could think of.

"Okay, men, let's get him out of the water."

Mary Ann slid off her rock and held up a hand. "Before you screw everything up, I'd like to make sure you check for a small caliber handgun on his person. I have reason to believe it's the murder weapon in the cases of Bobby Rainwater and Dale Bremer. It might also have been used on Mike Russell, but then the body was cut up and we couldn't tell."

"What are you talking about?" asked the deputy.

Mary Ann stepped forward to introduce herself. "It's Officer Sarzo. And you are?"

The deputy seemed puzzled, but shook her hand anyway. "Al Burns. We're looking for a weapon?"

"He was going to kill me, plant it on me, and claim I smoked the bro's."

"Pardon me, but what were you doing here all night?"

"Surveillance. Have a look up past the trees there, and you'll see why."

The three men turned the body over.

Burns was stunned. "Good God . . . Terry Gardner."

"The man on the take," said Mary Ann.

Burns scowled. "And my immediate supervisor, if that matters. Let's see here." He fished around in the man's waterlogged uniform. "Nothing doing, I don't see a piece. Sorry."

Gawley walked back to Gardner's rental boat. "Here we are, under the seat."

"Don't touch it! Get a baggie!" ordered Mary Ann.

Deputy Burns produced an evidence bag from his patrol boat, dumped the gun inside, and held it up for all to see. It was a High Standard .22 caliber SK100 with the four-inch barrel.

"Somebody got killed with this, this . . . toy?" he asked.

"Several people. But not by me," said Mary Ann. "I have never touched that thing. Be careful, I think you'll find Gardner's prints all over it."

"This is the damnedest thing I ever heard of," said the deputy.

67

THE AMADOR COUNTY Coroner confirmed that Deputy Terry Gardner died from asphyxiation due to an obstructed trachea — drowning, in effect — at approximately ten PM, give or take. He made note of multiple skin abrasions. He also reported head trauma consistent with the force of a blunt instrument sufficient to concuss the deceased. He did not discover any gunshot wounds.

Mary Ann was examined at Sutter Amador Hospital in Jackson. Aside from scrapes earned in the heat of battle and the previous cuts on her hand, she was found to be in good health.

"You're doing okay for someone who just got beat up. How'd it happen?" asked the nurse practitioner, a mature woman with a no-nonsense demeanor.

"I burned myself in a bonfire that got a little too big. I smacked into a tree. I fell on a rock. And, before all that, I crushed a small salt shaker in my hand."

"Sure your boyfriend isn't involved?"

Mary Ann snorted. "I don't have a boyfriend. I'm a cop. Line of duty, blah blah blah."

The woman smiled. "The officer who brought you in told me the story, but I had to ask."

"Yeah, I know. We take the same courses in cop school."

"Right. So I'm going to paint some Betadine on the worst scrapes here, and prescribe Amoxicillin just in case that hand got infected during your adventures."

On her way out Mary Ann found a trash bin in the women's restroom. She placed a foot on a pedal, and the bin's lid flew open. She pulled her used tampon out of a pocket and dropped the last of her magical ingredients inside. The lid slammed shut.

"You know, I'm feeling better already."

▼

Twenty-four hours later, when Mary Ann showed up at the Book Nook, her arms and face were still covered in orange-brown stripes. The bandage on her hand was the size of a boxing glove.

"Look at you — wearing war paint today," said Lorraine.

"I was in a gun fight," replied Mary Ann, as casually as possible.

"What — ? Someone shot at you?"

"And I shot back." She paused for dramatic emphasis. "Forty-two rounds, by my count."

Lorraine nearly fell over. "You're joking . . . "

"I didn't hit a thing. But now, since I fired my weapon, I have to go through counseling."

"Great, you can say your ghost made you do it."

"Very funny." Mary Ann took a seat in front of the computers while Lorraine made espresso.

"What I don't understand is, the moment Chief Ibañez got run off the road, my ghost disappeared. Not a flicker since."

"That is strange," Lorraine agreed. "You've got me haunting the web, pardon the expression. Visitors are peculiar, even for ghosts. Maybe they don't really travel through time. Maybe time runs backwards for them. There's some speculation about this at Wraiths-Of-America-dot-com if you dig around. Or, maybe they need to take care of unfinished business, the crap you read in storybooks . . ." Lorraine trailed off.

"I think Ibañez was onto the bad guys — we still don't know what's really going on — and wanted to tell me all about it."

"Ectoplasmic visitors can't talk."

"I suppose he found that out. Tough on both of us."

"I'll say. When the day arrives, remind me not to come back." Lorraine placed a macchiato in front her young friend.

Mary Ann took a sip. "Or maybe he wanted to tell me just enough to . . . I dunno . . . get me going. That would be like him, he would do that." She thought about it for a moment while staring at the milky swirl in her coffee. "And I say it was Ibañez, but my visitor didn't even know his own name, so maybe these things are all just . . . real flaky."

At that moment the front door slammed open, and Tom Wagstaff barged in with a whoop and a holler.

"Hey, Mom, here's the latest — be on every newsstand tomorrow morning. Check it out!"

He was holding up the front page of the latest *County Courier*.

The headline was set in end-of-the-world size type:

LOCAL POLICEWOMAN SOLVES
AMADOR COUNTY CRIME WAVE

Lorraine took the paper from him, revealing Mary Ann sitting nearby.

"Hello, M," said Wagstaff. He was not absolutely completely surprised to see her.

Mary Ann registered the headline for what it was, a tribute, and stood up. He moved closer, opened his arms. She fell into them. They hugged. They shared a long kiss.

"Hey, don't make it look so desperate, right in front of your mother," Lorraine complained.

When they came up for air Wagstaff looked around, checked his watch. "Had lunch yet?"

The two women shook their heads.

"Well? Let's go."

Lorraine frowned. "Sure you want to make this a threesome?"

Wagstaff smiled. "Now, you bet." He looked at Mary Ann. She looked at him. "Later on . . . maybe not."

68

MAYOR TEASDALE was in her office with Gordon Hollinsworth, conferring on the choice of a new man to run the Golden Hills Tri-Town Police Department. She interrupted her study of the likely candidates' résumés to cross the room and flip a switch, igniting a gas-fed fire in her decorative little fireplace. Above the mantelpiece was the same signature Headwall Mine photo found in the police station.

"Cold today," she said, staring at the brave miners posing there.

"Turkey day is almost upon us," Hollinsworth said absently. "Who do you like?"

The mayor warmed her hands at the fire for a moment, then returned to her chair. She sipped coffee while she pushed papers around on her desktop.

"Well, there's a lieutenant in Sacramento wants to come up. He's got a good record, done some administration. What's his name . . . Gahagan. What do you think?"

"I wonder, will he actually take the job, once he knows more? There's a pay cut to go along with the title boost. What if he can't sell his house — it's too far to commute."

"Hmm. You're right," agreed the mayor. "We're beggars, not choosers. Who then?"

"The other guy who looks good to me is this character Fabriano, from Placerville. He's flying a desk right now, but he's been out there on the line, too. Broke up a stolen car ring a couple of years back."

"Too macho? Won't he get bored up here where it's quiet?"

"Probably not right away." Hollinsworth held up his copy of the *Courier* for the mayor.

"Yes," she acknowledged, "we've had our share of excitement. All over now, I hope."

"Vera, it's not all over. It's just starting."

She put down her coffee cup. "What do you mean?"

"Jesus, am I the only one you ever talk to? That fellow Gardner wasn't the bad guy, just a cop on the take, working for someone who could afford to pay for his services."

"Who?"

"Who do you think?"

"Are you suggesting this involves my good friend Sally Cruz?"

"I'm not suggesting anything. He's my client."

"Don't be silly. He's as honest as you are."

Hollinsworth couldn't help smiling. "What does that mean? I'm a lawyer."

"What are you getting at?" Mayor Teasdale was scowling.

"Just this. There will be further investigations. I have heard it said that the state will step in. Questions will be raised about Chief Ibañez' death. Possibly the DEA will come calling." He ran a hand through his silvery hair.

"Fingers will start to point. To Cruz and, sadly, to Rainwater. Those damn poppies your rookie cop discovered were growing on Hilltop property."

"I don't believe it."

"It's a shame. I have to tell Rainwater that the Feds still haven't recognized his little band, in spite of serious campaign contributions to several influential politicians. Contributions paid by Rainwater, but he doesn't have any real money, so draw your own conclusions."

"Thank God I'm out of it," said Mayor Teasdale.

"But you're not out of it. Once the gears start grinding, the Feds will be looking at your buyer with suspicion. They will stall. The locals who don't want gambling in their neighborhood will have some ammunition. And Mr. Rainwater will circle around to you wanting his money and his hotel back."

Mayor Teasdale went pale. "Could that happen? Would I have to return it?"

"Probably not. But you may have to explain how you didn't know it was a long shot to build a casino on your Auburn property. If he sues, it will be a public spectacle. More *Courier* headlines."

"Tell me you wouldn't encourage such a suit or represent him."

"Good Lord, Vera, of course not. I'm on your side."

"Well, then, I think it's best not to step in any cow pies. I'm going to ignore it all."

Hollinsworth stood to leave. "My idea, go with Fabriano. He's local, understands the foothills, and the other cops will respect him."

"Thank you, Gordon."

He showed himself out. On the street he looked in both directions and crossed over to the Pick & Shovel, where he ordered a pumpkin-flavored latte. He was standing on the sidewalk inhaling its spicy aroma when he spotted Billy Rainwater walking his way.

"Mr. Hollinsworth."

"Hello, Billy."

"I just wanted to say, we've submitted our plans — wait till you see them, it's going to be fantastic — and we're very anxious about those permits."

"Yes, I know. The planning commission bureaucracy. Worse than the DMV."

"It's been more than a month," said Rainwater in an accusative tone.

"Almost two," amended Hollinsworth, sipping his latte. "These things always take more time than you think."

"You're supposed to expedite. We paid a lot of money to get this to happen."

"Here's the problem, Billy. The poppies. You really shouldn't have let them grow on ancestral land. That looks very bad."

"I knew nothing about it. We can't patrol every acre day and night."

"I suppose not. Lot of ground to cover. But the Feds don't know that, and they don't care."

"Meaning what?"

"Meaning the Hilltop Band will lose its fight for tribal recognition. Your permits will be denied. We can appeal, we'll take it through the courts." He measured out a professional smile. "I'm sure we will prevail . . . eventually."

"That will take months."

"Years, more likely. That's just a guess, you understand."

"Sweet Jesus." A dark cloud was descending over Rainwater's countenance.

"Do you want some advice?"

"I want my casino."

"Yes, well, here it is anyway — put up a mall. I understand there's a Target nearby. A Sears or JCPenney would be a good anchor tenant. Add a Best Buy and a pizza parlor. That property can still become a lucrative investment."

"Are you telling me we're screwed? You want us to trade dollars for pennies?" Rainwater was bouncing on the balls of his feet.

"No, but you're a gambler — you've got to know when to fold 'em, like the man said."

"So, you! — the so-called lawyer! — Mr. Connection! How much are the boys down in Sacramento paying you to sell us out? That's it, isn't it? You're working for them!" Rainwater was white with rage.

"Not so, Billy, whoever 'them' might be. Call me when you calm down."

"You are fucked, Mr. Hollinsworth. Totally fucked."

Rainwater turned abruptly and walked down the street to his Honda Ridgeline. "Fuck you." He reached into the compartment under the load bed and pulled out a nylon pouch. He started back toward Hollinsworth, who was now strolling away in the opposite direction.

"Wait up, Counselor. I forgot something."

Hollinsworth turned, cocked his head, sipped his pumpkin latte.

A block away, Ricky Moss was writing a parking ticket when he heard the noise.

Pop! Pop! Pop!

Not very loud, but with a metallic snap that suggested gunfire. He dropped his citation book and ran toward the sound.

People were peering out of windows and doors all up and down Applefield's Main Street, staring at Billy Rainwater and Gordon Hollinsworth. Rainwater was standing in the middle of the sidewalk with an open nylon pouch dangling from one hand and a Taurus 605 revolver drooping from the other. Hollinsworth was flat on his back on the concrete. Two red splotches were spreading on his white shirt. The pumpkin latte had splashed all over the place. The front tire on a nearby car was hissing out air where the third shot had penetrated.

"Hold it right there," said Moss. He loosened the strap on his holster and drew his weapon. Rainwater, looking dazed, raised his revolver toward the cop. Moss had never had a gun pointed at him in his life, but he did not flinch.

"Point that thing down. Put it on the sidewalk."

Rainwater looked very confused.

"Hear me? Down!"

Rainwater leaned down and gently placed his gun beside Hollinsworth's coffee cup.

"All right, now you! Down on the ground, face down, hands behind your back!"

Rainwater's eyes were misting up. He hesitated.

"Right fucking now, asshole!" barked Moss, shifting into righteous cop mode.

Rainwater slowly got down on his hands and knees and flattened himself on the sidewalk as instructed.

Moss cuffed him, then holstered his weapon, taking notice of a gathering crowd. At a radius of ten feet, the awestruck citizenry of Applefield already had him surrounded. He fetched his mobile phone from his duty belt and dialed 9-1-1.

There was a knock on Mayor Teasdale's door. The fire department dispatcher poked her head in.

"Ma'am? You should come have a look."

Mayor Teasdale was huddled under her desk, where she dove when the shots rang out, obeying the stern advice of a corporate safety lecture she had once attended. She unfolded herself and stood up, trying to recover some dignity.

"What happened?"

"Looks like that Indian fellow shot someone, right here on Main Street."

Mayor Teasdale's eyes widened. She covered her mouth with her hand.

That evening Wade Gawley and Mary Ann bought drinks for Ricky Moss at the Palomino.

"He pointed the gun at you?" asked Gawley, full of envy.

"It happened so fast I didn't have time to crap in my pants." said Moss.

"You the man!" said Mary Ann.

Moss gave them a modest shrug. "I've never been in a situation before, but you know, the training kicked in."

On their second round, the speculation began.

"So, okay, Gardner shot Bobby." said Gawley, toying with his beer.

"And, boy, that started everything." Moss shook his head in wonderment.

"Why would he do that?" A plausible motive eluded the acting chief.

Mary Ann surveyed the room, trying to figure out who might be listening. Nobody looked suspicious, but she lowered her voice anyway. "I think Billy's casino was a crooked deal with this guy Cruz, some kind of dirty money, and Bobby didn't want the Hilltop Band to go for it."

"Bobby was a straight shooter," said Gawley with a sigh. "What about Russell?"

"Good old Mike. What if he set up Bobby, and someone thought he was going to talk about it? We know that slimeball couldn't be trusted, and maybe his employers felt the same way," said Moss.

"Bremer?"

Moss wrinkled his nose. "Another low man on some damn totem pole."

"Gardner was under pressure to solve the case," said Mary Ann. "Hey, we're the ones who put him under pressure. Once he arrested Bremer, that's when everything started to slide."

"And our fearless leader?"

"That's the tricky one." Mary Ann shrugged. "Cruz was in the accident, if that's what it was, and Gardner was first responder. No one else showed up for at least twenty minutes. I think the chief was onto their scheme, and they did him in."

"What about the heroin? That's what bothers me," said Moss.

"What about it? The coroner's report says overdose, more than enough to kill him. If true, he would have been comatose, not driving a car."

"They injected him at the scene and faked the accident?"

"Damn right," said Mary Ann with conviction.

"That's awful complicated, you ask me," said Moss.

Gawley stretched, yawned, checked his watch. "We'll never know."

"Not for sure," Mary Ann agreed.

69

IN THE DAYS AHEAD, the weather worsened. Snow fell on the upper slopes of the Golden Hills Tri-Town Area for the first time in a decade, duly noted by Mary Ann in her traffic advisories. As winter — cold, dreary, foggy, and wet — took hold, a number of riveting stories appeared in the *County Courier* . . .

RAINWATER PLEADS GUILTY
TO SECOND DEGREE MURDER

William S. Rainwater, formerly head of the Hilltop Band of the Hokyut Nation, pleaded guilty yesterday in Amador County Superior Court to the murder of Gordon Hollinsworth, a prominent local attorney and the Golden Hills Tri-Town Area's legal counsel. Rainwater was allowed to escape first degree charges, in spite of a public outcry that reached all the way to Sacramento, because the prosecution agreed with the public defender that his actions were the result of a "momentary passion."

"We just couldn't find any actual evidence of deliberate premeditation," said Jane Philips, the prosecutor in charge of the case.

Rainwater has expressed remorse. Sentencing will occur next month, and expectations are for twenty-five years in prison with parole possible after fifteen.

Mary Ann saw the article while she was out on Applefield's Main Street writing parking tickets. She was working her way toward the Miners Market when she came upon Salvador Cruz' green Range Rover, fresh from the body shop. It was angled into the curb not too far from a fire hydrant, with the right front tire barely touching a cautionary swath of yellow paint. She almost licked her lips in anticipation as she whipped out her book and scrawled a vengeful citation. Just as she was slipping it under the driver's side windshield wiper, Cruz himself burst out of the Apple Ranch restaurant wiping his mouth on a napkin. He hustled toward her.

"What is the meaning of this, officer?" he glowered.

Mary Ann pointed to the incriminating contact between tire and paint. "Sorry, but this is a no-parking zone. See the fire hydrant?"

"You are joking. The hydrant, it is five meters away."

"No joke, sir. I'm simply enforcing our local ordinance."

"This is outrageous. I will protest."

She looked at him with ice-cold eyes. "You do that. Take it up with the mayor. See where it gets you."

He rocked back, startled by her vehemence. "Or perhaps we can settle this here and now. I will pay you directly." He fished in his pocket and pulled out a wad of cash.

"Save your money, sir. I'm not for sale . . . unlike some cops."

"What are you talking about?"

"The department will never bring you in, Mr. Cruz. You're too shiny. But I know all about you. You and your alpaca operation. Talk about a joke."

"You know nothing about me."

"Oh no? I'm not the only one. The word is out. So why don't you just pay the ticket like the fine upstanding citizen you claim to be."

She turned away and continued on down the street. After a few paces her blood cooled and her heart stopped pounding.

Not long thereafter this news item appeared in the *Courier* . . .

SALVADOR CRUZ SELLS RANCH

Salvador "Sally" Cruz, who only recently purchased the land from the Dutch Flat Cattle Company of Lodi, has elected to sell The Golden Fleece Alpaca Ranch, his property on the outskirts of Tarvolo, to a Colorado company that operates a similar facility near Fort Collins.

"I know these animals, and I am saddened, but the new owners know them even better, and I have other business in San Diego that demands my full attention," said Cruz in a statement issued by the ranch foreman.

In announcing the transaction Cruz also paid tribute to the local citizens. "In my three years here, I have made many friends, and I leave with nothing but warm feelings for everyone in the Golden Hills."

Real estate professionals contacted for comment on this story estimated that Cruz' ranch improvements ran to more than $7,000,000, an impressive sum even in affluent Tarvolo.

▼

By Thanksgiving, all the big Sierra ski resorts were open full time. During her stints at KVIG, Mary Ann aired a dozen different radio ads trumpeting their 100-inch packed-powder bases. She herself was looking forward to a long weekend snowboarding with Tom Wagstaff and was down in Jackson buying gear.

As she emerged from the Mountain Madness sports shop with a new parka and boarding boots, she noticed a heavy woman across the street, shuffling along the sidewalk behind a cart full of groceries. The woman's free hand was clutching a cane. Well, well, if it wasn't old lady Crowfoot. Mary Ann crossed over to intercept her.

"Hello, there."

The woman stopped in her tracks. She turned as white as the snow on the nearby hillsides.

"What do you want?" she croaked.

"Officer Sarzo, Mrs. Crowfoot. Remember me?"

"Get back. Stay away." The woman raised her cane, ready to strike.

"Not what you expected, huh?"

"What do you mean?"

"The trap you set. It was clever, I was tempted. But here I am." Mary Ann spread her arms and did a little turn to demonstrate her good health.

The woman looked up and down the street, seeking an avenue of escape. Seeing none, she straightened up. "It was not a trap. It was a test."

"Oh sure. And I passed, is that it?"

"Goodness yes. I doubt I would have." The woman lowered the cane, but her eyes were darting every which way.

"Now I've got a test for you," said Mary Ann. "Leave me alone. Understand?"

Mrs. Crowfoot treated Mary Ann to her eerie smile. "Don't worry, young lady. I know an adept when I see one. Nothing I could throw at you would ever stick."

Mary Ann searched the woman's face for the lie, but didn't find it. Instead she caught a spasm of genuine fear passing across cataract-crazed eyes. Fear of the young woman now confronting her, Mary Ann realized. It made her feel guilty.

"All right then . . . watch yourself and, um, happy holidays." She waved and recrossed the street.

Mrs. Crowfoot continued toward her worn-out old car. As she opened the door she called out, "Wait a minute."

Mary Ann turned back toward her.

"You're good, but you're young, Sarzo. You don't know diddly-squat. So take heed — never conjure in fire. Water, that's the ticket. Much safer."

▼

Christmas time brought a dusting of snow to the streets of Applefield. Cars were slipping, sliding, and colliding in spite of many an urgent traffic bulletin from Mary Ann. People couldn't leave their homes to shop, and businesses were hurting. The political weather was even worse . . .

MAYOR TEASDALE INDICTED
FOR REAL ESTATE FRAUD

Vera Teasdale, longtime mayor of the Golden Hills Tri-Town Area, and the person often credited as the driving force in amalgamating Applefield, Ragtown, and Tarvolo into a unified administrative area with modern amenities and vigorous tourism, has been charged with real estate fraud. The indictment stems from a complex three-way deal that put her undeveloped parcel in Auburn into the hands of the Hilltop Band Native American group in exchange for an Applefield hotel.

State prosecutors claim that the sale was fraudulent, inasmuch as she knew, or should have known, that constructing an Indian-owned casino on the Auburn land was never a real possibility, and now they have the warrant to back them up.

"I will fight these false charges, and I will be exonerated," said the mayor. "This sale was made in good faith. Mr. Rainwater and his Hilltop Band were well aware of the extreme difficulties in pursuing their casino dream. I admired their optimism then, and I admire it still. I'm just terribly sorry their plans have been thwarted by cold-hearted businessmen and their political allies in the capital."

▼

In the first week of January, a warm Pineapple Express storm blew in from Hawaii and soaked the foothills, melting all the snow. The Whiskeyjack neared flood stage. The downpour kept the local cops busy with accidents and emergencies and overshadowed a changing of the guard that was dutifully reported by the *Courier* . . .

FABRIANO TAKES OVER
TRI-TOWN POLICE SQUAD

Dominic Fabriano is the Golden Hills' new chief of police. He was the Tri-Town search committee's "first choice," according to Helen Boxer, Applefield's fire department dispatcher, who was involved in the selection. Fabriano was interviewed for the job last fall, but winding up his duties in Placerville, where he was a detective sergeant, delayed the swearing-in until now.

"He's a pro who knows the ropes, knows administration, and I just want to arrest violators," was current Acting Chief Wade Gawley's reaction.

Fabriano laughed when asked what he foresaw as his biggest problem, now that the past year's events have been resolved. "Staying awake, I hope. Writing tickets on the tourists, probably."

▼

One fine day in February, when the fog had retreated down into the Big Valley, Mary Ann was patrolling the public park in the center of Applefield, showing the uniform to forestall casual crime. Someone had tipped the department that meth and marijuana dealers were doing business there, driving away the tourists who might otherwise come to admire the now-famous bronze prospector statue. Chief Fabriano, under pressure from the embattled mayor's office, was in no mood to coddle these lawbreakers and ordered a high-profile police presence.

Mary Ann saw no evidence of illegal activity on her rounds, but she did check the fountain, just to see how much trash had been thrown in there since her last shift. She was pleased to note that the town's undermanned work crew was on its toes. Nothing but a few pennies sparkled in the pool. While she was looking a small cloud passed over the sun, and a shadow crept over the surface of the water. Then the cloud moved away — but the shadow remained. An image formed in the ripples.

"Don't do that! You almost gave me a heart attack."

The ghost shrugged.

"What are you doing here? It's been months. Where have you been?"

The ghost rocked his head back and forth noncommittally.

"I know I sound like somebody's mother, but I called and called."

The ghost placed open hands over his eyebrows and turned them downward, like large eyelids.

"Been sleeping?"

The ghost nodded. He tapped a finger against his wrist, then jerked a thumb to one side.

"Gotta go?"

The ghost nodded again.

"You just got here."

The ghost raised his hands apologetically.

"Hmm." Mary Ann was silent for a moment, then her face fell. "So, you came to be polite and say goodbye, is that it?"

The ghost nodded a third time.

"Great, off on vacation to some tropical paradise, I bet."

The ghost rolled his hand back and forth, palm down, in a not-so-sure gesture.

"You may not know it, but I think you're Chief Ibañez. Work on remembering, okay?"

The ghost gave her a thumbs up sign.

"I mean it. Your name is 'Hector Ibañez.' You were chief of the Golden Hills Tri-Town Police Department. Got that? It's important, don't forget."

The ghost placed his hands together in the standard gesture of peace.

"Yeah, you too," she said.

The ghost blew her a big kiss, waved, and melted into the ripples on the water fountain pool.

She blinked away a dust mote in the corner of her eye.

"Hey, wait, you owe me, pal . . . "

But her shadowy ghost was gone.

▼

A week later, while tourists were swarming through the region during the Presidents Day holiday, the Tri-Town Area was rocked by a political bombshell . . .

TEASDALE RESIGNS UNDER PRESSURE
HOWARD TURNBOW APPOINTED MAYOR

In a shocking and unforeseen development, Vera Teasdale has stepped down from her post as mayor of the Tri-Town Area after eighteen years on the job. Although she stood firm following her fraud indictment, when many called for her ouster, she bowed to continued pressure in the form of multiple civil lawsuits.

Her fraud case never came to trial, but many have questioned the plea deal, which called for a cash reimbursement of $50,000 to the remaining members of the Hilltop Band and 60 hours of community service.

Hilltop lawyers have now brought suit in U.S. District Court in Sacramento, seeking to recover the lucrative hotel owned by the mayor here in Applefield. Another suit, this one filed by representatives of Robert Brannan, former owner of the hotel in question, seeks to unwind his earlier sale of this same property.

The mayor explained her departure to the *Courier:* "Although judgment was made in my favor, I now have to go through double jeopardy in the form of these onerous civil proceedings, which are without merit. Fighting a legal battle is distracting, and I can no longer devote my full attention to the towns that I love."

County supervisors have appointed Howard Turnbow, a well-known local businessman and former town council member, to fill out the remainder of Teasdale's term.

▼

Spring rolled around, and water roaring down the Whiskeyjack filled Upper Bar Lake to capacity. Almond trees in the Big Valley were white with blossoms and buzzing with bees. After a period of quiet hibernation, the Tri-Town Area suddenly came alive with gossip stemming from an obscure news report picked up by Tom Wagstaff and reprinted in the *Courier* . . .

SALVADOR CRUZ DEAD IN SAN DIEGO

The former owner of the Golden Fleece Alpaca Ranch in Tarvolo was found dead in his burned-out La Jolla mansion last week.

Cruz, a native of Mexico, was granted citizenship by an act of Congress last year. He was a generous benefactor of the Tri-Town Area and is given much credit for the economic development of the foothill region.

Cruz sold his Tarvolo ranch to a Colorado company last winter, and the operation has since become one of the largest suppliers of alpaca wool in the United States.

La Jolla police and fire departments are investigating the blaze as arson. If in fact the fire was deliberately set, the motive is unknown, but not without speculation.

"I think we're talking drugs, big time," said San Diego police spokesman Paul McFarland, whose department is assisting in the investigation. "There's not much left of this guy, but we see broken ribs on the skeleton consistent with bullet wounds. So I'm thinking he must have crossed up somebody important. A debt went unpaid, or maybe a rival group had a score to settle. Whatever it was, it shows us that the cartels have a long reach."

▼

The following week saw another crime story in the news, this one buried in the *Courier's* back pages . . .

BURGLAR PLEADS NO CONTEST

The man behind last fall's string of commercial burglaries in the Tri-Town Area has returned to face charges. Miguel Crespo, who previously operated a gas station and convenience store here, pleaded no contest to theft of groceries and dry goods taken from several local establishments. He was sentenced to restitution and 180 hours of community service after expressing deep regret for his actions, which he claimed were only meant to keep his failing business afloat.

▼

As spring moved on into May, the rain moved north, the grass turned a golden brown on all the hills, and the water level in the Whiskeyjack dropped enough for Tom Wagstaff to resume his gold mining hobby. Mary Ann went along for the ride on a warm afternoon . . .

RECORD NUGGET FOUND

A large gold nugget and dozens of gold flakes were dredged up on the Whiskeyjack this week by none other than the editor of this newspaper. An assay by Millwood's Gold Rush Emporium has confirmed that the nugget is a record-setter, the largest pulled from Whiskeyjack waters since all the hard rock mines closed in 1965. The nugget weighed in at 6.21 troy ounces. At current prices, its worth is estimated in excess of $10,000. "But I'm not selling," said the editor. "This is a trophy."

70

ON THE FIRST DAY of June Mary Ann drove down through Placerville and parked her Mini in the police department lot at the end of Main Street and Mosquito Road. She wasn't sure if she'd get towed from there, but decided she was on official business, even though she was wearing her civilian rags.

"Why do you want to join the Placerville police force?" asked the middle-aged HR officer from behind a steel and glass desk.

"I live here in town, and I'm commuting down to Applefield every day. It's a long drive."

The officer nodded sympathetically. "How'd you hear about our staff opening?"

"One of your guys just recently took over my department. Sergeant Fabriano? I guess he's the reason why you're hiring, right?"

"You're a cop? Sworn to the oath?" the officer seemed surprised, but not unpleasantly so.

"Yup, Golden Hills Tri-Town. I don't much look like one, huh?"

"Cops look all kinds of ways. You did POST somewhere, right?"

"Butte College in Oroville. But most of what I learned came from my chief, Hector Ibañez, while I was serving on the force."

"I met the man once. What a son of a bitch, pardon me."

Mary Ann's lips twisted into a wry grin. "Try working for him."

The officer leaned forward, folded his hands. "I hear there's been some action down there. Several murders."

"Yeah, six months ago we were pretty busy."

"Were you involved in the investigation in any way?"

Mary Ann was never that shy. "I cracked the case," she declared.

Her self-confidence drew a smile. "Unh-huh. All right. I'm looking at your CV, and it looks good. Recommendations from your fellow officers, including our esteemed former Sergeant Fabriano — hey, I'd like to have some of those." He nodded appreciation. "You might be a fit. Patrolling and admin detail at first, that okay?"

"Whatever."

"Aren't you supposed to sound thrilled?"

"Oh, I'm up for anything."

"But what?"

"Well, I want to become a detective."

"That could happen, but not right away, you understand. Seniority, we've got exams, budget cuts, the whole pizza, just like the Big City."

"I'm in no hurry, just hoping."

He paused and adopted a confidential tone. "I was wondering, you hear the damnedest rumors."

"Rumors?" Uh-oh. She knew what was coming.

"The story goes that one of your compadres down there was some kind of juju man, saw ghosts, cast spells. Know anything about that?"

Mary Ann couldn't help smiling. The off-target interview bullet was an easy dodge. "Not really. But that's the kind of goofy stuff I'd just as soon get away from, if you know what I mean."

"I hear you. Foothill towns, whew, bring on the gossip."

"So, when do I start?"

He slapped his hands on the desktop. "Let's do a little paperwork here and figure it all out." He picked up a form and a pen.

"Spell your name for me . . . ?"

"It's Sarzeau, S-A-R-Z-E-A-U. First name, Marianne, that's one word, M-A-R-I-A-N-N-E."

"*Marianne SARZEAU* . . . what kind of name is that? Canadian?"

She shook her head decisively. "No, no. It's French. My family comes from France, from a port in Brittany, by way of New Orleans, down in Cajun country. I've never been there."

▲ ▲ ▲